TREBUCHETS
in the GARDEN

By E.A. STEWART

ACCIDENTAL HERETICS SERIES
Book 1: *Bone-mend and Salt*
Book 2: *Trebuchets in the Garden*
Book 3: *Crux Lunata*
Book 4: *Song of Valerós*
The Mad Woman of La Catalane: A Novella
The Blue Door… and More Accidental Heretics Tales

LEGENDS OF VALERÓS SERIES
Wheel and Serpent: 1
Traitor: 2
Hero: 3

RAIN CITY INCIDENTS SERIES
(as Annie Pearson)
The Grrrl of Limberlost
Artemis in the Desert
Nine Volt Heart
The Pirate King

TREBUCHETS
in the GARDEN

ACCIDENTAL HERETICS: BOOK 2

E.A. STEWART

Jūgum Press

Third print edition: June 2018

ISBN 978-1939423924

Published by Jūgum Press
505 Broadway East #237
Seattle, Washington U.S.A.
www.jugumpress.net

For Jacyn, who wanted to read more.

Characters

House of Valerós
Pèire Leteric, seigneur of Valerós (pronounced like pear)
Beatriz, Pèire's granddaughter; Isabella's sister
Felicia, a ward in Pèire's household
Isabella, Pèire's granddaughter
Katelina of Naxos, Pèire's wife; duenna to Beatriz and Felicia
Sebastián, Isabella's son; heir to Valerós, Fontcours, and Montcava

Also at Valerós:
Anselm, the chaplain; a former crusader
Benito, master at arms
Guillem, marshal of the Valerós knights

House of Don Miquel of Cyprus
Don Miquel de Morella y Cyprus
Numa, Miquel's wife; a Kurdish noblewoman
Tomás, son of Numa and Miquel
Chrétien, Tomás's foster-brother

House of the Montcava Seigneurs
Durán, a Montcava footman
Eloïse, dòmna of Montcava
Henri, a donzel
Nicolau, Eloïse's older son
Renoud, Eloïse's younger son

Among the French Crusaders
Gerard, Viscount de Chartrain; a crusader
Hélène, Hugues de Beaurain's wife; a Montcava cousin
Hugues, Marquis de Beaurain; a crusader
Jean-Luc de Chartrain, a former knight

People in the South
Adalyde, a goodwoman from Toulouse, now in Laurac
Avraham, a scholar and merchant in Toulouse
Cebrián, a Catalan knight serving Pedro II
François of Rossynols, Paulette's husband
Jacques, a mercenary with Tomás and Chrétien

Joaneta, the soldiers' cook in Minerve
Lubos, a wayfarer
Marcos, a Catalan knight serving Pedro II
Marguerite, a business woman in Carcassonne
Pare Abát, "Father Abbot" of St-Féliz
Paulette of Rossynols, Marshal Guillem's mother
Raoul, a mercenary
Thierry, a mercenary with Tomás and Chrétien

Historic Figures

Arnau Amalric, a Church prelate
Bouchard de Marly, a hostage at Lastours
Folquet de Marselha, Bishop of Toulouse
Ghuilhem, mayor of Minerve
Innocent III, papal head of the Holy Roman Church
Maria de Montpelhièr, Pedro's wife
Mathilde de Garlande, Bouchard de Marly's mother
Pedro II, King of Aragón, Count of Barcelona; called *El Católico*
Pèire-Roger, the seigneur of Lastours
Philippe II, King of France; called "Philippe Augustus"
Raymond VI, Count of Toulouse
Simon de Montfort, Viscount of Carcassonne; a French army leader

In the Languedoc, 1210

IN 1210, FOR THE SECOND TIME, French lords and their armies came to the Languedoc for the crusading season, answering the pope's request that the land be cleansed of the so-called Cathar heresy. The Count of Toulouse had been excommunicated for not complying with the pope's demands. Some seigneurs, the lords of estates in the south, had pretended to comply the previous summer but then rebelled during the winter. Many seigneurs made plans to resist the invaders.

Simon de Montfort, the leader of the French forces, had been named Viscount of Carcassonne, after the previous viscount died in his own dungeons. Rumors flew: Simon would lay siege to the major city in the south, Toulouse. Or perhaps Termes. The unpredictability of Simon's plans fed terror.

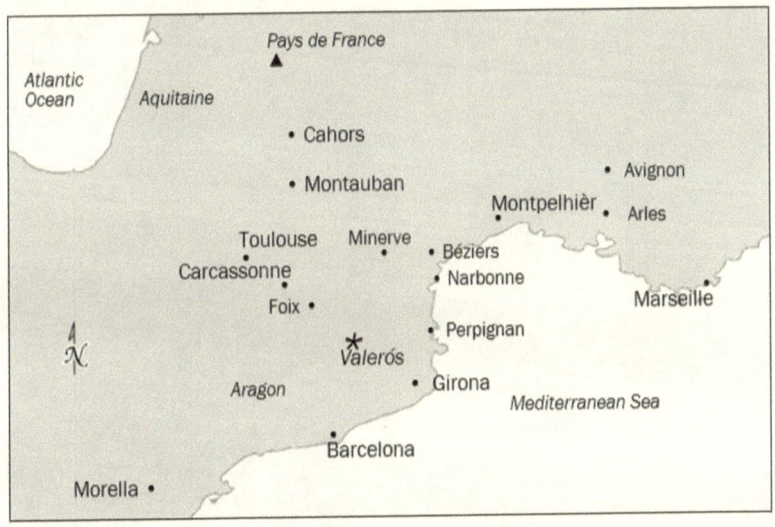

The Languedoc • 1210

TREBUCHETS in the GARDEN

A Dog-days Prelude

•

Toulouse, 1204

AVRAHAM THE TRADER GLANCED up as the morning sun broke over the city walls. White-gold light shimmered on the baubles scattered across his workbench. Across the square, a barefoot farm-boy tapped the rump of a desultory donkey with a stick as they picked their way across cobbles still warm from the previous day's sun.

"*Ai,* Toulouse in summer. Dung, dead dogs, and cabbage-ends, all ready to roast again in the sun." Avraham yawned as he settled his cap in place. His impatient guest had roused him too early in the day. "The air hasn't moved in Toulouse since Shavuot."

"Your people's festival of first fruits?" The visitor, a young donzel dressed in traveler's leathers, attempted to be polite.

Avraham's soft answer was overwhelmed by one of those black-robed street preachers shouting in the market square.

'It was the Dark One, Satan, who shaped Man from clay. That evil God made Man's carnal nature.'

"Sancta Maria, we have to listen to the foolish declarations of heretics all day long," Avraham's young visitor groused. "Souls migrate from beasts to men. A woman who conceives a child brings evil to the world. It can't be called philosophy, much less heresy."

"You and I believe in the same God, *mon amic.*" Avraham tapped his bench top as he often did to raise a point in their many discussions. The baubles on the bench rattled and scattered. "You and I cannot accept that God is both good and evil."

"*Òc.*"

1

That hoarse voice agreed with him in the common tongue of Toulouse but sounded tired, as if plagued by sleeplessness for a decade. Copper-colored hair escaped from a felted wool cap. The fine-boned face had no beard. His visitor's page, a mere child, crouched in the doorway, drowsy from rising so early. The donzel's rough clothes failed as a disguise. Nothing could hide that its owner came from among the pampered of Toulouse.

Avraham folded his hands on the work table, falling into the familiar discourse he enjoyed with his young friend. "A clear mind such as yours cannot espouse that this world is evil made manifest."

"If I consider my own life, that goodman teacher might make sense. But then, I would have to forget history, science, and reason." The visitor glanced out the door across the disorder and dust of the marketplace, fidgeting more than usual, hands twitching. "You always say you are a businessman, not a scholar, Master Avraham. Can we conclude this exchange quickly?"

The youth's voice rose to an agitated pitch but did not break. Even nervous and hoarse, it echoed the tones of Narbonne or the southern hills rather than the hawkers or parish priests shouting pieties to drown out the goodmen preaching in the market square.

"You want to trade Greek buttons?" Avraham held up a disc, pleased to tease his visitor. "You want to buy my precious manuscript with buttons and buckles?"

"These are real gold."

The buttons, which trailed threads from the tunic they had once decorated, were indeed gold but of modest value, and Avraham's scroll was worth more. His visitor appeared every fortnight, interested in any ragged manuscript the trader might have recently acquired. Occasionally, a few silver pennies appeared and a purchase was made, but the youth had never sought such a costly text.

Like a father in despair over an errant child, Avraham complained again. "These rubies? You pried them from what, donzel? Your father's dinner knife? Your mama's best goblets?"

"I have no mother or father. If you are trying to shame me, I lost all shame years ago."

Avraham continued his chiding. "These objects defy anything I've seen from you. This little pin," he held up a silver brooch shaped like a cross, "was maybe stolen from your mama's prayer beads?"

"It belonged to my grandfather, who was a true crusader. This is all I have to offer, Master Avraham. Can we strike a bargain?" Empty hands spread, beseeching. Nails bitten to the quick, rimmed black with ink.

"Why so hurried?" The dealer pushed back strands of his greying hair and then lifted another gem with wooden tweezers, peering at the stone for many moments. "You come here every fortnight to read my manuscripts. I always save what you want until you can afford to buy. But today, you think maybe the king of the Angevines will march on Toulouse before you can steal enough from your family? You make me miss my breakfast for buckles and stones?"

"We are leaving Toulouse today. It's my last chance to see you."

"This is sad news, donzel." After teasing all morning, Avraham felt true sorrow. "I don't know where I'll find such entertainment with you gone from the city."

"I'm sorry to say farewell to you. But I long to leave this stinking city more than I long for heaven." The youth pushed the pile of gems, buttons, and brooches into a mound. "Is this enough?"

Avraham shook his head as he always did at this point in a trade. "My scroll is a mere fragment, but it's said to be written by your St-John's own hand."

"Sancta Maria, it's in Latin. And only a fool would think it's a thousand years old," the youth said. "Just tell me yes or no."

"Avraham ben Yitzchak is not the one to argue over your saint's Gospel." Avraham was ready to cede the bargain. "At your last visit, I guessed that you'd want it soon. It's sealed in waxed parchment. Shall I break the seal so you can inspect it again?"

"I trust you."

"And I'll take your buttons and the stones you chipped from your family drinking cups. But you might as well keep this ring." He laid the bauble before the youth.

"You don't want it?"

"It's not worth the brass and glass it's made of. It's as false as you are, donzel." He almost dared to touch the youth's hand. "I shall miss you, ma dòmna of Montcava."

For the first time in their friendship, he called her "my lady."

▪

"How did you learn my name?" Senhóra Isabella frowned at the ring, a present from her now-dead husband at the birth of her son; of course, her sole gift from Nicolau proved to be dross.

"Last week I saw you come from your church on the arm of a man, with liveried servants behind you," Avraham said. "Was that your husband? He's a handsome man."

"No, my brother-in-law," she said. "It was a memorial for my husband who died on crusade. My father departed this world, too, on the road to Constantinople."

"I'm sorry for your loss, ma dòmna."

"It's sad about my father." Isabella grimaced. "But not about Nicolau. The indulgences he earned on crusade might buy him a place in heaven, which is the only way he could get there."

"Five years I've known you. You never say such things."

"You also know me now for a thief and a liar."

"Your minor deceptions are a fair price for the pleasure of your company," Avraham said. "And now you and your family are leaving Toulouse?"

"I'm going alone, with my son." She glanced toward the boy who slumped in the doorway. "We'll join my grandfather and sisters at home. I've stayed in Toulouse too long."

"*Way, way!*" Avraham cried words in Hebrew that he'd told her meant woe. He studied the boy. "Your son? Ma dòmna, why, you can't be more than twenty."

"Eighteen," she said. "If I were older, I'd call on the Count of Toulouse to help me. But instead, I must do this myself. After today, I'm no longer of the House of Montcava. So, please call me Isabella of Valerós."

"May the Almighty go with you, ma dòmna." He said it with unusual passion as he handed her the parchment package.

"Thank you," Isabella said. "Though I have long wished the Lord cared more for me than He seems to."

Excited to own anything so precious, she received the scroll with nervous hands. She tucked it into her satchel and hung the leather pouch around her neck once more, now containing just that worthless ring and the most beautiful calligraphy she had ever seen. Her son Sebastián lagged, groggy after being called from bed before dawn. She'd brought him to Avraham's only because she couldn't leave him alone with her dead husband's family.

"Come faster, Sebastián. If you were a crusader, you'd have marched a league already today."

"*Òc, el meu capità!*" He saluted her as his captain. "I am ready for duty."

As they hurried through the maze of alleys, she repeated the plan to Sebastián. "First we pack the silver we hid in the floor. Then at *migdiada*, when everyone is napping, we head for home."

"And take back Jerusalem from the infidels!" Sebastián crowed. He'd heard stories each night about his crusader grandfather Pèire, who had served the kings of Jerusalem. He gloried in the blunted knife she let him wear on his belt, playing Crusaders-and-Saracens.

"Not Jerusalem. What do the crusaders in our family call home?" Isabella prompted him.

"Castell-de-Valerós, the domus of the best knights in Christendom," he said. "And then I shall have a dog at last. And my own pony and a real bow. I shall have the best swordmaster."

It broke her heart that Sebastián had never seen their home in the Pyrenees foothills. Her grandfather Pèire hadn't answered her message when she begged to come home now that she was a widow. And so, she had to get away on her own.

Steal food and blankets for traveling.

Cut the buttons from Nicolau's clothes to sell.

Hoard every silver penny she could find.

Trade her dead husband's armor for a horse.

All because a six-year-old boy can't walk all the way to Valerós, though she could, if she were alone. Soon, Senhóra Isabella of Montcava would once more be just Isabella of Valerós.

The early-morning air, thick with humidity and dirtied by smoky kitchen fires, reeked of offal and sewage. Oxen yoked to overloaded carts dropped their own loads of filth while the farmers unpacked garlic and artichokes. Hawkers displayed sausages and honey under makeshift awnings. The more prosperous vendors had tiled roofs over their booths, backed up against the old city walls. Smoke from their open fires burned Isabella's eyes. That young man who hawked near St-Sernin, more handsome than God made most men, called out to everyone who passed him. "Fresh cabbages. For your table or healing your wounds. Cool your belly pain with these fine cabbages."

"Seljuk Turks. Turcopole archers." Sebastián identified strangers around them as enemies. An aged donkey passed, hauling a bundle of kindling. "The Kurdish cavalry of Saladin."

They skirted the market, ignoring the hawkers and dodging the black-frocked goodman who preached near the bakers' ovens, where women lined up for morning bread. As they approached the St-Sernin abbey, Isabella saw the burly frame of her confessor, Father Clémence, lumbering through the abbey's kitchen gate with a pair of chickens. He'd no doubt wring their necks with his own massive hands for the priests' midday meal. She wanted to escape the ugly, censorious Father Clémence along with her Montcava in-laws. Because she had grown up with trustworthy priests, she'd mistakenly told Clémence what the Montcava brothers did to her. Father Clémence declared it her sin and ordered hard penances. Once, for only a single happy week, she had a young lover named Jaume. When he died in an accident, she confessed that timid affair, and Father Clémence demanded torturous penances for two years.

Please God, may he not see us.

Although her prayers had never before been answered, a passel of mercenaries staggered by just then, laughing and smelling of wine and blocking the priest's view of her.

"Mercenaries!" Sebastián shouted, excited to see soldiers.

Those men wore the cross of the new crusade, like others just returning from that debacle in Constantinople.

"Now we fight for Burgundy," cried one amid a quartet of fair-haired Normans. "I'm happy to spank the Angevine King John, for Burgundy or any other lord."

"*Oui.*" Another Norman agreed, saying "yes" in the Frankish way, rather than "*òc*" as people did in the south. "Let's hope they pay better than the Venetians. May the dark angels take their souls."

"We can hope the Duke of Burgundy provisions better wine," the first man said. "We could pour that swill we had in Zara over the walls of a city and burn it during a siege."

Among those men, a suavely handsome but drunken mestitz man hung on the shoulder of a tall Celt, both a disgrace to the crusader cross stitched on their quilted tunics. Isabella's grandfather had such half-Saracen men among his knights, but all were abstemious and immaculate about their person, as were the Moorish merchants in Toulouse. That extremely drunken man collided with her in the way pickpockets do. Isabella drew her dagger as she shoved him away.

"*Ai Dèu*, put up your blade, man." He knocked aside her dagger with his gloved hand. "We're Christians. We don't fight our brothers." He spoke the common tongue of the south, but with the strangest accent she'd ever heard.

Laughing and hiccoughing, the tall Celt clutched at his companion's sleeve. "Sancta Maria, we never fight Christians," he said in the same accent. "Unless there's a war."

The Celt, who had a rebec slung over his shoulder, ruffled her son's copper-bright hair, which people seemed unable to resist doing. Sebastián offered his dazzling smile, appreciating the attention.

"This donzel must be the same age as your son," the Celt said, nudging his umber-brown companion.

"*Jhezu del tron*, could this one be mine, too?" The man called on Jesus in heaven. His words caused his comrades to fall on each other's shoulders, laughing.

Isabella sheathed her dagger and tugged at Sebastián. As those mercenaries rounded a corner, he sang a counting chant that began, "A mercenary I will be. *Ua, dos, tres, quatre.*"

"Not like those men," Isabella said. "You are a donzel of the great House of Valerós. You shall be a real knight one day. A man of honor. A guardian of our paratge."

The echoing curses of threadbare Norman mercenaries called up memories of Pèire grousing about the last crusade with King Richard and King Philippe.

> "Normans and Angevines like Richard Lionheart are the worst of the crusading brigands and thieves that floated like trash on the tide to Jerusalem."

She glanced back to make sure Sebastián followed closely and therefore nearly collided with a shaggy giant of a man at the end of the alley. A dusty, trail-weary man who smelled of horse and leather and clean sweat from exercise, the way a man should smell.

"Ça va? Uh...Are you all right, donzel?" The giant spoke the common tongue with a heavy French accent. He had ice-blue, piercing eyes. His probing inspection seemed intelligent rather than threatening. "Those fools didn't disturb you?"

"No, it's fine." She twitched a smile, which she didn't usually offer strangers, except he spoke kindly. Bearded, untrimmed—unlike most French fighters—he had the bearing of a knight, but a knight who'd endured a harsh journey.

"Do you know where..." The giant sought words, not fluent in the local tongue. "Where can I find a doss house? Or a brothel that lets pallets for the night?"

She did not know, despite living in Toulouse more than six years. "Ask in the St-Sernin market square."

He murmured thank you, in French, and then drifted down the alley toward the market.

Isabella and Sebastián crept through the narrow, deserted alley behind the stables of the Montcava villa. The high brick walls cast deep shadows, even in the glare of morning sun. They loitered beside a narrow alcove that even the most attentive passerby saw as just another reinforcing arch.

Pèire insisted that in the Outremer, the crusader-conquered lands across the Great Sea, every fortified citadel built an escape route, so crusaders who came home added secret passages to their villas. In the months after Sebastián was born, Isabella snooped through every corner of the Montcava villa, seeking such a passage, finding it in her husband's room. It served as the only access to freedom she had in Toulouse.

Sebastián stomped on the cluster of anise at the alley's edge.

"If you destroy their fields, they must become your slaves."

"Sebastián, stop that. A soldier of the cross who's a man of honor doesn't destroy without provocation."

She pushed aside the dusty veil of blue clematis and pawed through the tendrils of the vines that hid the entrance in the wall.

"Into the breach!" Sebastián croaked in a whisper.

He scrambled into the tunnel, but she reined him in to follow her into their enemy's house. For the last time. She was going to take them home, to their real home.

.

When Isabella exited the passageway and entered Nicolau's room, Renoud was pounding at the barred door and calling her name. She had one heartbeat to throw a robe over her traveling leathers and answer, pretending to have been asleep.

"You only hide to punish me, Isabella."

Renoud towered over Isabella just as his brother, her husband Nicolau, had done, telling her without saying the words: *I can make you do what I want.* Renoud, tall and with a lion's mane of tawny hair, he'd come home from Constantinople, where Nicolau died. The flower of the southern lords, that's what women in town called Renoud. But Isabella considered him vermin. The Montcava emblem embroidered on his sleeve suited Renoud: a scorpion with a red crescent moon.

"Isabella, *cor dolç*, this isn't a nice homecoming for a crusader like me, with you hiding and my poor mad mother turned heretic."

He moved so close that she could smell wine on his breath. He touched her chin and cheek the way one comforts a child, which repelled her. He'd come home with a cross tattooed on the back of his hand, little crescent moons picked out in red at each point of the cross. It was a badge of brotherhood among crusaders, he said, but none of Renoud's comrades resembled the dignified crusaders who served her grandfather Pèire Leteric.

"I am worried about you, dear sister." He caressed her shoulder, which always led to worse.

9

The pale, vexing wraith that was Renoud's mother, Senhóra Eloïse stepped in front of Isabella, blocking her way.

"You mustn't touch her," Senhóra Eloïse said. "She's filthy. Dirty with sin."

She endured more chiding and fondling from Renoud in front of Eloïse and the gossiping servants and, worse, a silent and sober Sebastián. Isabella pleaded a headache to retreat, and then she sat with Sebastián to comfort him, feeling him quiver in his struggle not to weep.

Then she heard hammers echoing from the passageway.

There was no longer a hidden exit from the Montcava villa. It was being nailed shut. After long moments considering her choices, Isabella removed her dagger from the traveling pack. She and Sebastián would have to leave through the front door, impossible to do while Renoud lived. But there would be blood. She hated blood. She tried to imagine fighting her way to freedom without blood touching her.

Playing beside her, Sebastián sang that nursery rhyme.

> I saw the wolf before the wolf saw me.
> I'll kill the wolf before the wolf kills me.
> God take the wolf and God save me.

In the alley beneath the balcony, the Montcava guards called to each other; Renoud's voice rose above the rest, and her whole body tensed with hatred.

She whispered, "We're going now, Sebastián. Carry this pack."

Letting her tunic sleeve fall over the hand that gripped her dagger, Isabella slipped through the upper hall and down the stairs. The wraith Eloïse again manifested, grasping Isabella's forearm.

"When you call up the Dark God, he comes." Eloïse wrenched away, raking Isabella with her claws.

Renoud's servant, Miró, held open the main gate. Renoud stood in the courtyard, raising his arms as if in supplication. She came behind him, preparing for what she had to do to escape.

"Who'd believe it!" Renoud shouted. "We never expected to see you here in Toulouse, senhór."

"God in the golden heaven with all the sobbing angels, why wouldn't I be here? Every other goat in town died but you."

Isabella called Sebastián to her side. She wouldn't have to touch blood to be rid of Renoud.

Her grandfather, Pèire Leteric, had come to bring her home.

PART ONE
Flying Souls

TO ARNAU, MY BELOVED BROTHER IN CHRIST,
As you bade me advise, I am convinced that Count Raymond of Toulouse retains the sins of pride and untruthfulness. Please recommend to His Holiness that he uphold the interdiction, so that people of faith in Toulouse will beg that the count comply. It serves a powerful lesson, that people cannot bury their dead in hallowed ground until Raymond truly repents.

As you and I discussed when last we met, the seigneurs of Toulouse fail to see what they owe His Holiness as the unifier and shepherd of the people of faith. You and I shall be happy to do as we are asked, to bring people here back into the fold.

> — *Esak, your brother in the Lord*
> *On the Eve of Pentecost 1210,*
> *the Eleventh Year of the Pontificate*
> *of His Holiness Innocent III*

1

Valerós in Chaos

Mon amic Gerard~

I write at Twelfth Night, asking you remember, the dire threat after my boy Vidal was killed and Miquel near about joined him? 'I saw the wolf before the wolf saw me...I'll take your mate and cubs.'

They're back, those Crux Lunata wolves, whoever they are. They're after my cubs and yours. Maybe Miquel and his boys. I'm asking you, who was always my true bonfraire in battle at Antioch and Jaffa and in the baking deserts of the Outremer, join me to fight back now.

You are Philippe's viscount, so you can best shelter my children when these wolves use this piss-ant's excuse of a crusade against us. I beg you to marry my child Isabella to keep those wolves from nipping at her heels. Bring her son Sebastián to your court until the dark angels take our enemies.

And when you marry my child, can you talk Simon de Montfort out of this tax he laid on my back, like I'm his own donkey?

I vow to help your boy that you raised with more strength and honor than we had in our day. We shall ride together to save your last cub from these wolves, to clear his name. Come to Valerós by Pentecost to help me fight these wolves.

Sodalitas, fidelitas, virtus
—Pèire Leteric, by his hand, who is your true brother

■

Gerard at Castell-de-Valerós, May 12

BEING A SMALL MAN, Gerard de Chartrain felt diminished when he gazed up at Castell-de-Valerós, hewn by giants from a steep limestone outcropping.

That untamed scoundrel Pèire will pour buckets of bitter wine and tell tall tales and have me married to his Amazon granddaughter before the moon rises. The Blessed Virgin can't protect me from Pèire Leteric when his battle strategy is set.

A lizard languished on a sunny rock, under which scorpions likely fed and bred. The horses kicked up dust, and the spring smells of mint and broom overwhelmed his senses. Gerard straightened his surcoat, sending a layer of trail dust to the wind, and waved to his seneschal to hold the Chartrain banner higher. And silently called on God to have pity.

Dieu ait pitié! Why did I say yes to that Catalan wildman? Habit from decades ago?

Except Gerard also hoped to find his own son, Jean-Luc, who'd insisted for six years that he must search alone to regain his name and honor. The last news Gerard had, Jean-Luc was at Valerós, playing at being a smith while making private inquiries—that is to say, spying—in advance of Gerard's arrival.

Hope? A weak word. He grasped the reins tightly, lest his hands shake or his heart beat too hard in keen anticipation

When the Valerós gates opened and Gerard rode inside, he smelled charred timber and wet wool. He expected to see Pèire, but didn't, and then surveyed all the people inside the gate, seeking his own very tall son.

Only a small, solemn young woman—barely a girl—came forward to greet him at the gate. She greeted him honorably, but coolly in more than passable French. She'd inherited Pèire Leteric's Catalan visage. Even the same dark eyebrows as when he'd first known Pèire. But she had gracious manners, though she resembled a child dressed up to pretend to be chatelaine for a feast-day parade.

"*Bon día,* senhóra." He guessed that was the proper greeting in the local tongue. "I have come to be of service. Are you Isabella, the woman I am to marry?"

"*Ai*, monsieur, welcome. I'm Beatriz, not Isabella. You came at a difficult time."

"*Bon día*, senhóreta." He was relieved to hear her speak in his own tongue, and relieved that Pèire didn't expect him to marry a mere child. He offered his hand in friendship. She seized it in her small hands and then did not let go. Her palms were creased with callouses.

"My...my...that is to say, your comrade Pèire Leteric has died of a sudden illness. He's been gone a fortnight now." Grief tinged her French more than her practiced accent.

"I am sorry to hear of your loss, senhóreta." He grasped her hands more tightly out of surprise, while unsure which of them he consoled. "Your grandfather Pèire was the finest of comrades, the most honorable man on God's own earth." *Aiieee, but we aren't that old yet! Pèire was too alive to be gone. And I just missed his passing, the grass not yet growing on his grave.*

"Now you've come all this way to help our donzel, Sebastián, and Isabella. But both left Valerós a few days after Pèire...d–died."

"*Dieu ait pitié!* Where did they go?" He released her hands, only to grasp her forearms, resisting the temptation to let grief overcome his good sense. This pale, overwhelmed child needed his help and comfort.

"Isabella rode with the Valerós knights to join Hugues de Beaurain, I think." Beatriz trembled as she spoke. "But she...monsieur, I'm sorry to tell you, but she declared she'd never marry you now that Pèire can't force her. And she says she's Master of the Valerós knights until Sebastián is of age. So, you've come all this way for naught."

No marriage! Thank God! He masked the jolt of relief that shot through his grief over Pèire. "And your nephew Sebastián is with her?"

"No. We feared he'd gone missing when the wool barn burned, but we've learned that he's gone to Toulouse with his uncle, Renoud of Montcava," Beatriz said. "I—I should have...would have stopped it, but I didn't know at first that Renoud seized him."

"Boys do best when they can study with their uncles." Another jolt of relief. Gerard couldn't guess what Pèire expected him to do with a boy. *I've long forgotten the fine art of corralling young boys' spirits, to teach them to ride and fight and—*

17

However, Beatriz was shaking her head. "Pèire doesn't…didn't think Renoud was an honorable man. He always refused to let him take Sebastián. And now God knows how I failed to prevent it. I've put the boy and everyone in peril."

"Surely, you aren't responsible, senhóreta." He released his hold on her forearms, clasping her hands again, feeling her grief and care flow into him. This child carried too great a burden. He listened to her, to learn how he could take up some of her load. Yet he let his attention drift for one heartbeat, when a figure in the village courtyard seemed taller than most men. But wasn't Jean-Luc.

"Yet the dancing angels in the golden heavens," she repeated one of Pèire's favorite epithets, so familiar from long ago, "left me to care for Valerós."

"Surely not all on your own, senhóreta." In most every word and gesture, Beatriz seemed kind and capable—and too young to be commanding a castle.

"My sister Felicia and I are crusaders' children, and therefore we shall do our duty and take care of the people left at home. Come, monsieur, let me offer refreshment while others care for your men and your horses."

∎

Beatriz gave rapid commands to the young house-knights and mews-boys who'd already begun helping his men stable their horses. When she returned her attention to Gerard, she said, "My sister Felicia sends regrets. She's delayed for a few moments from welcoming you."

Beatriz led him to a table in a courtyard, where a repast was being laid, with a stew of game bird and lentils. Little brown ones like he remembered eating in the Outremer. While she served food, she talked about difficulties in the castle village, but the few heartbeats of distress she'd revealed earlier now seemed smoothed over with great bravado, leaving only the sense of a young woman consumed with thoughts and worries about her castle and villages. He gave her his full attention, resisting the desire to inspect everyone who passed. *Time enough for my desires. Jean-Luc will find me if he's here.*

"Please forgive our disarray, monsieur. Our wool shed burned, and we're still recovering what we can of the season's wool, since it's our only hope for paying taxes." Over a heap of what they'd call an escarole salad in Gerard's country, she sprinkled sheep's cheese and ground hazelnuts. "And you see from the commotion that we're busy provisioning. Pèire says...said that our villages must prepare for possible siege by French forces."

"Why? Valerós is outside Toulouse county." He puzzled this new surprise. "And Pedro d'Aragón is...was Pèire's liege lord. The pope didn't call Pedro to send knights for this expedition." *And who ever charged a woman with provisioning a castle?*

"Some of our holdings, a castle called Arracheuse, are under the viscount of Carcassonne," she said. "So, Simon de Montfort called on Pèire to pay taxes and send knights to him by Pentecost. But since our wool barn burned, we can't pay those taxes."

That oily, animal smell of burnt lanolin added to the sense of tragedy in everything she described. "Senhóreta, Pèire asked me to help, especially with Simon, but why aren't Pèire's marshal and Katelina of Naxos here to guide you?"

"Marshal Guillem took that woman to a nunnery, when the knights left for Fontcours." She'd used up a portion of her bravado, and again sounded grief-stricken and exhausted, as if she sleepwalked through daily life. He grasped her hand again, since he sensed that simple touch comforted her, and it was all he could do for her.

A nunnery wouldn't suit the brave Katelina who ran our camp life in years past. Gerard knew Katelina of Naxos from the old days. She was devoted solely to Pèire. *That cannot have changed.* Fumbling for words, he said, "Your priest and confessor must have advised you of the best course."

"Father Anselm went with Marshall Guillem." She released his hand and instead gripped a pitcher handle, white knuckled, to pour his wine. "I believe you knew him in the Holy Land."

"Anselm d'Orleans?" Gerard last saw Anselm after the siege of Jaffa, when the man left Philippe's army to stay and fight alongside Pèire Leteric. *Anselm a priest?* "Why didn't they wait for me?"

Anselm and the other bonfraires knew Gerard had an unbreakable obligation to Pèire. He sipped biting Roussillon wine. *They left you behind because you need to tend these children, like when you drew the short straw at Jaffa and had to lead the women and children to shelter before the Saracen siege. Miquel himself declared it noble work.*

She said, "Pèire sent messages for you to rendezvous at Fontcours, when he joined Hugues de Beaurain. Instead of coming all the way here, like he originally asked." His blank look—he couldn't recall where Fontcours was—must have prompted her to remind him. "It's near Toulouse. Sebastián inherited Fontcours from his other grandfather, a crusader named Don Miquel. Perhaps you knew him?"

"*Dieu ait pitié!* Ah...yes, I did." Gerard stuttered an answer, after calling on God's mercy. *Miquel as grandfather to Pèire's scion? What myths did Pèire feed his children?*

"Don Miquel died, you know. Last year. Pèire heard of it not long ago. So, now Fontcours belongs to Sebastián." Beatriz continued, not knowing she'd stuck an arrow of grief in Gerard's heart. "We are surprised you came here, monsieur. Didn't you meet Pèire's courier?"

"No, senhóreta." In fact, Gerard had been worrying about his own missing courier, who brought news from his son Jean-Luc not long after Easter, but then never returned again. "But Pèire is too old...was too old...to be chasing soldiers across the south."

And I'm too old to cross a continent to take care of these children.

His seneschal hovered several steps from where Gerard dined with Beatriz. The extra-vigilant girl seemed to notice even before Gerard did.

"Please, won't you join us, monsieur?" She gestured to an empty bench.

"You are kind, mademoiselle. We were offered dinner in the great hall. My lord," he addressed Gerard, "your horse needs a shoe. One of our men claims he can make the repair, with your permission."

"*Aiieee!*" Beatriz exclaimed. "I'm sorry we don't have a smith to shoe your horses." She turned to Gerard, her hand on his wrist resting on the table. "The castle's smith is working at Arracheuse. Pèire employed Jehan to help here—we knew he was your man. But he left the same night that Pèire died."

That was the worst blow, though the tiny girl didn't see that, since she didn't know "Jehan the smith" was Gerard's son Jean-Luc. *The worst blow, though I know better than to hope. I pray hourly to avoid hope of more than the Resurrection. I knew—*

"*Ai*, monsieur, my apologies." Beatriz seemed to sense that he'd been distracted by his own thoughts. "I pile my worries upon you unfairly. Please rest while we welcome your knights and settle your tired horses."

"Thank you, mademoiselle." He turned over his hand so he could grasp hers again. "You are kind and brave. You must have inherited Pèire's courageous heart."

Her lips twitched as if she wanted to smile. Or weep. She seemed closer to tears than he'd witnessed during the recital of her troubles. Though he'd meant to praise her, he'd touched her sore heart. And regretted it, seeing her tears brimming, never falling.

He pushed aside his mug of wine and didn't attempt the salad or bread. This sad, burdened girl had won his heart, beyond his sworn duty to help and protect her.

Beatriz suddenly jumped up. "*Ai*, monsieur, please meet my sister Felicia."

The scents of lavender and mint followed the young woman Felicia when she joined them. She was small and brown, but by far the prettier of the two girls, with lively brown eyes and a small smile, as if a man had just murmured amusements in her ear. She offered Gerard a gracious bow but seemed shy compared to Beatriz.

"My sister did good service for your man Jehan," Beatriz said. "She stitched him up when a brigand attacked Sebastián in the lower gardens."

That story proved breathtaking, especially when it broadened to mysterious attacks against Isabella inside and outside the castle, and repeated attempts to snatch Sebastián. Pèire was right, the wolves were attacking his children. At the end of the stories, Gerard offered gratitude to Felicia. "I appreciate your service to my…man Jehan. Did you know the smith, other than to mend him?"

Felicia seemed startled by his question, lavender perfuming the air when she stirred. "No, my lord. I mean, yes, I helped to nurse him. We knew the smith was your man."

While Beatriz conferred with the kitchen girls, Gerard quizzed Felicia. "How did you learn that the smith was my man?"

"It was common knowledge, senhór…I mean, monsieur." Her French wasn't as successful as her sister's. Crows called from the battlements like the voices of the disconsolate dead, so that he strained to hear her soft voice as she said, "I can't say how we first came to know it. And he left without offering any farewell."

•

Gerard felt a sense of doom, like a physical illness. *All this way from the center of the Pays de France and already failed all promises. This is too much for you. Though you have to proceed.*

Beatriz gave him an austere room, where he shed his surcoat and changed out of dusty traveling clothes. He needed to clear his thoughts, yet found he was too tired to say more than a brief, habitual prayer of gratitude. He wasn't prepared to discuss with God all the travesties he'd just learned of.

Gerald came to Valerós to do as Pèire asked in that alarming missive. *Fraternity, fidelity, virtue.* The maxim of La Confraria de la Crotz, their bonfraires' brotherhood formed decades ago in the Outremer. He couldn't refuse, because Pèire asked, that bantam rooster of a heroic crusader.

Distressed by Beatriz's grief and his own disappointment, Gerard needed occupation, not a nap. It had been days since he'd made field notes, so he sat at a small battered table, likely rescued from a campaign. But before he opened his travel pack, he found similar notes on the table in Pèire Leteric's handwriting.

Gerard sat back, moved that the little Beatriz had done him the honor of offering Pèire's own room for his use. Then he thought to look for any evidence that Pèire had encountered Jean-Luc, who'd been condemned to wander. But only that scroll on the table remained to indicate who had lived there. He unrolled the scroll, seeing familiar names from when he'd first been on crusade with Pèire, Hugues de Beaurain, and their rowdy friend Miquel de Morella. Gerard hadn't been much more than a child, and it was more than fifty years ago, but he felt comforted seeing familiar yet nearly forgotten names of long-ago comrades.

Someone had recently annotated the list with a finely sharpened quill and lamp-black ink. Beside half the names, a dot had been place. Another quarter had open circles beside them. Beside another ten names a cross had been drawn.

Not just any cross, that peculiar *crux lunata*, with a crescent moon inked at each of the four points. That old insignia for the boys' club some of their comrades had formed, pretending to be a secret order seeking glory like the Hospitallers or Knights Templar.

It was as if Pèire were in the room, whispering in that backcountry growl of his. *They're back, those Crux Lunata wolves, whoever they are. They're after my cubs and yours.*

Dieu ait pitié! Pèire had been at work with a helper—these marks were too tidy to be Pèire's writing—to find who plotted against their children. Studying the list, Gerard hoped to see whether Pèire had determined who harassed them.

He answered a knock on the door to find a tiny woman, so old the castle might have been built around her. She smelled of garlic and grease and yeast, as a kitchen mistress does. Gerard struggled to penetrate her backcountry accent, first learning that her name was Ermessen.

"I have a message for you from Master Jehan the smith. Such a brave, sweet man," she said. Though she knew only his son's spying name, her praise warmed Gerard to a foolish degree. "He saved Seigneur Pèire's grandson's life and took a bad hurt doing it. It did my heart good to help the senhóretas Beatriz and Felicia with his healing."

His highest hopes and worst fears tumbled together, sharp edges rubbing in his mind. He asked the woman more about Jean-Luc's injuries, since it seemed inappropriate to ask the young women.

"Our dòmna Katelina taught those girls battlefield medicine," she said. "Felicia stitched the long slash on his thigh as if she'd spent her life treating warriors like your man Jehan."

He didn't have to press for more, since she was happy to talk about Jehan. "Us in the kitchen were half in love with that good man. We were lucky to have him here during all these bad times. "

"Do you know more about who attacked him?"

"'Twas a Greek man, to hear Jehan tell it. He saw the man's cuirass and fighting knife, and claimed the brigand was Greek. Which we think, those of us talking in the kitchen, proves Jehan must be more soldier than smith, because he knew the brigand for a Greek from seeing his cuirass."

"That's all he saw?"

"That, and the crescent moon cross on the man's hand, which still didn't help a soul know why a Greek kind of man wanted to snatch our Sebastián. Hope that's not who got the boy on the day when he went missing."

Gerard heard his own breathing, a wheeze. Like an old man tottering at the edge of his tomb. A hand with a Crux Lunata sign took a knife to his warrior-son.

The old woman tugged a bundle of fabric from within the bosom of her apron. "I'm proud to say the smith trusted me with this message, if you came to Valerós."

He received it from the woman's warm, worn hands, not even masking his excitement to have a message directly from Jean-Luc.

"I'm sorry it came to harm in the fire," she said as she released it. "It's hard times here, all of a sudden. You'd think we've earned more of the Good God's blessings than He's shown us. Else it must be that a bad moon still shines on Senhór Pèire's children."

For lack of parchment and pen, Jean-Luc had scratched a message in charcoal on a rag of canvas sacking, the edge burned and still reeking of fire, like the rest of Valerós. The remaining words were badly smudged. Gerard stared as if the message required divination. Jean-Luc begged Gerard to care for a woman, but only a ragged, burned edge with a single initial remained of her name. It began with an E. Or perhaps an R?

"Do you know the woman he talks about in this letter?"

"No, senhór. I suspect he had a maid, since he asked for a love philter from me. Master Jehan is a man after my own heart. He calls on the luck of stones and iron that his mother gave him."

"Jehan asked for a love philter?" His son Jean-Luc, the least superstitious man on God's earth, prayed to the Holy Mother and made his own luck in the world, though Gerard found the idea of a love potion rather sweet.

"Òc. Now I've given you the message, it's back to the kitchens for me."

She left him alone to read that ragged message again. With a part of the message lost, all Gerard knew was that now he had to keep three promises.

Protect Pèire's children from a secret enemy, who may still be lurking and ready to do more harm.

Find his son Jean-Luc, who had battled that enemy.

Shelter a woman for the sake of his son.

He fought impatience, that he couldn't scour the castle, seeking anyone who had news of Jean-Luc and the woman to whom he'd given a love philter. How to find the woman whose name began with—what? E? R? F? B? A badly drawn G or K?

Jean-Luc never dabbled with serving women. That left the two ladies on the castle. The diminutive Beatriz had the pinched look of a care-worn orphan. Gerard calculated her age. If she'd been born after Pèire last returned from the Outremer, she must be no more than fifteen or sixteen. Too young to be the woman Jean-Luc asked him to protect.

F, however, could be the quiet, impenetrable Felicia. He hadn't elicited anything from Felicia when they talked earlier that might indicate she was the woman Jean-Luc loved, except for her perpetual smile, like an artful woman who kept her secrets.

His heart lurched toward truth in a way that his head decided it must be Felicia.

He stared at the indecipherable message in charcoal until, frustrated, he instead picked up Pèire's ancient list of crusaders who may, or may not, have been Crux Lunata initiates. Who might be responsible for putting all these children in peril.

And Miquel and Pèire both dead? How had the angels managed to seize those two rascals in the same year?

∎

Rather than paradise on earth, as Pèire always claimed, Valerós was a dangerous place, where Pèire's children were under assault by Crux Lunata wolves. To uphold his oath as a bonfraire, Gerard had to protect this castle and Beatriz and Felicia (who must be Jean-Luc's love), while most of his army was leagues from here.

But Gerard had also made another promise, to join the Marquis de Beaurain's peacekeeping effort in the Languedoc. He seemed to hear Pèire's laughter echoed from the castle walls.

"Better pack up these girls and take 'em along. Keep 'em safe."

Therefore, later that night, Gerard finished a long conference with his seneschal, determining which of his men should stay to help defend Valerós against intruders and which should travel to Toulouse.

"How soon can we leave?" Gerard hated to ask it of his men, who needed a rest from the saddle as much as he did.

"As soon as the women are packed and ready to ride." The seneschal looked thoughtful. "Can they ride? We don't have to bring wagons, do we?"

It didn't take a moment to decide. They were Pèire's children; they could ride. "We don't have time for wagons. Before midday tomorrow?"

While returning to his borrowed room, Gerard paused in the open gallery above the kitchens to gaze at the stars and pray. Women's voices rose from the veranda under where he stood. A flash of light mirrored against the wall across the way.

"Ermessen, did you make this charm?" The woman spoke in a conspiratorial murmur. Felicia's voice, from the accent and soft manner of speaking. He understood just enough of the local tongue to guess what the women said.

"Ai, xiqueta, it's you?" Ermessen was the old woman who'd visited Gerard earlier. She called her visitor *child*. He guessed that's what the word meant. "I've been thinking on who it might be that robbed his heart."

"I can't tell if I'm ill from losing him or if—"

"I can see it on you, *xiqueta*. Do you want me to help free you from it?"

"No! Only heretic goodwomen think it's evil to bear a child."

"Not one goodwoman alive thinks that. The priests who say that are telling lies." The old woman spoke sharply. "But if you're happy to have a child from him, keep this charm he left you. It's the good luck he received from his own mother. You'll need it."

"Please, Ermessen, you mustn't tell anyone."

"You can keep this secret only so long, *xiqueta*."

A young Gerard would jump down from the gallery to see the woman. But his bones no longer moved that way. He settled for being content to have found the woman Jean-Luc wanted him to safeguard.

She said, "Ermessen, can you make a summoning charm?"

"I don't know if you can fetch him back with charms. But I'll try."

"And please make the charm call God's safekeeping for him."

A shadow flitted and was gone. Gerard came down from the gallery to the kitchen, seeking the old woman. When he asked about the girl, Ermessen folded her arms and denied she'd had any other visitor.

Of course she wouldn't say. It was dishonorable of him to ask.

"Will you please," he begged, "make the same summoning charm for me? Then we'll have twice the power."

Once she agreed, he also negotiated a balm for saddle sores and willow bark to ease the jostling of old bones. Too old to leap from the wall. Too old to undertake a journey from his home at Chartrain. Too old to protect a passel of children. *But you have to do it anyway, you old baquelar.*

He glanced around, again hearing Pèire's voice echo from the castle's stone walls.

Gerard had only this one night to sleep in a real bed. Then it was back to sleeping in rocky Languedoc campsites. His promises all merged into the same complicated, anxious task. *At least I don't have to marry the Master of the Valerós knights. But can Felicia ride while carrying a child?*

That rascal Miquel laughed at him. "I'm here to tell you, my bride did. Look what a hardy child she got for me. Women know how to take care. Better than we do."

"*Ai*, and look at us," Pèire said. "Heroes? We all did better after we had wives."

"But your girls can take care without a man's help," Miquel said. "Katelina taught them as good as we ever taught our sons."

"But nowadays," Pèire said, "we got this swindle of a false crusade that the pope and Simon are running here."

"However, our virtuous comrade Gerard," Miquel laughed, "thinks he gets a special pass for being French. He hasn't seen the wolves in his own yard yet."

"'I saw the wolf before the wolf saw me,'" Pèire sang. "'God bless the wolf and—'"

"Beware Crux Lunata!" Miquel cried.

Gerard jerked awake, looking around for the taunting ghosts of his comrades, who proclaimed even more danger beyond Pèire's bone-icing message.

2
Street Fighting in Toulouse

Jean-Luc in Toulouse, May 12

JEAN-LUC, ONCE KNOWN AS THE BEST of French knighthood, but now mostly forgotten, made it through the gates just as Toulouse was locking itself up for the night.

Only one common clown in ragged motley tossed his colored balls in the square, not even hawking for pennies. Everyone skirted the clown as just another obstacle on the cobbles.

A few small boys gleaned rusks near the ovens and trimmings left beside the vegetable vendor.

A voice wafted across the square from a tavern: a lord had immortalized his dalliance with a shepherdess, now a song that a lone jongleur performed for his supper. The best verses belonged to the shepherdess.

In the nearly deserted market square, he scrambled among the vendors, seeking to buy food before they packed up to leave for the night. Given the thick coat of dust on the cloth-merchants' shutters at the market's north edge, most had left off business weeks before.

"Where is everyone?" Jean-Luc asked at a *carnisseria*, after he'd bartered for a double fistful of coarse-grained sausage rolls.

"This town locked itself up tighter than a queen's quim when the *gavatx* came marching back." The sausage-maker called the French invaders throat-speakers—a common insult, accusing him of sounding like a frog. She was older than his grandmother, as irreverent as the old crusaders at Valerós, and as tiny as Felicia (whom he loved beyond reason though now she was secretly married to a man he called friend).

"May the angels bless you, senhora! Your sausages are delicious."

29

"You like my *salsiccia fresca*? This is the last of it. I'm joining my cousins in the Montagne Noire till you *francimandalha* invaders take your sorry arses back home. Did you come to Toulouse to hire out like the other rabble?"

"No, I'm seeking a man." Jean-Luc hunted the man who had betrayed him in Constantinople, destroyed his name as a knight, condemned him to hell with the excommunicated, and forced Hugues de Beaurain to call the hangman. "A one-eyed man who was injured at Constantinople."

"A handsome man like you should seek better." She judged him, tipping her head because he stood so tall above her. "A woman, perhaps? A friend? A blessing?"

"A good thought." Jean-Luc had decided on his rapid ride up the road from Carcassonne that he should first seek Sebastián of Valerós, to ensure he was safe. And then he'd hunt for his betrayer like a dog set to hunt rats in a barn. "Can you tell me where to find the Montcava villa?"

She pointed to a street leading off the market square. Her hand tremored with age. "Fifty paces after you go round that corner. But no one's there except the footmen and a gatekeeper. Maybe a few *esbirros*." She meant paid henchmen that families used to protect their villas. He waited for her to say more about Renoud. "Seigneur Renoud came home yesterday, then rode out this morning with some *francimand* knights guarding the bishop."

"The bishop's gone?" Bad enough that Renoud of Montcava was gone and likely took Sebastián with him. "The bishop is gone from Toulouse?"

"Gone to a council in Carcassonne they say. But if you have sins that need forgiving, there's priests who'll forgive your sins for three pennies, even though it's forbidden under the interdiction."

"It's not my sins that I suffer from..." He prevaricated. "But tell me, no bishops' court come Monday?"

"Not for a fortnight. But the bishops only hold heresy trials now. On account of..." She tugged his jerkin, pulling him down to gossip in whispers. "The Count of Toulouse is excommunicated. Any of you Catholics die here, the priests aren't allowed to pray you into heaven. Unless you find one who'll sell you prayers."

Then Jean-Luc and Count Raymond were both outside the fellowship of men in Christendom. All the count had to do though, was hand over heretics for judgment and take whatever punishment the pope assigned. The count had done it before, could do it again. Jean-Luc's case seemed harder.

The drumbeat of curfew sounded.

"Best get inside, senhór *francès*. The streets aren't for the likes of you after curfew. Even if you're too handsome for your own good."

"I'm not one of Simon's crusaders," Jean-Luc said.

"*Gavatx* on the street in the day, *gavatx* at night. Most see your kind as spies for the siege that the priests' dog, Simon, plans."

"I'm fortunate that you reserved judgment, senhóra, and shared your sausages."

"They'd go bad by tomorrow. Better a *francimand* vagabond than a wild dog."

"You are gracious. And I am grateful."

Although the denizens of Toulouse never regarded curfew as anything other than the drum-banging that separated day activities from the night, Jean-Luc intended to heed the sausage-maker's advice. However, the doss-house he used when last in the city had shuttered its doors. At the last call for curfew, he headed to the stable where he'd left his horse, prepared to offer a penny to sleep in the loft.

But he slammed into a gang milling in the alley, black kerchiefs masking all but their eyes, knitted and felted caps pulled down. Some were farmer-vendors in linsey-woolsey leggings and linen smocks. Some wore the half-armor of infantrymen from the last crusade: Constantinople, where Jean-Luc had lost everything.

"*Bona nuèch*." Jean-Luc hoped he voiced the local nighttime greeting correctly, though knowing his couldn't get the accent right. More than a head taller than any of them, he hunched down, intent on being just any man they might pass on the cobbled street. Of its own accord, his hand rested on the hilt of his sword.

"*Ai, com se n va*, moon-sew-war?" one man said, asking how it goes in a local tongue but parodying Jean-Luc's French accent, and spoiling for a fight.

"Pardon, *mon amics*. I am seeking Ranemiro's stable. They say it's up this lane."

"*Ai, pech,* invaders don't come down this passage." One man growled from behind his black mask.

"But we're happy to cram a wee heretic up your back passage, Senhór *Francimand*." Another joined in, the lighter sounds of a youth whose voice hadn't yet broken.

"I'm not looking for a fight, donzels, just a night's rest." Only four of them, none armed with more than sticks and cudgels. Jean-Luc didn't believe they intended more than a tussle, but he wasn't in the mood to be bruised for no reason.

"*Ai, ai,* 'donzels,' he says." The heaviest of the lot snorted in disdain. He stood closest to Jean-Luc's right hand. "Lordly as we can be, goat man. Toulouse welcomes the *francimand* invaders."

As that young man made his move, Jean-Luc pulled his sword—no easy feat in the narrow alley—and knocked the man's stick from his hand. Amidst the shadows cast by the waning moon, Jean-Luc sought who might strike next, hoping none of the masked youths felt the need to bring knives to a street fight.

He'd disarmed three of them, one with only a well-placed kick, and made two of them dance with a swing of his sword that he never meant to harm their limbs.

"Stop! Halt!"

Stronger voices drowned the clatter of sticks. Three *esbirros* appeared, wearing fashionable city-men's armor: embroidered surcoats over light chainmail. They advanced with swords drawn.

The *esbirros* leader called out, "Go brawl with the White Brotherhood. That's what your lords pay you for. God bids us to welcome strangers." As the black-masked gang retreated down the alley, the *esbirros* leader swung his lantern to see Jean-Luc's face, at the same time illuminating the scorpion embroidered on his surcoat.

"Pardon, senhór. We have no quarrel with our French guests. Forgive the exuberance of youth."

As the man held the lantern aloft, his sleeve showed another embroidered scorpion, an emblem of this lord's household. Then the sleeve slipped, baring his forearm which showed a soldier's tattooed cross. A lunar crescent at each point picked out in crimson ink. *Crux lunata.* Jean-Luc recognized the symbol of the secret order of knights that Tomás the swordsman warned about, enemies who sought to destroy the children of the old crusaders: Pèire Leteric, Miquel de Morella, Gerard de Chartrain.

Jean-Luc had been rescued from frivolous rabble by paid guards of the poison-barbed enemy. These men in scorpion surcoats served Renoud of Montcava, who'd pretended to rescue Jean-Luc in Constantinople but in fact helped advance his ruin.

Choking on the anger of that long-ago betrayal, Jean-Luc could only cough his gratitude for their intrusion into the street fight. Which he'd enjoyed more than this encounter. And damn if he was going to ask them directions to Ranemiro's stable.

He tramped up the alley, remembering where he'd seen that tattoo: On Renoud, when he pretended to help Jean-Luc flee Constantinople. And on the guard outside Hélène de Beaurain's pavilion when he encountered her in Hugues' camp near the Aude river. Was it only a few weeks ago that he'd fled from Hélène, who'd once more set out to lure him into sin?

Jean-Luc found the stable and traded a penny for the opportunity to sleep in the loft, where he stared at the rafters, wondering if his pursuit of the rumored one-eyed man was still his more important quest. He slept fitfully, waking repeatedly to worry. How was Felicia, the woman he loved, faring at Castell-de-Valerós? How well was she protected, since her secret husband was with the Valerós knights, on the way to Fontcours? Because no messenger had survived to warn his father Gerard not to go to Valerós, was his father in danger too? Were Isabella and Tomás succeeding in their quest to learn who was behind the Crux Lunata conspiracy?

He woke at dawn with that paralyzing sense of helplessness. He could do nothing to protect Felicia. He had no way to beg Gerard's help to combat their Crux Lunata enemies, or even to warn him.

He brushed straw off his coat and left the loft. Before he set off in search of the one-eyed man who might rescue his honor among knights, Jean-Luc buckled his sword in place and walked out into the streets of Toulouse with all the other vagabonds, merchants, and heretics worrying about what would happen next.

3

Before the Siege

Tomás at Laurac, May 14

THE FORMERLY HANDSOME TOMÁS of Morella, Cyprus, and St-Joachim, knight of Pedro d'Aragón, and the bridegroom of Isabella of Valerós, held out a sensible, dove-grey gown for his wife.

"You need to appear as a woman of wealth and paratge, not a dusty knight. You shall command respect for today's crusade against la dòmna Eloïse. Let's use this shed as your casa while I dress you before you enter Laurac."

The village of Laurac, where Isabella's heretic former mother-in-law lived, stood on the tallest hilltop amid quiet farms and gentle hillocks, a huddle of brick-and-stone houses built over animal pens, a few outlying stone cottages, and a tile-thatched village square. Below that hill, the Valerós knights were feeding and watering their horses in a deserted pasture. The tall grass in the pasture lay nearly flat having not recovered from the past week's assault by the tramontane wind.

That wind, which rose from the fetid desert where the dark angels abide, had slowed their travels, making it impossible to take to the road for several days. *The worst tramontane in memory.* They heard it everywhere they'd been forced to take shelter. Laurac had seemed unattainable while the wind howled and lightning flashed. But now, here they were, hoping against hope that Isabella's son Sebastián might be here—and eager to ask Eloïse of Montcava who had fathered her bastard sons.

"See, *kalila*, nice tight sleeves. You won't be plagued by waves of cloth like the gown you borrowed at Rossynols." Sweetheart, Tomás called her. Though Isabella was more than dear to him.

Isabella finally agreed to put on the gown. She let Tomás drape, button, tie, and pin a woad-dyed linen surcoat in place.

"I laid out good silver for this robe, Isabella. And look at my handiwork. Two gold buttons. I sewed them in place myself."

"You wouldn't pay a three-penny toll where Chrétien broke his leg, but you spent good money on gold buttons?" Isabella was hoarse from the wind.

"They're mine. I snipped them off a dead Frankish squire when the infantry rioted in Zara and then kept them sewn inside my jerkin."

Isabella stiffened under his hand, a quivering pulsation that always broke his heart.

"Why give me that look, ma dòmna? I didn't kill the man, and if I didn't take his buttons, another *baquelar* would."

"You had this robe in your travel pack, Tomás?"

"Yes, and I have a cap for you. I bought them from Senhóra Paulette's daughter. Let me help you with your hair. I do a better job than anyone can."

"Because you've practiced for years on your brother Chrétien? That's what he'd say, isn't it?"

"Someone had to do it for him, since my vain brother insists on masquerading as a Viking berserker, while claiming he's Samson and can't cut his hair."

"He's too thin for a berserker."

It all started playfully, but quickly shifted to her darker surmises about how Chrétien faired in Toulouse with his new friend Durán, seeking Isabella's son Sebastián. Finding Sebastián was the reason for this journey, for weeks in the saddle, through rain and repeated blasts of the tramontane wind. Renoud of Montcava, her former brother-in-law, had snatched Sebastián, not waiting for the bishops' court, where he'd accused Isabella of heresy so that he could be declared the boy's legal guardian. Tomás had his own wishes here, that Eloïse might confess her sins against Miquel, and give him proof that he was the proper inheritor of Fontcours.

"Perhaps Sebastián is still at Laurac." She sounded wistful, as she had for days, hoping to find Sebastián staying with her mother-in-law Eloïse, who'd joined this community of goodmen. Tomás, however, privately called them heretics because of all the trouble they'd caused everyone in the Languedoc.

"*Ai,* ma dòmna. Today we'll have good luck. Here, O Queen of Jerusalem, is your cap. Just a simple coif and barbette." He slipped the flat white cap onto her head while guiding the chin strap in place with his little finger.

"If I may choose, I prefer nothing at all or my felt cap. I travel better as a boy. And I don't need frippery."

"Call me foolish and extravagant, but I prefer you as a woman. Here, let's finish dressing you." Tomás wrapped his second-best belt around her waist, doubling it back and tying it behind, and then taking that opportunity to hold her close. She wiggled free, laughing with pleasure.

"No hose." She refused what he handed her. "I never wear more than light stockings after May-Day."

"*Eu vos amor.*"

"That wasn't an invitation, Tomás." Yet she touched the tender part of his ravaged face, where only her fingers had ever been allowed. "I'm not making love in a deserted cow-bier. Not today, anyway."

"Fine. Then let's go launch our siege on Eloïse of Montcava."

"As we discussed last night," Isabella drew the words out, "it's best that I confront Eloïse alone."

"And I still don't agree." He kept his voice low, not intending combat over this.

"Tomás, I know Eloïse's evil ways, how she prevaricates and hides from any truth."

"Still, it's my father Miquel that she betrayed, so—"

"Eloïse did worse by me during the seven years that I endured in her house in Toulouse than she did when she betrayed your father." She wiggled, adjusted her cap, her robe, the pins.

"Worse than marrying my father and then hatching two bastard sons who stole his land?"

"*Òc.* Worse. I escaped my nightmares by never thinking of it. Don't ask me to remember now just to satisfy your curiosity."

"As you wish, my dear wife." He never expected he'd speak that word, wife. "I shall imagine the worst and—"

"You cannot imagine it." She smiled and posed in her new robe, as if she knew how to soften any disagreement between them.

"Then I shall pledge myself merely to kill any remaining Montcava bastards who have ever hurt you."

"While you dream about that day," she said, "I'm going to go find out the name of the man who is our enemy. I'm not doing it for your sake alone. I want Renoud of Montcava to lose every hold he has over Sebastián and over me, in the bishops' court and everywhere in Christendom."

"And then—"

"Then we go to Toulouse in time for Pentecost and have a conversation with the bishop. You can use the secret entrance into the Montcava villa that I told about to confront Renoud and rescue Sebastián. After which, we go to Fontcours and find Sebastián, if we didn't find him in Toulouse. Then we serve beside Hugues de Beaurain for the summer, to fulfill all of Pèire's promises."

"Bless you, *kalila*." He still had hold of her hand, though it was time to let her go, like she insisted. "Please come back soon, my dear false heretic, so we can go to Toulouse. I want the bishops' court to forget it ever saw your name on any list of heretics."

"Don't interrupt, dear heart. After crusading season, then I shall sell the services of Valerós knights as mercenaries, so we can pay taxes and survive more than just this summer."

"But," Tomás masked his frustration over this idea, "I still believe that going to Pedro is a better idea."

"I'm not rendering castles to a king so we can pretend we're safe." When she was this fierce, she was more beautiful than that gown and headcloth could make her. "Valerós is independent and owes only vows of honor. We shall live that way from now until the Resurrection."

.

"I'd still rather go with you," Tomás called once more after Isabella as she walked up to the village to ask Eloïse of Montcava the name of the man with whom she had betrayed Don Miquel. "You can call me your bodyguard if you don't want anyone to know I'm your dutiful and obedient husband."

Isabella waved, shaking her head, that new smile lighting her face as she waggled one finger, warning him off. "It's better this way. Me, alone. And is likely to produce a result faster, which we badly need."

Then she continued, each step taking her farther away than Tomás had endured for the past fortnight. An empty space opened before him as the heat rose from the valley, shimmering.

"*Renrén, fadrin.*" The ghost of his father Miquel called from the hedgerow, greeting him as a fool. "*Ai*, mooncalf, stay with her. You can't trust women. Take my word."

"Have mercy, Father," Tomás muttered. Miquel still dropped by, uninvited, like he had since the hideous two nights on Cyprus a year ago, when Tomás had endured pain and fear, trapped in a cellar by his enemies. "A cord links us, keeping her with me."

"If you leave a wife to her own devices, there's no telling what you will lose."

"What I want to lose is your nagging," Tomás said. "It's one more blessing that whenever she's with me, you are not."

"I'm as discrete as the next monkey milker."

"Ha!"

"Yet I stay away as a favor to you," Miquel said. "Since we aren't at war yet, *fadrin*, you don't need me and every other *peccador* in the army listening while you two do the sweet thing."

Tomás watched Isabella climb the hill to Laurac, his arms folded over his black leather jerkin. He'd taken off the Valerós hauberk and chainmail, as had the rest of the knights to the show the villagers they weren't crusaders, yet he knew he couldn't be mistaken for anything but a warrior.

．

Only a handful of Valerós knights had ridden to Laurac with Tomás and Isabella. The rest remained behind at Marshal Guillem's casa, still recovering from the camp sickness that had felled most of them when they worked at the refugee camp at Vale of Roses.

The knights knew their mission: to protect Isabella while she sought her son. The knights knew Renoud as Isabella's disreputable brother-in-law, an enemy because he'd stolen Sebastián and falsely accused Isabella of heresy. They did not know him as the bastard scion of an enemy who worked secretly to destroy Pèire and Miquel and their children for an unknown enmity that began years ago in the Outremer. Renoud's unknown father was the real enemy Tomás hunted. And Tomás desperately needed Eloïse to identify that man, so he could take proof to the bishops' court that he alone was the inheritor of Miquel de Morella's lost lands in the Languedoc.

When Tomás joined them, the Valerós knights had already made a comfortable camp. The horses tended and all the camp chores done, the men lazed among a circle of boulders and benches that a shepherd must have once dragged into place, decades before. Tomás sat with them.

"This game is called riffa." Tomás pulled a set of three dice from his jerkin, proposing a true game of chance.

"*Ai*, jet dice," Lázaro said. "Your old dad Miquel had bones very like those."

"These were his."

"Can't no living man win against your papa's black bones," Bonanat said. The tall, thin knight bent like a crane to see what Tomás held in his hand.

"Any man can win as well as another," Tomás said. "You roll until you get a pair, then you roll the third bone. That's your score. High score wins."

They began their turns, and indeed, Bonanat and Lázaro lost to Miquel's bones. After long sunny days spent gambling with the Valerós knights, Tomás had begun losing intentionally, so the knights had enough silver to keep the game going. He didn't care to win their daggers and protective charms, which was all they had left at the end of most days. Some lost because they paid attention to the stories being told, calling out corrections if a familiar tale strayed from the collective truth instead of attending to the game. Bonanat and Lázaro lost because they suffered from a kind of gamblers' blindness.

Yet again, even playing riffa, Tomás had to sneak silver back into those men's pockets, finding no graceful way to lose to them. It'd be a sin to keep taking from them when they offered friendship.

"We're out here enjoying this grand adventure." Bonanat mused while he counted out the silver pennies that Tomás insisted he'd won. "What do you think the *peccadors* who stayed home at Castell-de-Valerós are up?"

"Whatever Senhóreta Beatriz tells them to do." Lázaro shoved his pennies in his jerkin without counting them. "She's Pèire Leteric's own grandchild, who was always taught the right ways. She'll do like Senhóra Isabella and step up and keep the peace, make things right. Isn't that so, senhór?"

He meant for Tomás to answer, who couldn't respond truthfully. It wasn't Renoud snatching Sebastián that forced them into this adventure. It was Beatriz's tantrum and lies, misdirecting everyone so they'd each ridden out of the castle, chasing phantoms. Perhaps Beatriz now commanded proper action at Valerós, but she'd created the chaos they'd traveled through.

And she wasn't Pèire Leteric's own grandchild. That falsehood had spawned a storm, worse than this blasted tramontane wind. Some of these men, having been with Pèire for decades, must know the truth, that Beatriz was Pèire's daughter.

"When Father Anselm joins us," Tomás said, "we should pray for Castell-de-Valerós."

4

A Specter, Perfected

"It's BETTER THIS WAY. Me, alone."

Isabella waved one last time and trudged up to Laurac atop the hill. Each step felt like a rending in the fabric of her new life with Tomás as she walked toward the pain from her old life. Dressed again in woman's clothing, Isabella found it cooler without gambeson and hauberk, quieter without chainmail chiming at every move. But she felt exposed as she sought her mother-in-law Eloïse in her new lair.

Summer rose from the pathway around her, butterflies springing up from the purple salvia to flit away. Swifts swooped to skim the mid-height wheat fields and then soared up toward heaven. New greenery tumbled over the path's edge, mixing oregano, mint, and wild strawberries. As beautiful as any farmland could be. But the grape vines hadn't been tended.

Every step tore away at the new connection to Tomás, from her breastbone down through her loins.

"*Hola*, senhóra!"

A woman hailed her from among a cadre of women weeding patches of beets and beans outside the village walls. Then all the women vied to call their goodwoman's greetings and offer hospitality: shelter, food, provender for her knights' animals, provisions for traveling.

"Senhóra Isabella!"

A goodwoman coming down the path proved to be Adalyde of Toulouse, a senhóra from their old neighborhood near St-Sernin. With high coloring and white hair shot through with black strands,

41

Senhóra Adalyde stood as tall as Isabella, but was raw-boned. She did not press a goodwoman's handshake; her fingers, roughened from hard use, curled inward as if from infirmity.

"We fed your son last week," Adalyde said after they exchanged greetings, each surprised to see the other in this remote village.

Isabella pretended to be calm. "I trust he is traveling in very good health?"

"*Ai, òc.* He couldn't hope for a more careful protector than his uncle," Adalyde said. "What a handsome young man Sebastián has become. But he always was a charmer. I remember him in your courtyard, shooting his toy arrows."

"I remember also that he hacked your young almond tree with his dull knife, pretending to practice his swordsmanship. I must apologize again."

As they walked toward the village, Adalyde repeated what the Valerós band had heard elsewhere in the Aude valley. Simon de Montfort's men rode through the towns to root out what they called heretics, employing gold-dousers to seek hidden wealth, shouting in disgust when they found nothing to loot and only old beans and chickens to forage. But among Simon's men, discipline won out: villages weren't torched in pique. Here at Laurac, only a few natives remained; most had deserted the town for the higher hills. Many current inhabitants were rich women and their servants, come to live the simple life of goodwomen or sent to the countryside by their families, who all expected Toulouse to come under siege this summer. The good-humored Adalyde said the provisions these goodwomen brought to their retreat were hidden in cow byres and root cellars, so they possessed a wealth of food to share with visitors.

"And cows and chickens?" Isabella asked. "Don't you goodwomen abjure the fruits of animal flesh?"

In good humor, Adalyde said, "Children can't be badgered to become perfected. We trade what we grow with our neighbors for other goods."

Isabella followed Adalyde to the village square, where two dozen women sat spinning and knitting in the sun, singing songs that had been sung when the first huts and bread-ovens were built in this valley. As they approached, Isabella said, "Your good Christian life has always sounded so austere to me. It's hard to image Senhóra Eloïse living such a life."

"From the old days in Toulouse," Adalyde said, "*Òc,* it would be hard to imagine."

·

As Isabella remembered it, in the latter part of the bad old days in Toulouse, Renoud towered over Isabella: *I can make you do what I want.* And her wraith-like mother-in-law Eloïse insisted: *She's filthy. Dirty with sin.* While the two of them sinned against her, with every breath Isabella took.

In the Laurac village square, women stopped sewing to press their Good Christian's handshake upon Isabella. She returned the welcoming gesture while too aware that she had to answer Renoud's false charges of heresy. Yet here she was in a heretics' community, seeking news to help her new husband, with only five days to produce the proof Tomás needed to claim Fontcours as his inheritance from Miquel.

After all the delays on the road, she was in a hurry to gain answers from Eloïse and then to find Sebastián. Beyond the threat of the too-imminent day for the bishops' court, she felt her heart beating with trepidation. If she failed to elicit truths from Eloïse, Isabella would have to ask Tomás, the man she loved, to drink from a chalice of bitter gall. To give up his hopes to secure justice for Miquel, to simply let Sebastián have Fontcours as inheritance from his Montcava father.

·

Adalyde said, "Eloïse will surprise you, senhóra. Your mother took the Consolamentum at Twelfth Night."

"Your ritual for people who are dying?" *She's only my former mother-in-law. My own mother was never cruel.*

"No, the Consolamentum is to give up the battle between light and dark before death hovers nearby." Adalyde pointed to a woman in the square. "She has become one of our perfected."

Eloïse, the solitary specter who'd haunted the Montcava villa, came across the square to join them, squinting to see in the bright sunlight, her skin now a tawny gold and her hair snow white, free of the costly headcloths she formerly wore. Recognizing Isabella, Eloïse rushed to her, arms open, silver eyes flashing in the sunlight. The same spectral-thin woman, boney fingers, swans-down wispy hair, and haunting eyes. But for the first time in her life, Eloïse embraced Isabella with warmth.

"I salute and adore the divine light within you, *ma bel criatura.*" Eloïse, who had despised Isabella, called her *my lovely child.*

"*Bon dìa,* senhóra." Isabella murmured in greeting.

Eloïse petted Isabella with affection while introducing her to the other women as the brilliant mother of the young knight Sebastián they'd met days before. Stunned, Isabella listened as the familiar thin-lipped mouth poured forth accolades instead of spewing bile.

"*Ai,* my child, I cannot shower sufficient praise for what a good man you have made in Sebastián. He is a joy."

"It's been a long while since we've met, ma dòmna *sogra.*" Instead of calling her "mother" as had been insisted in the Montcava household, Isabella called her "mother-in-law."

"Call me Eloïse, child. We don't regard titles here. I owe kitchen duty this afternoon. Please join me, so we can talk."

"Your new faith has transformed you, Eloïse."

Eloïse laughed, silver notes never heard in former days. "*Ai,* faith is for old wives who tell tales and for priests who want us to believe the unbelievable. We need only to attend to our daily work to be righteous."

They passed through a shady alley between houses, entering an open space along the steepest side of the hilltop. A few younger women called out, "*Bon día,* senhóras," as they hustled and hummed under a thatched portico, away from the ovens and open hearth beside the village's low stone wall.

Still stunned by the changes in Eloïse, Isabella joined her at a worktable and accepted a task, to cull chickpeas in large crockery bowls. Perhaps the new Eloïse would answer her questions immediately, so she and Tomás and the Valerós knights could be on their way quickly.

"I've had much to learn here," Eloïse said. "The younger women think magical wisdom comes with taking the Consolamentum. But I'm like a child learning from her duenna."

"But don't you goodwomen refuse food and die after your rite?" *To commit suicide and deny the Resurrection*, as Father Clémence and the other priests said. Isabella scooped the scum of bean-hulls floating in the bowl's water and dropped it into a smaller wooden bowl.

"*Ai*, child. Such wrong tales are told," Eloïse said. "Yet, you've seen more than one ailing old man or woman turn their head to the wall when it's all over. Roman and good Christian alike, we know when it's our time, when food no longer sustains."

Eloïse pounded cooked peas in a mortar and pestle. Isabella couldn't see the old Eloïse in her new companion but began asking what she needed to know.

"I'd hoped to find Sebastián here."

"Renoud said you'd come. But Sebastián is safe at Montcava, where he should be. I can guess your other reason for coming." Eloïse glanced down to ensure no peas escaped her pounding pestle. "You can rest easy for Sebastián's future. Last week, I gave Renoud my portion of the Montcava estates."

"How kind." Isabella now worried that Renoud intended to take everything from Sebastián. Her son knew what was due him, from his father and grandfather, but could a twelve-year-old battle his greedy uncle without her help? Trepidation made her heart beat hard once more. Except, of course she'd be with her son. In just a few days. Then she recalled Pèire's claim about the true purpose of this crusade. "So, now the French crusaders can't steal Montcava?"

"Given all the lies being spread about heretics' gold?" Eloïse laughed. "What I did is purely practical. I don't want those invaders forcing Sebastián or Renoud to sacrifice for my choices. Now, no harm can come to my son or yours because of me."

"It's kind of you to give up your wealth for Sebastián." Isabella continued culling soaked chickpeas.

Again, Eloïse laughed. "You'll see that it's not a sacrifice when you are ready to hear what the goodmen teach."

"I'm not sure that will happen. But I came for another purpose." She settled her hand on Eloïse's. "I'm here to learn what only you know, ma dòmna. Tell me who fathered Renoud and Nicolau."

"*Ai, mi criatura*. Only your Roman Churchmen might care. Their records prove that my husband fathered my sons."

"A knight as dark as Don Miquel never fathered sons as fair as Nicolau," Isabella said. "A crusader in the Outremer didn't father a son in Toulouse."

"Did Pèire Leteric send you to plague me again?" Eloïse laughed again, her eyes flashing.

"Pèire died last month." Isabella closely watched her former adversary, who was now perfected. "Sebastián didn't tell you?"

"*Ai.*" Eloïse set aside her mortar and pestle. Her silver eyes, once so frosty with accusation, were soft, concerned. "I hope Pèire endured a good end."

"There was never peace while he lived, Mother." Isabella called her that again, like in the old days, when she believed Eloïse to be the mother of all evil. "Thanks to you."

"Upon my honor, I don't know why you'd say that, child."

"Your honor?" Isabella whispered. "Your honor didn't protect me while your sons tortured me."

"Your imagination carries you away."

"No, Eloïse. Besides what I endured from your sons, someone makes havoc for the children of Pèire, Miquel, and Gerard de Chartrain. We believe it's your son's father. Who was that man?"

Eloïse bent over her work, crushing peas in her pestle. "Adalyde says the women spied a Moor among your knights. Is it Miquel?"

"It's my husband, Miquel's real son. Don Miquel died last year."

Her eyes as beseeching as a begging puppy, Eloïse said, "Please tell me that he found a good end."

"Miquel was injured by enemies. He lingered in great pain for years. So, no, not a good end."

Eloïse burst into tears, burying her face in her hands.

Perhaps now Isabella could extract an answer from her weeping mother-in-law.

5
Eating Loneliness

ON A MISTY MAY-DAY morning, after rain from the Mediterranean washed away the burned wool smell, Gerard de Chartrain left Castell-de-Valerós, to do his duty by his old comrade Pèire Leteric. The trail from the upper hills was steep, rocky, and unreliable, with some portions washed away with the melting snow. His coterie of knights rode with Felicia and Beatriz, who did as well as his men riding down steep trails. The women never complained, showing good spirits—after a long argument while Gerard convinced them of the need to travel for their safety.

Their traveling party wasn't plagued by the infernal wind and lightning his knights had endured on the ride up to Valerós. Gerard drove them all at a pace he could himself hardly maintain wanting to push on to Toulouse with speed, worried and eager about what he might find there. Isabella and the Valerós knights? Young Sebastián? *Dieu ait pitié*, his son Jean-Luc? Gerard hoped to meet Hugues de Beaurain there, who could help him solve the puzzle of that list he'd found on Pèire's table. Hugues could help guess which of their old Crux Lunata rivals might be perpetuating the troubles at Castell-de-Valerós.

Two days from Valerós, when the travelers reached the lower, gentler hills, a hot sun warmed their journey. Lizards crawled on the rocks after the sun steamed them dry. The heat woke the cicadas and crickets, and their incessant whirring and chirping seemed to sing the same song as Gerard's unrelenting worries for the chore he'd undertaken, to shepherd two young women away from the chaos and dangers inside Valerós.

At Limoux, Gerard's traveling party crossed the Aude River. His men identified a superior campsite in a swale that smelled of new spring grass. Hiding in the trees and old stone walls, black redstarts jingled *whee-tic-tic* rather than singing like the orioles.

Gerard and his seneschal guessed that the journey to Toulouse would take another five days, if their luck held. Now they needed to replenish supplies. He set out toward the local village to ask permission to camp, but the mayor came down the trail from the village, his arm around the village priest, calling a greeting in the pope's name first, and then in the name of Our Lord.

Gerard exchanged the usual greetings and inquired about purchasing fresh food for his Valerós charges and whether his men could camp in the swale.

The mayor spread his hands. "*Aiieee,* monsieur. We have no booty and no heretics. We gave our spare food to Simon's foragers last week."

"I'm not on campaign, senhór." Gerard addressed the man respectfully, in the local tongue, however poor his accent. "I want to purchase food, not take it from you."

But the mayor huddled like a kicked dog. He tugged at his priest. "Tell him, Father. Promise that we are Catholics."

Dieu ait pitié! This man fears me!

In the first moment, Gerard found the idea ridiculous. He was as old as the mayor's grandfather and stood only just tall enough to reach up and put his hand on the man's shoulder.

Gerard repeated, "Senhór, I'm not leading a raiding party. We want only your kind permission to camp here and purchase food."

"*Ai,* monsieur. We can do better than mere water and fodder. I beg you to accept hospitality in my house." The fellow offered hospitality as a defense. Nothing Gerard said offset the man's pure fear.

The mayor's trembling solicitousness washed over Gerard like icy water. Gerard had undertaken Pèire's chores, while believing that this affair wasn't a true crusade, but merely a magistrate's demand to pay taxes and do as the pope commands.

Yet here in Limoux, grasping the mayor's trembling hand to accept his hospitality, Gerard understood that people in the Languedoc feared for their existence. That Gerard with his dozen French knights struck terror in people's hearts.

"You are too kind, senhór. I would indeed enjoy your company for a meal." Gerard allayed the mayor's fears and accepted clean, safe beds for Pèire's children, seeing that he'd undertaken more than a simple chore to offer protection. Pèire had said as much in his message. *"Those Crux Lunata wolves…They'll use this piss-ant's excuse of a crusade against us."*

He broke bread with the mayor, listening to stories of the terror French marauders had fostered the previous summer. Gerard offered sympathy while feeling horror inside. These were ordinary country people, not enemies to Christendom.

"Try some of these sausages," the mayor said. "Every village will tell you that their sausages are the best. But you'll find ours are true perfection."

Gerard agreed, affably. Wasn't that what he was known for, at home and in the old days on crusade? Yet for the last six years Gerard had supped on loneliness for breakfast, dinner, and supper, hearing his dead wife repeat, *"God took them all from me."* He needed to heed Pèire's message, and what Pèire's ghost had said at Valerós. Their Crux Lunata enemies still pursued his son Jean-Luc.

After he acquitted himself over supper with the mayor and the village priest, Gerard decided to better explain their mutual peril to the women he'd sworn to protect. *My son and I are in peril, too. It's more than Valerós.* That's what he'd explain.

•

Gerard went in search of the women, hoping they rested comfortably in their borrowed quarters.

Felicia sat alone, not touching the needle work in her lap. Tears streaked her cheeks. Against his own character, Gerard trespassed on her solitude. Sitting beside her, he put his hand over hers, hoping to offer comfort, but she moved away at his touch.

"Senhóreta, I know you carry secrets of the heart."

"You can't know my secrets, senhór."

"You don't have to tell me yours. But I beseech you to hear mine. The man you knew as Jehan the smith is my son."

"I must beg off this intimacy, monsieur."

"Please hear me. You're too young to have felt this, to understand how I love my son. How my heart calls to him every moment of the day. His exile keeps us apart and creates more grief than God should ask me to bear."

"This isn't fair, my lord." She wrenched her sewing work in her hands as she spoke. "Confessing your sins...it...it's embarrassing. No one except God cares whether you fathered a bastard."

"But the smith—"

"Don't speak to me again of that man. If you please." She pointed to the door, wanting Gerard to leave. "Beatriz is in the chapel if you seek a companion."

That was fair. She couldn't retreat from him in a stranger's house. But he left in profound surprise. A bastard? Had Jean-Luc told Felicia nothing about who he was?

And he'd failed to explain the real dangers for which he'd taken the duty to protect her.

·

Wanting to calm his turmoil after failing with one woman, Gerard visited his knights, finding that the mayor had delivered measures of grain for the horses and the same fresh bread and sausages that Gerard had enjoyed. As dusk approached, Gerard returned to the village to find a few moments of peace in the chapel.

There, he found little Beatriz alone, prostrate and weeping, pounding her head on the stone steps leading to the altar. As much as he hurt from long days on horseback, he knelt on the floor beside her, taking her up in his arms to comfort her.

"I am such an unholy sinner," she said through her tears. Never as pretty as Felicia, Beatriz's face now did not have even the fresh, young innocence that was her most attractive feature.

He tried to console her the way he used to comfort his wife. A young girl couldn't possibly know about sin, but he kept quiet and let her tell her grief.

"Did you know Katelina of Naxos was my mother and Pèire my father?" she said.

The question shook him, though now that she asked, any man should have seen Katelina's features together with Pèire's in her countenance.

"You didn't know?" she said. "They kept it a secret from most of the world."

Gerard murmured about the enormity of the deceit, although marrying a Greek schismatic was a secret Pèire's enemies could use against him and his children.

"They told me my mother died," Beatriz sobbed. "They said I was an orphan. But the woman who cared for me, who I loved like a mother kept this secret from me."

"I didn't know." Gerard stroked her head, the girl's hair tumbling from her head covering. "But it's true, we were all pursued by enemies. They killed Pèire's son Vidal and swore to destroy his entire family."

"But Pèire—I still want to call him Grandfather—let Katelina run the castle as if she were a servant." Beatriz sobbed for a few moments. "Before she left, Katelina insisted that he'd always honored her as his wife when they were alone. That she could not have loved me more, even if I'd been taught to call her mother."

"It must seem vile." Gerard had no experience to know how to say the right words to her. "They did it to save you. The danger Pèire and Katelina sought to escape was real. When I tell you, perhaps you can forgive them?"

He told the story briefly, how Pèire called upon him because they'd both lost children to a dangerous secret enemy, who'd assaulted them through Church law and secret assassins. "You might be alive today, senhóreta, only because our enemies don't consider you Pèire's child. Pèire and Katelina managed the life they did because the Church never discovered that he'd married a Greek schismatic. Can you forgive them?"

"There's nothing to forgive. It's I who am a monster. I lashed out in anger and caused horrible things to happen." She stumbled to her feet, pacing in the little chapel. "I helped my father's enemy achieve what he desired by sending my mother away, destroying my family. I put our land in jeopardy. If anything happens to Katelina and Isabella, it will be as if they were killed by my own hand."

"*Ai*, child, use your faith." As Gerard said it, he felt what a weak argument he offered. "You will be forgiven, as your confessor has taught you."

"What good is God's forgiveness, if He is so arbitrary?" Her anguish caused her to tremble. With his arm around her, he could feel pure grief. "God let me hurt Katelina, because I didn't understand Pèire's lie. It's the same kind of evil as the burning of Béziers in His name. Do you see that?"

"What I see right now is the mistake I made, thinking of you as a child," he said. "I forget others carry grief with them, while I sin by thinking only of my own sorrows and how my own children have been harmed."

He's choose another time to explain more about the perils they faced. Her current danger, he felt, was that she might be swept away with grief and remorse. He coaxed her up from the cold stone floor and away from the chapel, to walk in the pretty village by the Aude, forgetting all his worries while comforting her. When it was dark, he left her at the cottage the mayor had offered for Beatriz's and Felicia's use.

Then Gerard was alone again with his own thoughts. The first one that sprang free from the evening's emotions: How could Isabella—or Sebastián—be the Master of the Valerós knights if Beatriz was Peire's child?

6

Whispers and Rumors

Jean-Luc in Toulouse, May 14

"OVER THERE. SEE? THAT'S the poor *baquelar* with one eye." The pocket-size mercenary pointed with one dirty hand while holding out the other for a silver penny as he craned his neck to look up to Jean-Luc, "and one leg."

"But that's two different men." Jean-Luc was disinclined to part with the penny.

Though it was only May, Toulouse baked each day into a stale early-summer stink. The former soldier batted away the flies. Skinny as a javelin, wearing the shreds of a studded jerkin, the man stood at the market corner where mercenaries came to sell their services to anyone seeking protection. The one-eyed and one-legged kind found day-work, boarding up villas for merchants who'd sent their families to live with relations in Montpelhièr or Narbonne. Everyone said it.

The French will lay siege to Toulouse this summer.

Which must be why Jean-Luc found no one at home when he knocked at the gate of the Montcava villa that morning to ask for Sebastián of Valerós. Not even the *esbirros* he'd met two nights before, though the villa hadn't yet been boarded up.

Jean-Luc dropped the promised penny in the man's hand, disappointed again. He'd ridden hell-bent for Toulouse and then spent days tramping through every neighborhood, from dawn until long after curfew, searching every hell-hole and brothel low enough for a mercenary to afford. In the alleys and doss-houses, he found a dozen men missing a leg or an eye, but none were the repentant man who'd been overheard confessing that he betrayed a man in Constantinople.

Jean-Luc suffered that betrayal. One day in 1204 during the Norman attack on the city, Jean-Luc's whole life was stolen from him when other men bore false witness, claiming he'd stolen booty during the sacking of the city. He was excommunicated. Banished from Philippe's lands and army. Sentenced to hang.

His years-long search for anyone who could prove he was innocent of crimes in Constantinople had taken a turn since Gerard had asked him to visit Valerós. Now his hunt was colored by perpetual worry about whether a hidden enemy might harm Felicia or his father. All that remained of Pèire's intention to meet Gerard in Fontcours were the baking bones of Gerard's courier and Pèire's messenger, which Jean-Luc had found in the hills below Valerós. Jean-Luc would run to help Gerard now, if only he knew where to run to.

Heat blasted Jean-Luc's face as he entered the cheap wine house where he intended to spend the evening. Once more he regretted sacrificing his beard when Tomás commanded it a fortnight ago. Feeling exposed to anyone who might recognize him, Jean-Luc hunkered over his wine cup and spread his legs and elbows to claim most of the bench, a signal to anyone with half a wit that he did not want to be bothered. Drained from that day's efforts, Jean-Luc fell into his old habits; first he guessed one man's story and then another, anything to keep from pondering his own sad tale.

The low, smoky room with its rotting rushes and rackety, hacked-up tables contained the maimed and scarred soldiers, foragers, and baggage tenders that Jean-Luc had known since he left his mother's home. Jean-Luc picked out the ones that might have become sergeants except their captains noticed excess cruelty or stupidity, faults that discipline could never repair. And there was the scrappy bantam who could rouse his companions in battle but couldn't organize himself for more than another dice game once the battle ended.

"Seven!"

A grizzled man, his leathery face wrinkled up in disgust, called out as if his heart had broken when the dice were tossed. Jean-Luc knew dozens of the man's brothers, bitter about losing their crusader booty in the gambling dens, sure the world owed it back to them. Yet if the man got a new fortune in another crusade, he'd lose it to another toss of the dice, which meant such men were always available to supply the next captain who needed soldiers.

At curfew, the innkeeper took a gamble: he doused the hearth fire and half the candles but didn't send anyone away. Jean-Luc agreed: it was better if the wine-tooters stayed here and gambled away their shirts. The streets were filled with the White Brotherhood, the bishop's vigilantes, plus the neighborhood ruffians who baited the Brotherhood into deadly street fighting. However, the room became too dark for Jean-Luc to find amusement by guessing strangers' fates, so he chewed at his own soul again, like a trapped rat. How many more empty nights would God force him to live through, watching as other men also wasted their lives?

A man dropped heavily onto the bench opposite him, and Jean-Luc glanced over to see who ignored the signals to keep at a distance: a short, squat man from these southern lands, with the pugnacious look of a bully seeking a fight.

"Are you the giant Frankish son of a bitch who's seeking a half-blind man what was in Constantinople?"

"I am. But my mother was a good woman."

"All Franks are sons of bitches. I lost my sister in Béziers, and no man can deny me when I say Franks are bastard sons of the devil."

"I wasn't at Béziers. What do you want with me?"

"You been asking people all around." The man spoke with a back-alley Toulousain drawl. "What's in it for him who might know such a man?"

"A cup of wine or ale. A loaf of bread."

The man spat in the rushes as an answer.

"I've chased too many rumors. I'm not paying for more falsehoods and bad wine-dreams." Jean-Luc had few pieces of silver left and damned little hope.

"In Constantinople I fought beside a man called Enego. He lost an eye, which ended his work as a crossbowman. The surgeon-barber sawed off his leg on the journey home after an accident with a supply wagon. Back here in Christendom, Enego spent all his time sobbing in church. Is that the man you want?"

"Could be. Or maybe not." Jean-Luc gripped his wine cup to hide his excitement.

"What do I earn if I tell you where the man is now?"

"Alive?" Jean-Luc asked. His lost brother Yves whispered a warning. *This isn't a man to trust.*

"*Òc.* You bastard Franks think everyone is as crooked as you in their hearts."

"By the Blessed Virgin, I swear that's not so," Jean-Luc said. "If I find this man, I promise that you will have a soldier's place in a lord's court."

"A big promise. What do I have until then? Moldy crusts?"

"I'll give you a letter. Take it to the Viscount de Chartrain or the Marquis de Beaurain at Fontcours, in the valley east of here. They'll find a place for you."

"They be southern seigneurs?"

"No, they're Philippe's men. But you'll be treated fairly. They aren't the Franks who burned Béziers."

"How do I know your letter don't say for them to cut my throat for a thief?"

"Have a priest or a clerk read it to you."

The man considered it. "Starving is worse than asking a Frank for bread," he said at last. "My friend Enego followed a priest to Carcassonne at Easter. You can probably find him in a church there."

"What priest?"

"A gold-douser priest from St-Sernin who heard his confession. A big man, ugly as a vomit-eating dog. Called Father Clémence by some and 'lecherous sack of wine' by others."

Father Clémence was that priest who'd been murdered at Castell-del-Valerós. How had his fate once more been bound into the dealings with Pèire Leteric and his family…and the sweet woman protected at Valerós, whom he loved?

This is who you listen to now? Yves whispered again.

•

Come morning, Jean-Luc knocked at the door under the neatly lettered, modest sign, *Avraham el Comerciant*. First, he pawned his best knife, because his pockets were nearly bare. Then he gave Master Avraham a few pennies for twice-scraped parchment, lamp-black ink, and the cheapest quills. With the kind permission of the shopkeeper, he stood at a tall table and wrote three messages.

First, he wrote the letter he'd promised the man in the tavern, begging a place for the man in Gerard's small army.

Next, he inked a warning to his father, using the crude code Gerard taught his sons when they were eight, with a crusaders' life in their eager dreams. *I'll meet you at Fontcours as soon as possible. Meanwhile, beware Crux Lunata. You know them from days of old.*

Last, an anonymous warning for Hugues. *Beware Crux Lunata, from the old days. From a loyal knight and your bonfraire.*

Then he went in search of the fellow from the previous night's tavern, to pour three pennies in his hand and send him to Fontcours with these messages.

Jean-Luc had no faith any messages would find his father or Hugues, but as with every endeavor in his blasted life, Jean-Luc had to try.

7

Susannah amid the Goodwomen

AFTER ELOÏSE FINISHED WEEPING and wiped her eyes, she stared off toward the hills. Impatient for answers to her question, Isabella tapped her mother-in-law's hand.

"I need to know, Eloïse."

"Does your husband hurt you?" Eloïse spoke low. Isabella bent close to hear. "With men like that, Moors I mean, they say the man's member hurts a woman. And such men enjoy that."

"That's ridiculous. Whoever—" Isabella stopped. "Is that what Nicolau's father told you? To make you afraid of Miquel?"

"It's common knowledge."

"No. It's monstrous and untrue."

"Forgive my ignorance," Eloïse murmured.

"Forgive you?" Isabella spoke in a furious whisper. "How can I forgive what you let your sons do to me? And then you and Father Clémence blamed me."

Eloïse again mashed peas in her mortar and pestle. "*Ai,* forgive me in the common way people mean forgiveness. Because we are the same, you and I."

"We are not alike, Eloïse." These beatitudes were driving Isabella wild with anger.

"*Ai, òc,* child. The Dark God of this material world lives inside us both, deceiving us about the struggle between Good and Evil, tugging us to do evil. That evil provoked your brothers."

"I did no evil in your house. Evil was done to me, ma dòmna *sogra.* Nicolau came after me just to be cruel."

"That's the Dark God inside us. The evil in women draws out the Dark God in men. Nicolau could not resist the power of evil within you."

"Renoud was as bad then," Isabella said, "and now he's worse."

"My son tries to be good. But for men, the evil inside a woman can be too powerful to resist." Eloïse spoke like a pious teacher. "When men are provoked, we are too weak to stop them."

"Provoked?" Isabella quelled the fury coursing through her, hearing the unspoken words in what Eloïse claimed. *Because we are the same, you and I.*

"Did that man force you?" Isabella asked in Catalan.

"I never can understand that crude mountain tongue you and Pèire speak."

Isabella repeated the question in the common tongue of Toulouse. "Nicolau's father raped you?"

Eloïse winced, her sun-kissed face going white, so that familiar blue vein throbbed at her temple. "It was just as all men do."

"No, all men don't do that. Not all men are evil."

"All except Don Miquel." Eloïse seemed to pity Isabella, smiling in a sad way. "I have always loved him. Because he was strong enough to resist evil. He never forced me." Her laughter had lost its warmth. "But he left me after the Dark God inside me provoked another man."

A clash at the fire-pit startled them both. A young woman failed at hanging a pot over the fire. The hook swung and clattered against an iron cauldron. While Eloïse helped hang the pot, Isabella searched for new words to evoke truth from her mother-in-law. The world shifting under her feet.

When Eloïse returned, Isabella said, "Don Miquel was indeed a good man. We must set the world right again. Please help us, Mother. Tell us that man's name."

"I can't help you, child. I look only to my own good end. I no longer live in the world of hate and lust and desire."

"Yet Sebastián and I must still live in this world."

"Renoud loves you. Ask him to help you."

"If he loves me, why is he trying to kill me?" Isabella cried.

The singing stopped. Women glanced up from their tasks at Isabella's outburst.

"Your imagination defeats your better nature," Eloïse said. "He's your brother. He wants to protect you and Sebastián."

"He's not my brother-in-law now. Nicolau is dead, and I have my own knights for protection." Isabella begged. "Please, Eloïse, who fathered your children?"

But Eloïse rose abruptly and joined her friends, calling for them to hold hands for a blessing. Isabella did not cry out again. What hell had the dark angels created for Eloïse?

·

For a quarter turn of the sun, Isabella endured a sewing-and-spinning circle, her mind drifting to Tomás and how he might be passing the time until she returned with answers from Eloïse so they could go to Toulouse. All through that afternoon, though it was a peaceful spring day, Isabella's agitation grew. She'd failed to evoke the truths she needed from Eloïse—and there wasn't another plan, another way to bring proof to the court, to either help Tomás or to stop Renoud's machinations.

The tramontane wind had exhausted itself, so the late afternoon grew warm. Bees came out, buzzing in the nearby garden. With the buzzing Isabella's fears and frustration grew. She'd wasted this day to learn only that Eloïse was no longer cruel and had herself been treated cruelly long ago. Frantic, Isabella darted from one idea to another, for what more she could say to elicit the name of the man who had destroyed Miquel and sought to destroy Pèire and his family.

She needed the proper words, like a hedge-witch's spell, that would ensure Sebastián's safety and her own, and that would satisfy Tomás's quest to restore his father's honor.

Meanwhile, Eloïse spun flax with a distaff and spindle and chatted with the other women about how the Dark God created this world and thereby manifested evil. When that topic faded, they discussed how to manage the kitchens and food supply. Isabella offered guidance for maintaining the fields over summer, knowing much more about farming than these city-born women.

Before sunset, the women returned to discussing spiritual matters, with Eloïse leading a round of question and response—and Isabella arguing, like Susannah among the Elders.

"We all feel that our bodies serve as the battleground between light and dark. What is that evil in you?" Eloïse spoke as if it were a philosophy discussion, and not what she and Isabella had quarreled about earlier.

A young woman busily sewing a hemp food sack said, "It is not your true self, but the Dark God's grip on the material world. It's why we choose instead to live together like sisters and brothers, instead of licensing lust, the Dark God within."

Isabella repressed laughter, having recently come to appreciate licensed lust as better than the burning evil of loneliness. Or the evil she'd formerly endured living as sister-and-brother with Renoud.

Adalyde asked, "If the sacraments are of no value, must we worry about confessing our sins, as Catholics do?"

"A sin is when you choose to hurt your brother or sister by manifesting the quarrel between the Good God and the Dark God." Eloïse lit up with pleasure, offering this answer. "Avoid hurting others and you thereby avoid sin."

"Our own actions cause evil, not a dark angel quarreling with the good God." Isabella stared at Eloïse. "Our choices can affect others, across generations. The sorrows our choices create for our children and grandchildren, that…" Isabella tapped a finger on the palm of her other hand "…that is the sin for which we must beg forgiveness."

Eloïse finished spinning and removed the empty distaff from her belt, busy with the heavy spindle in her hand, ignoring Isabella.

"Why would a God who is supposed to be all-powerful let us choose to do evil?" Adalyde said.

Isabella saw, then, how to evoke an answer from Eloïse. "Even if you have been more sinned against than sinning, some sins go with you everywhere. God's grace shines a light when truths are revealed, if you confess and—"

"*Ai!*" Eloïse jerked as if startled, flinging her spindle aside. Isabella put up her hand to protect her face. Instead, the spindle pierced her hand. A small river of blood flowed into Isabella's lap.

"You're hurt!" Eloïse exclaimed.

All the goodwomen scrambled to do good for an injured disbeliever, but Eloïse strove to be the first among these equals.

•

Isabella wanted to appear brave, out of a foolish desire to compete with the asceticism of the goodwomen. But she closed her eyes as Eloïse pulled the spindle free and then washed Isabella's injured hand. The sight of blood still sickened her.

"We must come as close to God as possible in everyday life," Eloïse said. "With every breath and deed."

"That's why we pray, so our sins don't keep us from God." Isabella bit her lip as Eloïse pulled the linen bandage tight.

"*Aiieee*. People want priests to intercede because it's frightening to come naked before God."

"But you are afraid, Eloïse." Isabella froze a smile, trying to mirror Eloïse's warm friendship, though she didn't feel it. This woman, now kind rather than cursing, once again held Isabella's fate in her trembling hands. "Why won't you answer me?"

"As a good Christian, I can't aid the killing of a man. And that's what you mean to do."

"The quarrel with Nicolau's father is my husband's problem. I only seek safety for Sebastián and me."

"And Renoud?" Eloïse said. "I saw you standing behind him with your dagger, that day in Toulouse when Pèire came."

"The war Renoud and I wage is not about his father. But you can help stop a perilous war. That man and his agents have attacked me. And Sebastián. And others, some of whom have died. I believe he intends to kill the king of Aragón. If you want peace, then—"

"I cannot name the man when you seek to kill him."

"Mother, you are afraid. I can see it." Isabella couldn't argue with Eloïse's claim, because Tomás had said as much about his desire to revenge his father. "Be brave and answer me."

"*Ai, ma criatura*, I fear for you. And Sebastián. Nicolau became wild with grand ideas when he met his father. You are a much weaker vessel."

"I am stronger than any woman you have ever known." Isabella said it because it felt like truth. "There's so much evil around me now, you cannot make it worse."

"But, my child, you argued all afternoon that you don't believe in the truth. Go back to your husband now. You seem to believe in him."

8

The Pall of Marriage

TOMÁS PEERED THROUGH WINDOWS and doorways in Laurac searching for Isabella, twice tripping over feral cats that bounded, snarling, out of alleyways when startled. He found her already in bed, alone in a tiny cottage.

"Have they converted you yet?" Tomás slipped into bed beside her. Isabella's first shiver felt delicious. He touched every part of her, wanting to learn all about her once again after the long day apart.

Her hand was bandaged. "What's this?"

"A sewing accident. As I have always worried would happen."

"Did they hereticate you?"

"No. Their beliefs are for old people busy preparing for the next world. And people who want a license to sin."

"They blame women for dragging the world into evil by having babies." He stroked her neck and hair, to coax her to relax, but he couldn't evoke it as he had in their first few nights together. "Isn't abstinence even less appealing than forgoing meat?"

"If I listen to those teachers, you'll be out of luck, *amador*." She tucked in under his arm, as he had grown accustomed to. "You know what Beatriz says about goodmen?"

"'Why don't they just dig their own graves and drag the dirt in after themselves?' Pèire told me."

Tomás threw his leg over hers and pulled her closer. "But if you listened to our own priests, we'd have congress only to add to the next generation for God's glory. You and I would be up to our necks in children before you could say, 'Lead us not into temptation.' Come and sin with me."

"Tomás, are you even a Christian?"

"I know, I'm blaspheming again." He nuzzled her, not thinking about his soul at all. He wanted to kindle warmth with her. "My mother was raised a Maronite. Do you know about them?"

"They're Christians in the east who were separated from the Roman Church until the crusaders came."

"Yes. Mother became a Catholic when my father married her." He twisted a lock of her hair. "Though she'd have become a Sufi or a Bogomil or anything else my father asked."

"She taught you better than you behave."

"My teachers were *conversos* and Muslims and old Catalan knights who saw too much crusading. My father had friends among the Knights Templar, the Hospitallers, and the Ransomers."

"What did you learn?"

"I tend to believe what my father always said."

"What's that?"

"He said his life proves that God doesn't care."

She shivered again. "But don't you believe that we have to do as we were taught?"

"Let's not talk about priests and heretics, *kalila*." He whispered in her ear, her hair tickling his nose as it cascaded over him. "Unless you want to play intemperate heretic maiden, and I'll play the wicked village priest who saves you."

"There are good priests."

"Yes. Father Anselm, and—damn me, I forgot the name of the other honest one I met. I think it was in Jaffa or Antioch. Or was it in Burgundy? I know it wasn't Zara."

"Stop teasing."

"Stop talking philosophy and let me get closer to you."

"You can't get any closer, Tomás."

"I want the thrill of trying." He touched her the way Isabella had professed to love. Yet she didn't move toward him as she had earlier that morning. "*Kalila*, what's wrong? Did those heretics make you doubt the world we live in?"

"*Òc.* Tomás, Eloïse didn't desert Don Miquel for another man. She was raped."

"That's her story, then?"

"Don't laugh like that. I believe her."

"And that's why you aren't in love with me tonight?"

"No. My hand hurts."

"Then let's just be brother and sister tonight. We'll sleep instead of playing." When he spoke, she tensed under his hand, as rigid as a virgin, as if it were their first night again. "What's wrong, *kalila?*"

"Eloïse spoke so much evil. I'm struggling to forget. Can you tell me the story again? About how we shall move forward?"

Tomás whispered the story, how they'd wring truth from Eloïse. "Then you shall lead the Valerós knights and ride to Toulouse to prove in the bishops' court that you aren't a heretic and that Font-cours should never have been taken from my father Miquel. We shall embrace Sebastián there and secure his inheritance. Then we shall join the Marquis de Beaurain at Fontcours, to fulfill the promises that Pèire made."

"*Ai.*" She murmured as if she listened, but she still lay stiff, un-yielding. The rhythm of her breathing meant she remained awake, but she didn't answer him. After a long while, she sighed, "*Aiieee, my hand hurts.*"

Tomás wanted to punish that Montcava witch for disturbing Isabella's peace. He still didn't know when that chance might come.

·

Weeks before, Anselm had conjured a divine union in that vaulted chapel in the Vale of Roses. Since he'd married Isabella, Tomás slept more at night. He didn't know if that came from the celestial being lying by his side or because Miquel mostly left him alone.

He woke at dawn, when Isabella ran from their borrowed stone cottage to be sick amid the garden's patches of mint and spinach. She returned, fumbling with the pitcher of water on the trestle table, spilling on the dirt floor as she splashed while washing. She stood over Tomás, who was still in bed, sunk in ungodly joy at seeing the dawn light shimmer on her damp face.

"I feel ill." She sorted among their clothes, tossing his jerkin aside before finding her robe.

"Yes, I noticed."

"Then what are you smiling about? And my hand still hurts."

"I'm sorry for you," Tomás said. "Come back to bed."

"You'll bother me, and I don't feel well." She cast aside his hose, searching for her own thin stockings.

"I won't bother you, I swear it. Let me hold you before we have to stir for the day."

As she shook out his clothes, a packet fell from his jerkin.

"Now what?" she asked.

"Read it."

She studied the marriage contract Father Anselm had forged with the knights.

"You gave everything to Sebastián." She seemed puzzled, though he'd hoped to please her.

"No, just Fontcours. The rest is divided among our children." With Isabella sick each morning, he had to tell her. "Besides Sebastián, I have another son." He tugged her down beside him. "Please don't be angry. Anyway, he's your son, too, under the pall of marriage, the same way Sebastián is now my son."

"Does this child live on Cyprus?"

"He's in Cairo with his mother."

"Why don't you keep him with you?"

"For the usual, tawdry reason that his mother is not my wife." He touched her forearm to coax her back into bed with him, feeling her pulse throb above the bandage on her hurt hand.

"You abandoned your child?" Isabella eased away from him, a sensation that jabbed at his heart.

He sat up, moving to the edge of their cot, still touching her. "When I was fourteen, one of my swordmasters in Cairo asked his step-sister to remove my naiveté. She was an old-fashioned courtesan, more than twice my age, and I was an eager student. Then she declared I'd got her with child. Though people say that women of the world know how to avoid that. I hadn't thought of it at all."

"Do you see your son?"

"She ran away," Tomás said. "Our people searched two years to find her so I could provide for them. I saw him once when he was three and then when he was eight."

"Why did she run away?"

He tried to pull her to him again, then stopped when she resisted. She hadn't softened into his loving wife since she returned from her conversation with that Montcava woman.

"My father made me into a monster." He found nothing to say in the present moment that would warm her to him, but he proceeded with what had needed telling. "I kill people for money. There are nicer words for what I do: mercenary, *soldadier*. In Venice, they now call warriors like me *condottieri*. The boy's mother saw what my swordmasters were making me into—she called me a manticore— and she didn't want her son forced into that life."

"What will become of him?"

"He's being educated as a scholar. Our steward in Cairo, for a family business there, makes sure he has the best teachers."

"What's his name?"

"Yusuf."

"Is that the same name as Joseph?" she asked. "Who was sold by his brothers into captivity?"

"Stop it. I'm doing better by him than Nicolau did for Durán or any other bastard he fathered."

"Why do you care about Sebastián?"

He settled back beside her. "He reminds me of Pèire. He reminds me what it's like to be a boy. And anyway, I couldn't shake him loose if I tried."

"And Yusuf never gets the chance to know you," she said.

"It's what his mother wants. Please don't think about it," Tomás said. "I never think about how you got your son."

"I never think of it either." She rested her head on his arm.

"*Ai, kalila.*" He pulled her close to him. She didn't resist, yet she didn't come to him. "I'm not the bad husband you had before. This man understands the priceless treasure he holds."

"But I need to say—"

He stopped her with a kiss.

"Isabella, I've never been so happy. Say what I long to hear."

"It's you, *amador*. Only you."

Hearing that always made him happier still. And then she settled into the peaceful way they greeted each day together.

9

A Villa in Carcassonne

Jean-Luc in Carcassonne, May 14

"JE M'APPELLE MARGUERITE." The woman led Jean-Luc to her room after he paid for a cleaner place to sleep than any doss-house in Carcassonne could offer.

Tall and willowy, Marguerite had a curious back-street accent from the Pays de France. Her dark hair streamed across her shoulders and tumbled down her back when she undid her headscarf before preparing a basin-bath. She was strong and efficient: in a few brief movements she relieved him of surcoat, shirt, and hose, and then she gently, thoroughly laved his bare body with herb-scented soap and a linen rag.

"There seem to be more French women here than in other Languedoc cities." Jean-Luc didn't know how to converse, having never purchased a night with a woman.

"Simon de Montfort's wife has come, bringing reinforcements for the army." Marguerite laughed, ruefully perhaps. "The rest of us traveled here with last year's army, as my mother traveled to Jerusalem, and her mother before."

"Journeying with those who took up the Cross?"

"The Cross, *oui*. Do you think the pope's dispensation for crusaders extends to the crusaders' own whores?" She playfully kissed the top of his head. The soapy smell competed with other spices when her bosom pressed close. "Though we probably haven't killed enough heretics and Saracens to please any of the popes."

Jean-Luc relaxed, grateful to give up the sweat and soil of travel. But as she rubbed the folds of his body, he stirred—any man would—and so stayed her hand.

"Madame Marguerite, I only want to sleep. Your greater services are not required."

Her smile twisted, mocking him. "I don't meet your fine French standards of excellence?"

"My soul belongs to another and with it, my body. I require only your good company and comfort."

"Perhaps you've just been in the south too long. Here, let me shave you."

She hummed a song as she worked, her touch gentle, efficient, sensitive to his every move. He listened closely. It was the song "*Amours mi font souffrir,*" the suffering lover's refrain. When she finished her task, he again tried to make safe conversation.

"You have much nicer quarters than travelers I've met with other armies."

"I suppose you'd say I'm lucky." She rinsed her razor, wiped his face clean, and moved to tidy the room after his bath. "The French lords and captains have taken over all the villas, but few have yet to send for their lady-wives."

"That's why all the houses look like military quarters? I visited here a decade ago. These austere villas were all courts of delight then."

"A soldier would notice that."

"And you have the luck of a room outside a bawd house."

"*Oui,* I traveled here with Robert de Beauvoir. Simon rewarded him with this house after Carcassonne was defeated last year."

"This is his house?" Jean-Luc rose to leave, remembering Robert from Constantinople.

She pressed him back to his chair. "He was killed when Simon attacked a Trencavel village up the Aude valley. Then Simon convinced Robert that's where the heretics' gold was to be found."

"There is no such thing as heretics' gold."

"Perhaps it is as you say."

"It is as I say. The goodmen give all their wealth away."

She shrugged, in the way only a woman of the Pays de France can. "Simon's gold-dousers say there is wealth buried in the cow byres and root cellars all over the south. Do you have another shirt? A clean one? I will pass this one to the laundry women."

Allowing her gentle care, he surrendered his tunic and slipped into his other shirt. She excused herself to make a brief foray to the villa laundry. When she returned, Marguerite resumed her own story. "I hope to live here a while longer. The villa passed to the count who was Robert's liege-lord. The house remains untouched, because that count hasn't journeyed south."

"But you have to work for a living."

"That's true." She shrugged again. "Soon, some man will come and force me to live outside the walls with the others. Life will be a little harder now that the city's own bawds are returning to the area. But many men, like you, prefer to hear their own tongue spoken."

Jean-Luc agreed that French sounded like music in this lonely, alien land. "From the marketplace, it appears that the hawkers and fishmongers and poulterers have also come back," he said.

"Wherever you go, a city wants its belly filled."

"Yet I saw plenty of French laborers in the mews and taverns."

"It's the water-boys and stable sweepers who came down the Rhône with the army," she said. "They stay because life is easier in the south. This past winter was certainly warmer."

"Will you stay?"

"Perhaps I'll find another French protector. People here foolishly think that the army will go home again, like last year." She put out the rushlight, pitching the room into darkness. "They don't know Simon yet. His army, and me, we're staying. Let's go to sleep now, since that's what you paid for."

Lying back on Marguerite's cot, Jean-Luc stared into the dark and rubbed the twisted burn scar on his arm, though it made him think about his brother Yves whenever he touched it.

"You have so many questions for me." She crawled under the coverlet to lie beside him. The scent of lavender and peppermint wafted up as she settled the covering. "What's a man from the Pays de France doing here, if not working for Simon?"

"I'm searching for a man named Enego that I knew in Constantinople." A slight exaggeration. Jean-Luc did not remember the one-eyed soldier who might have confessed to Father Clémence about having ruined a French knight.

"Enego? That one-legged bowman from Toulouse? Who lost an eye on crusade?"

"You know him?" Jean-Luc whispered to cover his eagerness.

"Last week he was drinking in the same tavern where I met you." Marguerite rolled over, her warm backside pressed against his damaged thigh. "He signed on as a mercenary for one of those southern rebels with all the castles. Termes, perhaps."

"Are you sure?"

"No. Perhaps it was Arques or Queribus." She shifted, one body seeking warmth and comfort beside another. "Some seigneurs who don't want to be ruled by the French are recruiting among men Simon won't hire. Their agents quietly pass word in the taverns and brothels."

"Who can I ask, to find where that man went?" His excitement echoed in his voice. And he sat up too suddenly in the bed.

"No one will answer a French knight asking such questions. You'd put yourself in danger."

"*Aiieee*, that's wise advice, madam."

"Then sleep now, monsieur."

He tried to find sleep, having come so close to finding that man, and failing again. A familiar gulf opened inside him. He should look for his father, since there was no more he could do at the moment for his name and his future.

Used to the physical sensation of hope waning, not to be eclipsed by sleep, Jean-Luc turned on his side, wrapped his arm around Marguerite, and savored the prickle of a woman's hair on his clean-shaven face, the peppermint odor from her locks redolent of summer days. Her body, relaxing into sleep, sent ripples of calm through him.

He curled more closely around her, thinking of a small woman who once pitied him and let him lie in her arms, promising she'd wait for him. When he tried to forget about Felicia because she now belonged to another man, his brother Yves waited to pester him about bad choices and ill-kept promises. *Admit it now, there was never any reasonable hope.*

He needed a good idea of what to do next, since there was no more he could do now to salvage his name and his future. He wanted to find Gerard, but the next step to achieve that must be to rejoin Senhora Isabella and the Valerós knights. That would eventually lead to Gerard, perhaps at Fontcours. He could also ask Tomás more about his claim that secret Crux Lunata agents pursued them. He could not, however, find a way to learn whether Felicia was safe at Castell-de-Valerós. He had only prayers, that Gerard rode to Valerós, found Felicia and her sister, and was protecting them. But he couldn't seek his father yet, because he should return to Senhóra Isabella and Tomás, to let them know they had ten days' reprieve since the bishop was gone from Toulouse. Then he'd ride with them to Fontcours, to find his father and be useful, since he couldn't help his own life.

Isabella and Tomás must still be in Laurac, and all he risked by making the half-day's ride from Carcassonne was a possible encounter with Guillem, the marshal of the Valerós knights. Who considered himself to be Jean-Luc's friend and bonfraire comrade. But who'd secretly married Felicia before he left Valerós, and therefore separated Jean-Luc forever from any hope for happiness.

.

Jean-Luc found Isabella, Tomás, and Father Anselm chatting in the corral at the edge of a bog-water meadow. The Valerós knights loitered under the shanties near the corral, gambling and repairing chainmail. The sweet odor of half-rotted grass filled the late-afternoon summer air. Swallows swooped over the field. Farther up the valley, cicadas and crickets droned.

He punctuated their mutual greetings with the question that mattered most to him at that moment. "Do you have news from Valerós?"

And then heard Isabella asking her question. "Did you see Sebastián in Toulouse?"

"People in Toulouse say he's gone with Renoud to Carcassonne. People in Carcassonne say Renoud left for Fontcours."

Jean-Luc watched her face, her cheeks glowing with a high, almost feverish color. He couldn't see if she was reassured or made more anxious by his report.

They had no news from Valerós, but with relief, Jean-Luc learned Guillem had not yet rejoined them, having remained at his mother's house, waiting for some of the Valerós knights to recover from camp sickness.

"I have important news for you," Jean-Luc said. "The bishop is gone from Toulouse for a fortnight."

"We don't have to rush to Toulouse?" Tomás said.

"Except to find Sebastián," Isabella said.

"There's no court until the twenty-seventh of May." Jean-Luc should have hurried his news, but Tomás and Isabella interrupted at every other word he spoke.

"That's one less worry for today." Isabella seemed excitable.

Tomás said, "We still need to bring Valerós knights to Fontcours as quickly as possible."

"*Mon amis,*" Jean-Luc interrupted their discussion about what to do next. "The bishops' court is delayed. But, swordsman," he pointed at Tomás, "the court only meets to examine heretics."

Tomás's face lost all its happy excitement over the delay.

"What?" Isabella seemed puzzled, white lines around her frowning eyes, like a woman with a fever.

"Count Raymond is excommunicated. There's no Church business in Toulouse. The bishops' court examines heretics, but it won't hear others' pleas. No justice. No marriages. No masses, or confessions, or marriages or—"

"Tomás can't plead for justice over his father's inheritance." Isabella sounded disappointed, even sad, while Tomás remained still as a stone. It wasn't Tomás's way to be silent.

"That's what I understand," Jean-Luc said.

Father Anselm broke the silence that followed. "We haven't made you welcome. Isabella brought us food to share from the heretic women's kitchen." He offered to share what he had of a white bean potage with chopped spring greens, olive oil, and garlic floating on top.

"Will you leave for Fontcours today?" Jean-Luc had believed Isabella came to Laurac in hopes that her son was with her mother-in-law. "Since that's where Sebastián is."

"Not yet," Isabella said.

Tomás explained. "Eloïse of Montcava holds secrets that she needs to share with us. And she isn't forthcoming."

"Secrets." Jean-Luc's thoughts wound around that word.

"The specific secret," Isabella said, "is that the father of her sons is not the man she married. We think—"

"We know," Tomás stole her words, "that's who is behind the plot that has damaged all of us. And we need to know who that man is, to protect both Isabella and Sebastián."

"And while I try to convince Eloïse to be forthcoming, I've had to spend far too much time with spinster heretics." She offered Jean-Luc the remains of her own dinner, claiming she wasn't hungry. "I feel like a dog left to howl in the kennels, biting its own tail."

"Don't let their false ramblings disturb you, ma dòmna," Father Anselm said. "You can't change their minds."

"But I'd trade all of Valerós for decent conversation," she said. "Did you know the souls of dead innocents fly all around us, looking for newly conceived babies to take for their new bodies? They can jump in your mouth while you're eating."

In the middle of a bite of black bread heaped with white beans, Jean-Luc winced at the idea of flying souls.

Isabella said, "If it's someone wicked, their soul goes into a dog or a rabbit. But not a fish or a turtle. That's why it's acceptable to eat a trout but not a rabbit."

"Do only women have to worry about swallowing souls?" Jean-Luc asked.

Isabella and Father Anselm laughed with him. But Tomás said, "Why is that any stranger than believing the bread and wine are the actual body and blood of our Savior?"

Isabella berated Tomás for heresy while Father Anselm only seemed amused.

"There's a great deal of difference," Isabella said. "Holy men have pondered these mysteries for a thousand years, and we receive their wisdom from writing and debate. It's not the wretched imaginings of weavers with no knowledge of history or philosophy or of the Gospel itself."

Tomás tugged at a lock of copper-colored hair escaping her coif. "Still, it comes down to arguing that one person believes one thing and another doesn't. There's nothing to prove either side."

Isabella went into a tirade, deploring his apostasy, before seeing that he was teasing. She pummeled him with her unbandaged hand, but Tomás caught her fist and pulled her close to him.

"*Ai*, Queen of Jerusalem, I'm no heretic. Save your rancor for true believers." Tomás dropped his voice. "With my body I thee worship, my queen."

And, Jean-Luc saw, the swordsman's wife adored him. Also, the sodding mercenary had never been in love before, but either divine inspiration or pure passion led him to talk love as elegantly as he talked rubbish while fighting. Jean-Luc was about to admit privately that perhaps Tomás was no longer the arsewit he'd pretended to be. Then, walking behind them on the path, Jean-Luc heard those fateful words.

"Please, Isabella. You'd do as I ask if you loved me."

All the exotic sweet talk, and it came down to the same sad thing as every losing bastard tried with his lover. *You'd do it if you really loved me.*

The swordsman would cock up his love affair in the same way he wrecked a good fight. Jean-Luc felt like shouting a warning, the way a good swordmaster does.

Stop! Look out behind you!

You've left your middle open!

Check your footing!

Lubos in Transit

Come evening on the plains, when he wanted a good meal and a warm bed, Lubos went looking for a woman to give it to him. He just smiled and asked, then said thank-you the way he did whenever his own woman Aykuna called him her angel. His father, Père-Izsák, taught him that when your body leads you to find comfort with a woman, it is correct in the eyes of God. He wants your seed in the vessel created for that purpose. But to do so with a man offends both the greater and lesser spirits of God.

And it's a man's duty, as the incarnation of spirit here on earth, to end abominations. Just like it's a woman's duty to feed a man and take care of him.

On the hillside, an old woman dug in her garden. When Lubos approached, she offered the greeting that filthy heretics give, wishing him a good end. She touched his hand, offering the deluded good cheer of a soulless woman. His hand burned where she touched him. He felt defiled, curling his enflamed hand into a fist.

Two days later, after he found a safe place to camp, Lubos killed a lamb with the first arrow he shot. Père-Izsák would admire how his skill with the bow was improving. Not sorry to be alone, Lubos spent the evening roasting that lamb over a spit. To celebrate.

With half his bidden tasks done, Lubos was blessed with the good fortune to meet Père-Izsák again. He told about his successes, laying out the stories of the men's death like sacrifices on an altar.

"*Petrus mortuus. Petrae disiectae.*" Père-Izsák spoke with satisfaction, a smile on his face. His father's words of praise rained down on Lubos like a balm. This must be how Jacob felt when he stole Esau's blessing.

"You are my angel." Père-Izsák touched the curls of Lubos's hair as he blessed him.

The spirits in the stones sang a song with the souls Lubos had trapped in his sword, using the words of Père-Izsák's blessing. One more Rock to tumble. Then Lubos could find a son for himself and go home to Aykuna.

The sun was setting by the time the lamb's flesh grew hot enough to eat. He tore into the meat with pleasure, finding it bloody and tender.

Tomorrow, he'd hunt again.

Inquiry into Iniquity

TO ARNAU, MY BELOVED BROTHER IN CHRIST,

The bishops in Raymond's county and the related provinces, whether appointed through the righteous offices of the Holy See or received through simony from their princely cousins and brothers, support the teachings from the Synod of Toulouse to varying degrees. Of interest for His Holiness to consider is Canon Five, which forbids marriages between blood relations, asserting that the line be drawn at the seventh degree of consanguinity.

We find that the practice of only three degrees of separation is rampant in the county of Toulouse and the other environs so rich with heresy. And among the hereticated, brothers lie with sisters, mothers with their sons.

We, together with all the legates on this business of faith, must recommend to His Holiness that the next council strictly impose prohibition to the fourth degree. Among the princelings and their lords, this may help draw wives from lands that have sworn fealty to the Holy Roman Church.

We must work to stop the spread of this pernicious heresy, starting from the cradle.

— Esak, your brother in the Lord
15 May 1210

10

Fontcours, in Splendor

"SENHÓR RENOUD BIDS ME make you welcome." The Montcava-steward greeted Gerard and his party when they arrived at Fontcours, his livery embroidered with a crimson scorpion. The steward held out his hand the way southerners do to greet each other. When he released Gerard's hand, the fellow's sleeve fell back, revealing a *crux lunata* tattoo on his forearm. "Our master insists that you consider this your own home."

After riding all that way, seeking safety for Pèire's children, Gerard had taken the two women into a nest of scorpions and Crux Lunata wolves. He had to find Hugues de Beaurain as soon as possible, while keeping Beatriz and Felicia away from the Montcava scorpion-men. He'd spied Hugues's banner in the distance when they rode into this valley.

But first, Gerard de Chartrain had to greet the rest of his men, who had set up camp while waiting for him to return from his Valerós expedition. As he toured the encampment, one of his captains remarked how tired the viscount looked.

"Take my pavilion, monsieur, while we pitch camp for you."

Behind the captain, his men roasted a slab of pork fatback and stirred a pot redolent of garlic. The sounds of his small army busy making camp left Gerard yearning to settle in with these men.

"I'd best stay in the manse with the women." Gerard had to remain close to them, given Fontcours might be as dangerous as Castell-de-Valerós.

"Thank you, monsieur," Beatriz said. "You are a comfort to us." Her brown hair had escaped its head covering, such that she again appeared as the earnest chatelaine. She fretted about why the Valerós knights had not yet arrived at Fontcours, though they'd left two weeks earlier than their own party.

Sadly, God had not chosen to award Beatriz with the beauty and tranquility of her half-sister Felicia. Except, as it turned out, Felicia was no relation at all to Beatriz.

"However, I'm not comfortable using the Fontcours villa in its master's absence," Gerard said.

"It belonged to Sebastián's grandfather," Beatriz said, "to be passed to the oldest son. Therefore, it now belongs to Sebastián."

"Sebastián would think us silly not to use his house. And we can sleep in real beds." Felicia sounded fatigued, not showing the same enthusiasm as Beatriz for exploring their proposed residence.

Gerard was relieved to at least get them safely into a clean, comfortable house. For the whole journey, the girls sat their horses just fine, never complaining. But every campsite had been fouled by other travelers, and all the villages were full of refugees from Carcassonne and Béziers, sickness and death everywhere. He also found it hotter on the plains than earlier in the spring, before he began his trip up into the backcountry hills.

"It's beautiful," Beatriz exclaimed. They'd found a stream running among herbs and rockroses in the villa's southern fields. "Isabella never told us about the vineyards and the cypress groves. And the gardens! Sebastián's land and manse are so handsome."

"It certainly surpasses the last town," Felicia said.

They'd traveled through Bram, where the entire village was sick and in despair. Gerard had diverted the girls so they didn't hear the tragic story of the Bram knights. He got his company on the road again before the town's sickness could spread to their own camp.

He went out again to see how his men fared, leaving the women to settle in as inhabitants of the manse. Hugues de Beaurain's men camped on the broad plains surrounding Fontcours, arrayed with the orderly efficiency that Hugues always maintained, his camp causing minimal disturbance in the farmlands. Gerard's captains had his men do likewise and then set routines to keep the camp functioning until word came to march.

One of his sergeants, Ogier, approached with deference, though the man was old enough to have ridden with Gerard when they returned from the unattainable Jerusalem.

"Monsieur, a ragged man came from Toulouse bearing letters from…your agent."

Ogier stammered, unable to say Jean-Luc's name aloud, and then handed the letters to the viscount, who managed to read the first one without betraying his awful weakness, his longing to see Jean-Luc again.

> The man who bears this letter is be given a place in the viscount's retinue, after judging his abilities. He has done me a service.

No name, just a rough sketch of Gerard's arms.

"You'll want to speak with the man," Ogier said. "But we've talked with this brute at length. He didn't know the name of the man he helped, but says his destination was Carcassonne."

The second letter was more comforting and more frightening. He traced the words his son had written in the old code they shared.

> I'll meet you at Fontcours as soon as possible. Meanwhile, beware Crux Lunata. You know them from days of old.

·

Later, surveying his men's work from a small hillock, fingering the scrap of letter in his pocket, Gerard spied a tall figure riding toward the camp, sitting his horse French style. From the size of the man, it had to be Jean-Luc.

Gerard straightened and walked rapidly, eagerly down the hillock to meet him. But coming closer, the man presented greater bulk and less height. So, Hugues then.

The tall rider reined in his great destrier and tossed aside his aventail. "What is your name? French or foe?" the man cried.

It was Colomb, Hugues's half-brother. Similar to Hugues, but only half-carved from the same block, rough edges everywhere in manners, temperament, physique. Where Hugues incarnated *cortezia*, as seigneurs call courtly honor, Colomb made one think clown.

"Bonjour, Monsieur Colomb. *C'est moi*, Gerard de Chartrain. We haven't met since Jaffa. We both rode with Hugues in those days.

Pèire Leteric asked me to guard his grandson's land while Simon's army is marching this summer. We bring a portion of the force that Pèire promised to send to Simon."

"Did that old goat-legged leper let his chainmail rust up so he can't ride anymore?"

"Pèire has passed to the other life and is now awaiting God's judgment."

"*Jésus dans le ciel*, I expected that old bastard would have pleaded to escape his sins long before now." He slapped his thigh as he guffawed. Colomb's big horse danced sideways, as if barely under his control.

"He was a good man and true to his friends. Which is why I have come here in his stead."

"*Flic floc.* I'd forgotten you were such a sassy one, Monsieur Gerard. Does Renoud know what you're about? He was no friend of Pèire's, save for that witch who married his brother."

"Renoud joined plans with Hugues and Pèire for this summer's arming." Gerard felt ire rising in his gorge. "Hugues certainly expects to see me, and Valerós knights are coming also."

"Valerós has knights that can ride? *Qui s'ho creu?*" Again with the thigh-slapping and the dancing horse, asking who'd believe it?

"They ride as well as any knights in Christendom." Gerard hid his resentment, pushed back at anger. "Better than most."

"We shall see, we shall see."

Riding up to join Colomb were the usual bullies and toughs that Gerard remembered the man keeping company with in the old days, all armed to the gills, and one larger man, so menacing that even the others in the coterie kept clear of him, had *crux lunata* tattoos up and down each arm.

Colomb waved for those men to follow him as he rode away, not taking the common leave between gentlemen.

Unsettled, Gerard sought the Fontcours chapel, to give thanks for this safe—safer—haven for Pèire's children, if he could keep them out of reach of Montcava men and Colomb's bullies. Instead of praying, he meditated on how to find Jean-Luc, rather than waiting for who knows how long until his son came to Fontcours. He fingered the letter again, considering what the letter-bearer had said. *His destination was Carcassonne.*

Only a day's ride from Fontcours. But rather than allow his impulse to mount a horse and ride there, he'd wait for Hugues, who'd return to his standing camp soon enough.

After that day's work, Gerard ventured to visit the manse again, where he found Colomb had taken the greater portion of rooms and kitchen, placing a small garrison of rough soldiers at too-close quarters with Gerard's charges.

Seeking the two women, Gerard found Beatriz kneeling beside Felicia, who had gone to bed with camp fever.

That many days on the road, and instead of bringing them to safety from enemies and marauding crusaders, he'd brought them to a standing camp of Crux Lunata wolves along with one of the worst dangers of a soldier's life.

Dieu ait pitié! I'm trying, Pèire.

As hard as I've ever worked on any campaign.

Our enemies remain unhampered, and trip us from their hiding places.

11

Warning the Queen of Jerusalem

JEAN-LUC INTENDED TO LET the swordsman find his own fate, yet he felt stirred to protect the woman, as a valiant knight should.

"How long will you remain here?" Jean-Luc asked Isabella when he walked with her up to the village, a huddle of houses too close together, all made of cold southern stone and tile.

"We're staying until we persuade Eloïse to name our enemy," Isabella said. "I hope it's soon. Our knights are eating their way through the heretics' food supply. It's like laying siege, except some of these old women are so hereticated, they believe they can live on light and water."

"But there's no court where Tomás can take his proof," Jean-Luc said.

"Whoever fathered Renoud and his brother," Isabella said, "is the sources of the Crux Lunata plot to destroy us. And seeks to kill Pedro d'Aragón."

"Then we all want to know what she says. I'm convinced now, too, of Tomás's claim about a Crux Lunata plot." Jean-Luc hadn't believed that their intentions in Laurac mattered to him, until he'd become convinced about Crux Lunata at the end of that street fight in Toulouse.

She pointed to the deserted benches in the center of the village, where the women had been spinning when Jean-Luc first arrived. He sat beside Isabella in the quiet of the evening, the summer dust on the horizon becoming burnt carmine as the sun sank behind the Pyrenees, the murmur of heretics' prayers drifting on the breeze. In the day's last light, Jean-Luc saw that her love affair had turned Isabella almost beautiful, yet she seemed fragile in a new way.

"What will you do?" Jean-Luc asked. "When will you leave?"

"Tomorrow, perhaps. I hoped that the rest of the Valerós knights would rejoin us by now. Since we don't need Eloïse's confession immediately, we should meet our date with Simon, to bring Pèire's knights. I shall convince Tomás that we can come back here later."

"What happened to your plan to get Valerós knights hired as mercenaries?" Jean-Luc asked.

"Tomás believes we should go to Pedro instead."

"They are your knights," Jean-Luc said. "Are you prepared for the same disasters that struck the last queen of Jerusalem?"

"Because this crusade is like Saladin's attacks?"

"No, I refer to what happens when an heiress gives her kingdom to a bad husband."

She glared. Her face was flushed, as if she were feverish.

"He's making you submit to him," Jean-Luc said. "He wants to turn you into something you're not."

"No, he's not."

"You let him weave flowers in your hair. You look to him before you speak. He's changed you."

"He's my husband. He loves me."

"He's also ruthless. Revenge turns a man into an animal, though it's not clear Tomás was ever human. You are diverting him. I hope you are civilizing him. But he'll soon return to what his father built him for. And I fear he'll force you to submit to his desires instead of regarding yours."

"You are wrong," she said. "And you can't speak of my husband like this." Spots of fire burned in her cheeks.

"Ma dòmna, I want to be wrong. But I am a knight of the bonfraires and I am also sworn to uphold the oath Gerard de Chartrain made to protect you."

"And I'm the queen of Jerusalem." She flushed hotly, squaring her shoulders. "I don't need a nameless knight or a false smith to protect me."

"I am not Jehan the smith. I'm Jean-Luc de Chartrain, the viscount's son."

A spark of anger flared, but because of the frailty he noticed earlier, she had no fuel to keep it burning.

He said, "Tomás warned me about deceiving you, ma dòmna. But I won't apologize, because people are always happier not knowing my name."

She tipped her head back, her eyes closed. Shadows subsumed the last of the afternoon sunlight, but her face was lit from the fire inside her, and her voice was hoarse and rocky when she spoke.

"When I was a child, Pèire and Gerard intended that you and I should marry. I saw it in letters my grandfather saved."

"We would have been unsuited to each other," Jean-Luc said.

"You don't have to rescue me. Tomás will never harm me."

"I won't speak ill of your husband again. But please, think of me as your brother and ask for help whenever you might need it."

"A brother?" She sunk to the bench beside him in the twilight. "If Felicia hadn't chosen Guillem, you'd be my brother."

Jean-Luc bowed his head when she mentioned Felicia, as if he'd been kicked in the belly. He forgot why he'd hectored Isabella.

"I have to see her again." All the weakness in his soul could be heard in his voice.

"No, you mustn't. Let Felicia go with her husband."

"I spend every night trying to forget her touch and the sound of her voice, but she said she loved me. I was sure she meant it. She said she'd wait for me."

"She's too young to know what that means."

"If you hold someone in your arms night after night, you know that person's true feelings."

"But you just said I don't understand Tomás." She laughed, a high-pitched chime he'd never heard from her before. "Anyway, it's too late for you."

"I think I gave her a child."

"*Ai Dèu.*"

"God and the Blessed Virgin both know I tried."

"Maybe that's why she married." Isabella's voice seemed unnaturally high.

"Perhaps. I have to know why she forgot what we swore to each other."

"My poor brother."

Isabella kissed Jean-Luc, offering her sympathy. He let the kiss linger too long. The too-familiar feeling of insufferable loneliness fell on him like the shadows of the night.

"And you, O Queen of Jerusalem. Let me help you when you most need it."

12
Crossing a Threshold

Tomás at Laurac, May 15

As twilight settled, Tomás paid his gambling debts and headed for the village to join his wife. He leaped to the top of the village's modest wall, high enough to keep geese from straying if their flight feathers had been nipped. Jumping down to the pathway, he again startled those half-wild cats, who were now stalking a bevy of pigeons pecking in the hens' grain. Birds flapped upward and swooped away, cats screeched and darted in all directions. The stealthy warrior Tomás, a knight of Pedro El Rei, had entered the heretics' lair.

His tooth hurt again, so he checked through deserted cottages and the heretics' kitchen, hoping but failing to find cloves. Passing through the alleys, he came upon a wattle-and-stick cottage so small, it couldn't contain more than a cot and perhaps a stool, with scarcely room for a body to move about. But the rushlight inside cast the shadow of a spindle and distaff in use.

Miquel stood at the open door.

"*Bon nuoit*," Tomás said. "Shall I join you?"

His father brushed his greeting aside, as he had when Tomás-the-child pestered him a score of years ago. Tomás stepped to the doorway beside his father.

"You came to kill me." Eloïse, the Montcava witch, sat on a stool, drawing flax from distaff to spindle. "All these years, and you still want to murder me."

"Can this senhóra see you?" he asked Miquel.

"Every time I close my eyes," the woman said. "I was so young then." Her silver eyes darted from her winding thread to Miquel, who now looked more like a Provençal courtier than a warrior. "When the

Count of Toulouse called you away, my father's old friend came. He said I betrayed my soul, giving myself to an infidel's son."

"Damned by wedding a half-breed Moor?" Tomás bristled. Her thin, high voice cut through the pain in his head like a knife. Miquel touched his arm to silence him.

She pulled fiber from the distaff to feed to the spinning spindle. "The man begged me to let his love save my soul."

"You gave away your honor." Tomás scowled, feeling his insides fill with hatred for her. "All that courtly southern talk about paratge, and you betrayed my father."

"The man forced me. He said you'd do the same, but worse. *Ai*, Miquel, that isn't true, is it?"

"No, *kalila*. You needed more time to be ready for a man's love. You were afraid," Miquel murmured. "Then I find a dead goodman's soul flew through the air and landed in your belly."

"I remember you standing in the doorway, just like now. I feared that you'd strike me dead."

"Never in this life, *kalila*. I mean, in my life that was." Miquel spoke warmly, with kindness Tomás had not heard since he was a child. "You can't make love to a woman who doesn't want it. Or if a cord binds her heart elsewhere."

"I will find the spit-licker who held that infernal cord and drag him to hell with it," Tomás said. Miquel gestured for silence again, in the fatherly way that forces a child to obey.

"The only cord is the one that ties my heart to you, Miquel," Eloïse said. "The Consolamentum. My new faith. Old confessions. Nothing has broken that tie. Or stopped the longing."

"Ma dòmna, how could I know?" Miquel said. "I wronged you."

"I've endured soul-searing pain since that day you rode away. You hurt me worse than that other man's evil."

"Your old friend tortured us for half a lifetime," Tomás said.

"*Calla!*" Miquel ordered Tomás to shut up, and then dropped to his knees. "Ma dòmna, I owe you recompense."

"*Ai*, Don Miquel. Always the honorable knight." She placed her hand on his head. "Nothing can repair the hole that man tore in our world."

"I'll stay with you now, ma dòmna. We can repair the world."

"Father, what are you doing? She destroyed you."

Miquel crouched beside Eloïse, taking her hand in his. She laid her head on his shoulder.

"No, *fadrin*. Don't you see? I helped that man destroy this senhóra. That must stop now."

"I gave you my oath, Father. I still mean to find our enemy."

"What can you give my son, ma dòmna, to quell him?" Miquel whispered in her ear. The words carried across the great divide that had opened between Tomás and Miquel in the heretics' silent town.

Eloïse struggled with the folds of her gown. Miquel kept her close by him. "I made this years ago, when I still hoped you'd come to make the world right again." She presented a small parchment packet. "Is this sufficient to satisfy your son?"

Tomás unfolded the packet. The first thing he read, written in lamp-black ink, was the signature of that priest Clémence they'd buried at Valerós. It was dated the previous year, when Eloïse joined the goodwomen at Laurac.

> I, Eloïse of Montcava, attest that my wedded husband was not the true father of Nicolau of Montcava and Renoud of Montcava. May the God of Moses and St-Peter have mercy on my soul.

"This isn't enough." Even a few days earlier, Tomás would have paid the Angevine king Richard's ransom to hold this testament for the sake of revenge. But now, since there'd be no bishops' court except to judge heretics, he didn't know what use her testament would be. Instead of offering the thrill of possible revenge, holding it felt...heartbreaking.

"It's attested by a priest," she said.

"*Ai*, that makes it so much better." Tomás tasted bile as Miquel wrapped this pathetic, white-haired woman in his arms while she huddled against him like a helpless girl. "A truth attested by a leprous, lying monkey of a priest."

"What more do you need?" she said.

"The man's name," Tomás said. "Your old friend caused my father to be enslaved among the Saracens."

"Tomás, it wasn't her fault."

"When Miquel didn't die, your leprous weasel friend worked to destroy us on Cyprus. And then this." Tomás barely touched her chin, lifting her head. "Can you see in this rushlight what your son did to me? Tell me his father's name."

"Tomásino!" Miquel held up his hand, but Tomás went on.

"We know it wasn't Geoffroyde Conflans or Calvet de Villeroi or Robert d'Aunoi," Tomás said. "I found each of them while hunting last year, and they denied it."

She and Miquel regarded each other, but neither spoke.

Tomás rolled the dice to win. "But the Beaurains lived next to you then, and it was the marquis who educated your sons."

She made a sound like a trapped animal.

"It's not Hugues," Miquel said.

"But it is. Look at her weep," Tomás said.

"I won't surrender a man to be murdered," Eloïse said. "And knowing the man's name will only bring more danger and fear into Isabella's life. Let Renoud protect her. Forget vengeance."

"Renoud stole her son," Tomás said.

"To protect Sebastián from danger. Only Renoud can protect that boy."

"What danger? Who wants to hurt Sebastián?"

"All of the Dark God's evil world." She pounded her palm. "You will only make it worse if you continue a crusade for revenge."

"I will persist," Tomás said. "Renoud has only brought a devil's rash of evil to Isabella."

Eloïse denied it. "She's wonderful, but wrong-headed. He's her brother. Renoud always does what's best for her."

"Jove's pissing monkey! This is so wrong."

"Stop, Tomás. I must stay here to undo the evil that I caused this senhóra," Miquel said. "Take that confession rag and go back to hunting, *fadrin*."

"Are you certain, Father? Is this right and honorable for you?"

"What can happen? I'm already dead."

"*A Dèu*, then."

"As if God ever helped me with anything." Miquel reclined on Eloïse's cot. "Travel well. And take care of your wife, *fadrin*. Better than I did mine."

.

Tomás tripped over the threshold and ran across the village square in three leaps, wanting to find Isabella, to show her the scrap of parchment.

Across the way Tomás saw his wife kiss the giant Frenchman, and then they walked together to Isabella's cottage, where they kissed again.

.

His tooth screamed in his head, as he watched the big Frenchman wander down to where Father Anselm camped in the pasture. Tomás wanted to pursue the man and kill him. But he hesitated; the pain pounding in his head could lead him astray.

Feeling Eloïse's folded packet in his hand, he resented that no bishops' court would meet to restore his father's honor. First, they needed to be on the road at dawn, to find Sebastián in Toulouse. He would kill Hugues de Beaurain. If not tomorrow, then very soon. But who to show Eloïse's note? The Count of Toulouse? No, he remained under interdiction. Go straight to Pedro? He had no legal power over Fontcours, since the Count of Toulouse owed his position and power to Philippe of France. What would to do?

Find the Crux Lunata leader. Stop any future evil from that quarter.

That solution wasn't from Miquel, but his own decision.

As he walked through the village, headed again for Isabella's cottage, Tomás heard a baby scream in the cellar of one of the empty houses. He stepped inside the open door, the cry echoing in the cellar. The door slammed behind him, which thrust him down the steep steps and pitched him into the dark. He leaped back up the stairs, throwing the full weight of his body against the door, just as the latch clicked shut. Recoiling from the blow against the door, he stayed still to hear what else breathed in the dark with him.

The dark. It felt as if the room were alive, though it was his own pulse he felt, not anything in the cellar with him.

"Father, are you here?" he called, first in Catalan, then in the local tongue, then in French.

Something brushed against his leg, and he fought an unreasonable jolt of fear, his fingers trembling, the tips stinging with cold. Miquel had deserted him for that Montcava witch.

"Help!" he cried. "Please help!"

If he allowed one more shout, it would be a shriek of fear, like an animal. "*Un, dos, tres, quatre, cinc.*" He counted to twenty, and then shouted again.

For interminable moments, he heard nothing but his echo. With a hand on the wall to keep his bearings, he bent to heave up the contents of his stomach, then stepped back, trying to remember where the door was. It couldn't be more than a few steps upward.

A cat meowed. The wailing infant he'd heard. After he found the door, Tomás knelt and called for the cat, wanting it nearby.

"*Aquí, aquí, gat!*"

It came close and let him touch it. When he begged, the cat came up into his arms and burrowed against him. He sneezed and then held the cat tighter when his sneeze frightened it.

"*Vint, dètz-e-nòu, dètz-e-uèch.*"

Counting down, he waited, frantic to shout once more for help, holding the cat closer when it stirred.

"Help!"

Sweat prickled under his clothes and in his hair, running down the back of his neck. Holding the cat with one hand, he took the knife from his boot, preparing to defend himself. He listened for rustling in the cellar, hearing the wretched symphony of foul sounds from the dungeon in Famagusta. Something live touched his foot, and he screamed.

The cellar door creaked opened, and the cat leaped from his arms into the sudden gap of starlit night.

"*A mal punt, senhór?*"

It was Jean-Luc, calling it an unpleasant situation in the local tongue, with his wretched Frankish accent.

Tomás shoved past him, needing to be out of the dark before he screamed in terror. He leaned against a nearby cottage, hands on his knees while he could his breath.

"Are you all right, swordsman? You seem ill."

"Go to hell."

"Beat you there. But I'll move over so you have space to burn."

"I saw you with her." Tomás rushed at the Frenchman, putting his knife to the man's throat. His hand shook, more from leftover fear than jealousy.

Jean-Luc batted the knife away with the back side of his hand. He shoved against Tomás's sternum with the heel of his other palm, and Tomás stumbled.

"You've lost your edge, swordsman."

"I saw you." Tomás still wanted to rip into the man. He folded his arms to keep from striking the man. That left him helpless again. Like the relief and failure of Eloïse's useless letter. Like seeing Miguel offer his enemy comfort.

"Don't be a nit, swordsman." Jean-Luc didn't take Tomás's anger seriously. "Do you have any human feelings besides murderous rage and inane jealousy?"

"I'm not insane." His let his anger free, hoping it washed away the residue of fear from that black cellar.

"I said inane." Jean-Luc straightened his surcoat, preparing to walk away. "*Bon Dieu*, man, your wife is not capable of disloyalty. Her only fault before God is she loves you. Don't cock it up."

"I saw what I saw." He resisted Jean-Luc's provocation, like he'd resisted overwhelming fear in the cellar. To keep from striking out again, he carefully restored his knife to his book.

"If you're so jealous, why not put her in a harem? Isn't that how your people protect women?"

"My people are Christian Cypriots. And why should I take advice from you, Jean-Foutre, about how to take care of my wife?"

"Because I wasted enough of my life with jealousy. It destroys men. Your wife is true, and you fail her if you doubt." Jean-Luc remained calm, which continued to aggravate Tomás.

"Damn you," Tomás said in Catalan.

"I'm already damned. And I'm turning my back on you now and leaving. I shouldn't, but if your wife trusts you, then there must be something in you worth regarding."

13

Consolamentum

"WAKE UP, ISABELLA. WE'RE leaving. I packed while you slept. What's this ring I found in your sleeve?"

She thought she answered, but Tomás must not have heard.

"Isabella, wake up. I have an answer from Eloïse, so our days of hell in Laurac are over. Get up and dress. It's time to go."

"I'm sick."

"You've been sick every morning for days. You'll be fine once you're up."

"My head hurts. My hand hurts."

"Yesterday it was your stomach. What is this ring?"

"I stole it from the abbot at the Vale of Roses."

"Whatever for? You need to control your impulses. Come on. I'll meet you with the horses. I know you want to saddle your own."

Only a moment later the knights Bonanat and Lázaro pounded on the door. "Senhóra, we're waiting! Marshall Guillem arrived this morning, so all the Valerós knights will ride with us."

Then everyone stood peering down at her. The light hurt her eyes. Father Anselm unwrapped the bandage on her hand.

"Sancta Maria, who tended this wound?" he exclaimed.

He was shouting, and all the noises in the room hurt her ears. Tomás. Father Anselm was shouting at Tomás.

"The bed is drenched from her fever. How could you not notice?"

"I wasn't in bed with her."

"How could you be in the room and not feel her fever? This wound has to be opened and scraped clean this moment."

Someone gave her water and grasped her throbbing hand while Father Anselm tended it. Tomás. It was Tomás who cradled her. And Guillem held her down. Tomás whispered in her ear, but she couldn't hear what he said because it hurt so. She saw Father Anselm, who held a knife in his hand, dripping red. When she cried out, Guillem put a belt between her teeth.

"Bite down, ma dòmna."

She couldn't make her body obey. She could hardly spit out the belt when she had to be sick. Then she was shivering. Father Anselm stayed beside her on the cot, rocking her.

"Tell those women I need more wet linens to help cool her off. And no, I don't want any of those crazy witches in here."

All the noises except Father Anselm's voice shattered and refused to form into words.

"She can't ride. Not today, nor tomorrow. She needs to be in bed."

Much later—very much later, after she'd been sick every way possible, and then sick again, and then lost count of how many times she shivered or felt as if she'd catch fire—Jean-Luc sat by her and said prayers to the Holy Virgin.

"It's not what you think," she said.

"What is it, ma dòmna?"

"No one has ever held me all night. Even when Katelina came, I was too big to hold. She only held Beatriz and Felicia."

"It's all right. God will keep you safe."

A cold cloth touched her head again.

"He'd never harm me, Jean-Luc."

Father Anselm wiped her lips with water and tipped her head so she could swallow.

"Jean-Luc isn't here, ma dòmna. He and Tomás went to find Sebastián. We'll see them in a few days at Fontcours. Drink this water so you can be well again."

·

Father Anselm prayed for her, saying the same words over and over. Then he sang a psalm in plainsong in his sweet voice for a day and a night. The music replaced her burning-hot dreams. She flew over Valerós like a hawk with just the psalms and the wind.

Then the song went away and the prayer changed. Hands touched her head, but without the cooling cloth and Father Anselm's gentle words. The prayer was in the common tongue, not in Latin.

"Now, to receive this prayer, you must repent your sins and forgive all others."

Father Anselm's voice thundered across the room. "For the love of God, get away from the senhóra."

"We're consoling this woman in her final moments."

"Get out!"

The scuffling shattered in her ears.

Father Anselm was beside her again. He held her good hand and placed a cool cloth on her head, while he prayed in Latin. *Pray for us, O Holy Mother of God, that we may be made worthy —*

"Where is Tomás?"

"Don't you remember, Isabella? He went to find Sebastián."

"Am I better?"

"I don't know, Isabella. If you are still burning in the morning, I have to take your hand. You can be strong for that, can't you?"

In the night, though she couldn't open her eyes to be sure, people touched and turned her again. She shrieked when someone brushed her hand. Crying out, she begged for water, but the words wouldn't form. She just wept until she slept again.

Then it was morning. She could tell because larks had beaten back the sounds of the nightingale in dim, grey light. She felt whether her hand still burned as badly before. It was important to be better, though she couldn't remember why.

Someone stirred nearby.

"Tomás?"

"No, I'm Brother Gilabert." A voice hovered behind her.

"Where's Tomás?"

"If he's one of those heretics, they sent him to Carcassonne." The voice sounded aloof, disgusted.

"Tomás isn't a heretic. Where's Father Anselm?"

"In Carcassonne. At least those Christian knights guarding you fought like men. They couldn't be stopped until we called on the names of the pope and the king."

"Who are you?" She tried to see him from within in the sweat-sodden nest where she lay.

"I'm a brother in Christ who travels with the crusaders." He was young, perhaps her own age, the angles of his face as sharp as the razor that had shaved his pate. He touched her again, with dry, cold hands. "Let me see your hand to dress it."

"You won't take it from me?" Her hand still hurt while the brother prodded it.

"What?"

"My hand. It's better, isn't it?"

"The pestilence isn't spreading. It's not as hot as when I first tended it. But I don't know how much use it will be when it heals." He remained aloof, uncaring. "I'll wrap it for you, and then we'll be on our way."

"Are we going to Carcassonne?"

"No, Lastours. We should be there before nightfall."

"But Lastours is two days away."

"We've been traveling since we found you yesterday in that den of heretics. We'd be there sooner, only it takes so long to drag carts over these goat paths."

"Where's my horse?"

"All the heretics' goods were seized, senhóra. I assume your horse went to Carcassonne, too, to serve Simon de Montfort." He shook his head in dismay, the way that priest Clémence used to when she came to confession. "It amazes me how you heretics can find armies of Christian knights to defend you."

"I'm not a heretic," she said.

But the brother smirked. "God knows His own."

14

Burdens and Beasts

"MAY I SIT BESIDE her, too?"

Felicia grew more listless, suffering from camp sickness. Gerard plagued Beatriz for news.

"It's a humiliating illness, senhór." Beatriz's soft voice was the only thing in the world that soothed him now. She called from the chamber where she nursed her sister, while Gerard lurked outside in purgatory.

"I blame myself." He leaned against a tapestry: Charlemagne defeating the Saracens after Roland was slain. A scene unfit for a room where women lived.

"You mustn't, senhór. As you told me, blaming yourself is a weakness of spirit."

"I should have known better than to take you girls through Bram." It felt as if he'd failed Pèire before he ever arrived at Valerós.

"You'll make yourself ill," Beatriz admonished him. "You must sleep."

Later, after Felicia ceased being violently sick and only burned in fever, Beatriz allowed him in the chamber. Gerard stayed by the girl's bed, bathing her head and bared arms to help bring down the fever. He took advantage of Beatriz's good nature, making her listen to his soul-searching as they talked through the night. Yet he never said what burned inside him: he couldn't find Jean-Luc and he hadn't protected the women left in his care.

"I shouldn't bother you with my concerns when you are burdened with worry for Felicia."

Beatriz touched his hand. "I hope you'll be my friend," she said. "I have no other, besides Felicia."

"You'll have your friend again. God must promise us to make Felicia well." Gerard wept, a shameful display of weakness.

"Why do you care so for her? You haven't had a chance to know her since you came to us," Beatriz said.

"*Dieu ait pitié!* I've failed him. He never asks anything of me. The one thing he wanted. And I failed him."

"Pèire never asked you to rescue us from fate. You must rest."

She mistook his concern, as if he meant his oath to her grandfather. Gerard didn't correct her. He had three promises to keep, and he was exhausted in the pit of his soul with the effort.

.

Colomb allowed riot and rot amongst his top captains, as Gerard had seen in the past, never understanding why Hugues stood for it within his own well-ordered ranks.

"Blood is blood," Colomb said over the evening's meal, where he'd insisted that Gerard join him. "That's why we're here. Hugues's wife is a Montcava, and they always protect their own. Or get us poor bastards to do it for them. Renoud is good at that."

Gerard steeled his gaze. "Fontcours does not belong to the Montcavas. It belongs to Sebastián, Nicolau's heir."

"*Ai, oui.* But the Montcava estate is just down the valley, and Renoud asked us to bivouac here. Just as well. We have more water and our horses have the sweetest grass in the valley."

After the principal part of the meal, Gerard came to understand that Colomb and his cohorts had brought wenches from town. When fruit and cheese were carried to the table, the purchased women joined them, heads uncovered, robes half tied.

"I don't know if my men got the count right," Colomb said. "Perhaps you'll have to share if you want to join us."

Gerard had lived in harsh, long-standing camps in the Outremer, and there couldn't be much in this world he hadn't seen. But Fontcours was right here in Christendom, a hare's leap from the St-Féliz-de-Fontcours abbey, two timber-walls from where his charges rested. He demurred from participation and tried to raise the flag of camp-sickness, but Colomb waved away the concern with a laugh.

"One little girl with the stomach-heaves? Not enough to alarm this squad. We're clean enough for your sort, aren't we, *putana*?" He slapped the haunch of the woman in his lap. She answered in the local tongue, not understanding Colomb's French.

That one loutish giant with the *crux lunata* tattoo stood apart from the rest, like a lord's own guard, not looking at the women, just heaping hatred on Gerard with his gaze. Was this the demon-wolf the Crux Lunata knights set to wreak havoc on the bonfraires? Or one wolf in a large pack? Gerard needed Hugues's help to sort the puzzle.

"Thank you for the good dinner," Gerard rose. "I'm not used to these late southern meals. I'll bid you adieu for the evening."

·

Colomb groused over a message from Hugues, who remained in Toulouse. The marquis wanted men at work in the fields.

> "*Mon cher frère*, our men consume the people's food, trample their fields, drink dry the streams and wells where herds of horses never camped before. It is our duty to God and our brothers in Christ to return good to the land."

"Brothers in Christ! My hairy hind-end," Colomb exclaimed when he summoned Gerard to show him Hugues's orders. "Every last man and woman in this land, down to the lowliest whore and varlet, every one of them is a Satan-sucking heretic. What do I care if they starve next winter? The faster they go to Judgment, the better."

"We will, of course, do as Hugues asks." Gerard agreed with Hugues—in fact, he had already set his lower ranks to farm tasks.

"Don't we always? A bastard cannot choose." Colomb continued to rage, until Gerard gradually coaxed him into breakfast and a more rational mood.

As servants laid out bread, duck-egg omelets, and sheep's cheese, Gerard asked what he'd been wondering over the days.

"Why are you here, Colomb? Isn't there greater glory and booty for you with Simon? Hugues is here to keep peace. There's not booty to be shared at the end of this summer's work."

"To protect Fontcours. I owe that to Renoud."

"I don't understand."

"The Montcava brothers grew up next over from our lands. I raised Renoud and Nicolau up in the army. Like an uncle you might say." Colomb sneered, another of his private jokes. "Renoud learned to fight. Nicolau—well, nothing said is best said. I've led Renoud this far in life. He needs to not cock it up by running around with honor-free southern rebels."

Then Colomb went off into his verbal rampages again for a long while, expanding on oaths and condemnations of the whole of the heretical south.

"I am happy to guard Fontcours for Renoud, the way Renoud takes care of that whelp Nicolau got on Pèire's witch-girl. If Simon challenges this land, God forbid, I will be here to protect it."

"But the old Count of Fontcours gave Fontcours to Miquel of Morella. Then this land passed to Nicolau as oldest son. This isn't Montcava heritage land."

"The so-called Don Miquel, that braggart spy and womanizer? You remember that I was with Hugues in Jaffa? I know Miquel well for what he is. That gambling cheat met his own ill fate when the Church took Fontcours and gave it to Nicolau."

"Miquel is dead."

Colomb spat. "Thank God for that. The world is better for him being gone. And Nicolau? Wrong color to be the son of that black-amoor. And now his son has a heretic for a mother."

"Master Colomb, peace! You're a good fellow. Why this bile?"

"Renoud is holding Fontcours for the Montcavas, using his friends in the Church. If Renoud slips, or if he's mistaken for just another lying seigneur of the south, Simon will seize Fontcours. I am sworn to help prevent that."

Gerard steeled his gaze. "Fontcours does not belong to Renoud. It belongs to Sebastián, Nicolau's heir."

"But Renoud is Sebastián's guardian and steward."

"No, he's not. I am. Or I soon will be. I am marrying the boy's mother soon."

"Then a truly magical witch she is, indeed. When last I saw him, Renoud crowed that his cousin Louis is marrying her."

"Renoud is mistaken."

"*Ai*, well then, good luck with that." Colomb ripped another handful of bread from the loaf on the wood plank before them. "Those Montcavas like to keep it as close as consanguinity laws allow. Lord knows I tried to break into that tribe years ago. But me, not the right blood lines, didn't bring enough land to the bargain. Hugues made it into that clan by wedding his faithless wife. They don't like any Montcavas escaping the fold without a grand, wealthy bargain."

"The Montcavas have nothing to say about who Isabella of Valerós marries. She's of age." Gerard felt Colomb's rude ideas disturbing his rational thought. "Our marriage was arranged through Pèire Leteric."

"But as you said, Pèire's dead. Her remaining relatives are Montcavas. And if you make yourself first in line for marrying that witch, you still have to convince the bishop in Toulouse she isn't a heretic."

"*Bon Dieu*, what are you saying, man?"

"You didn't know? And yet you want to marry the wench? Renoud let the Church know she's a heretic. Those women you're protecting are likely just as bad."

"None of the women in Pèire Leteric's household are heretics."

Colomb shrugged. He sopped up the remains of his omelet with a fistful of bread. "If anyone knows, it's Renoud. She promised to marry by Pentecost. That's tomorrow. And you're sitting here waiting for her. As is Louis of Montcava."

"I must write to the bishop. Or go to Toulouse to see him."

"She's supposed to be at the bishops' court on Monday, to prove she's true to the Church. Maybe she'll marry one of you poor bastards before then."

"*Dieu ait pitié!* May the angels sing!"

"Angels don't fly in protection of heretics. They're all consigned to Satan's care." And Colomb was off again, denouncing the hereticated whores of the south.

When he finally got free of Colomb, Gerard departed for his morning prayers in the chapel. Then, at the summer kitchen, he caught that crude guard of Colomb's, the one who never removed his leather cuirass and seldom unlaced his aventail, watching Beatriz as she instructed the laundry-women about Felicia's robe and linen.

"Aren't you supposed to be in the fields?" Gerard asked. The man was so tall—like Yves and Jean-Luc—that Gerard addressed the laces and studs of the man's cuirass. It was of foreign make, so that Gerard had to cover every league of his Outremer travels to recall where he had seen it. In the eastern empire?

"I'm not a farmer," the brute said. "And you are not my father. I serve only his commands."

15

The Knights at Lastours

Isabella, lost in the Languedoc, May 21

ISABELLA LIVED THROUGH EONS in each moment as the dog-cart jerked along the road. The tedium of the ride and the heat made the day seem interminable. Although she rode in a covered cart, the air seared like a village oven. Sweat ran between her breasts, so she kept pulling at her robe, afraid to find crawling insects. She yearned for water after emptying the flask the brother left her but kept quiet in hopes of finishing the journey more quickly.

When the sun hovered two fingers' breadth above the western horizon, the wagons stopped. Brother Gilabert brought her water. He helped her from the wagon so she could stand. Senhóra Eloïse paced nearby.

"What happened at Laurac?" Isabella wobbled when she took two steps.

"Several dozen crusaders came and carried everyone off to Carcassonne." Eloïse didn't turn around to answer her.

"But they didn't take us," Isabella said. "Why are we here?"

"Renoud sent his knights to help us when he learned the crusaders were returning to Laurac."

"Why aren't we going to Fontcours or the Montcava estates? Or Toulouse? Why are we out in the Montagne Noire?"

"Lastours is a safe place for Good Christians," Eloïse said. "Renoud wants us both to be safe."

"Where are my knights?"

"Only your priest and marshal and two other knights were in the village when the crusaders came."

"But the rest?" Isabella wanted to ask about Tomás, but then remembered that he went to find Sebastián.

"Let your brother take care of you, *ma bel criatura*."

Eloïse wandered toward her own dog-cart.

■

A servant at Lastours led Isabella to a sleeping room filled with women, most wearing simple linen robes of country folk.

Breathing rapidly, seeking air, frantic to know how she could get to Toulouse, Isabella asked, "What day is it, senhóra? It was three days before Pentecost when we came to Laurac."

"It's five days since Pentecost," the woman said.

"No! It can't be. I must see the bishop in Toulouse soon."

One of the women in the sleeping room said, "Welcome, sister." She kissed Isabella on the forehead.

Another woman led Isabella to a pallet where she could sleep. "We're happy to see any Friend of God."

"But I'm Catholic," Isabella replied to each greeting from a good-woman. Beyond the frantic sense she carried, her anxiety increased when each woman who greeted her could not answer the simple question, how could she get to Toulouse?

The next morning, Isabella feigned sleep when the women wakened and dressed near dawn, though she was well enough that she felt hungry for the first time in days. Alone, she rose and tried to straighten her gown, which was torn at the shoulder and impossibly stained. She rearranged her surcoat, the beautiful blue coat Tomás had given her, and found that the two gold buttons had been cut from it while she slept. Whether that happened in Laurac, on the journey, or here in this sleeping porch, she could never learn.

Isabella stretched, feeling the pull of pain in her hand. No one had tended the wound since Brother Gilabert wrapped it the previous afternoon, so she carefully pulled the bandage to see how she fared. The wound, now a long cut across her palm instead of the original stab wound from Eloïse's spindle, had crusted and sealed under Father Anselm's stitches. The scab was still pink at the edges. As she tried to stretch her palm, it ached, stiffened, and resisted. She couldn't close her fingers over it. With her left hand, she wrapped it as neatly as possible, feeling that she wrapped linen to hide a catastrophe. *It will heal. It will heal.* She chanted that to console herself, and went exploring, away from where the women were singing, and probably spinning, in the sun. Her fevered thoughts had been replaced with worries about finding Sebastián. And Tomás. How to escape this place?

After crossing through the kitchen gardens where children weeded under the supervision of two older girls, she came upon an open door leading into a room outfitted like her own scriptorium. A small white-haired woman wrote at a desk, working with great concentration. She resembled Eloïse, but when she turned to answer a voice out of Isabella's sight, her face was peaceful and benign; her eyes moved in intelligent, curious response to a hidden speaker.

A man's angry voice echoed in the room. "King Philippe gave in to the pope over a few confused old women who won't say their prayers right. Now he wants to make us live like Angevine serfs."

"As you have said." The woman spoke mildly to the angry man. "But you know that's not what this is about."

"It's not about how we say our prayers or whether we ask the correct priest to bless us. It's about who takes our taxes and names our bishops." The furious man pounded on the table where the woman worked. "They want to break Count Raymond's balls. They'll destroy a generation of knights and their lands to do it."

The woman spoke the southern tongue with a French accent. "It's Raymond they don't trust. Philippe is merely helping the pope gain obedience."

"I'm a soldier, ma dòmna. I know a captain doesn't get obedience from his men unless he lives by the same rules." The man tried to match the woman's calm tone, but his tension sharpened each word. "I can't obey the Church unless its priests and bishops keep the rules, too."

"I beg you to trust diplomacy. Don't make my son a pawn in this. Let him go." Though she sounded calm, the woman stabbed the parchment on her desk with a quill as she spoke. "Bram shows what happens if you push Simon de Montfort."

"Senhóra Mathilde, your son made himself a pawn when he rode into this country with the French crusaders. We shall not agree, but I bid you good day."

The man brushed past Isabella as he stormed out to the court-yard—a southern lord in late midlife, haggard and grey from worry, yet he walked with the carriage of a seigneur. Isabella glanced at the woman, who resumed writing at her desk. Hesitating, Isabella wandered farther into the next courtyard, gathering courage to ask for help to escape this place. Thyme, lavender, and mint carpeted the garden path. The dew had dried, so every step released spicy fragrances. Bees hummed in the wild roses beyond the garden fence, where a blue rock thrush cocked its head, trying to decide whether to sing or flee.

The rock thrush flapped up and over the outbuildings.

Isabella followed the thrush. The perfumed path led to another courtyard, where the bird perched in a yew tree and sang. A crowd of southern knights sat in the sun, their voices humming like the bees in the borage and thyme. Blinded, they grinned in ghastly, perpetual smiles, their noses and upper lips cut from their faces by the knives of Simon's army.

■

Isabella at Lastours, May 22

"If you're one of those goodwomen they brought here last night, you'll find the women's house by the kitchen gardens." The woman smiled coldly, as if still arguing with the angry lord.

"No." Isabella sat down unbidden. "I'm Isabella of Valerós. I shouldn't be here."

"You don't need to be afraid." The woman spoke softly now, but returned to her writing, dismissing Isabella. "This is the safest place in the country for goodwomen. Simon will never attack in these rugged hills again."

"I'm not a goodwoman. This trouble is none of my business."

"It's everyone's business now, *ma chère*, because your whole obstinate country has raised the Church's wrath." The woman spoke in a rich accent, sprinkled with French. "Don't be deceived. Even though all your lords sit waiting for the French to go home when it gets too hot. As if, like children, it will disappear if you just close your eyes. Do you all believe in magic?"

"I don't." Isabella couldn't keep her voice from shaking.

"Or perhaps you believe in miracles? That's what it will take to defeat Simon. He intends to win."

"This has nothing to do with me." Isabella's breath came as a sob. She covered her eyes, pressing hard, trying not to picture the blind, lipless men in the garden.

"You saw the knights from Bram?" the woman said. "It's shocking, but that's how Simon will force the south to obey."

"How can you be so cold?"

"I weep at night. In the daylight, I am pragmatic. You good-women should trade heresy for a rational view of the world."

"I'm not one of them. I shouldn't be here. I need to be in Toulouse." Isabella felt foolish and small, an uncomfortable sensation.

The woman regarded her sharply. "You are ill."

"Not so bad now," Isabella said. "But I haven't eaten for days. And I'm desperate to find my husband and son."

The woman called through the arched doorway for toast and broth to be brought. Then she gently unwrapped Isabella's injured hand. Her whole demeanor changed to warm regard.

"I am Mathilde, from Garlande in the Pays de France." Despite her white hair, Mathilde had the vibrance of a young woman. Her eyes shone with interest as she regarded Isabella. "My son is hostage here. Bouchard de Marly. Have you heard of him?"

"I live in the hills above Narbonne," Isabella said. "And I've been traveling, so I have little news. I'm Isabella of Valerós, but my son has an estate near Toulouse."

"Where's your husband, senhóra? Why are you here alone?"

"He went to Toulouse to find my son. The boy's father died in Constantinople, and now his uncle has stolen him away."

"I lost my husband Mathieu in Constantinople, too. There isn't a day I don't still think of him." She released Isabella's injured hand. "I can see you were very ill. Please rest."

"I can't. It's too important for me to go to Toulouse."

"Here's food. Let's start with that." When the food arrived, Mathilde served her as one cares for a child. "We'll find a bath for you and then see what we can do."

While Isabella ate, Mathilde chatted with easy, assured manners, though she talked about war and strategy. "My son Bouchard came to Lastours as an emissary for Philippe, not Simon. But he arrived just as the knights of Bram found their way here. Now he's a hostage."

"How did they travel, being blind?"

"Simon's men left their captain with one eye, to lead them. Any human hearts can understand why the seigneur of Lastours seized my son. Now we're in the middle of a stand-off."

"But you said Simon won't attack."

"Because the terrain is impossible. The Count of Toulouse sent pleas to Rome, but the pope's legates called him to St-Gilles, so he can't help. I send messages to Simon, but he says there's no negotiating with faithless southern seigneurs."

"I'm so sorry," Isabella murmured.

Mathilde didn't acknowledge the sympathy. "Simon doesn't have the forces to attack Toulouse. That's why he's going after villages."

"Those villages are empty," Isabella said. "Everyone has taken to the hills."

"So they say. And the towns bow when Simon comes and then kick dust in his tracks when he leaves. How did you come here, senhóra?"

"French crusaders came while I was ill. They carried away my knights, though we're Catholic and sworn to King Pedro. A priest I know brought me here."

"This isn't a time to be found in the wrong place," Mathilde said, "as my son learned. Now that you've eaten, tell me why you are so eager to go to Toulouse."

"My brother-in-law, from when I was married before, condemned me as a heretic to the Church. I have to answer to the bishops' court or I'll lose my son."

Mathilde slapped her hand on the table, like the lord had earlier. But it was the slender, fragile hand of an aging woman. "That's how you know this was a mistake. By all the evil it generates."

"What mistake?" Isabella asked.

"The pope calling this crusade. And Philippe for going along with it. Count Raymond for lying and hedging. Simon for thinking he's holier than the rest of us. I warned my niece when she married him. But now Alix is just like Simon. What about you and your new husband—the one you misplaced?"

"We haven't worked out yet what our life will be, only that we intend to always travel together. Only fate has separated us"

Mathilde said, "I went everywhere with my husband. Except I didn't go to Constantinople."

"And now?"

"After this squabble ends, I intend to make a difference for women who turn to the Church." Mathilde grew animated as she spoke. "There are few houses for women who have no protectors. I'll spend every silver penny I can badger from the abbots, bishops, and lords until there are enough good places for women."

"It's not a problem here," Isabella said. "We live with our grand-mothers, aunts, and cousins. There's always a home to go to."

"But what if you wanted to study? What if your husband was cruel? Then where could you go? If your new husband discards you, Isabella of Valerós, come to the convent I founded in Paris."

Isabella clasped her trembling hands, exhausted. "I don't think Paris would suit me. I hear it's cold. Besides, my new husband wants me. If he can find me."

"How shall I help you, senhóra?"

"*Why* should you help me? We've only just met."

"Because you're a rational woman and in distress. It would please me to solve at least one problem amid all this chaos." Mathilde tapped her cheek as if pondering. "I need to send a message to Toulouse to tell the bishop what's happened here. Can you ride with my guards? It's a day's ride for my guard. Two days when I travel with them."

"Òc," Isabella said. "I've lived in the saddle the past month."

"But you've been ill."

"It's only my hand. I can still sit a horse."

"Bold words. You're like a wraith after famine, you're so thin. Your robe is frayed and reeks of the sick-room. Your hands shake from fatigue."

"I'm sure I can keep up. Do we leave today?"

"Tomorrow. Let's find better clothes for you. I have a house near the count's palace where you can stay. My people can help you prepare for the bishops' court."

"You are too kind, Mathilde."

"You'll return the kindness to other women, won't you? The dispossessed? The ones who need protection?"

16
The Searchers

"LOOK, SWORDSMAN, THERE'S A BLACKSMITH on every other street in this quarter." Jean-Luc, now Tomás's daily companion, pointed to one across the plaza.

"They said at the inn I could find a Moorish physician one street over from here."

"A physician to pull your damn tooth? This is beyond vanity."

The pounding in his head kept Tomás from responding. He spotted the physician he sought, an older gentleman seated in a market stall under an awning stitched from old campaign pavilion tenting. A man doled out silver coins while the young woman at his side, her head bound in a cloth, wept silently. Tomás appeared when the couple departed.

"*Ai*, you are in pain." The physician spoke with a Toulouse accent. "My name is Nizam al-Mulk."

Tomás recited his name, while Jean-Luc stood to the side, his arms folded, announcing without words his disapproval.

Peering where Tomás indicated, Nizam al-Mulk said, "You were taught well to care for what our Creator endowed, Tomás of Cyprus. This is from the injury to your face, isn't it?" He didn't wait for Tomás to answer. "It will have to come out. I see you've brought a friend to help."

He handed Tomás a poppy-and-wine potion, which aroused memories of his mother's nursing when Chrétien fetched him from that wretched cellar. Without waiting for Jean-Luc to assent, the physician showed him how to hold Tomás as he prepared to pinch out that hellish tooth.

"Don't you have someone to beat a drum so he won't feel it?" Jean-Luc looked alarmed at the strange pliers the physician wielded.

"Your friend isn't able to feel much pain at this moment," the physician said, just as Tomás lost his ability to stand.

•

Tomás needed help to count out three silver pennies, and Jean-Luc had to take charge of the phial of poppy syrup Nizam al-Mulk prepared. He could follow where Jean-Luc led, though he walked about as poorly as after the worst night of too much wine.

Jean-Luc propped him on a stool at one of the market-place kitchens near St-Sernin and then procured a trencher of stew for himself and a cup of watered wine for Tomás. They lounged through much of the afternoon. Tomás nodded off and then woke when he tasted blood and his head began to throb again. He dreamily tongued the empty space in his mouth, hoping that by the next day he might at last be free of throbbing pain.

He missed Isabella. And Sebastián. Even Miquel.

After gaining so much since the Vale of Roses, he'd lost everything when he had to leave Isabella to Father Anselm's care. And Miquel chose to stay in Laurac with that witch Eloïse. He needed to find his brother Chrétien, so that he had a partner he could trust, and who didn't despise him, as the French giant did.

He needed to rest from riding all over the countryside, seeking Chrétien and Sebastián and Isabella.

They had first ridden to Carcassonne, to learn that Renoud had gone to Toulouse. They rode to Toulouse, to find Renoud had gone to Termes with Hugues de Beaurain.

They rode there, hopelessly, and returned to Laurac, where they found everyone gone, taken by French crusaders.

They rode in a fury back to Carcassonne, but were denied entry. No one at the gate had heard of Isabella of Valerós. And the knights of Valerós were held until a Roman Christian lord claimed them. Tomás's claim to be master of the knights was laughed at. They came back to Toulouse, hoping Renoud might have returned there. But people at the gate claimed he wasn't expected for a day or two.

"He didn't trust us with his travel plans," the little man at the gate said.

It couldn't be more cocked up if a bishops' court had been held at Pentecost and they'd missed it. Now, it was four days until Isabella had to plead before the bishops, but Tomás couldn't find her. The next ride would be to Fontcours, in hopes that either Gerard de Chartrain or Hugues de Beaurain were there and could intercede for the knights.

Jean-Luc answered a knock at their flimsy reed door.

"*Bon día*, senhórs." Benito, the Valerós master-at-arms, greeted them, dusty and breathless, followed by a brace of the knights who had stayed behind in Laurac with Isabella. "We found you by luck, senhórs, since we recognized your horses in the stable."

Tomás stood up too fast. He fell onto his stool again.

"She's here?"

"No. At Fontcours—"

"She's at Fontcours?"

"No. At Fontcours, we tried to find Hugues de Beaurain to ask his help. He wasn't there. We aren't sure where to find Senhóra Isabella. But we think she's at Lastours."

While they headed for the stables to prepare to ride, Benito related what had happened—at least, the part he knew about.

The Valerós knights who'd ridden to Laurac with Tomás and Isabella had returned from foraging outside Laurac to learn that Simon's crusaders had taken Isabella, Guillem, Anselm, and two other knights. Benito and the Valerós men followed the crusaders to Carcassonne, where they met an abbot, a friend of Isabella's, who said they'd find her at Lastours.

"But outside Lastours, rebel scouts chased us away," Benito said. "We couldn't convince them we aren't *francimand* invaders. Though we can't any of us bark a word of French."

"Can you ride, swordsman?" Jean-Luc asked.

Tomás studied the stirrup, endeavoring to see how to get his foot into it.

"Just get me into the saddle."

■

JEAN-LUC MARKED THE DUST coating Tomás's surcoat when they approached Lastours. "One look at you after this ride from Toulouse, they'll mistake your quest for a Twelfth Night mummer."

"But you, Perseus, can't open your mouth without people knowing you're French. We can't get inside any door in the south if you're the one who asks."

They'd ridden all night in great hope, heading east toward the Montagne Noire. As the road became steeper, winding up to three castles atop outcrops, they were stopped at the pike-gate below Lastours. The knights there denied them further passage. The day was spent negotiating for messages to be carried to the castle-lord. Tomás and Jean-Luc learned a few women had been brought to Lastours from Laurac to avoid French crusaders, among them, Senora Eloïse of Montcava. But no one knew Isabella of Valerós.

"At least the horses are rested," Tomás groused. "Isabella would have my hide for what we forced these beasts to do."

"Look there, Tomás." Jean-Luc directed his unhappy companion's attention to a new parade coming to meet them. A French lady, of an age near to his father's, walked down the trail with six knights, all French, all unarmed.

"*Messieurs*, my men report that you seek Isabella of Valerós." She said her name was Mathilde de Garlande.

"I knew your husband in Constantinople," Jean-Luc said. "He was an honorable man."

She stared hard, endeavoring to recognize him, but Jean-Luc remained silent, obstinate about not stating his own name while Tomás recited his pedigree, ending with "knight of Pedro *le Rei*" in the vain way he liked to do.

"Isabella of Valerós went to Toulouse with my knights yesterday. You must have set out to ride here just as she came to town."

Jean-Luc watched Tomás master himself, knowing the pain the arsewit experienced, separated from his love in haphazard ways.

"I think you'll find your wife waiting at my casa in Toulouse, not far from the St-Sernin cathedral."

In the same neighborhood where they'd dossed while seeking Sebastián and Chrétien.

17

St-Jordi and the Spirits of the Streams

Gerard at Fontcours, May 25

A SPRING RAN THROUGH a laurel bower, falling first into a stony pool and then trickling away among patches of wild thyme and rock roses. Steel-grey clouds tumbled overhead, smoky grey at the edges where vague sunlight filtered through.

Gerard, the Viscount de Chartrain, knelt by the stony pool to dip a small carved image of St-Jordi in the spring and pray for rain. The viscount wanted rain, because it might slow the command to move the armies into position for a siege, though the mud of the south would turn hard as stone within a day under the hot sun. He tried to pray the correct the prayer, the one bowing to God's will, but that morning it roused bitterness instead of peace in his heart.

"We promised you a trip home."

Another voice in the hedges: Colomb, the cracked-mirror half of the better Beaurain brother, always there to plague him. Too weary to get up and walk away, too disgusted with the man to even announce his presence, Gerard stayed kneeling by the pool, praying for St-Jordi to intercede.

"We promised you more than your share of all the heretics' gold we find," Colomb said.

Then Gerard head what must be the voice of their secret enemy.

"I don't want gold. I want a son. And to finish hunting my father's enemies."

From the clatter and yelps, Colomb struck a man in chainmail. "Damn your soul, you are commanded to remain with this army."

From the jangling of chainmail, the man was running away. "I want to go home!" he shouted.

More clattering and beast-like aggravation in the bushes. Colomb emerged, splashing into the stream, and then apparently regretting it. While he cursed his wet feet, he finally noticed Gerard in the grotto.

Colomb drew up to tower over Gerard.

"Stay away from my business, little man. Go play with your wee girls."

18
Toulouse, Awaiting Siege

THROUGH THE LONG DAY riding to Toulouse with the Mathilde de Garlande's knights, Isabella rehearsed her defense for the bishop's court, while also continuously repressing her fears. All she had to do in Toulouse was to find Tomás, who must have saved Sebastián by now.

Travel toward Toulouse slowed for Mathilde's knights as the roadway was filled with carts, wagons, and walkers leaving Toulouse before Simon laid siege.

Isabella hated cities, especially Toulouse, and her hatred kindled anew on the outskirts. Before one can nestle into the bosom of wealth and fine living inside the city walls, one passes through the edges of the city, where people lived in stick-and-mud huts, poorly protected by broken-tile roofs, the bare dirt yards full of cast-off trash and half-starved dogs, with no doors protecting the inhabitants because there is nothing to steal and nothing to trespass against.

After passing through the suburbs of despair and dirt, Isabella rode with a dozen of Mathilde de Garlande's knights into the stinking, twisted metropolis she detested. Too many people and too many animals crammed together into narrow dirty streets, with sewage and garbage running down gutters in the middle of the road. Vegetables rotted in the markets, offal lay in piles by doorways. The city seemed much worse now than in years past. Simon de Montfort's plans to lay siege distracted people's attention so they didn't take care of their streets.

The city stank to the heavens, as it would until the rains came in November. Summer cloudbursts could never be enough to clean away the filth. The heat, humidity, and dust clung to her, as it had years before, a sticky feeling she associated with perpetual fear and the need to be alert for danger. The humidity made it hard to think, the air too thick to breathe.

As she passed through a corner of her old neighborhood, she saw the towers of St-Sernin had grown taller with the stone-masons' endeavors in the half-dozen years since she was last here. A new-style church was being built near the river, its corners and arches spikier than the graceful rounded stone churches everywhere in the south. In the marketplace, many of the rough shanties by the city walls had been replaced with permanent merchant stalls, but the crude huts in the market center were even more haphazard and ragged than she remembered.

It was coming on evening when they dismounted at the top of the narrow street leading to Mathilde's casa. A throng of men marched down the street toward them.

"What's this?" Isabella asked the captain of the knights.

"Everyone comes to see Bishop Folquet preach at vespers."

"I'd like to hear him." Isabella was eager to take the measure of the man to whom she must answer in two days.

"It's not for women. The bishop offers a matins service for women. Let us take you up the street, senhóra."

As they stepped away from their horses, a stream of would-be worshippers separated her from the knights and pushed her along in the crush. She pressed back, trying to return to her guardians, but within a couple of heartbeats she'd been shoved a full street away and lost sight of Mathilde de Garlande's men. At St-Etienne, where the men filed into the church, she broke free of the crowd and leaned against the cathedral wall to get her breath. As the flood of worshippers disappeared inside, she glanced around the square to get her bearings and chose the street that led back to Mathilde's knights, who must be searching for her.

She slipped into the narrow alley parallel to the street she'd come up to avoid the rag-tag clusters of men who hung in the square to watch others enter the church. Dark was falling, especially in the alleys where there were no torches or cook fires. Startled by a sound, she glanced over her shoulder to find a tattered mercenary. His eyes seemed crazed, and he reached for her.

"*Mignotta!*" He called her the lowest of prostitutes, as Nicolau used to when he was angry. "*Putana!*"

She ran, bursting out of the alley into a passel of servants carrying a sedan chair.

"Caution, senhóra!" A servant shouted in warning as she collided with the chair, nearly upsetting the bearers. To regain their balance, they set the chair down for a moment. In the commotion, the abbot of St-Féliz-de-Fontcours stepped out of the chair.

"*Bon Dèu!*" she cried.

She dropped to her knees before him and prayed for mercy, never so glad to see her old friend. Down the alley, the ragged man retreated into the shadows.

"Senhóra Isabella! God bless me, I'm so surprised to see you." The abbot clasped his hands as if in prayer.

"Mathilde de Garlande sent me with her knights, so I could see the bishop. *Ai*, Pare Abát! I am happy to see you, too."

"Are you reconciled with your brother Renoud?" he asked.

"I haven't found Renoud yet to discuss things with him."

"Let me escort you to your house. It's just around the corner."

"Senhóra Mathilde invited me to use her casa, Pare Abát. But the crowd pushed me away from her knights, and I'm trying to get back to them now."

"You can't be on the streets alone, senhóra. It's not safe in Toulouse these days, but especially at night. Come to my house. It's right here at this turn."

Which meant she was just outside the gates of the Montcava villa, and therefore had stepped into the wrong alley from the square at St-Etienne.

"Please lend me an escort to go to Senhóra Mathilde's casa."

"Nonsense. You can't prefer to importune strangers instead of honoring me as my guest. We'll send servants to fetch your things from your friends."

In the end she accepted, glad to step into any safe haven.

∙

Pare Abát fussed over Isabella while they enjoyed an evening meal together, picking at a simple rabbit stew with ginger and onions, fresh purslane in vinegar, a sweetened cheese with jellied fruits. He said that as bad as his vision was, he could see that she had been ill, and so she recounted her adventures, describing all that passed since they met at the Vale of Roses.

Well, not all. Many omissions and prevarications were required.

"I heeded your good advice, Pare Abát, and married. The Church can see that I am obedient."

He exclaimed how pleased he was. She didn't correct his assumption that she had married Renoud's silly cousin Louis.

"You will want this letter back then." The abbot rummaged in his leather pocketbook, the one he always kept beside him. "I haven't seen the bishop since we last talked. But you don't need me to play messenger, since you are here. Tell me about your misadventures."

Setting aside her dismay over all the trouble to write and send that letter he never delivered, she explained the happenstance of being in Laurac in search of Sebastián and being carried away to Lastours with Eloïse.

"How is the senhóra of Montcava doing, living in the bowels of ignominy with those heretics?" The abbot looked up from his meal to study Isabella as she answered.

"Senhóra Eloïse is well and happy. She has many friends among those people. Perhaps that's the allure for her." Isabella hesitated. "I found the heretics' discussions tedious. These people's views of God and salvation are simpleminded, or at least wrongheaded. It's hard to see how this heresy is worth the wrath of popes and kings."

The abbot pushed at the food with his knife, arranging it on the wooden platter. "*Ai,* so it seems. It's sad that Senhóra Eloïse fell into Satan's clutches in this way."

He did indeed sound saddened, which encouraged Isabella to speak with him. "Pare Abát, can you pray for me."

"Your heart seems to bear a heavy burden," the abbot said. "I cannot absolve sins while the Count of Toulouse is excommunicated. But you can unburden your heart to me, like in the old days, and I shall pray for you."

"That would be kind of you." Isabella tried to describe her burden simply and quickly, without revealing everything else about the Montcavas and her imperiled friends. She didn't consider these to be sins, but yes, a burden.

The abbot said prayers for her and assigned the lightest of private penances. "You have paid heavy tolls already for your sins and those of others." Then he offered her a light wine. "From the Rhône. I think you'll find it refreshing."

"Pare Abát. I must ask. Have you seen my son Sebastián? Is he with Renoud?"

"I saw him a week ago. The lad seemed hale and hearty."

She had to be satisfied with that unsatisfying news. After the servants cleared away their meal, the abbot rose to say good-night. He had to travel early the next morning, and it would be late into the summer before he could return to either Toulouse or the abbey near Fontcours.

"You'll cease fretting now, I hope," the abbot said at the end of the farewells. "You'll see your son soon, and do as your family wishes you to, for his sake and your own."

19
Street Fighting Redux

Tomás in Toulouse, May 26

TOMÁS AND JEAN-LUC FOUND Mathilde's house in Toulouse easily enough. But no one there knew anything about Isabella. The house-steward who answered their hail at the gate had heard that Garlande knights conveyed a woman to Toulouse. But no one knew where the knights had left her, and those knights had already returned to Lastours.

"The devil's own adulterous sister couldn't make a better pudding." Tomás felt impotent frustration embrace him, while the veil of the day's headache blocked his view of the next street corner.

"Now we walk the streets, swordsman. We'll find her." Jean-Luc beat road dust from his gambeson. "But we need sleep first."

Tomás was pouring out his dissent when Jean-Luc added, "Because we need to start our search at the Montcava villa."

After they again stabled their exhausted horses in Toulouse, Tomás had to spend extra silver pennies on decent lodging. They were exhausted.

While Jean-Luc dozed or daydreamed on the cot in their rented room, Tomás huddled over the brazier fire, trying to warm his aching bones. Spring in Toulouse shouldn't require a fire, but the stone-and-brick house hadn't warmed with summer, and so he shivered in his raggedy undershirt while the landlady washed his clothes.

Tomás curled up by the brazier and hoped that today's headache would go away. He closed his eyes to find a moment of comfort, which meant his vision of lying beside Isabella, her pale skin glowing under his dark hand, her wild copper hair falling all around him. He strained to remember how it felt to touch and taste the softest parts of her and to hear her moans in the dark of night.

Longing to find Isabella and make her safe, Tomás wrestled with the temptation to scour every house between Toulouse and Lastours. But he turned to the most crucial business: how to rescue Sebastián and how to answer Isabella's summons to the bishops' court. If Isabella didn't appear the following morning, Tomás would stand in her place, his right as her husband.

"Are you feeling sorry for yourself?" Jean-Luc sat up on the bed to drink water from a pitcher.

"What?"

"You're tapping your knife on the floor and beating your foot on the wall. The innkeeper is bound to wonder what we're doing."

"Do you think she's safe?" Tomás tapped his own knee.

"A dozen knights brought her to town. We know the knights arrived in the city. She just found other friends to stay with."

"But she hates Toulouse. She doesn't have friends here."

"You'll see her tomorrow at the bishops' court."

"It was lunacy to leave Isabella in Laurac."

"She insisted Sebastián was in danger," Jean-Luc said. "It made sense to leave her at the time."

"Because she was out of her head with fever. Now it's days and days since we saw her, and it's all cocked up."

"Now she's somewhere safe in Toulouse, tying her hair up in red ribbons and putting rue in her shoes."

"Why would she do that?"

"It's a charm. Girls do it to get men to come back to them."

"Isabella doesn't use charms. She reads Aristotle. She's rational."

"At least one of you is."

"Maybe if I'd read more Aristotle I'd have an idea what to do."

"Stick to the plan," Jean-Luc said.

"Which one? I started out revenging the evil done to my father. Then I wandered up in those hills, where Pèire Leteric kicked me sideways when he made me promise to protect his children. I spent a full turn of the moon trying to keep one woman alive. Now I have to rescue her son and save her land from the Church. Then I must find her knights so she can sell their services to the king of Aragón, who owns my life because I walked down the wrong alley one night. And my wife is lost somewhere in Toulouse."

"She's not lost. We just don't know where she is at the moment."

"I'm lost." Tomás recalled Miquel as he had last seen him, consoling Eloïse of Montcava. "As soon as I find Isabella and Chrétien, we're leaving this hell-hole and going home to Cyprus. Forget revenge. Forget Fontcours, and all the rest."

Jean-Luc said, "That's sensible. I'd go home if I could."

"The one time I proposed Cyprus to Isabella, she cried *'viech d'ase'* and called me a betrayer."

"That means donkey's cock in your tongue, doesn't it? She might be correct, but you should teach your wife to avoid street-talk."

Tomás let the jibe pass. "Isabella says I'm now responsible for every sheepherder, chicken thief, and vineyard serf in the upper Corbiéres hills."

"They don't have serfs in the south. You're thinking of Normans and Angevines and English."

"Like that codfish Simon de Montfort," Tomás said, "who stole Valerós horses and knights."

"In your list of daring deeds that must be done, after we find Isabella, we'll get Guillem and Father Anselm out of Carcassonne. With or without your horses."

"St-Vitus and the dancing angels. All I wanted was old-fashioned revenge, like a man of honor. I do not want to get involved in this God-forsaken crusade."

"Me either."

"And I did not want to chase a wife all over the Languedoc."

"No, you very much want to chase after Isabella," Jean-Luc said. "For a know-it-all sod, you have a blind spot that prevents knowing your own self. Or your true love."

Jean-Luc set bait for a quarrel, but Tomás considered whether he was right. "I don't pretend to understand her. Isabella was ill in Laurac, but I believed it was because she's carrying a child."

"Is she?"

"Only the hand of God could prevent it. Did she tell you?"

"No, we hardly spoke. I said you were an arsewit assassin who'd cause her heartache. She said I was wrong. I told her my real name and that I love her sister."

"Then she kissed you?" Tomás said.

"She felt sorry for me. I have a talent for making women sorry for me. They forget me a heartbeat later."

Tomás again tongued the hole where the bad tooth had been. "I hope the pollution in her blood didn't hurt the child."

Jean-Luc laid down and faced the wall as if he wanted to sleep again. "God gave you a wife who loves you."

"If I can find her."

.

Tomás stared at the parchment scraps in front of him.

First, his parents' marriage contract, which proved that his father Miquel married a Roman Christian, not a schismatic. That contract proved the Church had no legal basis for taking Fontcours away from Miquel and giving it to Nicolau of Montcava. With this record, he'd convince the Church to restore Fontcours to Tomás as Miquel's legal heir.

Second, his own marriage contract with Isabella, which made Tomás Sebastián's legal guardian, freeing the boy and Fontcours from Renoud's intrusive guardianship. In this contract, Tomás gave Fontcours to Sebastián, negating that the boy would otherwise lose Fontcours when the Montcava heirs turned out to be bastards.

Third, the charter written the last day Pèire breathed, which declared Sebastián a knight of age and Pèire's heir as seigneur of Valerós. This gave Isabella the reassurance she needed. Sebastián was Master of Valerós.

Finally, the written confession he'd wrested from Eloïse of Montcava. He felt a surge of pleasure whenever he read this proof that Nicolau and Renoud were bastard sons of an unknown father. And, therefore, they were not Tomás's brothers, born of Miquel's first wife, and could inherit only bastards' portion of the House of Montcava, unequal heirs among thirty-two cousins.

He didn't need any of these to say what must be said in the bishops' court. As her husband, he could directly plead Isabella's innocence as a heretic—which would free her from Renoud, forever. And as Isabella's husband and Sebastián's guardian, Tomás was the virtual ruler of Valerós, Fontcours, and Montcava until Sebastián was ready to serve as master of his lands.

Except.

Until Tomás was allowed to prove to the bishops' court that he alone was Miquel's legitimate son, then he was also Nicolau's brother and therefore had no legal right to be married to his brother's widow.

Eloïse's confession meant Tomás was legally free to keep his wife. Except her confession meant Sebastián got only a son-of-a-bastard's sliver of Montcava, the same size as the portion that Durán could claim.

However, Pèire had asserted that Valerós was enough for Sebastián. Except Beatriz might challenge Pèire's charter declaring Sebastián his full heir, since she was Pèire's sole living child.

With the proof of his parents' Christian marriage and his own marriage contract, Tomás could offer Sebastián the inheritance of Fontcours, Morella, and the villa in Barcelona from Pèire. And the money fiefs on Cyprus. Without Valerós, it was not a grand collection of seigneurial worth. It wasn't what Isabella insisted the House of Montcava owed Sebastián: all of Fontcours, the seigneur's portion of Montcava, all of Arracheuse through Isabella's father. And all of Valerós, from Pèire.

Tomás held the only proof that Beatriz was Pèire's child in that baptismal record he'd taken off those crusader-bandits on that dark, dangerous night. He could choose to never show it if Beatriz challenged Sebastián's inheritance.

Resolving to find a better course, Tomás laid Eloïse's letter and that baptismal record on the brazier. The dying coals slowly heated the parchment until blackened holes appeared and ate away at the ink. Then those records smoked and burned and disappeared into limp curls of ash.

"What's that smell?" Jean-Luc said.

"History."

"Sancta Maria! You burned your letters! How will you get your land back?"

"If I prove Nicolau was a bastard, Sebastián loses his legacy."

Jean-Luc groaned. "I can't fathom you, swordsman. One moment you're the world's best lover, the next you're a jealous fool. You ride all over Christendom seeking revenge and retribution, then you throw it away to protect a boy who's not your own."

"He's our bonfraire, Perseus." Tomás rose, ready to urge. "Get up and arm yourself, *compadre*. We're going out to find food and a good fight."

"I don't feel the need."

"Sure you do. Think how great it'd be to smash faces among the bullies who skulk around at night scaring people and pretending God is on their side? What sounds better?"

"There's always sleep."

"All you need is a dagger and a gambeson under your tunic. Even a sword is too much. There isn't enough room to use a long blade in these melees. And besides, it wouldn't be fair if you did. The pukes in the White Brotherhood don't know how to fight, only how to mob the defenseless."

"You go, swordsman. I'll stay here."

"No. I need you. If we stand back to back, it's easy to take six or even ten of them between us."

"I don't want to smash faces for fun."

"Yes, you do. You need practice as much as I do. You haven't had a real test since your leg was cut. And I need to know if my injuries from last year still temper my timing."

"That's not reason enough," Jean-Luc said.

"Come on. We're going to draw the Montcava weasel's guards out of his den, and then go in after the scrofulous weasel. You want a piece of that glorious fight, don't you?"

20
Sheltered by the Abát

Isabella in Toulouse, May 26

"WHAT'S THAT NOISE?"

Isabella called down from the balcony on the abbot's upper floor to the courtyard. A footman was rousting dogs from the kennels to serve as guards through the night.

A quavering voice answered. "The White Brotherhood is out, ma dòmna, seeking sinners. They are just a few streets away. But there's nothing to fear."

Queasy from breathing the smoke from the fires, Isabella gave up hope that there might be peace in the city at night.

Early the next morning, the day before she had to appear in the bishops' court, the abbot of St-Féliz left to travel again at the Church's command. In the courtyard, she found Miró, whom Sebastián called *fada d'atri*. The fairy of the Montcava courtyard had aged, his face deeply creased, but he recognized Isabella immediately and bowed deeply to greet her. Renoud of Montcava let most of his servants go when his wife died, Miró said, and now Renoud was shuttering his villa because of the unrest in Toulouse. But his old lord had graciously found other places for everyone.

"I'd rather go back to the farmyards," Miró said. "But we can't choose our fate, can we, ma dòmna?"

All through that day Miró played both footman and personal servant for Isabella. She sent him to the Montcava villa four times to ask whether Renoud had returned and to leave messages at inns and doss-houses, seeking Tomás of Cyprus. Disappointed every time Miró returned with no results, she stayed inside, hating Toulouse too much to believe she might find Tomás if she set out on her own.

She crept into the abbot's study to borrow scrolls and books, and then read by candlelight, until her eyes burned. If she didn't read, she couldn't otherwise calm her mind.

She worried about Sebastián now more than she had when Renoud first snatched him, not knowing what recklessness Renoud might undertake, since Eloïse had deeded all her property to him.

To not think of that man, she wondered how everyone at Valerós was faring without a seigneur or marshal or steward to lead them. Had Beatriz stepped forward to lead at Castell-de-Valerós, like Chrétien thought? And how was Felicia dealing with her dilemma of a French outlaw lover and Norman Sicilian husband?

As soon as she concluded business at the court with Tomás (he would appear in time!), they needed to find a champion to plead for Father Anselm, Guillem, and the other Valerós knights who were at the mercy of the French invaders at Carcassonne. Hugues? Gerard de Chartrain? They'd have to go to Fontcours in hopes of finding help.

But she didn't worry about Tomás, because it seemed disloyal to not believe he'd appear at the bishops' court. When he came, all would once more be well. If God were good, then Tomás's wit and skill must have brought him to Sebastián.

Isabella ceased entertaining the idea "if God were good." She continued reading St-John and didn't venture away from the text until she'd let the saint burn his wisdom onto her stinging eyes. Standing at the balcony, seeking the source of the noise and the odor of that night's fire, she rubbed hard at the scar forming on her palm, hoping to get more movement in her fingers. She glanced at the abbot's ring on the table, which she'd stolen on impulse at the Vale of Roses, and now intended to use to forge a letter proclaiming her innocence. She'd found letters in the abbot's study, so she could imitate his handwriting, but she hadn't opened them.

She didn't know yet if she could hold a pen.

And she was a foolish liar. She gazed out over the city rooftops. She wasn't worried about whether God was good. Rather, she just wanted Tomás. To see his eyes flash by rushlight as they lay in bed together. To hear him call her *kalila*, beloved. To touch the scar on his face and make his lips twitch. To find her own lips burning all day with the taste of cloves.

Miró tapped timidly on the door, the only one in the household who ever came to her room.

"Ma dòmna, I brought the clothes you asked for."

"You are kind, Miró. I'd nearly forgotten."

Though she hadn't. She'd worried why it took all day for a simple robe to come from the market, fearing she'd have to appear before the bishop in the grey linsey-woolsey robe she'd borrowed in Lastours.

"The laundry was slow, ma dòmna. I've been there every quarter of the day, begging them to hurry."

"The laundry? Why were they sent to a laundry?"

As she received the garments from him, she saw why: rather than new clothes, Miró offered robes from her chest at the Montcava villa.

"*Ai*, Miró!"

"Ma dòmna, when I saw what poor quality your few coins would buy in the market, it made me remember the much lovelier robes in your home, so I fetched them."

"You shouldn't have."

"It was no problem, except for having to harass the laundry women. On the way home, I remembered the poor state of your shoes, so I stopped for slippers, too."

"This is too much consideration," she said. A paralyzing worry gripped her.

"Not at all. The seigneur said I did the right thing when I met him this evening. He gave me a silver penny for my effort."

"The seigneur?"

■

Behind Miró, Renoud leaned against the door frame.

"*Bona nuoit*, ma dòmna. My sister, my love."

"Senhór Renoud."

"You needn't be so formal. I am your brother, after all."

He made the subtlest motion and Miró, his faithful servant for decades, disappeared. Renoud came in and closed the door. He prowled the room, touching the shift lying across the foot of the bed, turning over papers, and examining the objects on her table.

"Who's your father?" She persisted in that quest.

"I'm the son of Don Miquel of Morella, who abandoned his wife for a crusaders' life. But look here, Isabella. This isn't yours." He held up the abbot's signet ring, which she'd left by the pen and scrolls on her table.

"The abbot dropped it when he was at Vale de Roses. I meant to return it to him."

Renoud examined the ring against the candlelight and then slipped it on his little finger. "I'll take it, to save you from being known as a thief. I hope you brought back everything of mine you stole."

"What have I ever stolen from you?"

"The heir of Montcava. My heart." He stroked her chin, playing wounded lover. "I haven't seen you since the abbey at Fontfroide. Our reunion was interrupted."

His two fingers, which she'd damaged in their fight at the abbey, trailed down her neck and then rested in the hollow above her collarbone. "Isabella, let's forget these troubles. Come home with me. Nicolau and my wife are gone to heaven. We can be together now."

"No, we can't."

"Don't toy with me," he said. "I've written you a hundred letters and sent a dozen messengers to Pèire, begging for you and Sebastián to come home."

"Who sent Montcava mercenaries to throw me off the castle wall? To shoot arrows at me? You must be mad."

"I would never hurt you. I do my best to protect you, while you keep running away." He pulled off her head-covering and stroked her hair, imitating a tender gesture.

"You are using the Church to destroy me."

"Only to help push you and our son home." He acted like a sympathetic, caring man. "I only want to protect our child."

"Sebastián isn't yours."

"We both know that he is. And now, with this crusade, I can only protect you both if you stay with me. I'll keep you at Fontcours, where I have a string of lovely Arabians and books for you." He touched the scrolls on the table. "You see, I know what pleases you, Isabella. Don't provoke me anymore. Just say yes, and I'll make all your troubles disappear."

Isabella stared into his wild eyes, intending to use reason and refusing to feel fear. Which meant feeling nothing at all. She wasn't a child this time, but he was still larger than she was.

"I'm married, Renoud. My husband will be there tomorrow to stand with me."

"After the years we had together?" He slipped his hand under her hair, cupping her head. "Don't be foolish. Stand in the bishops' court with me tomorrow and tell them Sebastián is my child."

"I can't, Renoud. I'd be confessing that Sebastián is a bastard."

"Sebastián will have a share of Montcava. He's better off as my son than how you've kept him." He squeezed her neck until it hurt. "Tell the world Sebastián is my son. Tell the truth. No lies."

"Sebastián would lose Valerós if you claim him."

"Those backcountry sheep farms don't matter." He yanked her to him as if she were made of rag, and then kissed her as he always had, without expecting any response.

She slipped her hand down to the knife in her robe, but before she touched it, he pinned her arms and held her immobile with one hand while he wrestled the knife away. Renoud tossed it across the room, and then toppled her back onto the bed.

"Don't." She was trapped under the weight of his body.

"Come on, Isabella. You make me so excited. Don't change your mind now."

"Don't do this. I have a husband."

"You had one before and it didn't matter. And it's so exciting when you struggle. You always let me hold you down."

"Let go of me. Please. All the weeping angels beg you."

"I love it when you beg, my sister, my love."

Perspiration beaded on his skin like a film of slime on a vile creature. The odor of spunk and sweat and garlic was the smell of wretched, deluded Renoud, which turned her stomach. She tried what she'd always done before, to turn off her mind. Like blowing out a wax candle. But every movement, every touch was wrong. She would not allow it.

When he tried to lift the skirts of her robe, she bit his ear. Ferric, salty blood filled her mouth, choking her.

He screamed.

21
A Torch Goes Out

TOMÁS'S SPIRITS ROSE AT the prospect of a street fight as a prelude to real action. He badgered Jean-Luc out of the bed, and they both dressed for a hand-to-hand skirmish.

"When you carry only two daggers, the best advantage is one in your boot top and one in a baldric," Tomás said. "The trick is—"

"If you remember, I fought on the battlements at Jaffa while your mother was burning your swaddling rags."

"But you're a knight, born of a race of knights. You ride horses and lead men. You don't know the pleasure of hand-to-hand sorties with street rabble."

"The only way you could best me is to cheat, swordsman, as we've already seen. Please don't instruct me."

"All right. But remember this is just for fun, so you're only trying to disable, not kill people."

"I will treasure such invaluable advice, swordsman."

Once they reached the hawkers' stalls in the market, their spirits lifted at the scent of food. It was getting late, and most hawkers were eager to pack up and be off the streets before dark descended. Tomás and Jean-Luc found one stand where a young man and his mother still ladled out *escudella icarn d'olla*, a mélange of sausage and chicken with turnips, chickpeas, and cabbage in a thick sauce with enough pepper and mustard to please any man whose tastes had been shaped in the Outremer.

"Last of the cabbage and turnips from the past harvest," the old woman said. The two men dug into the food she served them in bread bowls. "We thank God the French invaders missed our farm last season. By mere luck we got our crops in the ground this year. Pray God and the blessed saints help us to a good harvest after the French ride home."

Tomás found he could chew on one side, but then the spices hurt the wounded part of his mouth, and he ended up giving Jean-Luc the wonderful stew and settling for the woman's offer of chickpea broth with rosemary and parsley root, as mild as it was unfulfilling. As the woman and her son packed up their portable kitchen onto a wheelbarrow, she discovered one last loaf of her day's bread and gave it to Tomás with a handful of prunes, so that at least his stomach settled.

"If you've finished stuffing your lice-riddled face," he said to Jean-Luc, "let's find what quarter the White Brotherhood intends to assault tonight."

In the square outside St-Sernin, they asked passersby where Bishop Folquet preached that night, and then followed directions to a smaller church, St-Etienne, where the bishop held forth, expostulating on the evils of the so-called perfected heretics, preaching against the seigneurial protectors who allowed the evil of Jews cheating Christians in the marketplace and Mohammed-loving Moors who traded steel and spices for silver to buy Christian wives.

Tomás, having heard the same vitriol spewed a hundred times before, smiled like a half-witted *converso* and crossed himself whenever the bishop spoke the Savior's name while he scanned the crowd for the leaders who'd drive two dozen scabied young men through the streets to assault any poor soul suspected of the travesties the bishop preached against.

As everyone bowed their heads for the bishop's blessing, Tomás slipped the hood of his tunic forward to hide his face. When the priest departed, a chant started among those in the chapel who, like Tomás, were pulling their hoods up to hide their faces. As the chanting crowd moved to depart, Tomás remained kneeling in prayer, blocking Jean-Luc from leaving the chapel.

"Move it, you stupid sinner." Jean-Luc gave him a gratuitous shove, insulting him in the local tongue, with a wretched accent.

"Did you like the service?" Tomás asked.

"I've preached that sermon a hundred times." Jean-Luc moved with him into the street behind the mob. "It stirs men's hearts and makes them forget to be afraid when the battle starts. But I didn't know the part about Moors stealing souls and wives."

"You've now been cautioned."

They followed the chanting throng toward St-Sernin. When the crowd was a few streets away from the marketplace, Tomás and Jean-Luc moved into the back alleys, where Tomás showed him how to spot the lurkers who waited to fight for sport. Then he pointed out those who were part of the Black Brotherhood, a haphazard collection of southern rebels who liked to fight the bishop's makeshift militia. Tomás quickly spotted two men he'd fought beside before, in both street melees and on the journey to Constantinople.

"I'm not surprised to find you here." Tomás greeted his former comrades, who clapped him on the back. "Are you freelancing or does someone pay you to lay in wait in the alleys?"

"We're headed back to Burgundy soon," one man said. It was Jacques, a blond Norman who'd shilled for Chrétien in dice games in Zara.

His smaller, broader brother Thierry said, "We wanted to get in shape before we hit the road."

"I'm surprised you haven't joined your countrymen on crusade here," Tomás said.

"Bah to that," Jacques said. "If I'm to kill another Christian, it better be in a fair fight, with one honest lord against another and no backstabbing priests in the middle."

"And none of their gold-dousing priests will ever sniff out any heretics' booty," Thierry said.

Jacques laughed silently, miming that Thierry's jest slayed him. "It's more likely that those fakers will just shit gold."

Tomás posed the problem to them: how to find more companions and then use the street fights as cover to attack an enemy.

"I met a few scrappy lads two streets over who will join us," Jacques said.

By the time they reached the street leading to Renoud's villa near St-Sernin, six men had joined Tomás and Jean-Luc. They agreed on a

rough plan to start a fight at the villa gates and then lure the Montcava men out to join them. The melee began when a flank of the White
Brotherhood entered the square, chanting for the salvation of heretics
and infidels. Tomás's band of volunteers sprinted toward the Montcava villa to take up their planned positions.

Upon hearing the white-hooded chanters call for purifying
Christendom from the filth of heretics and godless Moors, Tomás
let his hood fall away. He stepped into the torchlight and called out,
"While you howl in the street like dogs on a *francimand* leash, we
Moors are having your sisters and wives."

"You arsewit," Jean-Luc breathed at his side. "This is too much."

Tomás grinned, feeling happier than he had for days. "'Too
much' could make this more fun."

However, Tomás's jeer brought a flank of the rebel Black Brotherhood into the street, seeking to protect any southerner, even a taunting Moor. From that moment, nothing went quite the way Tomás
planned. First, his comrades ceased turning to Tomás for direction
and turned instead to Jean-Luc, as if he were a lodestone drawing
their iron blades to attention. The Frenchman apparently assumed
it was natural for those around him to obey any command he called.

Most of their band of volunteers snatched up staves or poles in
the marketplace. Tomás held only his dagger and a leather strap he
swung for distraction. He fought with his back up against Jean-Luc,
who cursed him continuously in French for a half-breed whoreson,
but when Tomás glanced over his shoulder, Jean-Luc also grinned
broadly as he struck down one ill-trained vigilante after another.

As planned, Jacques started a fire at the gates of the Montcava
villa and then called to the household to save itself, while Thierry
launched makeshift grenades over the wall: oil-soaked rags stuffed
in clay bottles and set aflame. The burning gates of the villa opened,
and the Montcava mercenaries ran out, shouting and seeking their
hidden attackers.

With the distractions in full play, Tomás and Jean-Luc sprinted
into a side street, striking down a handful of white-cloaked attackers
with the butt-handles of daggers or with a well-placed kick to mid-
section or groin. Tomás grabbed a torch from a fallen attacker and

swung it around, igniting the tunic of the man who hacked unsuccessfully at Jean-Luc. Then the two of them ran from the melee. A hundred paces around two corners, they found the alcove leading to the tunnel, just as Isabella had described.

"There's nothing here but offal and vermin," Jean-Luc said.

"You aren't supposed to find the door. That's the idea."

Tomás probed with his dagger around the seam at the back of the alcove. At the sound of metal against metal, he pressed his blade upward and felt the catch loosen.

"We're in!" Jean-Luc said.

"*Merda*, it's dark. You go first."

"Give me the torch."

"No, I'll keep the torch," Tomás said.

"Then you go first, swordsman, because I can't see without it. I can't even stand up straight. They must have built this tunnel for dwarflings."

"Or Satan's own angels."

.

Tomás always knew the torch would burn out, leaving them in the dark, somewhere the tunnel.

"*Jhezu del tron!*" He grabbed Jean-Luc's tunic in the dark.

"Sancta Maria, you scared the devil out of me. Let go, swordsman. I can't move."

Tomás dropped his hand but stayed so close to the Frenchman that they bumped several times in the journey through the passage. Toothache gone, he could feel that day's headache beginning. His vision had clouded before he entered the tunnel; needles and pins prickled his face and arms. It seemed as if half the night passed in total blackness as they inched forward, searching for the door into the villa.

"This is it."

Jean-Luc stopped so suddenly Tomás collided with him.

"Isabella said it was boarded shut from this side." Tomás heard desperate fear in his voice, sure Jean-Luc heard it, too. He wiped his sweat-drenched hands on his tunic, wanting to push past Jean-Luc and claw his way into the villa, where there would be light.

"I can feel a rough plank," Jean-Luc said. "I'll just pull—*Ai!* What crawled over my hand? Scorpions don't go where the sun never shines, right?"

Tomás held a hand over his mouth to keep from screaming. All the abject fear he'd felt in that Cyprus dungeon flowed in his veins again. The creak of the boards changed to a clatter, and finally Jean-Luc pushed the door open.

"Have your dagger ready," Jean-Luc said. "If anyone is in the house, dead or alive, they are sure to have heard us."

The windows of the room they came into—Tomás recognized the bedroom of Nicolau of Montcava because he'd once prowled it when studying his enemies—let in a rosy glow from the fires Jacques and Thierry had ignited.

"Are you all right?" Jean-Luc whispered. "You're wheezing."

"Yes." Tomás's voice croaked. "The dust."

"I don't hear anyone coming, so we might as well explore."

Together, they methodically checked nearby alcoves and rooms and then searched the central living quarters. They encountered no one, only signs of men camped in the villa without enough servants to keep order.

Moving into action behind Jean-Luc, Tomás slowly felt in control again. As they entered the next wing, Jean-Luc whispered, "The servants may be hiding. More caution here, swordsman."

The interior kitchen was deserted and the fires had been cold for days. Any cook in residence must have moved to the outside kitchen at the back of the courtyard.

"They're boarding up the place," Jean-Luc whispered. "Anything of value has been moved out."

Near the end of the servants' wing, Jean-Luc toed open a door. Tomás stepped inside, holding his dagger ready against any attacker. But instead they found Chrétien, propped on his elbow, peering at them from the bed. Shadows fell across the sleeping form of Durán, with Chrétien's hand entwined in his hair.

Rather than speak, Chrétien motioned toward the next room. Tomás signaled for his brother to join him, and Chrétien gently prodded Durán awake.

The next door stood ajar, and again Jean-Luc silently kicked it open. Tomás stepped to where the boy lay sleeping, as unperturbed by the commotion as Durán had been. Tomás hoisted the sleeping boy over his shoulder, clapping a hand over the boy's mouth lest he cry out in surprise. He whispered, "We're here to rescue you. Don't say anything, donzel."

He headed back toward Nicolau's room in the other wing. Jean-Luc followed, but once they arrived, the Frenchman began searching the room.

"You go." Jean-Luc opened a chest and pulled out its contents. "I want to search around for my own sake."

"It's not safe," Tomás said.

"What? Renoud of Montcava might come back home through your ruffian friends and scare me? I'm fine. Look, here's a sword. I can take off the hands and head of anyone who tries to stop me."

"I need a torch then." Tomás heard weakness in his voice. He wanted to beg Jean-Luc to come into the tunnel with him.

"I'll fetch the brand burning at the end of the hall."

Tomás balanced the boy across his shoulders, the torch in his hand and the dagger in his teeth, and then set out into the tunnel. Inside, it was silent as a tomb except for the boy breathing in his ear and Tomás's footfall among the debris as he slogged a thousand leagues through the tunnel, hoping that the blessed singing angels in heaven would keep the torch lit.

As they emerged from the tunnel, the boy whispered, "Where are you taking me?"

"Back to your mother."

"Are you taking me to heaven where my mother is an angel?"

Emerging in the fire-lit alleyway, Tomás saw it wasn't Sebastián he'd carried, but a small colt who must be Renoud's.

"Jove's pissing monkey!" he swore.

There was nothing to do but take the torch and go straight back to hell. The boy followed him. Tomás didn't have time or patience to stop him or any idea what else to do with the boy.

The sputtering torch flickered out midway through the tunnel.

22
Ending Choices

BECAUSE HÉLÈNE HAD PLANTED the idea that Renoud contributed to his ruin in Constantinople, Jean-Luc pawed through boxes and clothes in Renoud's room and then in what had been Nicolau of Montcava's private room. The only weapon in that room was a sword with empty gem sockets on the pommel. No other sign indicated the room's owner had been a soldier, much less a crusader.

Listening for changes in the sounds of the melee outside the gate, he crept through the family quarters. On the upper floor, most of the rooms had also been stripped bare. No papers, no personal treasures. At the end of the wing of rooms, he found another woman's room, preserved as if the woman would return soon to take up residence. The only disarray was a single opened chest, its contents draped across the lid. Otherwise, the room had been cleaned to an obsessive degree. A sound on the balcony disturbed him, and Jean-Luc stepped quietly to the open door with Nicolau's jewel-less sword in one hand and his dagger in the other.

Sebastián leaned against the balcony wall, peering down to the streets, though the walls were too high to see well. He was dressed in traveler's leathers, a long dagger at his side.

"I know you from the bonfraires. Else, I wouldn't have allowed you to come this close to me," Sebastián spoke without glancing over his shoulder.

"Donzel! I thought Tomás carried you away."

Sebastián's face cracked open with joy. "Don Tomás is here?"

"He just left. I thought he carried you out of the house."

"It must have been Henri. Will Don Tomás come back?"

"*Òc*, the devil take me for a leper, I am back." Tomás growled, his voice hoarse. He dropped heavily on the bed, resting his head in his hands. "Sebastián. Where on God's own earth were you?"

Sebastián said, "I came to the balcony when the fight started below. Then I prepared to leave when I saw Perseus creeping through the house."

"Are you all right, swordsman?"

Jean-Luc shouldn't have asked, because the swordsman wasn't well. The man's hands shook when he wasn't grasping them to hide the tremor, and sweat shimmered on his brow, more like the glossy shine of a fever than the healthy lather of a man in the middle of an adventure.

"I'm fine." Tomás's voice sounded more like the cry of an animal, and it rang far too loud. The noise on the street stopped.

And just then, Renoud of Montcava had his dagger at Tomás's throat, having come past Henri into the room. A second man swung a mace, a sword in his other hand, blocking Jean-Luc's return from the balcony. Renoud held a sword ready in his right hand, but it should have been no problem for Tomás to disarm him, even as he slumped ill on the bed.

Yet Tomás made no move to protect himself.

"Your good health is reassuring," Renoud said, "but what the hell are you doing in my house?" He studied Tomás a moment. "You're that *poulain* bastard of Miquel's. The one who killed my men on Cyprus."

"*Òc*, I killed them."

"I should have recognized you at Castell-de-Valerós. How were you allowed into Christendom? Hélène says you are an animal."

Jean-Luc started at the mention of her name, and Renoud glanced over, recognizing him in a heartbeat.

"It's Cain. I haven't seen you since Constantinople, when you kicked my brother in the head and killed him. And then I pushed your brother onto your sword. That seems fair, don't you think?"

Stunned, but not bothering to answer, Jean-Luc tried to see how this could play out with the swordsman paralyzed on the bed. Renoud had a fresh wound on the side of his head, perhaps from the street fights, and he brushed it against his shoulder every few moments.

Though the lord of Montcava controlled the scene, he jittered at every movement. Jean-Luc counted that at least two men in the room were not rational.

Renoud said, "My father wishes you'd stuck to killing your brother Yves and left my brother alone." He looked from Jean-Luc to Tomás. "Hélène threw you over when your face was spoiled, didn't she, *poulain*? My cousin is fastidious about some things, though I bet she still likes doing the sweet thing with Cain, even though he's broke and horseless now."

Chrétien appeared in the doorway. He edged Henri into the hallway. Jean-Luc let out a breath in relief, but then saw the Celt was unarmed, half-dressed, and leaning on a cane to favor a splinted leg.

"Take the boys away, *mon fraire*," Tomás said in a flat voice.

"Sebastián remains," Renoud said. "This is his house, and he might as well hear about his sorry friends."

Tomás said, "Chrétien, get the boys out. Take them to our old hostel. I mean to kill this man, and they don't need to see it."

"I want to stay with you, Don Tomás," Sebastián said.

Renoud turned to the boy, perplexed and amazed.

"Obey, bonfraire," Tomás said.

Sebastián crossed the room, skirting Renoud without a glance.

"Shall I stop him, Senhór Renoud?" The man with the mace spoke for the first time, his nasal Toulouse accent more like a street hawker's than a noble knight's.

"No," Renoud said. "The boy will come back on his own as soon as he can."

Sebastián stopped at the door. "I don't like you, Uncle. Did you think otherwise? And I'm not a donzel. I'm a knight of Valerós."

Renoud's face froze in a mask of hatred as he stared at Tomás. "We'll discuss it after I adjust your friends' view of their jeopardy." He notched the point of his dagger at Tomás's throat until a thin trickle of blood ran down the swordsman's neck. "My men are attending to the gate and courtyard. No one leaves without me. When I call, they will come to me."

"Sebastián knows the way through the tunnel. And if you call your guards, the Frenchman will make sure you die first." Tomás still sounded odd and flat, but he waved away Chrétien and the boys. His hands no longer shook. Jean-Luc relaxed just a touch. The swordsman had pulled himself together.

"Tell me who your father is, and then I shall make it hurt less," Tomás said.

"My father? *Ai, poulain.* You're unhappy because my father is alive and has power in this world, while your father died in a pool of slime, forgotten by everyone, whimpering from the pain my father dealt him."

"Any trifling sadness will end today, when I satisfy a burning desire to kill you," Tomás said.

"If you use the knife in your boot, *poulain*, you'll never find my father. No matter what happens now, he has already won."

"In truth, I've never understood the contest, whoever your bastard sire may be."

"You don't understand humiliation yet?" Renoud traced the longest scar on Tomás's face with the tip of his dagger. Tomás's chest heaved. "My family deals only in fairness. We want to return one man's humiliation to its authors and their children." Renoud's knife point rested on Tomás's scarred lip. An involuntary tic caused the knife to draw another trickle of blood. "I enjoy knowing my father was pursued for years by a landless bastard who only came close enough to get his face spoiled, but still can't prove anything."

"Your faithless mother gave me a letter swearing you're the only bastard in this room. Excepting, of course, your ruffian with the mace," Tomás said.

Renoud mocked him. "Will anyone in Christendom believe the ravings of an aged heretic? It's as unlikely as the hope that Cain will find his ruined name by seeking under every rock in Christendom." Renoud smiled at Jean-Luc, a ghastly expression. "And your father still grieves, Cain."

"Are there others?" Jean-Luc said.

Renoud, pleased to be asked, said, "My father finished with Pèire Leteric years ago. Pèire never had an ounce of gall after his son was slaughtered." He dragged the knife point down Tomás's face again, and Jean-Luc could see Tomás tensing to resist any physical response.

"But you continue to torture his children," Tomás said. "Picking on women like the coward you are."

"No, they aren't part of this. Isabella is my sister. Sebastián is our family's heir. We merely want them home again."

"I can't allow that," Tomás said. "The senhóra is my wife."

"The *poulain* thinks he got the senhóra?" Renoud threw his head back, laughing. "I'm not surprised she's pursuing a dark *poulain* this time, since she's tried everything else. But you Moors don't care what you get as long as it's white, isn't that true?"

Jean-Luc saw a storm gathering in Tomás while Renoud continued to provoke. "Does it take the two of you to satisfy her like it did when we had her? I know the noble Cain doesn't mind sharing Hélène. Isabella finds it more exciting when she has one to call *amador* and another to call brother. You can see it in the letters she wrote to me." Renoud tossed a packet of letters onto the floor at Tomás's feet. "As for me, I won't give up what's mine. Or didn't you know? *Ai*, I see it on your face, *poulain*. You don't know about the love my sister and I share."

Alarmed, Jean-Luc said, "Tomás, he's taunting you."

Renoud scratched a line down Tomás's check with his dagger. "She punished me by leaving when I was forced to marry. Isabella does as she likes while we slaves must be devoted to her."

Everyone in the room should have seen Tomás coiling like a cat, though he hadn't moved. Renoud still held a knife at his throat.

"He's lying, Tomás," Jean-Luc prayed the swordsman would come to his senses. "Don't believe him. Your wife is faithful."

"I had your faithful bitch just last night," Renoud said. "My marks covered those fading bruises on her collarbone. Were those your bites, or was it our friend Cain? I like my marks to last longer. You must have noticed. The mark on her belly is mine."

"Tomás!" Jean-Luc cried. "He's lying."

Renoud wiped again at his wounded ear, using the hand with the broken fingers. In a heartbeat, Tomás pressed his long dagger against Renoud's sword and jerked the shorter knife from his boot, circling it to draw Renoud's dagger away from the center of his body. The guard swung his mace back to bring it down on Tomás, but in the same moment Jean-Luc sliced the man's forearm open, wrist to elbow, and then chopped the man's lower leg half off with a long swing from high guard. The guard sank to the floor with a piercing shriek, howling as he tried to staunch the blood.

Calling for his knights, Renoud grinned wickedly as he stepped into the man-to-man fight stance taught in Hugues de Beaurain's training yards.

"Without a doubt, òc, I'm lying, you filthy heathen," Renoud said. "The truth is, I'll never share. You'll never touch her again, because I'll kill you like I killed the others. You can die knowing Isabella treasures her dead lovers. She drove Arracheuse into poverty, paying for dead lovers to get into heaven."

Renoud lifted his sword. He pressed Tomás's dagger upward in a gesture meant to call attention to his advantage over the swordsman, both in size and weapons. "How do you compare, *poulain*? Are you any better than her other dead lovers?"

Tomás, berserk, kicked at Renoud's hand to send the knife spinning across the room. Then he came in under Renoud's sword with his dagger. Wherever Renoud sought Tomás, the smaller man was already gone and, in a flash, so was Renoud's sword.

Then Tomás had his long dagger at Renoud's throat.

"Stop!" Jean-Luc cried. "We need to know more from him."

"Ask quickly," Tomás said. "This *peccador* does not have many moments to live."

Renoud smirked. "Even if you kill me, *poulain*, you'll never have her again without knowing she's mine. My own dear sister."

Tomás tipped his head as if struck, but at the same time he brought his smaller knife up and sliced into Renoud's middle until the cross-piece stopped at the man's sternum.

Renoud, shocked, stared down at the knife and then at Tomás.

"And always has been," he gasped and then fell.

"*Fou! Sot! Imbécile!*" Jean-Luc slipped into French, dismayed. "Look what you've done."

"Stop screaming!" Tomás hissed. "I hate that sound!"

Jean-Luc jumped back, thinking Tomás would attack him, but it was the bleeding guard Tomás went for. He grabbed the man by the hair, jerked his head back, and sliced his throat.

Rage throbbed in the pulse at his forehead and veins bulged in his neck as Tomás bent over Renoud. The man still breathed.

A bloody froth formed at his lips as he gazed up. Tomás sank to his knees at the man's side.

"I'll think of you always." Tomás again pushed his dagger into the man's middle, up under the ribs so it pierced the man's heart. The dead man stared up in surprise. Jean-Luc saw hope for restoring his own name flow out with the man's blood spilling onto the floor.

"You idiot-born mongrel!" Jean-Luc shouted. "How could you listen to the lying sod?" He stepped back lest he do harm to the swordsman. "We learned nothing from him! You prick arsewit, we're damned by you."

Tomás grasped Renoud's hand and studied it, and then pulled a ring from the dead man's finger and held it to the light, his face streaked with tears, sweat, and blood. He put the ring on his own little finger and then reached for the packet of letters Renoud had tossed on the floor, reading first one and then the next, as if he'd forgotten where he was and what lay around him. The dawn bell rang at St-Sernin, the ingenious new music of Toulouse that rang on the holy hours. At the sound, Tomás searched around wildly.

"The bishops' court!"

Tomás went to the door, and then came back for the packet of letters. In the hall, he headed for the stairs leading out into the courtyard.

"Where are you going?" Jean-Luc followed the swordsman, who seemed like a man in battle shock.

"To the bishop."

"Not out the front gate. We don't know if it's your friends or Renoud's guards in the courtyard. I don't like the odds for only two of us, and I won't let you commit suicide by going down there alone. Go out the way we came."

"I can't."

"You must. But you can't go drenched in blood. We have to find clothes for you here."

"I cannot wear that bastard's clothes."

"You can't be particular, having ended all the choices for us both just now."

23
A Bundle of Pain

THERE WASN'T ANOTHER TORCH in the family part of the house, and Tomás was being chivvied into the tunnel by Jean-Luc. Tomás held his breath and counted aloud through the number of steps from the entry to the exit, where he bent double, panting to get his breath before sprinting toward St-Sernin, his headache unrelenting.

The needles and pins had gone. Now, just the nauseating, pounding pain and the curtain over his eyes.

"You have a brother," Miquel said at his side. "You don't need more than that."

"Where were you when I needed you, Father?"

"If you must put your faith and heart somewhere, let it be in a man. Chrétien won't let you down. Or go back to the king. He's a fine man."

Tomás sprinted, outpacing his father without meaning to. At the street crossing, where one lane led back to the Montcava villa and the main way led toward the cathedral, he collided with a bald serving man, who dropped his bundle into the trash and ashes on the street.

"My lord of Montcava will have my hide!" the man exclaimed.

"He's in the mood for forgiveness," Tomás said. "What do you want with him?"

"I'm to deliver these garments to Senhór Renoud that he left in my mistress's room."

"He's forgotten them for all time. Send them back to your mistress." Tomás began to run again.

"The senhóra of Valerós left my master's house," the man called after him. "She returns them to the seigneur with her compliments."

"You lie!" Tomás stopped.

"Not I, senhór!" The serving man stepped back, afraid of being struck. "Our entire house will swear to it. The senhóra and Renoud had an awful row last night, and he left her bedroom in a rage."

"I can't believe it."

"I can't believe it either. When I served the Montcavas, whatever our master Renoud wanted, the senhóra complied. There wasn't any screaming and waking the whole house when he came from her room. I can't help wondering what's come over her."

Tomás grabbed the man. "Which way to St-Sernin? Where does the bishop keep his court?"

"It's right this way, by my new master's house."

Lubos, Dissatisfied

LUBOS LOOKED DOWN AT the man, while flies buzzed as loudly as the stone-spirits buzzing in his head. He hadn't heard the spirits in the city before, so he found comfort in knowing they were with him.

This was a bad man. The spirits sang it like a song.

That badness could not be allowed to rot into the earth.

Lubos took his knife, the special one that Aykuna gave him, and made a cut to let out the badness. The stomach is where evil lives. That's what Aykuna taught him.

The flies sang with the stone-spirits, and then came like crows, to clean up after battle.

He tasted the blood on his fingers, to see what bad men taste like. Dissatisfied, he thrust the coverlet over the man, to let him sleep while the flies fed on his evil.

PART THREE
Canços de Guerra

TO ARNAU, MY BELOVED BROTHER IN CHRIST,
Throughout this enterprise of peace and faith that His Holiness has charged us to undertake, each day we learn more. Simple, untutored souls have been defiled by the pernicious teachings of their diabolical ministers.

Their false bishops' teachings are like the howling of wolves and the wild savages of the north who nurture the Bogomils, with no resemblance to the sacred gospel taught by St-Peter and St-Paul.

— *Esak, your brother in the Lord*
27 May 1210

24

In the Bishops' Court

ISABELLA WAS BEGGING FOR a pair of footmen to walk through the streets with her when a herald knocked on the abbot's gate and proclaimed Hugues de Beaurain. Hugues explained that he came after hearing her story from the abbot at the St-Félix abbey, where the marquis had taken his wife to wait out the summer's crusade.

"I was sorry to hear about Pèire Leteric, Senhóra Isabella. Please let me do service for you today, in his honor. You need someone by your side."

"This is most kind." She was so happy to have a friend, she could have wept.

"If there's any service I can do for Pèire's children," Hugues said, "I beg to be allowed. Let me speak for you."

"Pare Abát told me what to say, but I would appreciate it if you walked with me."

Hugues nodded, agreeing to the request. "The abbot tells me that you have a new husband."

"I also have a son, and I misplaced my husband when he went hunting for my son. My brother-in-law Renoud has stolen Sebastián from our home."

Hugues frowned. "Should I speak to Renoud right now? I don't know if he'd listen to me, but I can beg him to be reasonable."

"You don't believe I'm guilty?" Isabella brightened. At least one man in the court might believe her innocent.

"Of course not. This is a fool's errand."

A coterie of Hugues's men shouted outside the abbot's gate, with the Valerós master-at-arms among them.

157

"Benito! Bonjorn!"

It was inappropriate to embrace him, but she did take Benito's hand and greet him in the Catalan manner, more as one greets a friend than as a salute to her guard.

Hugues said, "Your man arrived at Fontcours with some of your knights. He refused to be left behind when I came here to find you."

When she whispered, "News of Sebastián? Tomás?" Benito shook his head. She longed to hear more news of the Valerós knights, but she couldn't ask in front of Hugues. They crossed the square to the cathedral, where piles of brick and stone crowded around the masons' and carpenters' work-sheds. It was just another workday, and the tapping of chisel-and-hammer on stone rang around the square, together with the crank and whir of the windlass lifting another load of stone up to the catwalks.

"You know this cathedral, ma dòmna?" Hugues asked.

"Quite well." They passed the chapels at the east end of St-Sernin.

"But you haven't visited the bishops' court?" the marquis asked. "Did you know Bishop Folquet when you lived here before?"

"No," Isabella said. "I've heard his poetry sung." Nights, on the road from Valerós through the Aude valley, Chrétien taught more songs than she'd ever heard, including the poetry of Folquet de Marselha. "It's enough to make you believe in love."

"It's enough to make you believe—no, I shouldn't say anything." Hugues pressed her hand more closely in the crook of his arm. "Folquet left that life. He, his wife, his sons, they all turned to the monastic life. He now disavows his poetry and his former life as merchant and poet."

"Merchant and poet are a strange combination. A jump to a monk's life seems even more extraordinary." Isabella would have gladly left her old marriage for a convent. She couldn't imagine it now. She made a leap of confidence with Hugues. "I hope we are still allowed to hear his songs."

They passed a bas-relief in marble of God on His throne. The eyes of one of the angels seemed to follow her, as the people's lore claimed. But Isabella couldn't tell if the angel's eyes favored the side of pity or the side of scorn. Hugues indicated where Benito should wait for them, though Isabella disliked leaving him behind.

As they came down the walkway leading to the bishops' court, Tomás bounded among the colonnades, nearly colliding with Hugues before he saw them. He stepped back, as if in shock, his eyes darting from Isabella to Hugues de Beaurain. Sweat prickled on his brow.

"Senhór, I thank you for bringing my wife," he said.

"It was an honor." Hugues offered Isabella's arm to Tomás, who rendered the barest motion of either respect or gratitude. "If I can offer further service, perhaps you'll allow me to speak on your behalf."

"No," Tomás said. "I do not need your services."

He moved away abruptly, dragging Isabella with him.

"Tomás, I missed you so," she said. "Is Sebastián safe?"

"Restrain yourself before strangers, senhóra. When we are inside, only I will speak."

Dressed in black fustian, Tomás looked like a Toulouse seigneur in mourning, with only small gold buckles breaking the grim dress. He bent at the font where visitors could wash before entering, dipping his hands in the water.

"Restrain your impulses, senhóra, and answer their questions only if I ask you to speak."

The water in the center of the basin stained with rust where he rubbed his hands, and the sight of it made her heart thud.

"Is he dead?" she whispered, her voice sounding harsh even to her own ears. She breathed a silent prayer of both forgiveness and thanksgiving.

Tomás didn't answer. He rinsed his hands at the edge of the basin where the water was still clear, and then rubbed his face and neck. He wore the abbot's ring on his little finger.

"Do you understand, senhóra? Remain silent."

She smelled the same acrid odor of fear as their last night in Laurac. And the same as when he followed that assailant into the tunnels at Valerós.

"Do you understand?" Tomás said again, a dark edge to his smoky voice. One glance from Tomás alarmed her more than the entire fortnight's nightmares.

"Òc."

He took her hand in his damp one and placed it over his arm, standing away from her so that they barely touched.

Seeking signs of how dangerous the man by her might be, she missed the ceremony at their entrance. Gradually she could study the sea of faces in black robes standing at the edges of the room, with only the Most Reverend Folquet, Bishop of Toulouse, seated at a table. She searched for the poetic remains in the dry, brown-robed man buried in piles of parchment. Guessing from the pallor of his grey face, the sun had not shined on Bishop Folquet since Candlemas, though it shone daily in the Languedoc.

The barrel-vaulted stone ceiling of the hall echoed with footsteps and murmurings, gradually coming to silence as the bishop spoke in Latin to start the session, his voice as brown and grey as his appearance, no note of song coming from him. Hugues, standing among a handful of Frankish knights and southern seigneurs, tried to catch her eye every few moments, nodding in encouragement. The man whom Tomás said she should fear as her enemy wanted to comfort her, while her partner had removed his soul so far that she'd have felt safer standing alone. They stood beside each other for half the day while the bishop disposed of other cases. Tomás glanced at her only once, while her mind raced: what had happened?

"Senhóra Isabella, widow of Nicolau of Montcava, is asked to speak before the court on charges of heresy, murder, and harlotry. Is she here?"

Isabella clenched Tomás's arm, hearing the declaration, but he untangled her hand and dropped it at her side.

"She is," Tomás said, "but I speak for her."

"And who are you?"

"Tomás of St-Joachim in Barcelona. I am the lawful wedded husband of Isabella of Valerós and a knight of Pedro *El Católico*, king by Grace of God of Aragón."

"Is her accuser here? Who is her accuser?" The bishop glanced down at the pile of parchment on his table. The former merchant hidden within the bishop came forth as he studied his pages, as he clearly weighed each word he read as he must have formerly weighed his wares. "Renoud of Montcava, brother to Nicolau."

"Unfortunately, he has gone to God," Tomás said. "He regretted his accusations in past days, but he didn't live to tell you."

"How is this?" the man said.

"He was killed by street rabble in his home last night."

A murmur passed in a wave among the clerics crowded behind the bishop at his table. Isabella glanced at the Marquis de Beaurain, but Hugues showed no more interest in Renoud dying than the other lords beside him.

Tomás said, "This sad event has wasted your Excellency's time. Renoud of Montcava went to God knowing the truth of my wife's innocence."

"We beg you to convince the Church as you did Renoud of Montcava," the bishop said. The more Isabella heard him speak, the more she heard that the bishop no longer wrote or sang songs. "The first charge is heresy. We have her brother's declaration, saying Isabella of Valerós consorts with, offers support to, and travels in belief with the heretics."

"As a loyal Christian knight and as husband of the senhóra, I deny this."

"Who are you that we should believe your testimony?"

"I am the legitimate son of a crusader knight. The sword I have from my father was used to defend the Holy Sepulcher. I swear on his sword and on bread and wine that I speak God's own truth. As I have sworn allegiance to my Church and king."

"Is there any man here who will vouch for the honor of your name and position?"

"I will." Hugues's voice rang among the vaults. "The Marquis de Beaurain swears this man is a true knight of the Holy Church."

Tomás's face didn't indicate gratitude, but Isabella rendered her own thanks with a nod.

A cleric whispered at length to the bishop until they came to an agreement. The bishop said, "The swearing of an oath is enough testimony to your own faith, but it is your wife we are concerned with. The seigneurs here are plagued with hereticated mothers, sisters, and wives. The charge is against your wife, and we would hear her speak."

Isabella began to say what she'd planned, but Tomás pressed her hand.

"She is husbanded by me, and she thinks and acts as I command. It is not possible for her to believe other than I do."

Isabella flushed at this claim and studied the bishop to see how he reacted. Chomping at his lip, the bishop nodded in agreement with Tomás. "We shall hear the senhóra say her creed and profess her belief."

She looked to Tomás for an answer.

"Senhóra, please say what you believe," Tomás said.

Having listened to the gentlewomen in Laurac expound on the faults of Catholics' creeds, she knew the Apostles' Creed was sufficient testimony. She recited it in Latin, following the same cadence as she'd learned when Katelina taught them to read Latin. At the 'Amen,' which all the clerics in the room repeated, she continued, still speaking in Latin.

"I have always found it particularly inspiring to read what St-Augustine wrote about the second article, when he said—"

"Senhóra, these gentlemen care only about your faith, not your erudition."

Tomás squeezed her right hand in what might seem a gesture of affection to the clerics and the bishop, but she experienced it as pain, so her knees bent and her eyes burned.

Again, a cleric whispered in the ear of the bishop, who then said, "Don Tomás, would you show us your wife's hand, please.'

She felt Tomás freeze beside her.

"She injured it sewing last fortnight."

"If you would be so kind."

He unwrapped her bandage and spread her hand to display it on the table before the bishop. Glancing at Tomás, she found him staring at the mangled mess of her palm. The bishop, however, pushed up her sleeve and grasped her hand to study her wrist.

"We understand Pèire Leteric had a band of hereticated knights, and he branded them with the sign of the devil. Here." He touched her wrist.

"You mean this sign." Tomás bared his wrist to show the square burned there. "I was a seigneur of Pèire Leteric. And he loved Our

Savior as much as you or I. His bonfraires were a commune of the knights who prayed together for strength in battle. I know them, and most took up the Cross in the Outremer for years and then came home to Christendom to die."

"This isn't a sign of the devil?"

"It's an old crusader custom," Tomás said. "Pèire Leteric marked his men because it's often impossible to identify faces when picking up after battle. Any of you knows this if you traveled with the crusaders to carry the Cross to Jerusalem."

"I know." Hugues's voice again echoed in the stone barrel vault. "I marched with the crusaders to regain Jerusalem. And I'm proud to carry the same sign as this Christian knight does."

Hugues crossed the stone floor and bared his right arm, showing a white welt on the folded flesh of an old man's arm. While everyone gathered around Hugues de Beaurain, Isabella alone saw Tomás's amazed look, his eyes darting among the clerics and Hugues.

While the bishop made notes, Hugues stepped beside Tomás to signal solidarity with Isabella and her husband, his wrist still bared. Tomás edged away from him, pressing his hot body against Isabella's, but still he ignored her.

The bishop said, "The next charge states that Isabella of Valerós did cause the death of our priest, the holy Father Clémence of Toulouse, either by her own hand or by the Moor in thrall to Pèire Leteric. I assume the Moor is you, Don Tomás."

"King Pedro has accepted my forfeit. Although I cannot prove my innocence, he knows I did not kill that good priest. My wife was not accused of this crime."

"But in this letter, your wife stands accused. Does King Pedro speak for her, also?"

"No, I do. My wife could not have done it, for I was in her room all night, from the moment Pèire Leteric left me until Mass the following morning."

The clerics stirred in embarrassment, and the bishop glanced up, chewing his lip. Tomás clasped Isabella's hand. Uncomfortable with the easy falsehoods Tomás invented, she resisted his pressure, hoping he wouldn't hurt her again.

"I apologize to my wife, but I must reveal our indiscretion," Tomás said. "In truth, I practiced a seduction, but she never allowed it. We confirmed our betrothal and marriage that morning, so she celebrated her marriage as a chaste woman. I played the devil and she acted only as an angel. Neither of us learned about the murder until the following day."

"This is only hearsay on your part," the bishop said.

"Her sister and the Valerós master-at-arms saw me enter her room. They'll swear to it if you bring them here."

Hugues said, "The Valerós master traveled with me from Fontcours and is waiting in the ambulatory if you want to call him."

Tomás clenched his fist beside her, and she felt the same tension, not knowing whether Benito would know how to lie if they summoned him.

The bishop chomped furiously on his lip. "There's no reason." He read from his parchment for a moment before speaking again. "We have the final accusation: that Isabella of Valerós is a wanton and licentious woman who should be handed over as legal ward to her brother-in-law."

Sounding sad, Tomás said, "I had my wife say her creed, so you heard for yourself she isn't a heretic. I can bring a sister and a soldier to swear she didn't murder a priest. But how can I prove her chastity against slander? The only thing I can do is to swear by the Holy Cross this woman has never known any man other than her lawful wedded husband. One died on crusade, and the present one stands before you."

"Will the senhóra swear it, too?"

"My oath and hers are the same, for we are now one flesh before God. But our child will serve as testament later, since I'm one of the few men in Christendom with complete confidence he fathered the child his wife carries."

On Tomás's side, Hugues tipped his head and smiled at her, and she flushed, embarrassed at all the lies.

The bishop said, "I have before me the testimonies of a half-dozen men swearing otherwise."

Tomás said, "Your Excellency, this should be settled as a point of honor among men, rather than in your court. I challenge those men to meet me on the open field, all together, or each separate. And then I can answer their slanders in the way a man defends his wife."

"How did these men come to swear this?"

"Renoud of Montcava is with God, so it would be unkind to remark on why he acted as he did. But when I began helping to settle his affairs this morning, I found this."

Tomás set the abbot's ring on the bishop's table.

"This ring was stolen from the abbot of St-Féliz-de-Fontcours, who is a friend to my wife. I found other such anomalies among his effects. Although I'll buy indulgences asking God to accept the man into heaven, I believe Renoud was a thief and a liar who sought to injure my wife's good name."

Her hand aching with each pulse, Isabella swayed with fatigue. Tomás put his hand at her back to steady her.

"Show strength, senhóra," he whispered.

The bishop, whom Isabella now understood had absolutely abandoned poetry, said, "The charges against this woman are serious, but we must be guided by the love of God and the facts before us. In this light, if Senhóra Isabella of Valerós will be shepherded by her good husband, we believe both her name and her immortal soul shall be protected."

Isabella began to speak, but again Tomás crushed her hand, and she closed her eyes in pain as he said, "She will indeed be led by me."

"Do you know about this letter Renoud submitted," the bishop asked, "which bestows all of his mother's lands on the children of her marriage?"

Tomás said, "Renoud's mother lives among the goodwomen and cannot be persuaded to give up her false beliefs. But she surrendered her wealth to her Christian children."

"Then you, Don Tomás, are the only seigneur among the Montcava household and the family of Pèire Leteric?"

"Until Sebastián of Montcava comes of age, yes."

"Did Renoud of Montcava leave any children of his own?"

"We have discovered two children born outside the bounds of marriage," Tomás said. "One is of age."

"Did Senhór Renoud acknowledge these children?"

"Before myself and other witnesses, yes."

"Will you ensure they receive a portion of his estate? Do you know whether these are bastard sons, not the product of adultery?"

"*Òc*, your Excellency. As is the custom, these children will share in the family fortunes," Tomás said.

"Then God bless you and the children of your house. This court has no more business with you and your family as long as your wife is never again seen in the company of heretics. The clerk will give you a record of our judgment. You can wait for them."

The bishop flicked his hand in dismissal, writing notes without a glance around him. She had been prosecuted by a man who sold his soul to the Church, who didn't see a human before him, but a piece of goods whose worth he bargained over with her owner. She might have been a slave, though it was her soul that had been on Bishop Folquet's auction block.

However, he released her from all Renoud ever held over her.

Now she just needed Tomás to let go of her aching hand. And return to his true self.

.

Hugues de Beaurain stopped them outside the door, bowing to Isabella, but his eyes fixed on Tomás.

"You're Miquel's son. I must have been blind not to recognize you at Valerós. Why didn't Pèire tell me what he planned for Senhóra Isabella? The old fox. I congratulate you, Don Tomás."

Hugues held out his hand in greeting in the French manner, but Tomás ignored it, instead bowing his head as a Catalan knight would. Rather than taking offense, Hugues bowed in kind.

"Pedro is damned lucky to have Miquel's son with him. How is your father?"

Tomás stared at Hugues, his jaw clenched, as if he might end Hugues's life right then. Isabella grabbed his arm in alarm, but Tomás shook free. Hugues couldn't be insensible to so much hatred.

"My father died last year. While you visited Cyprus."

"I'm so sorry to hear it, Don Tomás." Hugues's face blanched white, and he spoke his condolences slowly. "Truly I am. We were friends, more than friends, in the old days."

"If you knew my father, then you know the wrong done when the Church took away Fontcours." Tomás's voice was smoky with anger, the sweet tones lost.

"I was in the north then," Hugues said, "with King Philippe."

"If you knew my father, then you know Renoud and Nicolau were not his sons."

Hugues met Tomás's piercing stare, and Isabella watched a tug of war: Hugues wanted to be a friend, but Tomás refused.

"Yes, but it wasn't my place to condemn her," Hugues said. "She was our neighbor in childhood."

"So I understand," Tomás said.

"I would give my life for your father," Hugues touched his own bonfraire scar. "But I couldn't hurt the woman. He asked that she be protected."

Tomás said, "You offered succor to the cuckoos in his nest. You rode to Valerós with Renoud when he carried threats to Pèire Leteric, and when he stole Sebastián from his mother."

"Renoud showed me a message from Pèire, begging him to take Sebastián."

"A forgery," Tomás said.

"From what happened in the bishops' court today, I now know Renoud was not your friend. But I wasn't part of what he did."

"You raised those bastards in the ranks of your knights."

"They were raised in my court, but I was in the Outremer then. I never met them until Constantinople. If my wife weren't a cousin, the relationship would have ended with that crusade."

"*Ai*, cousins." Tomás smiled.

Hugues understood the remark as an end to the tension, though Isabella saw the fire still burned in Tomás's eyes.

Hugues said, "Of course! You were cousin and sister to Renoud, ma dòmna. But then, people here all seem to be cousins. You'd think the Church would persecute the south for consanguinity instead of heresy."

"Sixth degree cousins," Isabella said. "Sufficient to pass the bishops' scrutiny."

But Hugues was attending only to Tomás.

"There's no reason for us to be enemies, Don Tomás. Please consider me a brother and call on me in the name of the bonfraires whenever you need it."

"Thank you for your service, senhór." Isabella hoped Tomás understood it couldn't be Hugues they pursued.

"Where are you headed now?" Hugues asked.

"To join my knights at Fontcours," Isabella said.

"To join King Pedro," Tomás said at the same time.

"We will all rendezvous in the fields near Fontcours," Hugues said. "Why don't you leave your wife at the St-Féliz abbey? That's where my wife is staying, out of harm's way. It's the safest place you can find in the Languedoc right now."

And so, Isabella noted, in the same way the bishops' court had done, Hugues transferred his concern for her to her husband, as if she weren't present.

Tomás said, "I intend to keep her safe in our own home."

Hugues bowed and left them, and Tomás steered her down an empty walkway to an alcove near the entrance, where they were alone together at last. Exhausted, Isabella leaned against the cold stone wall, wishing for a bench to rest, shot through with fatigue and longing to be close to Tomás again.

·

Tomás squinted, nearly blinded where the bright sun shone through the wide cathedral doors and reflected on the marble floor. That light didn't reach the shadows of the alcove where he stood over Isabella of Valerós.

"Your performance was inspired," she said. "But why did you risk telling them I was with child?"

"Don't be coy, senhóra. You were ill every morning at Laurac. And your courses never came while we traveled together."

"It was blood poisoning. I told you I couldn't get a child."

"But you had nothing to stop it. No herbs. No science." His outrage had grown since he'd encountered Renoud's servant on the street outside the cathedral. At last he could release that turmoil.

"Tomás, I can't."

"What did you do?" He whispered, furious. She might as well have struck him if she wanted to wound him in this way. He grabbed her wrists, in case she decided to attack him. "Did you have a heretic healer end it for you?"

"No. I can't have children. When Sebastián was born, I bled so badly, they thought I was dying, so they found an Arab physician, who saved me. But he had to take my womb to do it."

He let her go. She scrambled to the other side of the alcove.

"Why didn't you tell me?" He still whispered, the edge of his anger worn only by shards of pain.

"I did. On that first night. Couldn't you tell when you touched me? You know so much about women."

"It seems I knew nothing until Renoud served as my tutor." He yanked that bundle of her letters from his jerkin and threw it down at her feet. Then he put his fingers on the bruises, where he'd stared while standing beside her all morning. "What were you doing with him last night, senhóra?"

He tipped her chin with one hand. With the other, he pulled free the laces of her robe, revealing more bruises and scratches. Tomás whistled through his clenched teeth.

"*Amador—*"

"Don't call me that, Senhóra *Maliciosa*," he whispered. "You betrayed me with Renoud, that spawn of the devil."

"I would never under God's golden heaven betray you."

"Betray isn't a large enough word for it. Renoud could only tell me about those bruises if you lay with him last night."

"He hurt me when I fought him with my knife."

Tomás felt as dazed as when he'd been trapped in that cellar at Laurac. "You caught me in the game you played with Renoud. You call him *amador* in your letters."

"It's only you I care for, Tomás. I swear it on my mother's honor." She tied her robe closed.

"Renoud had your lovers killed. I thought there was no one else. How many, Isabella?"

"He killed them? He murdered them because of me?" Tears welled, but Isabella never cried. She did it to assuage his anger. "As I told you, no one alive has ever touched me."

"Renoud was alive then."

"I forgot about him, Tomás. I never think of him."

"Did Renoud tell me the truth about Sebastián? Is Renoud Sebastián's father?"

"How could I ever know? And what difference does it make?" She spoke with cold severity, as condescending as when he'd first met her.

"You're standing here, ready to weep over dead men. Are you weeping for Renoud?" He spoke so sharply, the words scratched as his throat. "Ask the dark angels for comfort. I cut Renoud the same way those wolves cut my father."

"He killed Jaume and Etienne." She murmured the words.

"Was I next? Like that priest and Renoud's mercenary?" He pressed the place at her neck where Renoud's bruises showed. "While I stood just now telling lies for you, I recognized that your knife went in the same way for both men. Where you chose to strike."

"Let go of me, Tomás. Renoud was a mad man. You can't hate me for his lies."

"*Ai,* I listened to Eloïse explain how nothing was ever her fault. How did my father refrain from sending that witch to hell?"

"Do you think it was my fault, what happened when I lived in her villa? You and Father Clémence are great judges."

"Did you kill that priest because he knew about you and Renoud? It's like incest, isn't it? Sleeping with your brother-in-law?"

"Don't let Renoud's lies make you play the fool, Tomás."

"I'm not a fool. By all the perished saints, I shall make sure Montcava and Fontcours come to Sebastián. You are my property. So, you'll stay in my control, as I promised the bishop."

"I won't ever again live with a man who hates me."

"You'll stay at the Montcava estates until I take the Valerós knights to join Pedro's army. Then Chrétien can watch over you at Fontcours."

"Let me go. Tell the Church I deceived you. Get an annulment."

"No. For Sebastián's sake, to keep possession of the lands I just lied my way into, I must remain your husband." He pointed to the bundle of letters. "Burn these. I don't want any more Montcava lepers using your sins against me."

"*Ai*, you're the same as a wolf in the hills, Tomás." She called after him. "What animus has stolen your soul, Tomás? You're letting Renoud destroy more than he ever could do on his own."

"Remain here until Chrétien comes for you," he said. "It will be but a moment."

•

When he was gone, Isabella picked up the letters, first reading the one tied to the top of the bundle, the letter the abbot of St-Féliz carried to Renoud from the Vale of Roses, with lamp-black ink still so fresh it shone on the parchment.

> My dear brother, I write to assure you that I shall do as you wish and be married by Pentecost. Sebastián shall come as a squire as you asked. Everything shall be as you desire. My tender regards for your care, as always, your sister Isabella.

She had written the letter so well that the sole deceit lay in offering tender regards. She leafed through the other letters in the bundle, though the lamp-black ink flaked from the parchment.

As she opened the second letter in the bundle, she remembered the day she wrote it, but now her eyes burned. The poor donzel Jaume died because a lonely fifteen-year-old girl shivered in Avraham's study at dawn and copied parts of the Canticles of Solomon into the common tongue, and then sent them in a letter. To a donzel who couldn't read.

> Amador, my dear brother.
> O my dove in the clefts of the rock, in the secret places of the stairs, let me see your face, let me hear your voice.
> For sweet is your voice and your face is comely.
> O that you were my brother who suckled the breasts of my mother. When I should find you, I would kiss you.
> I am yours. I am your sister, your love.

He killed Jaume and Etienne.

It was like once again seeing Jaume's broken body carried home after his horse-fall. But now she knew Renoud had paraded the dead boy in front of her. Too easy, then to imagine the terror and pain when Etienne died alone in Toulouse after their short-lived affair at Valerós, murdered by Renoud.

Tomás had been made to believe that these ancient letters were written to Renoud. People can be destroyed with steel, with poison, with knives and man-catching nets. This many years later, Renoud had used her foolish letters to kill the soul of her true love.

"Ma dòmna?" Benito's voice echoed in the walkway. "Shall we go away from here?"

25
Montcava Surcoats

JEAN-LUC FOUND THE SILENCE palpable after the door closed on Tomás's frantic panting, though he couldn't account for the sense of having pushed the man out to his own doom.

He dragged the dead guard out the same passage Tomás had taken. He stripped off the Montcava surcoat and left the body in the alleyway as just another victim of the street fights. Then he brought salt and sand from the kitchen to pour over the battle stains. After moving the lord of Montcava to the bed, Jean-Luc arranged and covered the body the way one lays out the mourned dead.

Then he stopped, as if waking from a dream, wondering what under heaven he was doing. It felt as if Yves were nearby, laughing at him, as he knelt and prayed to God, begging forgiveness for not knowing how to stop either man. By the time he finished praying, the heat of the day had already gathered in the room and the stain of Renoud's last wounds showed through the linen coverlet; desperate flies wanted to settle.

Jean-Luc started on his mission, to search the entire house, though he believed only Renoud's personal room might yield anything. As meticulously as he sifted through the objects there, he didn't find much: two golden candelabras and another Greek sword, though every man returning from Constantinople probably owned one like it. Renoud wasn't a man of learning, and Jean-Luc found only a scrap of a letter begging him to protect his mother. No signature or sign ending the letter.

When he finished the search, Jean-Luc threw off his stained clothes in exchange for a shirt and linen breeches from among

173

Renoud's things. He crept toward the central courtyard, sword in hand, curious about the hammering he heard.

Tomás's street-friends lounged in Montcava surcoats, eating cured meats and bread raided from the pantries.

"Bonjour, monsieur!" The man named Thierry hailed him in Norman French, reminding Jean-Luc of the horse trainers at his father's house. "We have established a foothold against your enemy and are manning the trenches."

Enormously thirsty, Jean-Luc drank several beakers of water and accepted bread and sheep's cheese offered by the new guards of the Montcava villa. He tried to explain the situation, how their friend Tomás of Cyprus was now the guardian of this villa.

"Like Raoul de Cambia, eh?" Thierry said.

"What?"

"You know, the song of the knight made mad when a count stole his estate? I met Tomás eight years ago, and every time we pass through Toulouse, he walked down this street and swore to bring down the thieving lord inside."

"The damnable street rabble destroyed the gate." Jacques grinned. "But we're nearly done rebuilding it."

Someone pounded outside the unsecured gate, and one of the new Montcava guards opened it to a small band of knights in Hugues de Beaurain's colors. Jean-Luc steadied his breathing, casually moving away from the gate, glancing over his shoulder to see that it was Colomb who led the coterie of Beaurain knights.

Colomb spoke in a thick French accent. "Our lord bids the men of Montcava to join us at midday where our horses are stabled. We set out for Fontcours."

"We'll be there, man," Jacques replied in French.

After the Beaurain knights departed, the men put their backs into finishing work on the gate-posts. Jean-Luc lent his own muscle to brace the door while others fitted the hinges.

"Are we really going with those knights?" Thierry asked.

Jacques said, "I'm not. I'm waiting for Tomás."

"I'm going." Jean-Luc decided the Fontcours estate was a good destination. He might find his father there. He might hear news of Felicia. Colomb and the knights offered a convenient way to travel there. "If you want to come, Valerós and Chartrain each has a company of men there you can join."

Just before midday, he put on the largest set of chainmail he could find in the villa and covered it with an ill-fitting Montcava surcoat, hating the gaudy crimson-and-gold embroidered scorpion. Despite the heat, he laced the aventail of his coif over his face. Among the arms they raided from the villa, the best sword Jean-Luc could find proved to be that one with the jewels missing from the pommel.

26

The New Master

OUTSIDE THE STABLES NEAR the hostel where he'd rented a room in the south end of Toulouse, Tomás heaved up bile onto the dung mound, and he kept heaving long after anything was left inside to cast up. The acid burned and corroded his mouth.

"Are you ill?" Sebastián asked, peering up at him earnestly.

Tomás leaned on the boy's shoulder for a moment and then propped himself against the brick wall of the hostel.

"Food gone bad, I think. That, and I haven't slept for days."

"Can I help you?"

"No, I'm fine. You shouldn't be out here alone."

"I saw you from upstairs and Chrétien let me come down. We've been at the hostel, waiting for you forever. Where's my mother?"

"She's going to the Montcava estates."

"Why? She hates it there. Doesn't she want to see me?"

"She's been ill." Tomás felt that he literally didn't have the gall in him to tell lies, but it was so habitual that he still managed to do it. "With so much to do, we have to split up. You and I are taking Henri to the Montcava estates."

"Then I'll see my mother?"

"No, we'll get there before her. Then you and I are going to Carcassonne. The French crusaders carried away Guillem and Father Anselm, and we have to free them."

"I can't believe she's letting me go."

"You're a knight of the bonfraires and the seigneur of Montcava now. You don't have to ask your mother's permission."

"I mean, I can't believe she's letting me go with you."

He put his hand on Sebastián's shoulder, mostly to steady himself. "Sebastián, I married her. Father Anselm did it, so she'd be safe from Renoud and other threats. That makes me your guardian."

"*Bon Dèu!*" Sebastián breathed, thanking God. "How could I be so lucky? What do I call you now? Are you my father?"

"You still call me Don Tomás. Let's talk on the road. We need to travel."

·

When Chrétien hobbled downstairs, Tomás sent Sebastián upstairs.

"Why was Renoud holding those boys?" Tomás asked.

Chrétien threw up his hands in that Catalan gesture of wonder, though it seemed unnatural coming from him. "I don't know. But I think Henri is Renoud's son and Durán is Nicolau's. Renoud treated Sebastián and Henri like sons of the household. And he treated Durán like a cousin. What happened today?"

"Too much. The Church made me guardian of Sebastián's inheritance, which includes Montcava and Fontcours now."

"Through a miracle of divine intercession?"

"No, simple laws of inheritance and marriage."

Chrétien's eyes widened. "The senhóra? Your dreams have come true?"

"Nightmares." Tomás told Chrétien, swearing inwardly that he'd never think about it again. "I have done as my father did and married my enemy's concubine." He finished the story. Chrétien murmured disbeliefs at every turn, as if Isabella had put him under her spell when they'd journeyed from Valerós. Tomás piled one more betrayal on the pyre that burned inside him.

Chrétien studied him without emotion. "Are you well, brother? You look all done in."

"I've had a toothache and I need sleep."

"No, I mean you look like the same devil's dung-beetle I pulled out of that cellar on Cyprus."

"I'm fine. Disappointed and tired."

"Did you have to come through that tunnel alone? Our French bonfraire didn't leave with you?"

Tomás couldn't hold his brother's gaze.

Chrétien said, "We'll take the boys to the knights at Fontcours right now. Then we leave this God-forsaken land. We can go back to the Outremer. Or go north. Burgundy is hiring mercenaries again."

"No, I made a promise."

"Not our damned oath to Miquel! Please spare me. Our father is buried, may God keep his soul. And keep our souls, too, after what our promises have dragged us through."

"No, it's what I promised Pèire. I need to get Guillem and Father Anselm out of Carcassonne, so they can keep Pèire's children safe. To protect Sebastián, we must also protect the sisters from hell."

"I'll be ready to ride in a heartbeat."

"You aren't coming with me."

"My leg is better. I won't slow us down a bit."

"I need you to be steward at Fontcours. Take Isabella there after the knights leave and keep her until I return."

They were quarreling over this when Durán joined them, belligerent.

"Don't pick a fight with me, donzel," Tomás warned, without even saying *bon día*.

"Stop calling me that," Durán said. "I have a name."

"Whatever Chrétien taught you about fighting, it isn't enough."

"*Òc*, Renoud, *que baqueler punxor*." Durán condemned Renoud as a bastard prick. "I heard what he told you, Tomás. And you believed him? What a fool you are."

"*Ai!* You didn't let Sebastián hear? I told you to take the boys away." Tomás felt the darkness of rage descend again.

"I took them away," Chrétien said. "I made sure the boys didn't hear one word."

"You're the same prick bastard as Renoud," Durán said.

"Was. He's dead. Go with Chrétien now. And mind your own business."

Upstairs, Tomás gave Chrétien one of the clerk's papers that declared Don Tomás of Morella and St-Joachim to be master and protector of Fontcours and Montcava, and he wrote his own letter naming Chrétien steward. Then he counted out silver pieces for hiring mercenaries.

"Is that enough?"

"It shouldn't take more than that to hold one woman in place," Chrétien said.

"Hire more men. Make sure they have their own horses."

"You're the master now." Durán sneered. "Renoud paid to keep a stable of horses. We can ride your own horses, noble master."

"Just get going." Tomás was too tired to quarrel. "Thierry and Jacques fought with us at the villa last night. Look for them in the neighborhood. But if you wait any longer, you'll lose Isabella."

"That would be better than throwing her away," Durán shot over his shoulder as they left.

Tomás begged water and bread from the landlady and choked down three bites of bread to calm his stomach. Then he asked her to prepare provisions so they could travel.

27

The White Brotherhood

ISABELLA AND BENITO WALKED to the brick villa in Toulouse that had formerly been her prison. Lurking in the shadows across the street from the Montcava villa, they tried to judge the house's fortification and the number of armed guards.

"I should have run after the Marquis de Beaurain," Benito said for the tenth time, "and begged him to wait for us."

"We'll be fine. I hid silver in my room once and I'm sure it's still there. When Pèire came to take me home years ago, I didn't waste time packing."

When no guards appeared, Benito knocked on the gate, prepared to lie to any enemy that might appear. A small, broad Norman appeared, dressed in Montcava colors and chainmail.

"Is the lord of Montcava home?" Benito said. "I have a message for him."

"Depends on who you mean," the Norman guard said. "If you mean the old lord, he's here but he's not talking much. The new lord of Montcava is Tomás of Cyprus. You want him?"

"Are you one of his men?"

"If I say yes, what's your business? Do you have a message for him or for the old lord?"

Isabella, despite having agreed to wait out of sight, stepped up beside Benito.

"I am the mistress of Montcava. Who are you?"

"Mistress?" The man gawked at her, then called over his shoulder, "Hey, Jacques, this woman says she's Tomás's mistress."

"She must be lying," a voice called back. "He never keeps them that long."

"I mean that I am his wife." Isabella crossed her arms and stood tall, eye to eye with the man. "This is my house, and I want you to let me in."

The Norman stepped back, his eyes wide with surprise. "And doesn't God give us something new to wonder at every day?"

After they entered, he barred the gate and then followed them as Isabella and Benito crossed into the foyer. The coolness of the house settled around them as soon as they moved out of the sun. Another man joined them. They were old companions of Tomás and Chrétien who had helped seize the house the night before.

"We're seeking the big Frenchman who was with Tomás," Isabella said. "Is he still here?"

"He went with the marquis's men."

"The Marquis de Beaurain?" Benito asked.

"Yes. One of his captains came, thinking we were Montcava knights, and said we were all to ride to Fontcours. But Thierry and me, we're waiting for Tomás."

"Ma dòmna," Benito said, "we should find the marquis."

"Benito, forget it. At least Jean-Luc is safe. Let's find what we came for."

Jacques and Thierry followed closely as Benito led the way up the stairs. Isabella didn't trust them to see what was hidden under the floorboards of her old room. As they climbed the steps, the air grew heavier with the heat of the day, smelling strongly of Toulouse. Benito opened the door to her old room, and then stepped back, blocking the door.

"*Dolç Jhezu!* You don't want to see this, ma dòmna."

"I'd better." She gently pushed her way passed him. But as she entered, the stench of death and incense roiled out. Benito handed her a rag and she clenched it over her nose. Only a half day had passed since Tomás left this place, but it was half of a very hot day.

Benito peeled back the thin sheet of linen spread over Renoud's face. Someone had laid his body out on her bed, attempting to give it the dignity due a seigneur, but the gore seeping through the linen and the flies destroyed any sense of nobility. The flies settled on the torn flesh at the man's ear.

"*Dolç Jhezu*," Benito moaned again.

Isabella pulled the sheet down farther.

"*Ai Dèu*, did Sebastián see this happen?" Isabella asked. Renoud had been laid wide open to the world.

"No, Chrétien carried the boys away," Thierry said. "Hope he's coming back with Tomás."

"Boys?" Isabella was eager to know. "Who was here?"

"That donzel Sebastián, who calls Tomás his master. And the wee one that looked like a whelp of this lord," Thierry said.

"And Chrétien's *bon amic*," Jacques said.

"You're jealous," Thierry accused.

"I swear I'm over it." Jacques shook his head.

Benito pulled the cloth over Renoud's face again, and then pulled a heavier coverlet from the chest to cover the body against the flies. Jacques and Thierry described what had happened.

"We didn't see it all," Thierry said, "because we fought the guards downstairs. When we came upstairs, it was too late to help."

"Not like Tomás wanted help," Jacques said "I've seen him in a dozen battles, but not like that. He always fights without passion."

"That's right," Thierry said. "He always fights like God's own assassin. No more passion than the reaper with his scythe."

"But the devil had him by the balls today." Jacques said. "Made me want to keep out of the way when Tomás ran out of men to kill."

"Would you fetch the death-cart men, please?" Isabella said.

She went into the hall, seeking clean air to breathe while Benito searched her old room for a modest treasure under the floor. The Normans returned along with the racket of a cart in the courtyard. While the death-cart men did their business, Isabella organized Tomás's men to clear out the house and board up the windows and doors. Isabella watched the death-cart bear her chief tormentor to the burial ground, thinking that instead of partnering with a crusader-hero, she'd slept with a butcher.

"What now, ma dòmna?" Benito said.

"We find the rest of the Valerós knights at Fontcours. Then we do what Pèire intended: serve the king of Aragón and protect ourselves from this wretched excuse of a crusade."

•

At dusk, when the work at the house was done, Isabella said, "I don't want to sleep here, Benito."

"The safest thing, ma dòmna, is to return to the abbot's house."

Although that was the safest choice, she couldn't bear the condescending stares of the abbot's servants, who had heard that hideous scene with Renoud. But no one at Senhóra Mathilde's casa had met Isabella, so she couldn't go there.

"We could rent a room," Benito said. They spoke quietly, away from where Thierry and Jacques nailed shutters over the last window. "We'll take my horse and travel with merchants in the morning."

"There's an inn near St-Sernin," Isabella said. "It's where Renoud stables his horses. We can find mounts there in the morning without wasting much of that silver."

"Let's go now," Benito said.

They were half way through the gate when Thierry called them. "Wait, ma dòmna! It's not safe on the streets at night. Tomás will have our balls on a stick if anything happens to his wife."

Benito and Isabella sprinted for the inn, but as they rounded the corner, Chrétien and Durán were coming up the street, leading horses. Isabella grabbed Benito's arm to run the other way, regretting that she was hampered by skirts and soft shoes. Every cobble jarred up against her feet as they bolted for St-Sernin, intending to circle around the cathedral and come to the inn from the other direction. But once again, she had the ill luck to arrive in the square as the White Brotherhood gathered for their evening Mass. She latched onto Benito's arm to avoid getting lost again. They padded down a side street, but a phalanx of the Brotherhood came up the same alley.

Benito pushed her into a doorway, shielding her with his body. She gasped, the stench and smoke of Toulouse burning her throat, a stitch in her side competing with her bruised feet.

The door behind them opened and a hand pulled Isabella inside. Benito followed close behind.

28
The Little Gold Madonna

Jean-Luc at Abbaye St-Féliz, May 27

"TAKE ME AWAY FROM this prison," Hélène whispered, her fingers tracing his eyebrows, nose, and chin. "Jean-Luc, I am so lonely since you last left me. I'll die here!"

Jean-Luc gently guided her hand away.

After the ride from Toulouse in the heat of the day, choking on dust at the rear of Hugues's train of knights, Jean-Luc welcomed the stop at the Abbaye St-Féliz-de-Fontcours. He unlaced his coif and wandered in the shade of a cypress grove, where he found a fountain and slaked his thirst, wiping the worst of the road dust from his face, and then chanced upon Hélène in the grove, playing with her lap dog.

"You've come back to us!" she cried at first, mistaking the intent of his presence.

But no, he explained. Hugues didn't know who rode with him, and Jean-Luc was only riding along to join other friends.

"Then you can save me from this place," she said. "Hugues dumped me here, like a dog he doesn't want. It's been two days and I'm already mad with boredom."

She made him sit with her in the grotto, which he found more ornate than he expected for a Fontrevist abbey. Hélène perched on her bench before a painted fresco of a Madonna and child, the child Jesus reaching out to angels hovering above and the Madonna in a cloak of the night sky. The fresco was Greek, unlike anything he'd seen in churches in the south and not like anything in the churches of the Pays de France. As he listened to Hélène's litany of woes, he saw that the whole wall had been taken from Constantinople and pieced together again here. A crack in the fresco split the Madonna's face in two, yet she still appeared benevolent and woefully consigned to the fate of the Holy Child in her lap.

He didn't want to think about what he saw in Hélène, clothed in red silks, complaining about her fate. She put her arms around him, leaving Galahad to jump to the ground, where the beast begged for Jean-Luc to take him up. He felt her pulse when Hélène put her white hands against his face, and the sweet smell of southern herbs wafted up from the heat of her body. He tried to remember if he had ever smelled a woman while his body baked inside dusty chainmail. At the corner of his eye, a grey flutter of wings disturbed the terebinth and honeysuckle. A small bird landed just an arm's reach away, and then abruptly changed its mind and flitted away.

"Why doesn't Hugues keep you at Fontcours with him?" he asked, interrupting Hélène's torrent of complaints.

"There's a woman there with a sickness that Hugues fears might be catching. I never catch anything. He knows that. He doesn't like me with him. Lord knows, Hugues has no need of a wife of any kind, and he certainly doesn't want me in the way when he joins Simon."

"Is Simon attacking somewhere?"

"They say—Hugues didn't tell me, but I heard them talking—that Simon is marching on Lastours."

"Simon lost at Lastours last summer. Why would he return to such a difficult place again? The terrain is impossible for deploying a siege."

"I'm telling you what I heard." Hélène pouted. "Simon chose Lastours because so many heretics fled there for protection."

"Sancta Maria!" Jean-Luc breathed, thinking about Tomás's mad ride to Lastours in search of Isabella. "Do you know if Senhóra Eloïse is still there?"

"Of course, she is. Renoud made sure she was moved there, and he'll make sure she's moved again. As ridiculous as my cousin is, he still takes care of his mother."

"Renoud is dead," Jean-Luc said.

She didn't seem to hear at first, and then her face softened and lost a degree of its unhappiness. After a few heartbeats, her face became placid as she spoke. "We shan't have to put up with either Eloïse or Renoud's villains when we stay in Toulouse now."

"It was your lover from Cyprus." Jean-Luc interrupted her calculations. "He married Isabella of Valerós, so he's Sebastián's guardian. He'll be the Montcava steward. Good news for you!"

"That *punxor!* He blames me for his face being ruined."

Feeling quite calm and almost enjoying Hélène's demonstration of her true nature, Jean-Luc removed her hand from where she clutched his arm.

"This place can't be a hardship, Hélène. This abbey is remarkably wealthy." He began to tally the benefits. "It's much cooler here than anywhere in the Languedoc in summer. Two streams run through the groves. There's a freshening breeze coming down from the hills. And it's always so peaceful to gaze upon beautiful art made for the glory of God. And there's so much art here."

"Thanks to Hugues. I swear he's given half his wealth to this abbey since I married him."

As she spoke, Jean-Luc spied a niche in the frescoed wall, which held another Madonna.

Hélène said, "He gave most of his booty from Constantinople to the abbey. I can't guess why, except he's always holier than any other man in Christendom."

"Is this from Hugues?" It was the little gold Madonna from the nightmare church, the one Nicolau of Montcava held in his arms when Jean-Luc tripped him.

"Yes. He gave it away, even after I begged to keep it."

"I'm sure you'll have a delightful retreat this summer." He was more than ready to leave her.

"Take me away with you!"

"Where can I take you, Hélène? I haven't a false bezant to my name. Do you want to dress as a knight and ride away with me in this heat? You'd have to leave poor Galahad behind."

"You have all the wealth of Chartrain."

Jean-Luc bent in the manner of Pays de France courtiers and kissed her hand, in the way that meant goodbye. "Perhaps Tomás will shelter you with his wife. She's a cousin of yours."

She shuddered with a sob, furious with him now instead of with Hugues. Jean-Luc knew her fury could be dangerous. But since his life was full to the brim with danger, a soupçon more wouldn't matter.

29
Almond Milk and Braided Bread

Isabella in Toulouse, May 27

"MA DÒMNA, PLEASE COME in and make my home yours." The man closed and barred the door as he spoke. "It will be morning before it's safe to send a messenger to your people. If I can offer you refreshments and a chair to rest, ma dòmna."

"Master Avraham!"

Her old friend, dressed as always in a brown wool robe, strained to recognize her in the candlelight.

"I know that voice." He looked closer at her face. His long hair was pulled back and tied neatly, but now it showed more white than grey. "It's Isabella of Montcava. I had no idea you were in Toulouse."

"I'm not." Isabella's voice was raspy from fright and from the dusty air of Toulouse. "At least, not for more than tonight."

"*Ai,* you always hated Toulouse. And now this peaceful city has become a place no man with an honest soul could love."

He brought Benito and Isabella refreshments: almond milk, filled eggs, and slices of braided bread with honey. And then he brought another chair to sit with them and tell stories. Isabella accepted with gratitude, hating how her illness left her weak. For a long while Benito sat with them, but at last Avraham pointed him to a bench where he could nap with a traveling cloak as his pillow.

"My wife will prepare a pallet for you, ma dòmna," Avraham said. "We can make you comfortable and keep you safe."

"Thank you," she said. "But sleep seems far away for me. I would like to talk with you for a while.

"You were a great one for questing after knowledge," Avraham said. "What have you been studying?"

Isabella said, "Lately, I study the sky to see if I'll be drenched or baked while chasing or being chased by someone whom I can't find. I read the fatigue in a horse's eyes and check its hooves to see if it is well enough to travel. It's like I'm driftwood pushed over God's own waterfall."

"Knowing how your mind works, I'm sure you'll find your way. But I'm surprised, senhóra, that you aren't married again."

Isabella swallowed a bitter taste at the back of her throat, thankful he expressed only surprise without admonishing her about the glories of married life.

"When winter comes," she said, "and the armies go home, I will, too. In truth, my friend, the past years have been an opportunity for calm work and I enjoyed myself, until these invaders came. And you? How are you fairing in this city?"

"Only as well as my brothers. We are thinking of taking our families to Girona, where we have cousins. It's not safe here for anyone, but especially for my people."

"I heard what the bishop is preaching. I'm sorry. And here you are, rescuing me. I have knights for protection and a safe home I could offer you, as soon as I can get home myself."

"We're fine for the moment," Avraham said. "We just endeavor to keep out of people's way."

"When winter comes, we'll all be safe again." She said it but felt it was a foolish hopefulness.

"Your bishops and pope and their French henchmen have opened a box of great evil. No one can vanquish this evil quickly. It'll be a generation, maybe more, before we see peace again."

"*Ai.*" She had also heard it from Mathilde de Garlande. They were right: the south would host more seasons of brutality. She'd seen the proof: in the blind knights in the garden at Lastours.

Avraham rose. "I have something I've longed to give you since I first received it. Whenever I see it, I think of you."

Beckoning her to his workroom, he offered her a tiny book, bound in chamois, its pages filled with tiny handwriting. In the dim candlelight it was only barely possible to make out the words.

"It's the Cantos of Solomon, in Greek. I remember you in those days, working to translate it from Latin. I bought it from a knight who carried it back from Constantinople. All this time, I've wanted to give it to you."

She reached to take it, grateful for his friendship, but dismayed to receive it today of all days. Avraham caught sight of her hand.

"Ma dòmna!" He set the book on the table and touched her injured hand. "What evil wrought this?"

He gently rubbed at the edges of the hideous scar in the middle of her palm. The wound itself was still tender, and he touched it with great sensitivity.

"You must see my friend who lives upstairs, ma dòmna. He's a great physician. Perhaps he can find a way to preserve the use of your hand. You always had the loveliest handwriting."

Isabella burst into tears at his kind words, since no one had comforted her after the crusaders carried Father Anselm away. Avraham put his hand on her head in blessing, exactly as her grandfather used to do.

30
Ululations on the Plains

Tomás, leaving Toulouse, May 27

IN THEIR RENTED ROOM in Toulouse, Tomás threw off the wretched clothes borrowed from Renoud and dressed in his own, and then tied his gear into a travel pack while gently questioning Henri, who leaped about, bug-eyed with excitement.

"Do you have a fever?" Henri asked. "You look like my mother when she had a fever."

"Tell me about your mother," Tomás said.

"They claim the angels took her, but I know she just died. She had a fever." Henri spoke solemnly. Other than the red hair, Henri was nothing like Sebastián, having full lips and wide cheeks, while Sebastián possessed Pèire's fine-edged Romanesque features. And Sebastián seemed a head taller than he'd been in April at Valerós.

"Who was your mother, Henri?"

"A senhóra. Our house was by the church at St-Sernin."

"And who was your father?"

"A crusader. He died fighting for the cross in Constantinople."

"How did you come to be with Renoud at the Montcava villa?"

"The nuns I stayed with told someone about me. One day Renoud came and took me to live in his house."

"Why did he do that?"

"He wanted to make me a gentleman," Henri said. "Then he went away and came back with Sebastián, which is much more fun than living there alone."

Tomás untied the bag of silver he'd retrieved the day before from his agent, a fellow Cypriot he paid to hold his goods and money in Toulouse. Though paying someone to hold money seemed absurd.

And the last of his silver from Burgundy was about to leave his pocket.

"All right, *fadrins*. Let's go. We've got leagues to ride before the sun sets." He stopped. "Henri, do you know how to ride a horse?"

"No, senhór."

"That's one less horse to worry about," Tomás said.

He led them through the alleys to an armorer he and Chrétien especially liked, where he traded silver for a mail hauberk, leggings, and a coif for Sebastián, small enough to be useful but large enough to accommodate how fast the boy was growing. Sebastián carried a sword out of Renoud's house, and he'd managed to keep the Castilian dagger Tomás gave him at Valerós. Tomás had to outfit him only with a shield, baldric, and belt. When Sebastián begged, Tomás added more silver for two javelins.

Next door, Tomás let go of more coins for a gambeson for each of the boys, though the smallest garment was swimmingly large for Henri. Then they followed the master's directions to a stall in the market where he purchased breeches and shirts for the boys. And ten steps away, he bought blankets. Back at the stable, he paid for the last of his horse's keeping.

"Sebastián, where does Renoud stable his horses?" Tomás asked.

"Near the east gate. Are we going there now?"

Sebastián latched onto the idea of stealing two of Renoud's horses, one to ride and a palfrey for their baggage. Tomás didn't remind the boy he was only taking horses from his own domus. The whole horse-stealing adventure took about as long as it would have taken to haggle with the stable keeper, but left Sebastián in a frenzy of joy when they gained the highway heading east to Fontcours. Tomás worked to keep up with him, riding with the light weight of Henri in his arms.

The small boy smelled rank, and the creases of his neck were a grubby grey. Whenever Henri moved, which was often, his head bumped again under Tomás's nose, and the smell of grimy boy-hair made Tomás think he held a squirming, unwashed puppy. Both Sebastián and Henri remained in sickeningly high spirits, calling out to each other silly names for travelers they passed on the road. The highway was crowded with merchants, mercenaries, and monks.

Half way to Fontcours, Henri fell asleep in the way children can instantly sleep anywhere, his small, thin body warm and pliable. His pulse showed in a vein at his forehead and throbbed against Tomás's chest, which he felt even through the weight of mail and gambeson. Holding the boy close, Tomás didn't know how he mistook the child for Sebastián, except he must have begun to think of Sebastián as an unprotected child after Renoud stole him. This boy was so much smaller and thinner, with a cherubic face. Sebastián was the boy-image of Pèire, all white-hot energy and determination, and Henri was the child-image of Renoud.

Whether the boy was Sebastián's cousin or brother, Tomás had to determine what to do with him. Chrétien couldn't handle a child while he took on serving as steward at Fontcours, and Tomás didn't want to see the Valerós knights yet. Besides, a military camp wouldn't suit a child from the city.

"I still don't understand why my mother isn't with us," Sebastián said. When shadows fell across the road, they slowed their ride, sparing the horses instead of stopping to rest since they were so close to their first destination.

"She's been ill," Tomás said. "She's upset about Renoud and there's business to take care of at the Montcava estates."

"What upset her? She always hated my uncle. Worse than she hated my father."

"I can't explain it," Tomás said.

"Does she know you rescued me? Was she worried?"

"Yes, she worried night and day for the past month. But she knows you're safe," Tomás said. "And she's proud you're riding as a knight of the bonfraires."

Tomás hadn't eaten enough to spew up anything, but his stomach churned at spouting lies and then flipped far worse when he contemplated telling Sebastián the truth. Instead, he focused his mind on how the two of them could travel safely, how to get Guillem and the other knights out of Carcassonne, how to deal with the Valerós knights, and how to fulfill Pèire's promise to Hugues de Beaurain. He didn't yet know whether Hugues was a friend or the final target for his revenge.

"There's the road to the abbey," Sebastián said. "We're almost to Fontcours."

"Let's stop at the abbey for a few moments." Tomás believed he had the answer to the problem of Henri.

The Fontrevists obligingly let the travelers in the gate, and the abbot's man met them in the court of honor, where Tomás told his tale while Sebastián fidgeted and Henri glanced around sleepily.

"Òc, the Marquesa Hélène de Beaurain is here."

"Her husband sent this boy as a page to her, knowing she needs company."

The brother frowned. "The marquis didn't mention anything when he visited this afternoon."

"This is her young cousin, seeking the same shelter as the senhóra. And the marquis offers ten silver pieces for the boy's keeping."

The brother refused Tomás's silver.

"The marquis already pays far too much for the keeping of his wife. One small boy won't make a difference."

"He needs washing," Tomás said.

"Don Tomás, I want to stay with you and Sebastián," Henri said. "I want to be a knight, too."

"You're too young." Sebastián saved Tomás the hassle. "We'll come back for you when the summer is over."

They left the abbey gates. Tomás asked, "Why come back at the end of summer?"

"When the crusading season ends, and everyone goes home, we'll get my mother and go back to Valerós. Won't we?"

"Fontcours and Montcava are yours now. You can live there," Tomás said.

"But I don't want to. Valerós is home. Montcava is just trouble."

"It has a better income than Valerós."

Sebastián shrugged. "I'd rather be a hermit or a pauper or a priest than live at Fontcours or Montcava. Mother always wanted it to be mine, but I don't care. Valerós is enough for me."

"If you'd told me, it might have saved me a lot of trouble."

"You didn't ask," Sebastián said. "Are we going to Carcassonne now, Don Tomás?"

He pondered it. "If we ride tonight, without stopping at Font-cours, we can be in Carcassonne by midday."

"Good. It drove me mad being in the villa day after day. Can we ride faster with Henri gone? The horses can see in the dark better than we can."

·

From the abbey, Tomás and Sebastián turned onto a country lane meandering in the direction of Carcassonne. The lane frequently degenerated into a goat track, but they saw no one along the way throughout the late afternoon. The sun gone, his headache gone, he felt almost as if he could breathe again. Still riding tirelessly ahead of Tomás as dusk settled, Sebastián halted at the top of a rise. As Tomás came up beside Sebastián, his horse's ears pricked forward, and then he too spied the band of soldiers below, beset by brigands.

"Aragón." Sebastián peered into the gathering dusk, trying to make out the surcoats of the knights fighting amongst brigands.

The four knights had been either unseated from their horses or surprised while dismounted. A fifth knight, slain or grievously injured, lay beside an arrow-shot horse bleeding away its life into the nearby creek. The brigands set upon the knights in a haphazard fashion, and the knights responded to their attackers without group-ing into a fighting formation. Outnumbered, the knights wouldn't last much longer.

"Do you see how we should ride upon them?" Tomás dis-mounted while they talked.

"I shall come from the east and you from the southwest."

"Yes. Lock your javelin against your saddle so you don't have to worry about it. You know how. Your sword is in your right hand and—what, donzel?"

"My long dagger is ready to pull if I'm unseated."

"If you're unseated from your horse, get your back up against one of those knights and keep it there. You can only protect three sides of yourself at a time." Tomás mounted his horse again.

"I've practiced it a hundred times."

"We're doing it in the real world now. Strike to kill, not just to wound. When we pass those trees, we yell enough for a dozen men and ride in circles after we arrive. Perhaps in this bad light they won't notice there are only two of us."

The ululations of the Bedouin cry Tomás learned in Cairo ripped from his throat and freed him from everything that weighed on his mind. He and Sebastián galloped around the fighters on the rocky knoll, but the limestone boulders and treacherous ground kept them from riding closer. Across the knoll, a gigantic man swung a nail-headed mace on a chain, waiting for Sebastián to come close enough, but Tomás was off his own horse in heartbeat, bringing his sword down on the brigand's forearm. The man's hand and the mace it held fell away, clattering down among the fallen boulders. The next stroke cut deeply into the man's neck.

Tomás shouted for the knights to form a circle, to protect their backs with each other as cover. Only one of the men turned to see who yelled directions. After a moment's hesitation, they began to regroup. Tomás, it seemed, couldn't command trained knights to save their own lives, while Jean-Luc could control ruffians with a single word.

Sebastián, still on his horse, struck down a lone brigand at the south end of the knoll. The man fell to his knees, and Sebastián leaped from his horse and bounded toward where Tomás fought three brigands surrounding one of the knights.

"Back to back!" Tomás shouted.

"*Òc, el meu capità!*" Sebastián shouted, saluting Tomás as his captain. He took the precise stance Chrétien had taught him.

"And the rest of you Aragónese hedge-pigs!" Tomás shouted. "Back to back. Get in formation. Fight like knights."

The two closest to Sebastián stepped into position with Sebastián and Tomás. Two others looked around, marooned from the knights by fallen bodies. One moved to protect the taller knight but was a half-step and two heartbeats too late, because two brigands burst upon him together and one drove a sword up the knight's groin in the gap between chausses and mail. The knight collapsed and died, shrieking in agony.

"Fall in!" Tomás yelled at the lone knight left standing. But the man was too far away to cross the gap to the other knights. Tomás leaped from a limestone boulder to land near the stranded knight.

"Get your back up against mine. And keep your shield in the middle of your body."

Sebastián backed up against one of the other knights, and together they'd nearly defeated their attackers.

"No quarter!" Tomás called. The brigands centered on the lone knight beside Tomás.

"But they cried mercy!" the knight shouted to Tomás. "And they're running away."

"And they'll be back tonight to cut your throat," Tomás called, running after the fleeing murderers to dispatch the last of them. He breathed hard as he ran, but wasn't winded, just pondering the two missteps he'd made in timing. He still couldn't respond with the speed and grace of past years. Before Renoud's men got to him.

He returned in a few moments, wiping his sword on a headcloth he pulled free from one of the brigands.

"You need to build your strength and your wind if you want to live long as a fighter," Tomás said to the tall knight as they climbed the rocky knoll to join the survivors. Then he stopped, seeing a fallen knight in a pool of blood, a gold circlet around the top of his mail coif.

Tomás dropped to his knees.

"*Ai, bon Dèu!* Not the king! This is the most cursed day since God created man. *Ai, dolç Jhezu!*"

He felt such a burden of grief and despair, he wanted to lie down by the king and die, too. Instead, he whirled in anger on the knight who didn't know how to protect a partner in battle.

"Damn you!" Tomás bitterly condemned the knight to hell in three languages. "Are you his bodyguard? You goose-livered vulture! You let them kill the king."

"I stood my ground and fought."

"You call that fighting? Look, you spit-licking cur. I hope you are man enough to say how he was slain. I don't need anyone thinking this is my fault."

"Your fault?" The failed knight sounded confused.

"Every bird that falls in Christendom, every goat that dies, somehow the story starts that I did it."

"This is too much pride, senhór. You've slain the surrendering brigands, but—"

"I liked the man. He was brilliant. I don't want him dead, but I especially don't want to hang for it."

"I don't think—"

"Exactly, senhór knight. You don't think to guard either your own middle or the man at your back. I'd barter my soul to ensure you never sell your services again, you scrofulous weasel."

"Tomás of Morella, isn't it?" The knight unlaced the flap of the mail coif covering his face, letting the coif fall back onto his shoulders. "I salute your swordplay. But could you shut up and let us catch our breath?"

Tomás glanced down at the dead man. Humiliation flooded his veins.

"He was wearing my armor," Pedro said. "Yesterday was his first day. He swore he was the greatest man-at-arms in Aragón."

"He lied about that. But is it honest on your part? To have someone pretend to be you?"

"I want to cheat anyone who seeks to deprive Aragón of its king. Three times we've foiled assassins this year."

"The man must have got the thrill of his life, parading as the king of Aragón," Tomás mused. "Then he found he couldn't parry a sword thrust to save himself."

"Would you like the same thrill, Tomás of Morella?"

"Failing to parry a thrust? No, thank you. I'd die of embarrassment if I did it as badly as he did."

"I mean for you to wear my armor, man."

"As in a masquerade?"

"As in being my bodyguard." Pedro gestured to the dead man.

"Now? You want me to put on armor that man just died in?"

"If you can put aside your fastidiousness, yes, it's what I want."

"You want me to walk around as a target, as a service for you?"

"Yes, though since I own your life, it's my risk and my possible loss," Pedro said. "But I forgot. You have knight-errant business to finish for Pèire Leteric. Have you made Christendom safe for his heirs yet?"

"*Ai*, in part. Pèire's heir is over there, the one who backed your other knights in the fight."

Sebastián pulled off his coif, flush with the thrill of his first melee. Pedro studied the boy before he knelt to clean his own sword with the head-rag Tomás had found.

"Saved by a boy and a mad Moor," Pedro muttered.

Tomás bristled but didn't say anything.

"I've been longing to ask you, Tomás of Morella, about this story going the rounds." Pedro put his arm around Tomás's shoulder, steering him toward where his men were gathering the horses. "People say there's a wild Moor who murders gold-sniffing priests, lay-brothers, and nuns. Last time, he stabbed a Fontrevist nun at the Vale of Roses abbey. Is it a cousin of yours? Do you think you could persuade him to stop?"

31
Choosing Sides

Isabella, leaving Toulouse, May 28

WHEN ISABELLA AND BENITO emerged from Avraham's shop in the early dawn, Chrétien and Durán waited in the narrow street with horses and half a dozen men, including Thierry and Jacques.

"Come, ma dòmna, we're leaving the city," Chrétien said.

Although Chrétien was to be her jailer, she mounted the horse he brought, eager to leave Toulouse. Benito rode behind her until they fetched his horse from its stable, and then they galloped out as soon as the city gates opened, leaving Toulouse behind, faintly glowing pink in the dawn light.

She preferred to ride hard. Chrétien accommodated that. At the first rest stop, she demanded riding clothes, and he didn't argue. Among the men, they assembled leggings, a shirt, and hauberk.

"Turn your back," she said. But she was so irate, she didn't wait. She began stripping to change. Benito held up a travel cloak, but she didn't care. In short order, she was once more a boy-squire.

Then they rode hard again, and by the next stop, everyone was ready for breakfast. The mercenaries made their own picnic further off, leaving Benito, Durán, and Chrétien with Isabella, who had sorted her feelings as they rode and found those feelings to be quite simple: she was furious.

"I'm not going to the Montcava estates." She ate bread and cheese, not remembering her last meal.

"That's where I'm taking you," Chrétien said.

"Did Tomás tell you what happened with Renoud?"

"Durán saw it." Chrétien glanced down, avoiding her eyes.

"And do you believe the lies Tomás heard?"

"I'm worried about Tomás. He might—"

"What? Slip and cut a finger while he's butchering people?"

"Tomás wasn't himself yesterday," Chrétien said.

"What was he?" she demanded. "Possessed by demons? Surely those were the most rational devils ever set loose. He stood in front of the bishop as lucid as any man in Christendom. Madness can't account for what happened."

"I can't speak for him, ma dòmna."

"Chrétien, please give your brother a message." She savaged the brioix, tearing it into hunks.

"And I can't be your talebearer, either."

"No? At least let him know he's hurt me worse than Nicolau and Renoud ever did. Tomás swears he's better than them. Now he has proof."

Chrétien touched her hand, which startled her. "Ma dòmna, in a while, Tomás will be better again. That's how it was the last time."

"When? The last time he slit a man's throat because he doesn't like to hear screaming? Thierry told me what happened."

"I mean last year on Cyprus. When he almost died."

"All right, tell me the story." Isabella shook off Chrétien's hand. "You mean to do it anyway."

"We came back from Burgundy to see our father before he died. Tomás went out to meet a woman. A company of thugs plucked him from her arms and imprisoned him in the cellar of an empty villa for three days, leaving him alone, with no water, unable to wiggle away from whatever crawled over him in the dark."

Chrétien stared off, stopping the story.

"And?" Isabella prompted him.

"They beat him with staves, making sure they hurt him. Inside and out. I guessed from his wounds and from what he wouldn't say."

Durán winced. "You mean they—"

"They humiliated him. Made him bleed. Made him beg."

"How did you find him?" Isabella said.

"I went to the woman's house when Tomás missed our rendez-vous. She let me in when I created a scandal shouting outside her door. Things weren't right. Her servants were dead drunk, the rooftop where the woman slept was a wreck. After I harangued her, she admitted her cousin attacked Tomás."

"How did you find him?" she asked again.

"I hunted down one of the thugs Hélène named, which took two days. Then I thrashed him until he led me to where they kept Tomás. I left the bastard there in exchange for Tomás, who was bleeding everywhere and nearly dead from thirst."

"And the other men?" Isabella asked, afraid to hear the details.

"Our father died the first night I was hunting Tomás. When he could walk again, Tomás spent weeks hunting the men who hurt him. Then he became more like his old self again."

"That's when he gave up women? Even though it was men who hurt him?"

"He said the memory of it left him revolted, and he was wasting his strength on base pleasures."

"But he still gambles," she said.

"That's mathematics."

"Chrétien, is this what ended your—" Isabella made a gesture, and then saw from the expression on Durán's face that she'd opened an untold story.

"Me sleeping with Tomás? No, that ended when we left the squires' barracks and became knights." He looked at Durán while he answered Isabella.

"Who was the woman he was with?"

"Hélène de Beaurain," Chrétien said. "And it was Renoud's men who beat him. The affair left him with a deep fear."

"He got over his fear of coupling with women," Isabella said.

"No, he's afraid of the dark. When Tomás wakes up after this frenzy—I think the tunnel at the villa set him off—he'll come to the Montcava estates begging your forgiveness."

"I won't be there."

"Ma dòmna, you must."

"Most of my family is dead or lost. I almost died last week. I don't know if I can write again. And I spent a fortnight humiliating myself with a man who said he loved me but suddenly believes I betrayed him. And he has stolen my son." Her voice shattered. "I will never again let any man punish me for someone else's sins."

"Your pain must be crushing, but—"

"Am I crushed, Chrétien? No, I'm furious. Someone raped him and he's afraid of the dark. Should I feel sorry or, God help me, forgive him? Just because he endured one night of suffering?"

"Three days and nights," Chrétien said.

"He should try six years of it and see who feels sorry for him."

"He'll calm down. Meanwhile, let's do as he wants."

"Last week I'd do anything he asked," Isabella said. "I'd crawl for him. I couldn't breathe if he wasn't nearby. But now he believes the lies my enemy told." Her voice broke. "I'm only ashamed that I let him hurt me."

"Isabella, he loves you."

"It's not logical, putting his name and the word 'love' in the same sentence. I'm sure it's not possible in Greek."

"We have to take you to the Montcava estates as he asked."

"No," Isabella said. "I'll go where I want and do as I like. You will either help or leave me alone."

"We can force you," Chrétien said. "Durán and I, with the others."

"No, we can't," Durán said. "It's not right. I don't want to do it."

"Tomás is my brother," Chrétien said. "Not everything we do is a lark."

"He's not your brother, and he's a *punxor*," Durán said. "This is wrong."

Chrétien, frustrated, dropped his voice as he pleaded with Durán. "We need to go to Montcava, Durán. Don't quarrel with me."

"There is no quarrel," Durán said. "I'll help Isabella go wherever she wants. You can choose. Go with me. Or go with your brother."

The two men stared at each other, but Durán broke away after only a moment.

"You can keep your brother's horse. I'll find another," he said.

"Durán, don't do this."

Benito helped Durán throw his travel pack onto his horse, and they prepared to ride together. Isabella got her own horse ready.

Chrétien called Durán's name.

"You can't stop us without force," Durán said. "Get your street friends to beat me, Chrétien, if you don't want to do it yourself."

He swung up behind Benito, who kicked his horse at the same moment Isabella kicked hers. Durán clutched the back of Benito's saddle, his eyes closed tight.

"Wait!" Chrétien shouted in the road. Moments later he caught up with them. "I'll go with you!"

They all reined in their horses. Chrétien tried to calm his mount.

"*Bon Dèu*." Durán still had his eyes closed, but tears streaked the dust on his face. "I didn't think I could do it."

"Where are we going?" Chrétien asked, pale as death.

Isabella said, "Fontcours first. We'll find Jean-Luc and the Valerós knights, and then we're going to be mercenaries. God knows where."

"All right then." Chrétien rubbed at his own dust-streaked face. "I know how to do that. Even without Tomás."

32

Gall in a Conquered City

Tomás in Carcassonne, May 28

WHEN TOMÁS FIRST AWOKE, birds sang and the scent of flowers perfumed the air. But he couldn't remember which country he was in to guess what kind of birds raised such noise, and he couldn't remember the season to guess what caused that cloying odor.

When he awoke the next time, he remembered everything. Larks and lavender.

And he was in a hell of his own creation somewhere in the Languedoc. After drinking all the water he could find and then sleeping more, Tomás woke again. What he remembered hurt worse than the throbbing behind his eyes.

"Do I have to give back your life since you saved mine?"

A silken Catalan voice purred nearby. Pedro, in a plain linen gambeson, hose, and breeches, appeared as calm and elegant as he had in Hugues de Beaurain's camp.

"The devil can have my life, if it's worth a brass bezant to him," Tomás said.

"You certainly fought like the devil's own man," Pedro said. "I've seen men walk around in a blind rage before, but I never saw it with such brilliant sword-play. However, as a Christian king, I forbid you to give yourself to the devil."

"You're a day too late, Monsenyor." Tomás grasped the goblet Pedro offered, though the fleeting idea of wine without food turned his stomach.

"But I've taken you back from the devil. You are in my camp now, so God and I will decide what your life is worth. Do you need a confessor?"

"God already knows what I've done, and a hundred pater-nosters won't repair it."

"God forgives you when you ask Him."

"I killed a man yesterday."

"You killed several."

"I mean earlier, before I joined you. I cut down a man in his own house because of what he said to me."

"Not another priest or gold-douser, I hope."

"No, a Toulouse seigneur." Annoyed that the king didn't take his confession seriously, Tomás fingered the long scar on his face, which itched and burned again. "It was the man who caused this, because his father hated mine."

"You murdered him?" Pedro finally became serious.

"He had a sword, and I only a knife. He intended to send me to the devil, but I went into a rage and killed him first."

"Sounds like sufficient provocation for God to forgive it."

"But I can't forgive myself. I let my heart and spleen rule over my head. I need to learn who the man's father is. That's my real enemy. But I murdered the man before he could tell us."

Pedro poured water and wine into his own cup from two stone jars on the camp table. He straddled a camp stool as he studied Tomás with a sardonic expression that left Tomás feeling even more humiliated and depressed.

"You were considerably more entertaining last night," Pedro said. "Even before the wine got the better of you."

"If I embarrassed you, you can hang me. Please do."

"On the contrary. It was amusing. Your excessive flattery half way through the wine was the only embarrassment. I shouldn't let you say those things."

Tomás couldn't remember what he'd said. His head throbbed with an orange glow again. "Where's Sebastián?"

"In camp with my knights, telling bloody stories and playing the hero."

"Will you protect him if I can't?" Tomás asked.

"Without a doubt. He's my seigneur. And a very impressive oath he gave me. In Greek and Latin." Pedro passed over his own cup. "Drink that wine. It's mulled and watered. There'll be food soon."

"Where are we?"

"At my camp, a brief ride from Carcassonne. Tell me, do you always drink like that?"

"No, never."

"Do you always gamble so recklessly?"

"No, I always win. Did I lose last night?"

"Only in the last few tosses, and only to me. Did you lose on purpose?"

"I hope so. God forbid I'm that cocked up."

Tomás tried to stand but settled for merely sitting on the cot, then realized exactly where he was.

"This is your tent."

Pedro made a gesture of dismissal. "It seemed wiser to bring you here last night. I wanted to make you stop talking."

"But this is your bed." Tomás glanced around, trying to determine where Pedro must have slept.

"It's of no consequence since you saved my life. Shall I also find you a nice estate and a wife to go along with it, Tomás of Morella?"

"I'm married already, as you instructed. One of Pèire Leteric's grandchildren." He sipped the wine, but mostly to hide his eyes as he talked to Pedro. "It secures Valerós and Arracheuse for you. Also, Montcava and Fontcours are under my charge, if you care about the Languedoc."

"Am I to congratulate you? Was it the tall, cold one or the little brown thing?"

"The taller of the two."

"In Narbonne, they say she's as frigid as a Pyrenees snowfall."

"Is that so?" Tomás felt bitter. "In Toulouse they say the opposite."

"Which is it? Will you be populating the upper Corbières hills with her?"

"The marriage is consecrated and consummated, but that's all." Tomás guarded against revealing more, rage rising again.

"You aren't keeping her?"

"Yes, technically. But not by my side. She's not that kind of wife."

"And what kind of husband are you?"

"The biggest fool God ever set down in Christendom. You must have noticed."

"In my experience, wives are always trouble, no matter where you find them and however much you admonish them." Pedro slapped at Tomás's knee, his hand lingering after the slap. "You can hardly blame yourself."

"Are you going to give me back my life?"

"No, you'd just throw it away, and I have use for it, if you can give up your mercenary ways and submit to my rule."

"I've never submitted to anyone in my life." Tomás tried to guess what Pedro meant by submission, but the king maintained a perfectly guileless expression, though his knee touched Tomás's. "Except my father and my swordmasters in Cairo. They never gave me any choice."

"Should I give you a choice?" Pedro said.

"If God insists I remain alive, working for you is better than any choices I've made. Give me work to do, Monsenyor, for if I'm idle, I'll go mad."

Tomás covered his eyes, the orange glow still throbbing at his temple. Pedro touched his knee again, and this time the touch felt like a comfort.

Pedro said, "You need to wash and dress. We're visiting Simon de Montfort tonight."

"Please, Monsenyor, will you get back the Valerós knights from him? And their horses?"

"Perhaps. I want you to wear my armor when we pass through the city."

"It isn't right. Lords wear their colors so they won't be killed in battle. You are worth a great deal in ransom."

"Whoever has tried to kill me, repeatedly, doesn't care about ransom. Take off your clothes and wash."

"What about Sebastián?"

"He's having the time of his life. My marshal will watch him."

·

At Carcassonne, people bowed and cheered as he passed, even though they meant it for the taller warrior at his side, dressed almost like him, but with a duller surcoat and no golden circlet around his coifed head.

"The hardest part of this job is keeping the aventail laced shut over my unroyal face," Tomás said.

"You're only a shade too dark to pass for an Aragón prince," Pedro muttered.

"We'll both roast in our own juices dressed like this."

"Too bad we can't lace your unroyal mouth shut," Pedro said. "The king of Aragón does not have a Cypriot's accent."

By the time they crossed the bridge and wound through the narrow streets toward the chateau Simon de Montfort now called home, the thrill had worn off for Tomás. Posturing as a king wasn't a challenge, because his swordmasters had made sure his bones and sinews learned erect carriage. The only effort was to be a taller man and to look people straight in the eye when he caught their gaze. Speaking quietly at his side, Pedro pointed out individual burghers and seigneurs who should receive special attention.

"It'd break my neck to be king," Tomás said, "all this nodding."

"Something else is much more likely to break your neck," Pedro said, "as recklessly as you stick it out."

"My father said God gave me a neck in order to risk it."

"God wouldn't waste that much beauty if He intended you to throw it away," Pedro said. "That man to your left is the mayor of Narbonne. Nod deeply and lift your hand to acknowledge him. His bishop is a whoring thief, so the mayor needs all the support he can get from his king."

"Strong words to describe a bishop," Tomás said under his breath.

"He's my uncle, so I ought to know."

At Simon de Montfort's chateau, Pedro's seneschal tended their horses and other men carried their meager baggage, while Pedro and Tomás were led through the courtyard into the center halls. All comfort had been stripped from the chateau. No rich tapestries. Few chairs provided comfort for visitors. No art decorated the welcoming hall. Alcoves designed to hold finery were now temporary armories that held bundles of arrows and crossbow bolts.

Simon de Montfort, in the same way he decorated his house, didn't waste effort with chamberlains and courtiers. He waited in the great hallway to receive King Pedro, the king who refused to accept his oath after Simon took Carcassonne and left the former viscount to die in the dungeons. Unlike everyone they passed on the ride through the city, Simon ignored Tomás, who still wore Pedro's crown. Instead Simon reached out to Pedro in greeting, bowing his head in only the slightest semblance of submission to a lord.

Pedro took Simon's hand and made no remark about the man's lack of good manners. But Tomás seethed. He'd seen Simon in action on the road to Constantinople, before Simon left at Zara to lead a band of disgruntled knights to the Holy Land. Simon possessed all the attributes of a warrior: strong as a bull, fearless, handsome, with a greater mane of hair than even the vain Richard Lionheart. Pedro's persistent Catholicism could be tolerated, because he recognized human folly in the mix of God's forces on earth. Simon had appointed himself to be the right hand of God.

But what galled Tomás that night was how the zealot greeted Pedro as an equal. To be sure, the Catalan seigneurs all fancied themselves as equal to their king. Charlemagne never really subdued these seigneurs. But Simon wasn't one of them. He owed allegiance to the kings of England and France, and Tomás knew the custom in those courts was that a lesser lord bent his knee before his king. Simon falsely adopted the title of viscount of Carcassonne, acclaimed by the French conquerors. But Tomás felt that Simon's greeting rose from a belief that he was Pedro's equal, not from adopting the court manners of the south.

Swallowing that gall, Tomás sank to his own knees and offered the circlet to Pedro.

"Your crown, Monsenyor."

Pedro accepted it without looking. He motioned where Tomás should wait and followed Simon deeper into the chateau, where the doors closed behind them.

.

Simon de Montfort cut off the lips and noses of the hundred knights of Bram and then blinded them. Or rather, he ordered it to be done. Simon let undisciplined French knights and ruffians from his baggage train burn Béziers. Simon rode through the valleys of the south harrying villagers and stealing food for his army. His handiwork resulted in the mud-sunk hopelessness of camps like the Vale des Roses, where a dozen nuns labored to keep hundreds of women and children from dying of dirt and hunger.

"Deus vult," Tomás muttered, thinking of how he'd viewed Pèire's hatred of Normans as a quaint prejudice born of resentment because he'd been stuck cleaning up messes left by the ruthlessly cruel Richard Lionheart. Killing a man in battle wasn't the same as slitting the throats of thousands of bound men, which King Richard did when the Saracens surrendered at Acre. It certainly wasn't the same as burning women, children, and priests, which the French army did in Béziers.

While Tomás pondered this, he ignored the French courtiers around him, refusing their hospitality and maintaining the posture of a soldier who would kill anyone that tried to step past him to get to his king. Pedro conferred behind that door with a man who thought he was God's own hammer, sent to pound the enemies of God into dust. But Tomás believed that Pedro, who worried about the well-being of the people God gave to his care, stood far above Simon in the company of men and angels. Even Tomás was responsible for far less evil than Simon.

Then, staring at the hilt of his sword, still tired beyond what sleep could cure, Tomás mistook it for the blade he'd used on Renoud and again saw that man's blood drenching the floor planks. When Tomás tried to remember what happened in the Montcava villa, he instead pictured Isabella standing in St-Sernin whispering. *Is he dead?*

"We've accepted our host's gracious hospitality for the night."

Tomás started as Pedro spoke to him.

A double brace of Pedro's men set a schedule for guarding the door of Pedro's sleeping chamber. Tomás started to claim his place in the schedule when Pedro said, "My bodyguard sleeps inside the door, in case any intruder makes it that far."

Following Pedro, Tomás barred the door behind them and studied the entrances and exits of the chamber that Simon lent to the king of Aragón. The fenestral latticework was covered with resin-soaked linen, the shutters framing them painted a deep red. Tomás flung open a fenestra to ensure no one could climb up the wall and enter in that way. Pedro tapped the table, indicating that Tomás should sit down. The trestle table, rubbed to a warm brown glow with beeswax, was loaded with provender, candles, quills, and parchment for the king's convenience.

Tomás refused the wine Pedro offered, having abused it too much the night before, and silently spread his surcoat and travel cloak in front of the door. He wrapped and rolled his chainmail in his doublet for a pillow. Then he stretched out, his dagger on one side and sword on the other.

"That's not where I intended you to sleep," Pedro said. "You aren't a servant."

"I won't be sleeping," Tomás said.

"Can I command you to talk ceaselessly, like you did last night?" Pedro unbuckled his jerkin and folded it neatly, his linen undershirt falling open as he straddled a chair. "I need your help to think pure thoughts after spending time with Simon de Montfort. Perhaps chess?"

Tomás joined him at the table and fetched a pair of dice out of his own shirt, shaking them from their leather pouch so they clattered on the table.

"Let me win back what I lost last night," Tomás said. "Al-zahr, or Hazard, as the Franks call it."

Pedro reached for the dice, his long fingers grazing Tomás's.

"I left your silver in my seneschal's keeping."

"A cowardly act, Monsenyor. We'll gamble for stories then. The loser must tell whatever tale the winner commands."

"Call me by my name when we're alone. I don't feel like being king tonight. What's the game?"

"Riffa. Roll until you have a pair. Then roll the third die for your total score. Highest of three rounds wins a story."

Pedro tossed first. When Tomás reached for the dice for his round, Pedro stayed his hand.

"Can I trust you?"

He wasn't asking about the game. Tomás again heard Pèire: *Your best bet is loyalty.*

"As much as you can trust any man on God's own earth." Tomás tossed the bones, matching Pedro's score.

"Why should I trust a lunatic Moor with no more than one brass barcelonese to his name and a reputation for murdering priests?"

"You have my life in your hands."

"But you don't value that."

"You have my oath, on my father's honor and my mother's."

Pedro tossed for the second round, and then Tomás had his turn, beating the king by a single point. When Pedro picked up the bones again, he stopped just before tossing them.

"Did you ever yearn for something so badly you couldn't ask for it, because you didn't want to hear 'No' from man or God?"

Without waiting for an answer, Pedro let the dice tumble across the table, scoring a pair immediately. He tossed the third die. They both studied the result.

Tomás picked up the dice for his turn. "I'm just like my father. I don't believe God answers prayer. You only get what you want by taking it, or by luck."

He tossed, and of course he beat Pedro on the last roll.

Tomás was determined to overcome his unease. "Tell me the story where a powerful knight, who could have anyone he wanted, instead chooses to put his hand on the knee of a disfigured *poulain* from the backwash of the Outremer."

"You're peeved because you can't win your silver back tonight, aren't you? Or have I offended you?"

"So far, you have only piqued my curiosity. Tell the story, *mon amic*."

"In the *cançós d'Arturo*, every knight has a secret. As does this knight."

"Is there magic in this story?"

"Magic transports the knight to another world," Pedro said, "where he quests forever. But his base nature keeps him from attaining his divine quest."

"No fair. No allegory. I want only the story."

"All right then. In Homer's story of the Trojans and Odysseus, you must accept that the gods enjoy interfering in men's lives. Otherwise, the entire tale makes no sense. In this story, you have to believe some men are anointed by God to lead and care for people."

"I'll grant you that," Tomás said, "though not all men will. Southern seigneurs won't. And neither will anyone who's been close to the kings of Jerusalem or Cyprus."

"They elect their kings in Jerusalem," Pedro said, "which makes no sense as a way to rule people. Unless you can stretch faith to accept that God would guide such an election and not allow the devil to—"

"Your story, *mon amic.*"

Pedro sighed in surrender. "If you believe God anoints kings and that once anointed, a king must give his life to the good of his people, then there is no room for the king to do as he pleases."

"I can't grant you that. The history of royal bastards is too long and rich to grant that kings can't do as they please."

Pedro hesitated. "Within the bounds of certain conventions."

"All right. I'll grant that. When do we get to the story?"

"The knight in this story, like Galahad, has slight personal knowledge of the world. He has never dallied with passing fancies and has known only two lovers. Oh, the devil take me, you'll count my wife, though she's hardly human and only counts as 'known' and not as 'lover.'"

Tomás sat back, surprised. "How can that be?"

"The knight believes in fidelity. And don't say fidelity is a mask for timidity. Or a coward's idea of safety. It's fidelity. To the heart and marrow. Don't think otherwise."

"I'm not judging," Tomás said. "I'm waiting for the story."

"For ten years, the knight endured the tribulations of the ordinary world by escaping into another world with—how shall I describe it? Castor and Pollux? Two friends closer than brothers could be? One of whom walked nearer to God than we can hope in this life."

"What happened?"

"God took the friend because he was too good for the ordinary world. Last year. The first time someone tried to murder me."

"*Ai Dèu.* I'm sorry." Then Tomás couldn't help blurting, "Was he wearing your armor?"

"No, I wore my own armor then. He never had a reason to wear armor in his life. Except that day."

"And the second one?"

"It was too long ago to make a good story." Pedro poured more wine, motioning again for Tomás to accept and was refused.

"And how does the *poulain* come to be in the tale?" Tomás asked. "Because he sees the powerful knight as closer to the ideal man than any he ever met?"

Pedro covered his eyes with his hands. "I really can't let you say things like that."

"The *poulain* comes from another world, too. One where most men fall far short of the divine nature God gave them."

"Stop it, please. At this point in the story, it's time for the knight to take a risk," Pedro picked up the bones again. "Otherwise, there won't be a story, just perpetual tribulations and disappointments, and a foolish hope that magic is possible."

"People who believe in magic are the easiest to cheat. Gamblers count on it."

Pedro touched Tomás's hand. "I didn't say believe. I said hope."

The next round passed with only the sound of the knuckle bones rolling across the polished table top, and it passed quickly. It would be unfair for Tomás to win.

With his familiar sardonic expression back in place, Pedro leveled his piercing, ice-blue gaze on Tomás.

"The first story I want is about what you cried out in your sleep last night. Scorpions? Rats?"

33
Into the Badlands

Jean-Luc on the road to Lastours, May 29

THE MARQUIS DE BEAURAIN, whom Jean-Luc had long had reason to believe might be his nemesis, addressed the Montcava knights before they departed the abbey near Fontcours, appealing to their family loyalty. Hugues still spoke elegantly, but he'd aged in the six years since Constantinople, the web of sunbaked wrinkles deepened. In the white, hot light of summer, Jean-Luc heard the gravel of age rattle in the marquis's voice.

Hugues said, "Although your master Renoud died last night, Fontcours and Montcava still need your service. But I am beseeching you as loyal knights to do one last favor for your old lord, to come with me and deliver Senhór Renoud's mother to safety. We shall return here tomorrow, and you can choose new masters."

With the laced aventail hiding his own face, Jean-Luc searched Hugues for a sign of his feelings about Renoud, trying to understand whether he'd submitted his oath to a monster over all those years. The marquis's gaze burned into the men he commanded. The same serious, dignified expression as always. But mostly, there was immense grief in Hugues's eyes, his cheeks sunken with restrained emotion. The other false Montcava soldiers looked to Jean-Luc, seeking how they should respond. As if by instinct, Hugues sought the man these knights treated as their leader. Lowering his eyes, Jean-Luc knelt before the marquis and offered his sword in service, as he'd done a dozen times in past years.

Always Hugues. In whatever lands they fought, Jean-Luc and Yves always gravitated back to Hugues as the best lord they ever served under. Thinking of Yves caused his hands to shake badly.

Jean-Luc grasped the jewel-less pommel tightly. He'd be back in Fontcours tomorrow, and then find his father.

But for now, Jean-Luc chose to follow Hugues for a day, to find out if he was lord or nemesis.

The Fontrevist abbot was coming with them, Hugues said, to act as a pleading voice if they needed him. Then Hugues, together with his half-brother Colomb, led them on the fastest possible ride across the Languedoc. At the lane leading to Fontcours, Hugues sent two knights off with messages and pushed everyone else onward, stopping only when the horses needed rest, and then setting up camp in the dark, when they were within a league of Lastours. They bivouacked without fires.

At dawn, Hugues rode with only the abbot and the Montcava knights, alleged southerners, on the trail up to the castle, presenting a white flag tied to his lance. At Lastours, the Montcava knights remained outside the gate where they could gaze across the rugged limestone hills cloaked in dark evergreens. The false Montcava men rested only as long as it took Hugues to return with Senhóra Eloïse on horseback, a small roll of possessions tied behind her saddle.

It was only six leagues to Minerve. But after they rejoined the Beaurain knights to begin the journey, the going was much slower, both to accommodate an older woman riding with them and to navigate the trails winding among the lower reaches of the Montagne Noir. They stopped often to accommodate the comfort of the woman. When they arrived at Minerve, their first sight was a view across the plain to the last red glow of sunset amid the curtain of dust over the Pyrenees foothills.

The walls of Minerve towered above two converging rivers. The plunging waters laughed at them while a lone soldier regarded them lazily from a narrow octagonal tower. The guards at the gates of Minerve wouldn't admit them, though the Beaurain knights remained behind on the plateau across from Minerve. Hugues begged conference with the mayor, who wouldn't leave his city gates to speak with a French marquis, but only listened from the battlements.

"I have here an honorable woman of your faith who needs shelter in your city," Hugues said.

The florid-faced mayor, Ghuilhem, stood at the gate, arms crossed like a stern father, but squirming in the hauberk he'd donned for the meeting. He said, "I'm sworn to protect my city, so I can't let the enemies of the Count of Toulouse in these gates."

"I am not an enemy of you or your people. I'm only seeking refuge for an old friend and relation," Hugues said.

Gradually the mayor was worn down with Hugues's eloquent pleas and allowed them inside the city. His guards relieved the visiting knights of their blades while Hugues and the abbot negotiated a place for the senhóra. In the end they were all invited to spend the night, and Hugues walked with his arm around Senhóra Eloïse as they went with the abbot to the mayor's house.

The false Montcava knights were left to the hospitality of the men guarding the walls of Minerve, and it didn't take any special intelligence for the newcomers to know they were hated. When Hugues departed with the senhóra whom Tomás insisted had once been the marquis's *amor*, Jean-Luc pretended to leer conspiratorially while chatting with their reluctant hosts.

"These lords, it doesn't matter if they're French or what, they want us to move heaven and earth for their high-class whores. Then we can eat dust, if you please." Jean-Luc spoke in the common tongue of the south, trying to hide his accent.

"Don't you know it," one of his sham brother-knights said.

"And do we get a woman to sleep with?" Jean-Luc joked with the Minervian guards. "Or even a bit of hot chicken on a stick?"

As he jested with their hosts, Jean-Luc saw a flash of red on the street and bent to pick it up. It was only a frayed snip of red yarn, but he held it tightly in his fist. Finding red was to find luck in love, the chance to make a wish. The idea of such absurdity after the past days' events caused him to laugh aloud at what a fool he was, searching for luck in cities in the south.

Behind the guards, where a collection of townspeople gathered to inspect the strangers, the same face appeared as followed him at the Vale of Roses. Jean-Luc stepped past the guards and advanced through the cobbled streets to find the man who stood as tall as Yves, with murderous pale eyes amid a matted tangle of beard and grey hair. If this was the secret enemy of his father and friends, then they'd have it out here, now.

Because it couldn't be Yves. Jean-Luc had held his brother in his arms while he died in Constantinople.

34
Poultry and Recognition

Tomás in Carcassonne, May 29

JUST PAST DAWN, TOMÁS slipped out of Simon's chateau with four men of Aragón, ostensibly to check their horses and find breakfast without disturbing their host, but really to just walk the streets and see life in the city. Two of the knights, Cebrián and Marcos, Catalan brothers from Girona, had been among the survivors of the brigand attack. They'd become Tomás's friends, gambling in Pedro's camp and helping to assert his worth among the knights of Aragón.

They walked in what could have been any marketplace in the south, except so few women helped pitch awnings and those women who worked at the portable kitchens kept no children with them. And the people coming through the gates entered quietly, without the cries to old friends across the square so typical in other markets. Like the supposedly pacified countryside, which in fact held hungry people hiding in cow-biers, this newly French city hadn't given its heart to its conquerors.

"It's not as if people are being tortured or starved," Pedro said through the half-laced aventail, his disguise as a knight of Aragón.

"You don't know what's below us." Tomás stomped the cobbles. "In the cellars and tunnels. Or in those towers. Simon has my men. Who else is chained up, dying of camp-fever like the last viscount?"

Pedro said, "Simon swears on the Gospel that people aren't dying in his prisons."

"Perhaps he's already buried them in the dung heaps."

As the other knights walked ahead, Pedro said, "Don't blame me, please. I'm doing my best to resolve this."

"I don't blame you, Monsenyor."

"And don't blame God either."

"No, I blame the devil whose house we slept in last night," Tomás said. "I hate the man. I can't help myself."

"And I can't allow myself the pleasure of hating him," Pedro said. "I have to work with him to end this."

Tomás should never have spoken. He'd almost fallen apart in the king's darkened room the night before, because he couldn't get rid of the images of his enemy dying and the stiff, angry woman he had hurt in St-Sernin. Then he learned that his companion couldn't close his eyes at night without hearing the cries of the thousands who perished in Béziers the summer before.

"Monsenyor, I want to ask after my friends today."

"I sent a message last night. We'll check with Simon's seneschal right now."

At the seneschal's casa, which was more a barracks than a home, Tomás spoke with the seneschal. The other knights of Aragón remained silent. Yes, the seneschal said, Simon sent word to release people from Laurac to Pedro's knights. Those men would soon be ready to join them. Meanwhile, the Aragón knights could wait at the manse of the viscount's councilor, the seneschal said, and break their fast at the inn near there. These things take time.

"One of the men is already gone," the seneschal said. "The marshal. His father claimed him yesterday. He's at the inn near the councilor's manse. He was coming back this morning to plead for the rest of them."

But they didn't find Marshal Guillem at the inn, only François, the Narbonnese husband of Senhóra Paulette of Casa de Rossynols. The man was so close-sighted Tomás repeated his name twice before the man knew who he was.

"Senhór Tomás, well met!" François greeted him. "Did you receive the same alarming message we did? Poor Paulette cried a storm of tears and then couldn't get me on my horse fast enough to go help Guillem. But you know how it is. You have to just sit and wait."

"I heard about it from the Valerós knights who rode to Fontcours," Tomás said.

"As did we," François said, "though we learned it in a roundabout way. Your men have spent a fortnight under Simon's guard.

At least your Father Anselm persuaded them not to house your men with the heretics."

"Where's Marshal Guillem?" Tomás asked.

Every question prompted a stream of words from the voluble François of Rossynols, but Tomás tried to remain patient because, as François remarked, there was nothing to do but to sit and wait. François said, "As soon as I could argue for his release, Guillem borrowed one of my horses so he could get back to his knights. Didn't have time to see his mother, even after scaring her nearly to death."

"I imagine it takes a great deal to scare Senhóra Paulette," Tomás said, "since her son has been a knight for forty years."

"*Ai*, you knights!" François exclaimed. "You don't have hearts like other men, do you?"

"Perhaps you're right," Tomás conceded, falsely, since he didn't have the energy to quarrel. "What of Father Anselm and the rest? Why haven't they been released?"

"Simon's men were persuaded to let my stepson go free because of kinship. But alas, they wanted a better Christian lord than me to plead for the others. I'm waiting for my brother to help free them. Let us order breakfast from our host here."

The torrent of words hardly abated between ordering the food and François's next topic.

"How is your wife, Senhór Tomás? Did you leave her at Fontcours? You must have planted enough seed that your wife is breeding now, eh?" He nudged Tomás in man-to-man jest and then turned to Tomás's companion. "This fellow did me the honor of celebrating the best consummated marriage in Christendom at my house. The one thing that makes you long to be young again is the sound of fresh, eager love in the night."

Pedro listened with a wry smile as the flood of words poured forth from François, who praised Isabella as the worthiest of southern senhóras.

"Not beautiful perhaps, or so my Paulette says, but your wife has the spirit a man wants by his side, plus the kind of mother-wit that leaves a man wealthier than before he found her, eh? Am I right, Senhór Tomás?

As François poured hot ale for Tomás, his quilted sleeve slipped forward and got wet with ale.

"*Ai*, Our Lady grant me mercy." François rolled up the wet sleeve, exposing a hideous scar in the palm of his right hand. Tomás reached out to touch it.

"Where did you get this?"

"Oh that." François laughed about it, and then a new story flooded out. "One of two mementos from my youthful indiscretions in the Outremer. All my brothers wanted to be famous knights and dragged me along. I suffered from swamp fever within a fortnight of landing. My other memento from the crusade. Sick out of my head, I disobeyed our captain. He was a mestitz tyrant, and to this day I don't know if I even heard the order. But he branded me a coward. That's what this means, if you haven't ever seen it."

Tomás had seen it before, but he kept his own counsel, studying François more closely than he had while living at the man's house.

François made a show of sadly shaking his head. "What the tyrant taught me was that a soldier's life isn't for me. My brother Hugues is welcome to it. He's brought all the glory the Beaurain family needs."

Isabella had made the same claim about François, when they stayed at the man's house on their second wedding night. He didn't believe it then. Now, he might find the truth.

"Do you know Renoud of Montcava?" Tomás asked, not meaning to grasp his dagger when he heard Hugues's name. He felt Pedro's hand on his shoulder, as if he needed to pull Tomás back from the edge of an abyss.

"By God's good angels, yes," François said. "Didn't want to mention it at my house. It's bad luck bringing up a widow's old family when she's honeymooning with a new *amor*, don't you think? I grew up at my grandfather's house, next door to the Montcava estates. Of course, it was lost to us before Renoud was born. By Our Lady's mercy, it's more than forty years ago. Renoud spent many summers with me at Rossynols when he was a lad, since his mother called on her old friends to help with her fatherless sons. I'd long thought to leave Renoud my land, like my uncle in Narbonne did for me. But now with Paulette's brood, and Renoud doing so well on his own, there's no cause. He's made his way just fine."

"He's dead." Tomás observed the man's every breath.

"Dead? How can that be? We saw Renoud at Rossynols only a fortnight ago, just before you came. Why, I said to Paulette—" François stopped and wiped his brow with a piece of silk he kept tucked in his sleeve. "I'm sorry. An old man gets used to hearing people have died, don't you know. But every soul lost reminds us of our own mortality. By God's angels, what about his mother? How is she dealing with this loss?"

"I haven't heard."

"How did the poor boy die?"

Tomás decided to tell the same story he told the bishop.

"There's terrible street fighting in Toulouse. Ruffians carried the fight into his house. He died defending his villa."

Conscious that Pedro heard the story differently this time, Tomás persevered with his embellishments while trying to determine how the news affected François. The man seemed more upset about the delay in their breakfast.

Tomás lied his best. "Renoud was gallant in a fight. He practiced it in Constantinople."

"He learned at the Beaurain court," François said. "His brother didn't have much more taste for fighting than I did. Renoud has a lot more talent. It's lucky we didn't lose him in Constantinople like we did his brother Nicolau."

"I never met Nicolau." Tomás gazed into the man's nearsighted eyes. After eight years of hunting, Tomás hadn't imagined it'd be like this. François gazed past him to the door, where a man waved extravagantly for the half-blind seigneur's attention.

"Ah, there's my steward," François said. "Strange about little wars like this. A fellow with anything extra can make himself rich. I brought along three dozen good laying hens, six roosters, and five cows. I'm going home with extra silver in my purse. As soon as I can get a guard for my wagons of fish from Narbonne to Carcassonne, I won't have to worry about how much silver is in my pocket for many months."

"Senhór, we can wait for your brother and the release of the others." Pedro spoke over Tomás's shoulder. "We'll be here for days on the king's business with nothing to do. I'll bet you're eager to get home to your wife."

.

"You didn't eat your breakfast."

"I'm not hungry," Tomás said.

"You are an elegant liar," Pedro said when they left the inn. Cebrián and Marcos lagged behind them on the street. "Do you prevaricate with me?"

"No, never."

"You won't lie with me, and you won't lie to me? Why does good fortune always come to me mixed in a satchel with disappointment?"

Tomás wasn't in the mood for light-hearted diversion, even though Pedro needed it. "That leprous weasel has worked to destroy my family for forty years."

Pedro laughed. "Your enemy is a talkative, randy old farmer-merchant who's selling chickens to French invaders. There's a moral to this story if we look for it."

They walked on without saying anything, crossing a few streets on the route back to Simon's chateau. The councilor said they needed to wait longer for the release of the knights.

"Fresh, eager love in the still of the night, eh?"

"Monsenyor, if you have no further need of me, I'd like your leave to go kill that man."

"But I do need you. And it's not that man. He didn't act like a man who lost a son, and he has no animosity for you. He didn't recognize you as Miquel's child, and you told me your beautiful face came straight from your father."

Tomás didn't remember such a conversation, but the argument was irrelevant. "Mere deception on his part. Or because he's blind as a bat. His Beaurain brother recognized me as soon as he got a good look."

"I forbid you to kill him without more proof. His only sin is wasting time driving cows to market instead of riding quickly to free the men of Valerós."

"I don't agree."

"You are needed here with me," Pedro said.

"All right." Tomás sought more patience than he'd ever owned. "I can wait, since I know where to find the man. What shall I do for you next, Monsenyor?"

"Go to Minerve and convince the mayor to surrender."

"Is Minerve under siege?"

"It will be soon. Simon picked Minerve for his next example."

"You can hardly use me as a diplomat."

"My counselors will take care of the diplomacy, though I'm sure it's preordained to fail. I want you to remain behind when the diplomats and legates leave. When the city locks its gates against Simon's war engines, you'll stay inside and persuade the city to surrender, to keep them from dying under siege."

"But no one ever follows me," Tomás said. "Your knights couldn't listen to save their lives. Why would anyone heed me in a siege?"

"You can practice new talents. Besides, you said you lived through the siege of Jaffa. There won't be anyone among the merchants and farmers in Minerve who can say that."

"I was nine years old."

"See? Your mother weaned you on Greek fire and you cut your teeth on Saracen steel. Who better can I find to advise battle-hating heretics on how to keep alive? You have a mercurial tongue and the wit to use it."

"Many people would say sending me proves you want them dead," Tomás said.

"But I don't. I stand for the Church, not the slaughter of innocents," Pedro said. "The heretics and their seigneurs won't listen to the Church or the French, or even my lords. But you might save them from themselves. You don't belong to anyone."

Tomás fell into a fugue hearing that, more like falling into a ravine than into a dream. He heard Pèire's voice: *How do you know who you are? How can others trust you if you're just a vagabond and a mercenary?*

Tomás gave his oath to a woman and her family, and it came to worse than nothing. His quest for his father's revenge was nearly over, awaiting only a final, tawdry rendezvous with the younger

Beaurain brother. Chrétien had left him in pursuit of true love. Tomás felt bereft at the thought that, indeed, he didn't belong to anyone. But then Pedro murmured close by his ear.

"Except to me."

35
Athene Intervenes

GERARD LEARNED HIS SON had come within a mile of Fontcours and yet hadn't stopped or sent a message. Gerard spent a long night asking God how and why it happened.

Pèire Leteric's granddaughter Isabella had arrived at Fontcours the night before, seeking the knights from Valerós. Gerard should have fallen to his knees with prayers of gratitude, since one more of Pèire's lost children had been found and was safe. But compared to her two small, compliant sisters, Isabella proved to be tall, burned by many days in the sun, and angry.

"Where's Jean-Luc?" Isabella demanded, immediately after saying hello. "He's supposed to be here.

Beatriz followed Gerard out of the sick room to hear Isabella's story. The girl had become his constant companion and consolation while they nursed Felicia. In better times, he'd have found Beatriz's conversation delightful. An educated, sensitive young woman, she never again mentioned the burden of sin she carried. Instead, she worked ceaselessly in service to others.

Gerard thanked God for the comfort he gained from Beatriz's friendship, but remained paralyzed with fear that Felicia might die. He struggled to leave it in God's hand. Felicia was awake more now, but she remained silent, weak, shrunken from her illness. He worried for her and he worried for the child she might be carrying. And meanwhile, sweet Beatriz nursed them both.

When her sister Isabella came, Beatriz seemed to sink back into the shy, unhappy girl he'd first met. He held the girl's hand while Isabella told the story of her journey across the south in search of

Senhóreta Katelina and Sebastián. In severe jeopardy, Isabella had placed herself under the protection of Don Miquel's son and then married him.

Isabella seemed to wait for Gerard's response, but all he felt was immense relief: he wasn't responsible for this wild woman dressed in men's clothes who paced the floor, impatient and overheated.

"You married Tomás?" Beatriz cried in dismay. "That half-Saracen scribe? Is he even a Christian?"

"Yes, he's a Christian," Gerard said. "His father was a great crusader. *Dieu ait pitié!* I can't believe his son is a scribe, though."

"He isn't a scribe." Isabella spoke as if their ignorance demanded great patience. "He's a knight of King Pedro and Pèire's seigneur."

Isabella finished her story, ending with the part that broke Gerard's heart: Jean-Luc left Toulouse with Hugues de Beaurain, headed for Fontcours. But Hugues had not stopped, and instead he'd gone on, for the sake of another errand.

Therefore, this morning, as Gerard prayed in the chapel, he guessed Jean-Luc didn't know his father was at Fontcours. Perhaps Hugues remained silent, sensitive to Jean-Luc's situation as an exile. Or perhaps Hugues needed Jean-Luc's help. Who better to help on any knight's business than Jean-Luc?

Leaving the chapel, Gerard found both sisters waiting for him, demanding his attention, though he wanted solitude. Isabella insisted on speaking with him, winning out over Beatriz, who seemed resigned to listening to her sister.

Isabella said, "I know you made promises to Pèire, my grandfather, and I am grateful for that. But I am taking my knights to join King Pedro. We leave as soon as we can be ready. I respect your bond with Pèire, but I do not want to be aligned with the French invaders."

"Your knights?" Beatriz said. "*Your* knights?"

"Sebastián's then, if you will."

Gerard said, "You are free to go. But you can't lead them yourself. Don't you want to wait for your husband?"

"He's gone to Carcassonne to free Marshal Guillem and Father Anselm. It's not clear how long that will take. I can't wait."

"I must protest, ma dòmna. You should be under the care of your husband."

"The Valerós knights are sufficiently skilled to offer me protection. We'll ride just after the Sabbath at the latest."

"Our knights are needed at home," Beatriz said.

"Where they'd be now," Isabella said, "if it wasn't for you."

Leaving the sisters to quarrel, Gerard slipped away to the solitude of the spring and his prayers for rain.

•

By keeping out of the house, Gerard managed to avoid both sisters, though he encountered Isabella twice as he toured the camp to check the well-being of his men. He found her with the Valerós knights, apparently dictating travel plans. Then he later found her with the ragtag mercenaries who came to Fontcours with her. These men camped near the Valerós knights and then commandeered a practice space in a closed courtyard. The senhóra was again dressed as a man and practicing close-hand knife fighting with a tall Celt. Gerard felt he should look away, but he couldn't quit watching the scandalous behavior.

Later in the day, his nervous anticipation for Felicia's well-being drove Gerard back inside. Felicia remained weak, with no appetite for either food or talk. She lay on the bed, swathed in clean linen for both her night-dress and her coverlet. But she stared listlessly at the wall, as if her two attendants weren't even present.

"My lord, I have to speak with you," Beatriz said. "I need to call on you as my friend."

"*Mais oui*, senhóreta. I hope I am one."

But then, a herald's cry echoed through the windows. Hugues de Beaurain had returned to Fontcours. Gerard ran down the stairs. In the courtyard, Hugues sat astride his horse, letting it cool down after a hard ride. The knights with him wore Montcava colors. Jean-Luc wasn't with him.

Isabella came from her knife-play in the courtyard. Gerard sensed that Hugues, too, was shocked to see how the senhóra dressed. As impatient as always, the senhóra didn't wait for the cooling of Hugues's horse. She held the huge beast by the halter, blowing in its nose while Hugues dismounted. Colomb, Hugues's brother, stayed on his horse, the great dancing beast coming too near to Isabella as she calmed Hugues's destrier.

"My lord, where is Jean-Luc?" Isabella's voice rasped as if the question hurt her to ask.

"Who?" Hugues seemed confused.

"My son," Gerard said. "Jean-Luc was with you."

"No, I've been riding with Montcava knights, on business for their former mistress."

One of the ragged men in Senhóra Isabella's coterie tugged at her sleeve and spoke in her ear.

"He was one of the Montcava knights," Isabella said. "Thierry says Jean-Luc left with them to join your men. Though these men aren't from Montcava. They are Tomás's mercenaries. Jean-Luc was the tallest of the whole lot. You can't have missed him."

Hugues leaned against his horse, his hand covering his face.

One of the so-called Montcava knights who'd arrived with Hugues spoke. "Jean-Luc is still in Minerve. He chased a man in the streets, and a soldier tackled him. When Jean-Luc shouted in French, they decided he was a spy."

Hugues spoke again. "I was in a hurry to return here. They didn't like having French soldiers in the city, and I didn't have time to waste for a knight I didn't know. I intended to send someone from Fontcours to deal with it."

Gerard felt elation blooming inside of him. He now knew exactly where Jean-Luc was.

"Words won't do for how sorry I am, Gerard. I didn't recognize him," Hugues said.

"He wouldn't want you to," Isabella said. "He didn't want you to compromise yourself."

"Compromise?" Hugues puzzled at the word.

"Because he's exiled and under sentence to hang. He didn't want anyone to have to take a risk for him."

"*Dieu ait pitié!*" Gerard did not mean to say it aloud.

Hugues said, "We'll take a band of knights tomorrow to bring Jean-Luc back. Where is your husband, ma dòmna? We need him. A southern seigneur can argue with Minerve's mayor better than I."

Before Isabella could answer, more traveling knights rode into the courtyard. One cried out to Senhóra Isabella, and she rushed to greet him. It proved to be Pèire Leteric's marshal. He'd met Hugues on the road after being freed from Carcassonne.

"Is Tomás with you? He was on his way to Carcassonne," Isabella asked.

"No, but thank God Tomás is going there," the marshal said. "Father Anselm and the others aren't free yet."

"Felicia's here," Isabella said to Guillem, her voice dropping. At the sound of Felicia's name, Gerard strained to hear what she said. "But she isn't well."

The slightest gesture from Isabella sent the marshal bounding across the courtyard and into the house, with another knight following him.

"He knows Senhóreta Felicia?" Gerard asked, though of course the marshal would, since Valerós was a small domus.

Isabella spoke softly, sounding almost kind. "Guillem is married to her. Didn't she say? Didn't Beatriz know?"

"No." He heard the hollow echo of weakness in his voice. "Did I fail to find the woman he asked me to take care of? He hasn't trusted me with anything else so important."

As they spoke, Isabella led him away from the courtyard, upstairs to where the marshal knelt by Felicia's bed with one of the Valerós knights at his side. Isabella stopped Gerard outside the door.

"Jean-Luc knows." She whispered. "Guillem doesn't. You must be a friend to both men and not say anything."

Beatriz came out of the room, pale, frightened.

"Guillem says Jehan the smith was traveling with you, then left for Toulouse with Tomás. Did you see him, Isabella?"

"Jehan the smith is Jean-Luc," Isabella said. "We talked about him last night. Hugues lost him at Minerve."

Beatriz wrenched her hands. She held a silver amulet that she rubbed in a gesture of anguish. She said, "My lord, I must talk with you. It's about your spy, Jehan."

"He isn't a spy." Gerard felt numb now rather than elated as he pondered Jean-Luc's ill luck. "He's my son. I want to help you, senhóreta, but please let me—"

"I'm pregnant," Beatriz said. The amulet was a silver boar's tooth, like the one Jean-Luc wore. After all this time, her accent was still so hard to understand.

"You, Beatriz? You?" Isabella cried as she slapped her sister. "*Pech, pech noía.* You stupid lying girl!"

Gerard put his arms around the raging woman to restrain her, surprised to find how strong she was. Isabella kept shouting at Beatriz over his shoulder.

"Do you know what you've done?" Isabella cried. "When he heard Felicia was married, it crushed him. He believes he betrayed his best friend. He's half mad for love. You fool!"

"Ma dòmna! Calm yourself," Gerard said.

She whirled on him.

"And you! Jean-Luc has worked harder than the devil's servant, to clear his name so he can come home to you. Why did you ever let him go away? It breaks his heart as much to miss you as it does to love my stupid sister."

"I'm not your sister." Beatriz shrieked, too, not doing anything to keep out of Isabella's reach.

"But you are a stupid, stupid girl!" Isabella shouted. "Jean-Luc loves you, and you almost killed him, lying about who you are."

Beatriz collapsed against the wall, crying. Gerard, who was always able to comfort his wife, didn't know what to do for either woman. He couldn't let go of the sister who screamed invectives or support the one who cried out that she wasn't a sister at all.

"Stop it. You girls weren't raised to behave this way."

The other knight left Guillem's side and came to the doorway, pulling free the hauberk's coif. It was Katelina of Naxos. Though Gerard hadn't seen her since Jaffa, she was just as beautiful as twenty years before, even while appearing as angry as the goddess Athene.

"You weren't killed!" Isabella cried.

"No," Katelina said. "One of the nuns was mistaken for me. Now, everyone, dry your tears. What do we do next to move forward?"

Lubos and the Bees

BEES SCREECHED IN HIS head. Yet his sword had been silent for so long. Lubos shrugged off the colored gambeson that Père-Izsák made him wear.

"I don't like your army, Father."

Everything came from his father, so he decided to keep the rest of the kit. That man who said to call him Père-Izsák—whether he was a priest or a knight, Lubos couldn't remember any more—was his father.

That was why Lubos didn't like the last unkind humiliation.

"People must not know you are my right hand, my hammer. You cannot come to me in the daytime like this."

"I want to go home."

"Haven't I been good to you?"

"Like the best father." Lubos spoke humbly.

"I have explained that it's best for you to stay near my side for a while. Why do you want to leave me?"

"I want to go home to Aykuna."

"It's not long now. But have you forgotten what I taught you? A man keeps himself clean. What have you smeared on yourself?"

Père-Izsák seemed sad.

To cheer him, Lubos said, "It's the blood of my enemy, Father. Bless me now, please. For I have feasted on my enemy."

"*Ai*, my son. What are we to do with you?"

Goodmen and Bonfraires

TO ARNAU, MY BELOVED BROTHER IN CHRIST,

You asked to learn the worst of the heretics' travesties, when their false words are exceeded by real action. Simon reports that it is common in hereticated villages to find our holy rituals turned upside down. Crucifixes are wrenched from the altar and dragged through the streets where men void their bladders and wives toss the offal from their kitchens.

Women in their unclean state stand with unbent knee in the priests' place before the altar in our churches. When the church contains a precious Gospel, children are encouraged by hereticated rabble to cast it down, and the sacred Gospel is trampled in the mud and slime of these perverse towns. As you advise, a siege will lead to more rapid purification of these lands.

— Esak, your brother in the Lord
1 June 1210

36
Street Cleaning

Tomás inside Minerve, June 5

TOMÁS STOPPED SLEEPING IN a bed. The chanting monks crept into his dreams. He couldn't marshal his thoughts while lying in bed. Besides, there wasn't time to waste sleeping.

Mostly, though, Tomás couldn't stand being alone. Solitude left him aware he was failing Pedro, having already failed Pèire Leteric.

And she wasn't with him.

After spending an intense week with Pedro, riding and practicing at arms, Tomás expected to miss that excitement. But instead, if any moment of silence came his way, her face and voice haunted him. Like those old crusaders in his father's villa, complaining about the aches in a ghost hand or leg lost in battlefield decades before.

Blessedly, the angels in the golden heavens seemed to take great care to ensure there was no time to rest. During the day Tomás worked two shifts on Minerve's battlements and another shift cleaning the streets. His only success with Mayor Ghuilhem was to convince him the city needed to prevent the accumulation of filth that had destroyed Carcassonne from within the year before.

At night Tomás did death duty with other men who were shunned by most in the city.

He built a death-duty crew to offer to the mayor by seeking others who ate alone: another mestitz man, born in Carcassonne, who went to work with a seigneur's mercenary force when he lost his home; a Norman who deserted Simon de Montfort in disgust after Béziers but couldn't find a place in any southern army; an older Saxon who had left the Angevine Richard's returning army fifteen years before for the love of a woman in Narbonne.

"Who is now with the blessed angels," the man said.

There was another solitary eater, a wild-looking Greek who spoke to no one. But before Tomás could approach him for death duty, the man went berserk and chased a passel of young donzels—including the young knight Sebastián—and cursed God as the bastard son of the devil. It took six guards to subdue the man, thrashing and pounding him against the cobbled street, leaving the wild man infirm and unable to speak.

"We got the devil sending us a plague of Frenchmen. We don't need pederasts," one man said. He walked away after delivering a last vicious kick to the man's throat.

At night, Tomás left Sebastián in Father Anselm's care. Days, Tomás kept Sebastián with him, except during street patrol. They gazed out over the battlements, and Tomás explained what Simon planned, dividing the army into thirds to cover all approachable sides of the city. And how the war machines were deployed.

"As much as I hate him," Tomás said, "I admit Simon has a general's brain. He knows he'll never breach the walls. We could set fire to his entire army before they ever crossed these canyons. But he's pounding along all the walls to make the people inside afraid. The same with the infernal singing monks. Who could listen to a hymn again in this life after weeks of their howling?"

Twice the war machines hurled a stray boulder over the wall near where he lingered with Sebastián, and far too many times crossbow bolts zinged past them, clattering against stone. One bolt bounced back to fall on Sebastián's foot. At those times, Tomás arrested his impulse to hug Sebastián to him, to drag him to safety so nothing could touch a mere boy.

.

After dark, he went with Sebastián to Father Anselm's infirmary where the boy stayed while Tomás did his night's work. The room had previously stored grain, so it was dry and free of vermin, though dusty. Father Anselm rigged a sail to draw fresh air down from the high slit in the stone wall. The sail, a skill learned in the Outremer, felt comforting to Tomás, who remembered such a sail in their home at Jaffa and on Cyprus. More comforting than the tiny altar with a wooden crucifix where Anselm knelt in prayer with three bowmen.

Sebastián set to the chores he performed for Father Anselm every night: rolling bandages the goodwomen left for the priest, burning herbs in the corners to keep down the sick-room smell, pounding other herbs for the salves and potions the priest used.

Tomás sat on the stone steps leading down to the makeshift chapel. When the priest finished, he joined Tomás there.

Father Anselm said, "Some people have gotten well. The woman with childbed fever went home today. I'm glad of that. The man they beat so badly still can't speak, but at least he'll be able to walk soon. Those men rushed to judgment too quickly for this poor tortured soul. You see him there. He's gentle as a lamb."

Senhóra Eloïse knelt beside the man, clumsily trying to spoon broth into his mouth. Adalyde, who'd been at Laurac, held up the man's head so he could swallow without choking.

"How did Adalyde get here?" Tomás asked Father Anselm.

"Pedro made such a fuss for your Valerós friends at Carcassonne, they let everyone from Laurac free," the priest said. "Someone told them Minerve was a safe haven, so they walked the twenty miles from Carcassonne."

"And the goodwoman Adalyde managed to make a nurse out of the timid Eloïse?"

"It's Senhóra Eloïse who is remarkable," Anselm said. "She brought me volunteers when she heard I needed help. She's a tribute to why they call them goodwomen."

Tomás said, "I'd die of a plague of boils before I ever let that woman nurse me."

"I heard you arguing with her yesterday. Nothing but acrimony passes between you."

"It's not acrimony on my part," Tomás said. "It's pure hatred."

"You have to let it pass, Tomás. It's too late to matter now."

The priest indicated the help he wanted from Tomás, to move a knight who'd been in the priest's infirmary for a fortnight, struck in the head by a French-launched boulder, no longer awake but not yet dead. The priest moved the man twice a day in a futile effort to ward off bed sores.

"Three people died today," Tomás said. "This time I knew two of them. Every day, I know more of the dead. I have to go bury them tonight, when it's late enough."

He didn't know why he called it burial, when they would only fling the bodies over the wall and into the canyon, hoping to place the dead among the shelter of the thorn brush and gorse below, out of sight of the families who'd lost them, which was why they waited until late at night to do it—to ensure that people wouldn't see bodies being fed to the crows and vultures.

Tomás said, "The goodmen let go of their dead more readily, especially if they have a day or two to pray over a dying friend. The mothers among the goodwomen, though, have just as hard a time letting go of their dead children as the Catholics."

He enjoyed the peace, grateful that Father Anselm knew an answer wasn't required, and grateful that the infirmary lay deep enough in the city that the sounds of the chanting priests could scarcely be heard. He rocked, his hands clasped as if he were another of the keening people the death-duty crew met when they came to carry away the dead.

Tomás said, "I wanted to be a great man like Pèire Leteric, but I'm so far from that, God could only think it a jest, me wishing it."

"You can't believe Pèire started life so grand. He was just a man. You can get there, too."

"As if I could leap the canyons of Minerve from where I am."

"I wish you could pray," Father Anselm said.

"It's too much like begging," Tomás said.

"Do you want to make a confession? You come here every night as if you want to talk, but then you sit and say nothing."

"Father, did you know she can't have children?" He whispered because he didn't want Sebastián to overhear while involved with his chores across the room.

"No, Don Tomás, I didn't know. If you want children, you don't have to stay married to her. If that's what's troubling you."

"What do you mean?"

"Let me be bold. I saw you with the king in Carcassonne. Is this an excuse to set your wife aside?"

"No, staying married to her matters more than anything. Though why I think about it so much, when we're stuck here waiting to die, I don't know."

"It isn't so dire," Father Anselm said. "The siege can't last more than another few days."

"How could she be two different people?" Tomás whispered frantically. "I wanted the chaste woman she pretended to be. When I found out it wasn't true, I was furious. But now I don't care. Except I just don't understand. *Ai*, I hate the idea of anyone else touching her. Yet I cannot stand being away from her."

"Whatever makes you think that our Isabella is not what you first believed?"

"She lay with Renoud the night before the trial. It makes my skin crawl to remember it."

"Why do you believe that happened?" Father Anselm spoke softly. "It seems so unlikely."

"He knew things about her. He told me how he'd marked her body the night before, and I saw the devil's marks. He showed me letters from all the years she slept with him."

"But only the devil in your own mind led you to believe she sinned. I know better. In your heart, surely you do, too."

"What do you know?"

Father Anselm said, "I can't tell you the secrets people confess."

"But I must know," Tomás said. "It's driven me mad, wondering how I could be with her, talking all day and most of every night, without knowing what she really is."

"What bothers you? That she had secrets? Or her chastity? What about your own secrets?"

"Before God in heaven, I had only one secret I kept from her. And it was nothing like her secrets."

"And your chastity, Tomás?"

"You're a man, Father. You know it isn't the same for men as it is for women."

"Perhaps it's been too long, but I don't remember it being different between two people who spoke vows."

"I've never loved anyone else on God's own earth. Isn't that enough? Please help me understand her."

"Suppose I tell you a story, then, the way our Lord used parables. There was once a country girl, smart, but young for her age, and overly sheltered."

.

Father Anselm whispered at the end of his story.

"Suppose the girl is strong enough to get away. You could see it as a glorious instance of the enduring strength of God's creation, how she grew free of her nightmares."

"Why didn't she tell me? We talked every night and day for weeks, but she never told me." Then it struck him. "No, she refused to tell me."

"If it happened to you, and if you were no longer forced to confess wrongly over and over, then why would you ever confess it again? To anyone?"

Tomás tried to speak several times before he found words. "How could Pèire let her stay in Toulouse?"

"He didn't know. No one did until she came home. She was a little girl who listened to an evil confessor. Then, when Katelina and I finally got the story out of her, she insisted Pèire not know. Whenever Renoud rode to Valerós, which he did at least twice a year, trying to get her to come back, Pèire fought him off just because she didn't want to go to Toulouse."

"How could a man do horrible things, all the while saying 'I love you'?"

"Who are you asking about? Renoud? Yourself?"

"Òc, I'm just what she called me: a wolf from the hills. An animal."

"No, much more human," Father Anselm said.

"Isabella can never forgive me. I let our enemy convince me to punish her for her own suffering."

"Knowing Isabella, the way her mind works, the question is not whether she forgives you, but whether she even remembers you by now. She's strong because she's very good at forgetting."

"Ai Dèu, how can I live with myself?"

"You don't have a choice."

37

Cher Malvoisine

AT THE CROSS-OVER MOMENT in the morning, the squeak and chirp of the birds died away, replaced by the persistent fiddling of crickets as the sun heated the ground and the shimmer rose. The bird cries ended earlier and earlier each day: songbirds fled the plateau with the arrival of the men who laid siege on Minerve. The crusaders who arrived late had to work hard to find material for shelter, reduced to weaving mats of brush and thorny twigs to create shade in the sweltering June sun. Only the locusts, scorpions, and field crickets were content to ignore the thousands of invading crusaders.

The silky skies held no promises for the sweltering crusaders, not a puff of cloud or prayer's chance of rain. The winds from the north remained too faint to ease the sweat from one's brow, and the occasional gusts blasting across the plateau only stirred up dust and drove it into their tents and beds, under chainmail so it clung to the folds of their skin, and into their food supplies so every meal was a chore, with sandy dust in every bite.

Before the Valerós knights could retrieve Jean-Luc from Minerve, the call came from Simon to join a siege there. Parched and dusty, riding two days ahead of the Chartrain foot-soldiers, the Valerós knights arrived too late to free Jean-Luc, because the gates of Minerve had already closed. They were too late to join King Pedro, who withdrew his knights as soon as the mayor of Minerve closed the gates. The king went to Toulouse, it was said, to beg his cousin Count Raymond once again to make peace between the stubborn southern seigneurs and the French crusaders.

By mid-June, the Valerós knights had been encamped for more than a fortnight, having arrived just after Simon positioned his men across the canyon from the walls of Minerve. Hugues de Beaurain brought his men just as quickly as the Valerós knights, anxious to prove his loyalty to the crusader cause after being caught by Simon's false rumors about Lastours. He wasn't the only knight in Christendom who had shepherded relatives into the trap that Simon laid for heretic refugees and their protectors.

The first few days at Minerve, they listened to the monks sing, proclaiming the Glory of God, if you understood Latin, and torturing souls inside and outside the city. When Hugues de Beaurain returned from Carcassonne with the remaining Valerós knights, they learned that Father Anselm, Sebastián, and Tomás were inside Minerve for the sake of King Pedro.

"Doing what?" Isabella asked, guessing that Tomás would do whatever Pedro asked, since he'd been so wild about the great king since they first met. Sebastián would follow Tomás over a cliff. Or into a siege city.

"It's not so clear," Hugues said. "But they say in Carcassonne that Tomás saved the king's life and has become his personal guard."

They said other things about Tomás and Pedro in Carcassonne, which the rescued Valerós knights—Bonanat and Lázaro—whispered around, adding to what Durán made known about Tomás's last day in Toulouse. Lying sleepless and alone in her tent, Isabella heard every innuendo as the men talked.

She didn't like the gossip. It weakened the bonds among men who had to trust each other in a fight. She listened the second night, hoping it would revive her anger, the safest emotion. The sole person she could question was Chrétien, but she never found him without Durán at his side. And Durán's opinion about Tomás was well known, with the word *punxor* repeated frequently.

However, even without private conversation, Isabella and Chrétien resumed their friendship in a tacit agreement to stop the gossip.

Chrétien sang *cançós de guerra* at night, singing about Arturo and Roland and sad songs about the loss of Jerusalem. She glanced around while he sang, looking for the effects of these songs on the men of Valerós, men whom she needed to respect her and—yes—respect Tomás as guardian of Valerós and Fontcours.

But, as always, Chrétien's songs were too evocative, and her mind wandered to where she hadn't allowed it to go. Did she want to allow feelings for Tomás? She should ask Chrétien again to explain why Tomás had turned madman on that horrible day at the bishops' court. She nursed her wounded heart, angry that Tomás had believed an enemy instead of her. But was she guilty of the same? Not listening enough to understand?

Chrétien sang until it was so late people were too tired to talk, which meant he sang until his voice wafted reed-thin, forcing him to switch to *cançós d'amor*, like the long song about Iseult and Tristan.

She hated the part where the sword lay between the two lovers.

∎

On the plateau, in the gathering heat of midmorning, Isabella, Guillem, and Benito lounged as the crusaders assembled Simon's war machines. Working behind a barricade of huge leather-and-wood shields, these soldiers wore the new brimmed metal hats the French crusaders had adopted.

"They're ugly," Isabella said, "but they make sense. No one in the south is going to attack with lance and sword. It will be fire and iron bolts raining down from city walls. There's no use roasting one's brains in a great helm."

"Armorers in the Pays de France must have earned a pile of pennies this past winter, hammering out those iron hats," Benito said.

A lizard crept out from the thorns to perch on a nearby rock, baking in the sun. The lizard moved its tail slowly, checking for danger, and then blinked once and became as still as stone.

"And didn't break their backs doing it, either," Guillem said. "You take strips of metal and pound rivets. I bet it kept the younger boys off the streets in the cold of winter, hammering away in the armorers' workshop."

"Warms my heart," Benito said, "knowing this war is paying to put food on someone's table."

"This isn't a war." Isabella mustered as much humor as she could manage. "The pope says it's an enterprise of peace and faith."

"The mamas in Minerve must say so to reassure their children when the stones hit the city walls," Guillem said.

Marshal Guillem had become bitter in the long days he waited inside Carcassonne, and now he only wanted this siege to end so he could fetch Felicia and ride back to Valerós. Isabella gave him leave to stay behind with Felicia, but he had refused.

One of the soldiers loading the trebuchet shrieked, jumping away from the pile of stones and dancing madly.

"Scorpions," Benito said. "They keep forgetting to look first."

The captain of the trebuchet crew came over to check on the man, sending him back toward camp and then admonishing the others as they hoisted stones into the trebuchet's sling. The captain's pure French echoed over the sun-parched plain. He was their favorite among the crusaders who worked the war machines. This man, Eustache from Hugues's forces, deployed one of the smaller machines within a day of its arrival, having it assembled and launching stones with great precision, battering a targeted tower. His talents were noticed by other leaders, for he and his men were moved to work the new giant trebuchet when it arrived on the plateau.

"They'll use this big machine to destroy access to the water," Isabella said. Guillem remarked the first day that Minerve would never surrender, because of the fortified steps to the well by the river. And a city of such a size stored enough food for a year. With a guaranteed water supply, the people inside had only to wait until the scorpion-chewed crusaders grew tired of the heat and went home.

"We'll see proper action now," Guillem said, "since the idea is to force surrender, not destroy the city. Too bad they didn't begin on the stairs to the well on the very first day. But with this monster machine, we can probably start packing to leave now."

"The angle isn't right," Isabella said. "They won't hit the stair walls consistently."

"They'll adjust it sooner or later. No one has anything better to do here than practice tossing stones at Minerve," Benito said.

"I hope they get it aimed correctly today," Guillem said. "The sooner the people inside decide it's hopeless, the sooner we can go home."

"It's been days, and yet their aim still isn't correct." Isabella's voice rasped from all the dust. "They're making the same mistake as with the other machines."

In the silence just before the soldiers released the beam-sling, Isabella's criticism carried across the sunbaked plain. Eustache, the master from the Loire Valley, came over to where the Valerós observers loitered. He folded his massive arms across his chest, confronting them.

"Bonjour, donzel. Do you and your men lack work?"

"We're King Pedro's men. We just watch," Isabella said.

"I fear the sun has burned your eyes, donzel. Cher Malvoisine, my great machine, is hitting exactly where Lord Simon asked. But perhaps, like all southern lords, you know better?"

Isabella crossed her arms, too. "You should be destroying the wall around the stairway. You're trying to hit the well itself, but it's impossible to aim accurately with such a big machine. Since you can only fire a few times a day, you shouldn't gamble on accuracy."

The French master looked where she pointed, squinting in the glare of midday light.

"Don't you ever look over there at night?" she said. "They laugh at you inside the city. They come down those stairs after dark, behind the wall. They bring water up in brigades. You can fire at the well until All Saints or even until Candlemas. It won't budge them."

Eustache studied where she pointed.

"I can't change the target without leave from our lords."

"The angle differs by this much." She held her fingers out to pinch the distance. "But you know that."

38

Chained in Minerve

Jean-Luc inside Minerve, Mid-June

ON GOOD MORNINGS JEAN-LUC woke feeling his faith growing again, as if an internal wound was healing over better than his burned arm ever had. Those mornings came after he'd stayed awake most of the night, reconstructing every moment he'd spent with Felicia, just to find comfort. Then he prayed ceaselessly until he felt his soul soar up through the slits in the stone wall, where God's own blue sky glowed over his head.

Those mornings, the scrape of chains on stone rang like the bells of the cathedrals in Paris.

On the bad mornings, the sound rang from the forges in the devil's charnel house, like knife against bone.

He gave up pondering how he got here, starting from when the world collapsed in Constantinople up till he chased that man through the streets. The man's face haunted him, transmuting from the disfigured wild-eyed creature in a motley suit of leather and chain to a familiar face.

Yves.

Yves who still spoke to him, but who died in his arms.

And disappeared, unburied, in Constantinople.

The man was a similar size, but shattered. The face: Yves lost his true face to Greek fire. This man—the more Jean-Luc tried to remember, the less clearly he could see it. Yves's face alone returned to him.

Then, when he most needed to pray, he could not look up and hope God was in His heaven. He fretted instead over the welts and sores growing where the iron bands chafed his wrists and ankles.

"Give me something to do!" he shouted on one bad morning, calling out as they shoveled his breakfast through the hatch. But his voice was still a hoarse whisper where they'd choked him in order to subdue and capture him.

"There's naught we can give you," the voice of the morning guard called to him. Jean-Luc never saw the man's face, or any others, since they'd chained him in here.

"Let me braid hemp. It would beat rotting in here, idle."

"You'd only hang yourself with it, and then your sin would be on my soul."

"Let me have a priest. You have sent me to hell on earth. At least let me confess my sins."

"We'll send you a goodman teacher."

"No, I'm not a heretic. I need a good Catholic priest."

"There are none here. The bishop threatened excommunication if any stayed, so they all fled as if their tails were on fire. We are as mired in our sins as you are."

While Jean-Luc tried to puzzle out the man's meaning, the mangonels started, one of them pounding the wall near his cell, rattling the pail for his slops. The sound cleared his numbed mind; he spent the day praying for the people of Minerve.

When the night guard brought a supper of bread with a meager slop of beans, Jean-Luc again begged for work.

"Make me useful. I can mend chainmail, sew a gambeson. Anything, man. Don't make me sit here while others might be dying."

The night guard laughed outside the door. "The great man you rode in with wouldn't take you away again. And we're not such fools as to give you a knife to cut our throats."

"Hugues?" Jean-Luc didn't mean to speak aloud. The name sounded like a gasp.

"Whatever his name, the old man paid us good silver to keep you until the summer ends."

"Let me go. I've been in a siege city before. I can help."

"Have a mad man help with the siege, eh?' The guard barked another laugh. "You have the sense and logic of the pope's own priests, and that's a fact. Hand out your slops."

39

Valerós, Hired

THE FEAST DAY OF St-Peter and St-Paul was like any other day. The Valerós men started arms practice before sundown, before the dust and the air cooled. Swifts whistled overhead, the shrill sound echoing off the city walls across the canyon. Red-rumped swallows cruised over the tops of the thorn brush, hunting gnats for their supper.

Chrétien, his leg still splinted, used his cane most of the time, but he had enough natural movement again that he could lead arms practice. He said, "This time, Isabella practices defense and Durán attacks. Benito, you take the other attack position and I'll defend."

"Why can't I be the attacker?" Isabella said.

"Because you attacked last time, and I'm the fight master, so you have to do what I say."

She wiped dust and sweat from her face, trying to clear her eyes enough to see. She still didn't feel completely well, and it frustrated her to know Durán gave her quarter just because she wasn't strong enough to win an honest fight. Before he came at her with his knife, Durán gave her so much time to be ready, their movements were more like stunts than a fight. Despite being so much taller than Isabella, Durán moved his weight so that when she parried and then struck for his middle, he was forced to duck and roll away from her, sprawling in the dust.

"Well done, brave soul!" Chrétien called, as if she were a child who didn't know when the game was rigged in her favor.

"You scrofulous dogs!" she shouted. "You'd lie to get into hell."

"Where can we find the master of the Valerós knights?" a voice asked in accented Catalan.

Isabella turned at the sound of a southern voice, her long knife still in position. A double-brace of Aragónese knights hovered at the edge of the practice ring, all sober as Bishop Folquet sitting in judgment. Most drew their swords as Isabella's blade flashed.

"At your service." Isabella sheathed her knife and bowed in the style of Catalan knights.

"Simon de Montfort bids us bring you his gratitude. They wouldn't have known how to attack the wall around the stairs to the well if Valerós men hadn't spoken."

"But we only spoke to end this quickly. Simon de Montfort doesn't owe us any thanks."

"Are you Marshal Guillem? Tomás of Morella said that's who would be leading Valerós. We expected someone older."

"Sorry to disappoint you. I am Pèire Leteric's child. Marshal Guillem answers to me."

"You are the secret child, then? The one Pèire claimed before he died?" the man asked. Tomás must have told tales all over Aragón, so this man mistook her for Beatriz. She didn't correct him. He said, "Tomás thought you'd quarrel over leading the Valerós knights. We believe Pèire Leteric made him responsible for the family."

"I am of age, and these knights go where I send them."

"Then, donzel, you are to send them to the camp of the king of Aragón. Valerós is now under the king's protection." The man still mistook her for a boy, so Tomás hadn't told all the family secrets.

She said, "We have no need of such protection. The Valerós knights have wisdom gained from experience, and I have Pèire Leteric's name. Right now, we're seeking a lord who will hire us as mercenaries, not protect us."

"Mercenaries, eh? Why not just fight as Christian knights and go home when the summer is over?"

"We're not interested in stealing booty from our neighbors. We're seeking silver to pay our taxes and help our villages."

"But Pèire's men are already sworn to the king of Aragón."

"If our king calls us, we'll come. But meanwhile, we need to earn money like honest people."

"Why should I pay for what I can command into my service?"

Hating that she'd failed to recognize the king, she should have offered southern-style homage. But the moment of salutation passed many moments before, so she pretended the omission was on purpose: she remained standing and studied the man who, they whispered in the night, owned her husband body and soul.

"Take me to your camp. We can discuss our business there," the king commanded.

Isabella walked beside Pedro, pointing the way in the dim light, maintaining the footing she'd established when she didn't know who he was, refusing to be afraid of him.

■

At their camp, Benito scrambled to bring another stool for Pedro, who had to bend to enter her tent, which scarcely offered enough room for the two of them. She lit a rush lamp while the king examined where she lived among the barest of camp comforts: a narrow cot, a table made from a box off the supply wagons, everything draped in horse blankets to guard against the sandy dust blowing everywhere on the plateau.

Along with the extra stool, Benito brought a leather flask of wine and two earthen goblets, the closest thing to hospitality they could offer without rousting the cook away from the baggage girls in the neighboring camp. Pedro accepted the flask from her and poured two cups of wine. From the ceremonial way he decanted and swirled the wine in one cup and then poured it into the other, she guessed this was how he habitually took the measure of, and also unnerved, whoever he kept waiting while he played servant.

Trying for the same cold Roman expression her grandfather used, Isabella gave Pedro nothing more to see than the grimy leggings and chainmail she wore, her head uncovered and her face filthy from sweating in the dust at knife practice.

The king sank on the camp stool, extraordinarily elegant in his silk surcoat, swirling wine in a stone cup, every movement as powerful and energetic as Pèire had described him. *"He's the kind of smart, bold king who can lead men into battle and make them happy to die for him."* Remembering how excited Tomás had been after he first met the king, she felt like a grubby child. The wonder was not how

Tomás had moved so quickly from her bed to the king's (if what they said was true), but rather why Tomás ever came back after he first met the king.

Pedro set a goblet before her on the rickety table.

"Handsome set of men you keep."

She shrugged, indifferent to discovering what he meant by the remark. As she reached for the wine goblet, he saw her wounded hand. His long fingers tracing the edges of the scar.

"You haven't recovered from this. You shouldn't be at arms practice yet."

"The poison is gone." She retracted her hand away from his. "There isn't time to lie in bed to cosset a weakness of the flesh."

He leaned back, as much as the small tent allowed, and sipped his wine while regarding her.

"So, donzel, you want to be a mercenary. It's not enough excitement to be either a crusader or a rebel?"

"Our lands are too poor to afford either." Isabella determined to begin boldly. "And this affair is unworthy of professional soldiers. Some of us believe what our mothers taught us."

"What was that?"

"A Christian who slays another Christian also sheds the blood of Christ."

He rubbed the deep line between his brows, and then spoke in a voice so low Isabella had to lean forward to hear him.

"I too dislike this exercise the pope is taking. Instead of skirmishes among Christians, I want to build an army. The real crusade should be to take back Andalusia for Christendom."

"You cannot build a real army by offering booty and indulgences," Isabella said. "You have to train men to be soldiers, which takes time."

"We are thinking alike here, Master of Valerós. And after you defeat the other army, you must go into the new country and make the people happy. You can't just camp in their houses and hope they'll become your faithful servants."

"The first crusaders tried that in Jerusalem," Isabella said.

"What happened there proves you can't slaughter them all either. If you try those tactics, it takes generations to make peace."

"You have a better plan, Monsenyor?"

"When we go into Iberia, we'll be ready to put administrators and peacekeepers in place. And we'll leave people in their own homes. We want to defeat their rulers, not steal from the people who live there."

"However, while you are training your army, the men have to be paid," she said. "They can't live on promised booty."

"You say your knights are wise, donzel. Can you send them to help train my army? It will take two years, if we can quit wasting time here, bullying other Christians."

"Two years of Pedro demanding service, or two years of being paid so our families aren't starving while the Church seizes our land for taxes?"

"How expensive are you, donzel?" Pedro said.

Caught for a fool, since she had no idea what price to set on her men and their services, she plunged ahead.

"I have twenty men, seasoned in the Outremer, who are each worth two gold marks a year for your purposes, plus their keep and armor," she said. "And land for each if they stay with you through two years and all the battles. We'll bring our own horses."

Pedro laughed. "Pèire taught you to negotiate, didn't he?"

"He taught me everything. Or made sure I learned it from men he trusted."

"Believe me, I can see the resemblance to Pèire Leteric in you. I regret deeply he's gone, and I regret he didn't introduce us before now." Pedro seemed bemused. Isabella regretted using Pèire's name to deceive him.

"Do you have parchment and pens?" Pedro asked.

She tugged the box of writing tools from under her cot and passed it across the baggage-crate table to him.

The king said, "Let's agree now, without quibbling. I need the wisdom Pèire Leteric gave his men, and you need to pay your bills. One mark a year for each man, and they report in Barcelona by All Saints. I will cover the taxes for Arracheuse with Simon. Shall I write the contract, or will you?"

When Isabella reached for the offered quill, she remembered she couldn't close her fingers around a pen to do more than sign her name.

"You write it." She folded her hands in her lap.

"Shall I get a clerk or priest to read it to you, so you'll know you're not cheated?"

"I can read it myself. Pèire didn't raise ignorant children," she said. Pedro looked up from his writing, still smiling at her. She didn't apologize for the outburst. "I don't even need to read it. I know you won't cheat me. Nor I you."

He bent his head again to finish the contract. Her heart raced. She'd done it: she'd sold the Valerós knights as mercenaries, without a husband to do her business, without fearing she might sign on with the wrong lord.

Pedro pushed the parchment across the table, handing her the pen, and she too bent her head to sign it.

"Master of Valerós, can you help me get a message to the woman Tomás of Morella married?"

"Give me the message. I'm his wife."

Pedro recoiled if he'd been struck.

"Then you aren't Pèire's child. You're a woman."

She jerked the parchment into her lap, so he couldn't snatch it away. "I am leading these knights as the only member of Pèire's family present. A boy trapped inside Minerve can't very well lead them, can he?"

"You deceived me, senhóra."

"You made assumptions, Monsenyor. I haven't lied to you."

"Tomás said you—"

"I am determined to save Valerós." She grabbed the edges of her hauberk under the table, rattling the mail rings, unexpected jealousy seizing her. From the familiar way in which Pedro spoke his name, she imagined how Tomás told secrets in the night, whispering across a linen pillow.

Pedro waved his hand, abandoning what he'd begun to express. "I'll put my own guardian over these knights and over Valerós, senhóra, until a man from your family can lead them."

"There's no reason for a southerner to do that." The rasp in her voice betrayed her tension.

"As your king, I prefer to have men lead the forces of Aragón, especially now. Valerós is under my protection."

"As regent for your loyal seigneur, I respectfully decline the offer. We are not in need of protection, whatever Tomás may have told you." She put her hands on the table, in control of her feelings again. "Rather, we can help you. There's nothing you can do to assist us, other than to hire our services."

"You are a bit rebellious for a loyal seigneur," he said. She couldn't read his expression.

"It is not rebellion to assert one's rights. Only Simon de Montfort thinks that."

"You are a woman in peril, without your husband to protect you."

"Mathilde of Garlande is in Lastours to argue for the release of her son, and she hasn't a husband to protect her. Alix of Montmorency led a thousand knights across Christendom without a protector. Women all over the south are running villages and estates without their husbands, because there is no other choice with these troubles forced on us. Whatever your experience with other women might be, a crusader's child does not need protection."

"You speak with heat, senhóra. Do you feel you have cause to rail against my decisions and actions?"

"You sent Pèire's heir and our priest inside the siege." She lied, because she believed Tomás had caused Sebastián and Father Anselm to be inside Minerve with him. But she didn't want to talk to Pedro about the jealousy gripping her.

"I didn't intend that. Sebastián your son, I assume?" Pedro didn't wait for an answer. "He sneaked in, and your priest refused to leave, even under threat of excommunication. The men responsible for guarding your boy have been punished."

"The situation does not argue well for me to accept you as a protector."

"But since I'm your king, you'll learn to live with it."

"Valerós serves you as seigneurs and as Christian knights, not as your children."

She tapped her fist on the table top in the same way Pèire always indicated that his mind could not be changed, but as she did it, even the tap hurt her hand. A hollow gesture. But Pedro didn't seem to notice her weakness.

"If I allow you to serve as master of the Valerós knights," he said, "do I have your oath?"

"Yes, the very same oath Pèire gave you. 'We who are as good as you, swear to you, who are no better than we,' and all that."

"It's kind of you to condescend so far as to consider me your equal," Pedro said.

"I can deliver better knights, but can any of your other seigneurs give you a better oath?"

"Tomás of Morella did," Pedro said. She felt him weighing her reaction. "He swore to protect my life as if it were his own."

Isabella laughed, which sounded frantic instead of scornful. She wondered whether Tomás also swore that he'd found his soul.

Pedro frowned. "Your husband forfeited himself to me for the murder of a priest. He's mine now. Do you need him back?"

"I want my son and my priest back. You can keep my husband. I have no use for him." She was lying as she said it, but she managed to heap sufficient scorn in her voice to aid the deception.

"Then we aren't competing for him, senhóra?"

"You're competing with the devil." She willfully ignored his meaning. "And right now, he's locked inside Minerve, waiting with my son and the rest of them to see whether God or the devil gets their souls."

"Senhóra, do not think…" Pedro grasped the clay mug, his knuckles white with tension. "Like Our Lord's care for every sparrow that falls, it breaks my heart to think of a single life lost in this endeavor. I sent Tomás to help me save lives, to talk Minerve into surrender."

"You should have sent Father Anselm," she said, "and kept Tomás out of it. No one does what Tomás says. Minerve will never give up now."

"That's what he said." Pedro rubbed the knot of tension at his brow again.

"And what else?"

"I'm sorry?"

"Your message for me from Tomás. What else did he say?"

"He wants you to be careful of Hugues de Beaurain's brother. He's convinced that's who your enemy is."

"Who is Hugues's brother?"

"The chicken farmer you honeymooned with. We met him in Carcassonne when he came to free your marshal."

"François of Rossynols? How ridiculous."

"You and I agree on that at least. I'll take my leave now, senhóra, and see your knights in Barcelona come All Saints."

After he ducked to leave her tent, she jumped up and ran after him. His knights presented a barrier between her and the king.

"Monsenyor, did you receive the letter I sent you?"

"No, ma dòmna. What was your message?"

This late, she didn't know why she hesitated.

"A warning to take care."

"Mercé. I already know about jeopardy. Is there more?'

"You can't rely on oaths," she said.

He was already walking away. "I'm from the south, ma dòmna. I learned that in the cradle.

She called after him, saying it aloud. "He's afraid of the dark."

Pedro didn't turn around. "I know. He told me."

40

The Music of a Siege

AT DAWN, THE SINGING monks' voices swelled, waking everyone who might sleep, when a refreshed brood of them joined with those who had chanted over the night. Then the wave receded to the daytime's usual singing, men's voices calling to God in repeated waves, like the ocean tide sweeping the Mediterranean shore, falling back to crash again.

"I love the music of a siege."

Miquel casually leaned over the battlements in the broad daylight, while Tomás could only peer through an arrow loop to avoid crusader arrows. A stone from a French catapult thundered against the wall. Miquel's white robe fluttered in the brief hot breeze of dawn. He dressed like Tomás's teacher in Cairo, in loose trousers, his unbound hair falling to his shoulders in the manner of Nizari swordmasters. His dark skin gleamed under the burning sun.

"When we traveled through Iconium, the mercenaries there told tales of an old god of war." Miquel spun stories in the tedium of every watch. They'd retraveled the entire path of the Second Crusade in the past several days. "I always wished a warrior god would guide me, one who's a good soldier, strict, leading men into battle."

"You told that story yesterday, Father."

"But think of it, *fadrin*, after all the quibbling with your mother about how to pray and who to call God, it turns out I'm more right than she was."

"Are you mad or only trying to drive me mad?"

A crossbow bolt whistled by, grazing his father and then clattering to the cobbles below.

"I can serve the master I want to now." Miquel grinned as he wiped at his cheek where the arrow passed.

"So, go do it."

"I'm stuck dallying here until you finish your oath. Isn't it time to step out of the sun, *fadrin*? You're dreaming while awake."

·

"You have a son, senhór. You know what I'm feeling."

Joaneta the soldier's cook declared herself too happy to live, she said, since her grandchild was born. She scooped a thin stew into the bread bowl she handed Tomás when he came down from a long morning on the battlements. His head only ached now after too much sun, which happened that morning, so it was hard to see past the headache's veil. Dead noon inside Minerve. The pitch changed among the chanting Cistercian monks, indicating a new bunch had taken over from those who sang through the morning. Sweat still trickled down his face, though he'd torn back his coif several moments before. The wind seldom blew, save at dawn and dusk, so the morning's sun left his scalp prickly while sweat ran in rivulets under his gambeson. The flies were as irritating as the monks who sang of God's love morning, noon, and night. He couldn't think which made his skin crawl more.

"*Òc*, my son is twelve. No, his birthday must have already come." Tomás scooped the meager stew with his bread. Joaneta meant Sebastián, but Tomás meant the son he'd seldom seen, who was older now than Tomás had been at the siege of Jaffa. "This is delicious, Senhóra Joaneta. I don't know how you do it."

"I have garlic and extra salt hidden under my bed. The marshals missed it when they put all the stores under guard. I'm happy to share with our defenders, but I'd rather give it to you soldiers myself."

A boulder from the war machines crashed in the square, sending dogs barking and women shrieking. Joaneta glanced over but didn't react.

"This isn't a safe place for your kitchen, Joaneta. Let me send men to help you move it under shelter."

"I'm fine here. The men have enough work and worry on their hands. Twelve is a great age for boys. Is he learning to be a knight like you, senhór?"

"He's studying to be a scholar."

"It must be a comfort to your wife, when you have to leave her. Or is she the kind of wife who likes to send men to battle? I heard some women do, though I don't understand it myself."

"She's not—"

"There you are, Don Tomás," a voice called. "Please come along with me."

Ghuilhem, the mayor of Minerve, had no use for Tomás, except when a message came from the crusader lords, and then he called on Tomás to explain what Pedro's opinion would be. Though Mayor Ghuilhem likely wanted only another opportunity to humiliate Tomás, as surrogate for Pedro. Scorn poured in a torrent from the mayor's mouth as soon as Pedro left the city.

"Your liege lord Pedro wedded Maria of Montpelhièr when the town begged him, after two other husbands spurned her. Which proves he'll sleep with anyone, even the pope, to expand his kingdom. We aren't interested in marrying into Pedro's dream of a greater Aragón any more than we care to have the pope thrust his overtaxing priests up our backsides."

Inside the man's house, though, the mayor's goodman hospitality gained precedence over his personal scorn for Tomás. A serving man helped Tomás out of his chainmail and gambeson, so Tomás came to the table in his shirt and breeches, knowing he stank beyond what humans can bear. Another man offered refreshments, which Tomás always refused, having resolved to accept no more than the rations served each day to the soldiers. Between the mayor and Tomás, hospitality defined the bounds of honor between them: the mayor offered; Tomás refused. For the real business they shared, Tomás offered advice Pedro might give. The mayor refused.

"You don't have to stand up there in the sun every day," Ghuilhem said. "It's not your city, it's not your battle. You aren't a believer."

"I believe the same as the other men standing there. The French have no business in these lands. Most of the defenders don't believe in God the way you do. They just fight because their lords set them to it."

"Pedro didn't lend me men to shoot bolts at Simon de Montfort. He won't lift his own hand against that monster."

Tomás drank from the water poured for him, judging it was the cup due him at midday. Then he prepared for yet another of the mayor's onslaughts against Pedro before he heard the new message from the French.

Ghuilhem said, "We needed his help, all of us. Pèire-Roger at Lastours, Aimery de Montréal, Raymonde of Termes, myself. And Pedro said he'd do everything he could for us. He promised us the moon and sun: all the men we need, his direct intercession with the pope. And we know the pope loves a good Catholic boy like Pedro, eh?"

Tomás didn't reply, since he'd taken the measure of the man as soon as Pedro left. He'd decided the goodman mayor would never listen to another man's advice, or ever consider that facts could be different from how the mayor understood them.

"And what must we give him in return?" the mayor said. "Nothing much, you say. We just have to bend down and kiss his arse the way the French pucker up for Philippe. Pedro will send all the men we want. We only have to surrender our castles to him."

"Rendability." Tomás said it but didn't want to argue it again. "He only asks that you agree to render any of your castles if he needs them."

"And what's the difference, if he rubs our faces in it or asks us to stick our noses in it ourselves?"

"He wants to show the pope that—"

"Pedro wants to show he can crawl up the backside of the south and take it for his own, so the pope will call off Philippe's dogs. And he knows what I think: French dog or Aragón Catholic, we'll keep our land to ourselves, thank you."

"Do you want to show me the message you received today?"

The mayor threw the parchment on the table, and Tomás read while the mayor continued to rant. "We aren't the men our fathers made us if we bend to an overlord," the mayor said. "These are our lands, gifts from our fathers and grandfathers and great-grandfathers.

We don't need to bow to a sodding king for the right to hold what has always been our own land."

In the message, Simon de Montfort, viscount of Carcassonne, by the grace of God, once more demanded full surrender and delivery of all heretics sheltered in Minerve, to be brought to account before the bishops. Else, Simon's war machines would destroy their city.

"Simon is days away from defeating you," Tomás said. "His big machine will destroy access to the water by this Sabbath."

"This is a boaster's bluff. You've seen how the heat is burning up Simon's soldiers. They can't hold out for another fortnight in this weather. We can survive. We've been stockpiling water since they began attacking the walls."

"Ask Pedro to beg mercy for the women and children, and then send them out now."

"No one is being held here against their will. They could have left if they didn't want to resist Simon."

"You must bargain with Simon," Tomás said. "He doesn't need another Béziers. The pope made that clear. Simon needs to show the other towns they'll receive mercy if they bargain with him."

"Bargain with a monster? We're not the same fools as once lived in Béziers. We'll never open our gates to him, even if he can get Philippe, Pedro, and the pope to sing us hymns in person."

"All right." Tomás tried to shift tactics. "If you want to survive this, you need to protect your water until the French go home."

"What do you propose? Pedro promised to leave me with a great warrior."

"Some of your men want to go out and burn the great trebuchet. You should let them."

"Who is proposing this?"

Tomás named the men who discussed it night after night, but only named those he believed could manage it. "They think they can go over the wall in the dark."

"It would buy the time we need," the mayor mused. "Eventually the French will get too hot and pack off for home."

Tomás rose to take his leave. He didn't want to press the idea further, for fear the mayor would reject it. The man at the door helped him back into the sweat-sodden gambeson and chainmail, the first mail Tomás had ever seen rust from the inside out. The mayor called to him one more time before Tomás made it out the door and back to the sweltering heat.

"Which side of the moon did Pedro promise you, *bon amic*? What leads you to stay here and ask us to bend over for the French day after day?"

41

Minerve, before the New Moon

Isabella outside Minerve, June 30

"WE ARE NOW EMPLOYED," Isabella said. "We've been hired to train an army."

"Do we know how to do that?" Chrétien said.

"Guillem and Benito do. The rest of us will just do what they say. Shall we join the knights? Will you sing tonight?"

"I think not," Chrétien said. "Let's go watch the city walls."

It wasn't the first night she'd slipped past the mangonels and the barricades to crouch on the stony outcrops with Chrétien, Durán, and Benito to watch the city. It was how they first heard the brigade on the stairs to the well. When they stepped cautiously among the boulders to find their favorite perch, it was long after the water brigades finished their work. The city was silent. Were it not for the monks, the night could be considered peaceful. A week before the new moon, they stared into the dark, letting their eyes adjust until they could make out the forms of soldiers atop the battlements.

"I'm not going to Barcelona," Durán said. "I don't want to be a mercenary."

"Then I'm not going. We agreed to stay together," Chrétien said. Isabella felt them move next to her but couldn't see what passed between them.

"I wish you'd come," she said. "To help keep my bravado in place, if nothing else."

Chrétien said, "You couldn't pay me a gold mark a day to—"

From above, a guard challenged them.

"We're knights of Aragón, the men of Valerós!" Isabella called up. It was the same guards who challenged them every time they came out here. Durán and Benito climbed back up the stone outcrop to prove to the guards that the men of Valerós hadn't changed into heretic marauders since the last time they watched the walls.

"How did you feel when you couldn't ever have him again?" Isabella whispered.

"That was so long ago."

"Don't tell lies, Chrétien."

"He told me he preferred women so he'd end up hurting me, because it meant more to me than it did to him. It pretty much crushed me for a year, since it was the first time I'd heard that particular goodbye. It prevented a lot of heartache, though, for the next dozen times I heard the same plea."

"He told me—"

"Stop thinking about it, Isabella. Now he belongs to the fish-lipped king of Aragón. Neither of us matters to him."

"We don't know if what they say is true."

"But we can guess. Though I shouldn't care because I'm happier with Durán. You shouldn't care because..." Chrétien trailed off.

"I was too angry that day to make Tomás see he was wrong."

Chrétien laughed bitterly. "Write him a letter and get a cross-bowman to shoot it over the wall. Then forget about him."

"You are as disturbed by him going off with the king as I am."

"I can't stop thinking I must be second best. Even though it shouldn't matter anymore."

Durán and Benito chivvied the guards above, Durán promising them on his mother's tomb to protect this part of the plateau from any invasion of Minervese heretics.

Isabella said, "Tell me again what happened on Cyprus."

"What do you want to hear, ma dòmna?"

"Do you think he has a soul?" Isabella said. "Did he lose it in that cellar? Did he ever have one?"

"He's my brother, Isabella. He's saved my life a dozen times." Chrétien's voice was charged with emotion. "I saved his life that one time on Cyprus. And when I saw him in Toulouse the day Renoud died, I saw he needed saving again. But he wouldn't take me with him. I'm his brother, and he sent me away."

Durán's voice called softly to them, and at the sound, Chrétien scrubbed his face with his sleeve. Benito and Durán scrambled down the rocks.

"Look over by the walled stair." Durán pointed where Malvoisine and other war machines had sent stones all day. A faint movement in the night showed against the wall. Ropes, with crawling bodies.

"Let's go down there." She slid off the outcrop to find the goat trail leading into the rocky canyon. The others followed close by, even Chrétien hobbling over the boulders, each as quiet as possible while stumbling through scorpion-infested rocks and thorn brush in the dark of night. She edged ahead, jumping from rock to rock and crossing the thin stream.

Durán hung back with Chrétien, and Benito kept whispering, "This is a really bad idea."

Across the canyon, they skirted the willows and brush, knowing from watching the walls for many nights, and from the smell, that Minerve's dead lay in the thicket. By the time they reached the walls, one last figure sprinted off into the night. The ropes still swayed from the weight of those who climbed down them.

"I'm going up!" She felt more excited at this idea than any in the past long, dusty, tortuous weeks.

"If you do it, I'm coming, too," Chrétien said. "And I'm telling Tomás you're still in love with him, the moment I see him."

"No, it's Sebastián I want to see."

"And I'm the legitimate son of the King of Jerusalem."

"Let's go. Benito, are you coming?"

"Chrétien and I will steady the rope, and then I'll come up behind you," Benito said.

She asked him to lift her so she could reach the knotted end of the rope.

"Wait!" Durán said. "Use this."

He wrapped her injured hand in a piece of chamois, and then hoisted her onto Benito's shoulders.

The rope burned her hands, even with the chamois and the multiple knots in the rope, and she ached in every muscle when she at last reached the top. With her arms as leverage on battlement, she struggled over its edge.

At the top, she leaned over the ledge to see how her friends fared, but the three never started up. They'd stepped away from the rope, and the guards who never recognized them as men of Valerós were shouting and shoving at them, which Durán hated.

The other three weren't joining her inside. And the men at the top of the battlement were preparing to hail crossbow bolts down on her friends' heads.

42

The Greater Weeping Angels

Tomás outside Minerve, June 30

A MAN FROM MINERVE WITH whom Tomás had shared a cup of water at midnight now hung from the beam of the trebuchet they failed to burn. The Minervese men set the fire with oil and rags as intended, but the flames only superficially charred the machine that doomed Minerve. Bodies hung from beams of the other machines. Tomás counted, hoping someone had escaped, but the numbers added up to total defeat.

He'd missed what happened to those men once his feet hit the ground and Sebastián landed safely beside him. Without a word, he and Sebastián ran in the opposite direction, wading through the stream and then sprinting through rocks and stones up the canyon wall. They missed the trail more often than they found it. And he couldn't stop imagining Sebastián skewered by a crossbowman until they crawled over the last of the canyon's rock outcrop.

"*Bon Dèu*, you're still alive!" Tomás breathed as they reached the top of the plateau, hugging the boy in relief.

"Let's get behind the barricades." Sebastián grinned at him. "It's first light. The bowmen of Minerve are already searching for careless crusaders to use as targets."

In the dawn light, they made their way to the Valerós camp, having spied it from the battlements when they were inside Minerve, staring out at the thousands of men who wanted Minerve to either perish or surrender all its wealth to the crusaders. However, on the plateau, Sebastián and Tomás couldn't penetrate the line of Simon de Montfort's soldiers surrounding the Valerós camp.

"What's happening?" Tomás asked men in the outer ring.

"Men from this camp were with the Minerve heretics who tried to burn the trebuchet," the man said. "Are you with these men?"

Tomás had left his surcoat inside the city. He and Sebastián looked like baggage ruffians.

"We're with the king of Aragón," Sebastián said.

"Then what are you doing here?" the soldier said. "Everyone knows Pedro is leaving today."

Tomás and Sebastián made as if to join their master but circled around to the other side of the Valerós camp. When Simon's soldiers departed, the war machines started pounding the walls again, and the monks began singing. Their voices echoed off the canyon walls, so they sang close harmony, making a ghostly choir, singing of perdition and God's judgment.

The ring of men opened, and they entered the Valerós camp.

"Sebastián!" Guillem the marshal grasped the boy's hands in a Catalan greeting and then hugged him. "Why, you're a head taller. Even more."

Benito glanced up from his work sharpening a sword. "Donzel!"

In a moment most of the knights circled around Sebastián, welcoming him back. But no one said a word to Tomás. Standing at the edge of the knights, Durán studied Tomás.

"Durán, why are you here? Is Isabella at Montcava with Chrétien, or have they already gone to Fontcours?" Tomás said.

"She preferred to be here," Durán said.

"Where is she?"

He advanced on Durán at the same moment that one of the knights stepped back from the crowd surrounding Sebastián. Though they jostled each other and Tomás begged his pardon, the knight didn't glance his way. Recognizing Bonanat, the skinny, crane-like knight that he had freed from Carcassonne, Tomás called to him.

"Bonanat, where is Senhóra Isabella?" he said.

The knight glanced over at the sound of his name, but then turned away again without a word.

"Jesus in the golden heavens, what is this?" Tomás exploded. "Where is my wife?"

"It doesn't matter to you now, does it?" Bonanat said. "You're the sodding bastard who spurned her, set her aside like the castle trash. But it's you that's not worthy of the devil's dung heap."

Sebastián stared at Tomás, ghost-white under his sunburn.

"You don't know what you're talking about," Tomás said. But Durán stood with his arms folded across his chest in challenge, which meant that every man in the camp must know what had happened in Toulouse.

"I weep for the shame on your father." Bonanat turned away again, like the rest of the Valerós knights.

Tomás felt his ears burn in humiliation, anger heating his sword hand. "I made a mistake. And I'm seeking my wife so I can beg her forgiveness. Please stand aside and let me find her."

"She's over there. She went searching for her son, whom you carried into danger."

The knight pointed to the top of the walls of Minerve.

"*Ai, Dèu!* How could she be?" Tomás felt like wailing. But of course, she did it in the same impulsive moment he'd bounded over the walls to find her. "Couldn't you stop her?"

"You should have been here to take care of her."

"*Jhezu del tron*, don't you think I know, man?"

"There's no evidence of that," Bonanat said.

"Let's go, Sebastián," Tomás said. "I have to report to Pedro."

Sebastián's face was as empty as the cloudless sky, resembling Pèire's so much that Tomás felt punched in the gut.

"Sebastián, let's go."

"You can't possibly think I would go with you." Sebastián's voice sounded so much older than a boy's.

"Yes, I do. I'm your guardian, as well as your master."

"I'll stay with my own men. It's where I belong." Sebastián crossed his arms, standing like Pèire would.

"Durán, you and Chrétien—"

"We promised Senhóra Isabella to stay with Sebastián if we found him before she did." Durán imitated Sebastián's stance.

"*Jhezu Cristo* and the weeping angels." Tomás felt as if he'd catch fire from anger. "The whole lot of you can go to the devil. Whatever you do to me, it's not going to help Isabella."

271

"It'll help my own sense of honor, though, to see you gone," Bonanat said. "Go serve the king of Aragón the way he likes it. No one wants you here."

As Bonanat again turned his back, Tomás bullied Durán away from the others.

"You cur!" Tomás shouted at him. "This wouldn't be anyone's business but mine except for you."

Durán shrugged. "You scorned her and left her. It's only too bad for you if people know."

"Just tell me, Durán, did she say anything?"

"She's taking the knights to Barcelona to be mercenaries as soon as the siege lifts."

"I mean, did she say anything about me?"

"She said you were the biggest donkey cock in the world. But she didn't mean it in a nice way."

Tomás resisted the urge to lash out at him, hating the smug expression on Durán's face. "Where are Chrétien and Jean-Luc? Why aren't they with the rest of the knights?"

"Jean-Luc is in Minerve. Didn't you have a chance to chat?"

"You lie."

"No, he went there with Hugues de Beaurain and then got left behind."

"Why didn't Chrétien take Isabella away as I asked?"

"He has more honor than that," Durán said.

Tomás clenched his fists, feeling the rocky plateau of Minerve crumble under his feet.

"Where is Chrétien? I need to speak with him."

"He's gone to tell Viscount Gerard where Isabella went. Gerard and Hugues de Beaurain just returned to the French camp."

"And where have they been?"

"Delivering Beatriz and Felicia to Guillem's mother at Rossynols. Gerard and the marshal wanted the women closer by, but where they'd be safe."

"*Jhezu del tron and* all the weeping angels! We are doomed!"

43

Dieu Ait Pitié!

GERARD LEFT HOME AT Easter knowing his body couldn't stand the torture of a full season in the saddle, but he hadn't reckoned for so much pain or so very many days riding.

Everyone at Fontcours regretted Simon's call to the siege at Minerve. No one had any heart for this crusade. Eloquent as always, Hugues called upon God to protect all, especially the unfortunate who were to be attacked. Gerard also prayed, but silently felt guilty about not wanting to spend time in the saddle. The first torture of the morning required half a day to overcome: walking to the chamber pot. Once he could put one foot in front of another without praying to God to lift the burden, he had to keep standing, because if he sat down too soon, he'd have to walk through the pain once again when he rose.

And then he had to govern closely the food he touched. No more sweet hot milk upon rising, which was easy enough to avoid because it was so hard to come by in the camp. A soft poached egg and boiled semolina, the same for supper with whatever fruit his man could bribe from the provenders. A bite of meat and bitter greens at midday.

On this morning, they'd ridden hard to return quickly to Minerve. They'd decided that Hugues's brother's house at Rossynols would be the safest place for the women. They could have sent their men to move Beatriz and Felicia there. But neither he nor Hugues wanted to leave that chore to others, Hugues because he damned himself for Jean-Luc's most recent bad luck, Gerard because it was his duty to worry about these women. This ride to Rossynols had been the most painful, and he felt anxious about Beatriz riding in her condition, however much Katelina of Naxos admonished him about misplaced worry.

After saying good-bye to the women, Gerard and Hugues left the domus at Rossynols when dawn's light was mostly imaginary and arrived at midmorning to the thunder of the mangonels and trebuchets beating against the counterpoint of chanting Cistercians and their Fontrevists brothers.

Not long ago he wanted to spend the rest of his earthly life behind Cistercian abbey walls, chanting the day long about God's love and His divine plan for mankind. Now, he had these girls to worry about, and the hope of Jean-Luc's freedom. The sound of this chanting affected him in the same way it did almost every other person on the plains outside of Minerve: it drove him close to madness.

Gerard hobbled off, leaving his horse with the boys, admonishing them to be sure the beast was cared for properly, but not taking the time to see that it was done. Which was yet another guilt he carried. He stood at the privy, painfully trying to make water. He'd ridden with Richard and Philippe in the hope of retaking Jerusalem. He'd faced Greek fire more than once in this life. He could surely face taking a piss after riding a horse twenty miles.

The serving boys laid out refreshments in the pavilion he shared with Hugues: dried meats, last season's figs, a carafe of wine. He only wanted water, but the camp supply was so brackish no one could drink it without cutting it in half with wine.

He silently offered prayers of gratitude to his Maker over the repast. Hugues grew impatient with too much prayer after learning he'd left Jean-Luc inside Minerve. Gerard had to agree: God was excruciatingly slow to answer.

Still longing for water, Gerard poured more wine, his shaking hands clattering the stone jug against the clay cup, which was already sticky in the heat. He studied the ring of sweet, dark wine drying on the rough camp table, thinking bees and wasps would be the next plague sent to them, when a mestiz warrior burst in. A knight. Gerard hadn't seen him before, but there was no mistaking who it was when the man pressed his knife at Hugues's throat.

"You have been out delivering innocents into the hands of evil," the young man said.

Hugues remained still. Once more Gerard watched ice run in his friend's veins. Hugues never showed any sign of fear.

"We are making Pèire's children safe, Tomás," Hugues said, "as we promised him we would."

Tomás laughed, but without humor. "The way you made Jean-Luc and Senhóra Eloïse safe?"

"I didn't know the siege would be at Minerve, else she wouldn't be there now. I didn't know Jean-Luc rode with me."

The young man's dark eyes blazed; hatred seemed to pulse through his whole body while the point of his dagger pressed close to Hugues's throat. But the only response Gerard saw in his friend was the throbbing of a vein at his temple.

"You are out to destroy us," Tomás said, "or to help others do it."

"Tomás, you are mistaken," Hugues said.

Gerard imagined Hugues must feel the man's hatred, hot in his face, yet Hugues remained cool, never looking away from his tormentor for a moment, even when another man stepped into the pavilion near Tomás.

"I cut Renoud down," Tomás breathed hotly, "the same way they did my father. And I'll do the same to any Beaurain wolf or cub I find. If it's not you who beget him, then it's your brother. I'm not going to worry any more whether I have the right man."

Tomás's hand twitched, scratching Hugues's throat and drawing a trace of blood.

"Stop, Don Tomás."

Pedro d'Aragón put his hand on Tomás's shoulder, drawing him away from Hugues.

"May all the angels weep as they dance in the golden heaven. It's the Beaurains who tortured us all these years. He wants to destroy us." The Moor's voice sounded so tight, the complaint rang out as grief rather than hatred.

"I'm a warrior, Tomás." Hugues didn't lift his hand to stop the trickle of blood at his neck, perhaps more surprised at hearing one of Miquel's epithets again than afraid of the blade. "If I had a complaint against you, which I don't, I'd fight like a man, not sneak around like a knave."

"Come, Tomás. This isn't the man you're seeking." Pedro called to the Moor softly, in the way one entreated a loved one.

"Pèire's children are with his brother in Rossynols." Tomás's knife blade wavered, as if he were uncertain.

"I'll send my knights to bring them away," Pedro said. "They'll be safe. Put up your knife and come with me now."

∎

When the Moor and his king were gone, Gerard found Hugues staring after them, his face grey and drawn.

Hugues said, "Your sons were squires in my court, Gerard. I can't contemplate the grief you must bear for them. Please don't believe I could ever harm either of your boys."

"I would never think so."

"Jean-Luc was a good soldier. He'd have been one of the great knights of France. And then, I didn't want to believe it, but they showed me proof. It was all I could do to keep him from being hung. I swear, nothing I did ever harmed your son. I just couldn't save him."

"Hugues, I don't believe you harmed him."

"And to hurt Miquel and his family? You know that's impossible, don't you?"

Gerard tried again to reassure him, but the marquis didn't hear him.

"Thirty years of chasing after him. I should be ashamed of it, if it didn't at least show constancy of heart." Hugues spoke evenly, as if talking would steady him. "I would be with Miquel, as close as two men can be, then he was off again. I never gave up until I saw him with that Kurd wife of his and their child. He didn't greet me any differently than any other man on the streets of Jaffa."

He peered up at Gerard. "Yes, it hurt, but I wouldn't do anything to harm him because of it. I couldn't."

"*Dieu ait pitié!* Hugues, don't torture yourself. Just pray to God to forget it."

But his friend paced while speaking in a jagged, emotional torrent of words.

"I waited ten years to put it behind me, and then I married Hélène because my brothers told me to. What a mistake. A man like me has no business taking a wife. And she's not what they promised. She wasn't bred to be a crusader's wife. She needs close guarding, and all I can do is give her money and put men that I trust in her way. And it does the man no good." Hugues rubbed his face as he paced and pulled at his hair like a man in mourning. "I'm sure it confused your poor boy Jean-Luc, but what could I do? Tell him to get on with it, because she doesn't interest me? That's what I should have done. Perhaps then he'd have stayed in Arles with her instead of following me to Constantinople."

Hugues stopped pacing. A beseeching look replaced the calm expression he'd held when threatened with a knife at his throat.

"Did you see his boy? Miquel's, I mean. I first saw him in the light of day at St-Sernin, all lathered about something, dressed in black like Miquel used to. And he tells me cold as sin Miquel is dead. I wanted to fall to the ground and weep. He is so much like Miquel, I wanted to embrace him. Can you imagine if I had? Right in front of the bishop, crying out how I loved Miquel more than I care for the salvation of my own soul?"

Gerard fingered the wooden image of St-Jordi in his pocket, mouthing a prayer for his friend, who once again paced as he talked, trying to shake off his grief.

"I wept through that fool's errand, going to Lastours to rescue Eloïse," Hugues said. "Weeping two entire days because Miquel was dead, when I hadn't seen him for fifteen years. The only reason I fetched Eloïse was because long ago Miquel cared about her. And can anyone ever understand that? The girl who was my next-door neighbor grew up to capture his heart, and she threw it away."

"I never understood it," Gerard said, "to this day."

"I tried again to catch that heart," Hugues said. "I went back to the Outremer when Miquel did and followed him right up until he disappeared on a raid near Damascus. But it was never any different. He liked me with him, unless there was a woman. And there was always another one parting the flap of his tent."

After a while, Hugues calmed down a bit. He poured wine, unable to sit still at the table to drink it. After a long while, he spoke again.

"We have to find out who is torturing his boy and hounding Pèire's children."

"Pèire convinced me that it's one of those Crux Lunata boys from the old days," Gerard said. "I keep running into younger knights with that foolish *crux lunata* mark. We knew all the knights that Miquel did. If we just think hard—"

Hugues went pale again. His wine spilled across the table as he cried out, sounding as if he might drown on his own words.

"His son came after me! That means Miquel thought—*Dieu ait pitié! Non!*"

44

Goat Spit

THE HUNDRED PACES TO Pedro's pavilion passed in a blur. Once they were inside the king's tent, Pedro slammed Tomás up against a packing chest.

"You spent four nights weeping in your sleep when you killed a man who deserved it, *mon amic*. How long will it take if you kill the wrong man?"

Tomás, exhausted, was unable to answer the questions Pedro flung at him. The perpetual noise of the singing monks and the idea of Isabella in danger drowned all other sounds.

"Have you eaten?" Pedro asked. "When did you last sleep? You need to eat and be ready to ride. And I'll send knights after those children. Though I tell you, that chicken farmer is not your enemy."

"Where are we going, Monsenyor?"

"St-Gilles. The prelates commanded the Count of Toulouse to appear for judgment. Raymond is my cousin, so I need to stand by his side since Philippe won't."

"What do you want me to do?"

"Put on my surcoat and coif again. Word has gotten around that it's unlucky to wear my armor. No one else will do it."

The food came sooner than Tomás was ready to eat. He toyed with it while Pedro cajoled him. Tomás finally interrupted.

"I couldn't stay in Minerve, Pedro. I wasn't doing you even a dram of good. The mayor hates you, which you might have warned me about."

"Lord Mayor Ghuilhem says I'm trying to crawl up the backside of the south while the pope crawls up mine, right? He's told me so more than once."

"He rebuffed any attempt I made to reason on your behalf," Tomás said.

"With more allegations of who's up whose backside? It's an obsession with him. But will he end the siege soon?"

Tomás recounted Ghuilhem's rejection of Simon's last entreaty.

Pedro rubbed the knot of worry in his brow. "Then it's just as well you came away. There's nothing left but to work harder on Simon to make an offer they can accept."

"Or you could send me to kill Simon."

"Are you mad?"

"I'm a better assassin than a diplomat. And it would assuage my feelings for the man and the terror he causes."

Finding the motions of eating tedious, Tomás set the bread and cheese aside, hoping Pedro wouldn't notice. The mention of assassination twigged the king and sent him pacing the tent, agitated.

"You're jesting, right? Listen, Tomás, you are bound to the oath you gave me. Spend your time making good on that."

"To protect you and yours as if those lives were my own? Why would you want that? I'm only alive because God isn't done punishing me."

The line deepened in Pedro's brow, which Tomás recognized as mild censure for blasphemy. Pedro said, "What about the other part? As if we were brothers sharing one heart?"

Without waiting for an answer, the king left the tent to shout to his men to be ready to ride. He called for a camp boy to bring water for washing, and then returned to Tomás, calmer, teasing again.

"Speaking of punishment, I met your wife. The senhóra said I could keep you since she has no use for you."

Tomás grimaced.

"She scared me, in spite of her generosity," Pedro said. "Pèire Leteric's child makes an unpredictable sort of wife, I imagine."

"I don't want to talk about it, Monsenyor."

"But I'm just imagining. My own wife is predictable to the extreme. If I have to see her, which I must when we pass through

Montpelhièr, there's a day's tirade on my inadequacies, followed by another day of aggressive pouting when I don't respond to her sermons. She's only quiet when trickery or a plague of bishops forces me to bed with her. Then I'm laid prostrate by her evil breath. Now your wife—"

"My wife is inside Minerve."

"*Ai Dèu*, how did that happen?"

"We climbed down with the men from Minerve who attacked the trebuchets. She climbed up."

"Are you taking command of her knights?"

"No, Sebastián and the Valerós marshal have them."

"In Toulouse, they say you swore to the bishop that your wife acts as you alone command."

"I lied. No one listens to my command, especially Isabella. And you must have noticed my oath isn't worth goat spit. I failed the oaths I gave my father and Pèire Leteric. I ruined the lives I'm responsible for, and I desecrated my marriage vows by listening to lies. I think my own brother despises me."

Pedro sat beside him, his hand on Tomás's knee, as serious now as Tomás was.

"You can't stay here to wait out the siege," Pedro said. "You'll drive yourself mad. And I need you."

Pedro's consolation brought him up short, though Tomás felt confused by it. And the ceaselessly singing monks would bring him to mayhem within the next half day.

"Where are your clothes, Monsenyor? Do you have a horse for me? And I left my chainmail inside Minerve."

"You have to wash before you put on my clothes. You stink of the siege."

45

Perplexity

THE MAYOR OF MINERVE had met Pèire Leteric several times in Narbonne. And one of the mayor's closest friends among the goodmen in Minerve was a man, Calvet de Villeroi, who traveled with Pèire in the Outremer years before. Coming over the wall resulted in only one moment of hazard before Isabella was greeted as Pèire's child. People she met didn't care whether someone was Catholic, which most all the soldiers on the battlement were. The people just didn't like agents of the Church sending hell-fire over their walls.

And everyone greeted Father Anselm as a friend who helped the sick and the sick at heart inside Minerve.

During the first days, she spent many daylight moments staring out at the bodies hanging from the mangonels, trying to see whether any of them could be Tomás or Sebastián. When she wasn't staring over the walls, she sought Jean-Luc.

"He's a knight of Pèire Leteric's." She lied, to urge the mayor to believe it was important to find Jean-Luc. "His father is the Viscount de Chartrain, who's a vassal of Philippe's. Upon your honor, you must treat him as a true hostage."

Ghuilhem the mayor said, "We haven't seen him. I understood he rode away with the knights he came with."

Frustrated by the mayor's lack of concern, she asked everyone she met about Jean-Luc, but it was as though he'd disappeared from this earth.

What she found inside the city was many people trying to live in too-small rooms. And great heat, but no freedom to sleep on the rooftops, because boulders flew over the walls. On the third day after

Isabella arrived, Malvoisine the trebuchet destroyed access to the well, and Minerve began to learn how to do without fresh water.

By then she had sufficient work; she didn't have time to worry about what happened outside the walls. A city stores food for a year, but the major stowage happened at last harvest, and the city had added soldiers and refugees since spring. She joined the several dozen people who marshaled the food and water supply, trying to keep people from hoarding or, more often, making foolish choices while in anguish. Everyone had lost family or friends to the French crossbow bolts and flying stones. Fevers found victims just because people lived so closely with each other that pestilence made easy leaps from a child to an aged grandparent to a nursing mother.

Isabella had to forget she hated blood, because there was too much for her to avoid. Mostly it was casualties among the soldiers on the walls, but one birthing mother couldn't stop bleeding, and a grandmother had a cough that became deep and bloody.

"But no camp fever," Father Anselm. "Thanks to your Tomás, the city has stayed clean. We aren't helping people to die in the middle of a bloody flux."

It was mostly the Catholics who came to Father Anselm. One woman came to beg a salve for a burn her child got from a fire-arrow.

"You look like the boy who used to work here," she said.

"He's my son. I came seeking him."

"Hope that mad man didn't get him, the one who chased boys in the town. He disappeared, too, didn't he?"

Father Anselm handed the woman the ointment of calendula and olive oil. "I don't know what became of the man, but Sebastián left the city with his foster-father. I'm sure he's quite safe."

After the woman left, Isabella sought Father Anselm for answers to questions she'd been afraid to ask.

He said, "Tomás takes better care of Sebastián than any father or mother could hope to."

"Did you know he's the bodyguard for Pedro d'Aragón?"

"We talked of it." Anselm rested his hand on hers. "He's very inexperienced in matters of the heart."

"Did he tell you that he has spurned me?"

"Isabella, he left here seeking you. He understands you better."

"You didn't tell him about Renoud? *Ai Déu*, he must hate me even more now."

"He loves you still."

"No, he's not capable of love," Isabella said. "You must have noticed that in his confessions."

Father Anselm hesitated. "He's only confessed to me once, and I didn't learn anything about him as a man. But I've seen him with Sebastián, and I know how he felt about the tragedies in this city. He's capable of great goodness."

"Did he tell you that he butchered Renoud?"

Father Anselm closed his hands over hers. "He got caught up in strong passions. It's a new experience for him, to feel for other people, and he made mistakes."

"He has a chasm where his soul should be," Isabella said. "I don't know if even a priest could help fill the hole."

.

On the fifth day Isabella spent inside Minerve, a man came to Father Anselm, troubled.

"I'm guarding a prisoner for my cousin Bertran, who has death duty this week. The prisoner begs every night for a priest. I'm to tell him there is none, but I can't bring myself to say it. You must see him. He needs to confess his sins in your tongue, since he's a *francimand* like you."

Lubos in His Father's Army

PÈRE-IZSÁK INSISTED THAT LUBOS must remain with his army.

"I want you to be safe," the knight-priest said. Lubos believed him, because he knew the man was his real father.

"But I want to be useful to you, Father."

Part of him wanted that, but most of him wanted to go home to his woman, Aykuna, who lived in the land where people talked like birds, whistling to each other. Where everyone could hear the spirits singing in the rocks and creeks and forests.

His savior-father hadn't punished him, though Lubos had failed Père-Izsák, being captured and lost too long.

"You will be useful, my son."

"And then I can go home?"

It seemed Père-Izsák didn't hear him, because he responded to a call that took him away and never answered before going.

Lubos hated the army before. And hated it just as much now.

So many men's bodies, too close together. He couldn't hear the stone-spirits speaking to him. Even the voices of the souls in his own sword sounded only like those bees buzzing in his head.

Secret Masses

TO ARNAU, MY BELOVED BROTHER IN CHRIST,
Despite the example of the current siege, their princeling lords persist in giving shelter to hereticated fools. They aid and assist in hiding the heretics' gold and withholding the dues and taxes owed our Mother Church.

Secular priests, those men unconnected with any order and not living under a Rule, are too untutored to guide their flocks. Please help His Holiness to understand that we need more teachers as well as more swords for suppression, else we will continue to see the Host defiled and our priests taunted in the streets.

— Esak, your brother in the Lord
8 July 1210

46

Crucesignati Reminisce

"I HAVEN'T REMEMBERED THAT story in years," Gerard said. "At the time, I was so much younger than you or Pèire and Miquel. All of you barely tolerated me following you around, though we served the same lord. Miquel was such a madcap. Anything for a laugh, at anyone's expense."

He and Hugues reconstructed what seemed the pivotal points in the story: Miquel at his wedding, half a day into the wine-and-aqua vitae portion of the ceremony, seeing the Beaurain brothers and cousins there, and remembering aloud the pranks at the camp near Antioch.

Hugues said, "The bonfraires' brotherhood was Miquel's idea. He convinced every boy in the camp we'd been initiated into a secret military fraternal order, descended from the Romans. 'Far older than the Knights Templar,' he said, 'more secret than the ancient rites of the Maronites and Coptics.' As if we could tell the difference then between Coptics and Seljuk Turks."

"Do you think that's where it started?" Gerard asked. They'd spent a day remembering what they could, back to when they first met each other.

"I'm not sure how. Miquel spun his fantastic ideas along about as far as he could." Hugues seemed lost in that memory. "It was Miquel who seized on the idea of branding us with a crossbow bolt. He had most of the boys begging for the initiation trials."

"Most squires in the camp were like me," Gerard said. "What were our lords thinking, dragging boys as young as us out among the Turks and Mamluks? There wasn't one of us with enough horse-sense to keep alive without God's own beneficence. Such lack of wisdom among the lords caused that crusade to come to nothing."

"That crusade certainly allowed boys like us to get in trouble," Hugues said.

"What do you call trouble?"

"That whole bunch of boys Miquel left out in a ditch, bare-assed, screaming to be saved. Miquel didn't understand his power over men. Those boys wanted him to choose them so badly, they didn't recognize an old-fashioned snipe hunt. Miquel betrayed their trust, solely out of ignorance."

"But you must have been humiliated, too, Hugues. No one passed the test when he and Pèire first created the bonfraires. He made fools of all of us."

"No, I passed. I was the only one the first time." Hugues bared his arm. "Miquel laughed at them, declared them piss-ants with no knowledge of what it is to be a true knight, a man of honor."

"Yet both the bonfraires and the Crux Lunata confraternities survived beyond all that foolery," Gerard said. "I've seen that sign, the *crux lunata*, on some of Renoud's men. Can it just be Renoud of Montcava that is the source of this evil? How could he carry an enmity from then? He wasn't even born yet."

"Most of the boys in camp went with Miquel and Pèire, grew up to be honorable knights. The only boys truly upset by Miquel's tricks were my cousin Thedisius and my younger brothers, Esak, François, and Colomb—"

Gerard gripped Hugues's arm where the bonfraires scar showed. "*Dieu ait pitié!* Miquel's boy could be right. Beatriz and the other women are in danger! But from a different Beaurain."

47

Whispers in the Night

Tomás on the road to St-Gilles, July 2

"AN OLD WOMAN, JOANETA, cooked for the soldiers. Bread, garbanzos, a squirrel stew. I ate with the soldiers, because the mayor and his goodman friends wouldn't host me. The soldiers almost to a man are Catholic and only fight because their seigneurs sent them."

Tomás whispered in the night, telling one story after another.

When they needed to rest on the journey to St-Gilles, Pedro selected a lord to honor with the opportunity to lend hospitality to the king and his two dozen knights. The horses were stabled, the knights given assorted beds, and the king offered the best room. But it was another man's house. Tomás felt nervous about the rampant rumors about his having become the king's constant companion. Yet he continued to whisper stories of Minerve.

"Joaneta had three daughters and one just birthed a son, the first grandchild. The family praised God for sending a son, which seemed a contradiction to what the goodmen preach. She sang all day, the bawdiest of ballads, children's rhymes, love songs. The soldiers near where she cooked sang with her, so we couldn't hear the chanting monks and because it made her so happy to sing with us. Then yesterday afternoon a stray stone from the mangonels flew over and landed on her chest. Crushed her in mid-song."

"Tomás, peace, please."

"The town had a sweet, simple-minded boy called Gonçalvo, who gave himself the job of carrying bolts to the crossbowmen. The job didn't need doing, since we hoisted up bushels of bolts using the windlasses. The bowmen found so few chances to let off a shot that we'd have bolts to last through two more Easters. Each man could carry enough to his station for the whole day. But Gonçalvo wanted work, so the men accepted the bolts he brought and let him say prayers for God's deliverance."

"Tomás—"

"Gonçalvo was telling me about the cats he hid in his grand-mother's cellar, because the men teased him about having to eat his pets soon. He stepped in front of an arrow loop—he couldn't have been exposed for two heartbeats—and took a French bolt right through the throat. Didn't even have time to be surprised before he tumbled over my feet."

"Tomás, stop. No more. I should never have sent you in there."

"I was honored you asked me. Honestly, at first I was thrilled at the chance to lead them away from ruin. If I could just understand what I missed."

"It's Mayor Ghuilhem's fault, and his seigneurs. Not yours."

"No, I mean what I missed from my father. They say I look just like him. And Miquel said I could handle sword, bow, and knife better than he ever did. But they also say my father could lead men into hell and show them out the back door. Now me, I can pour water for a dying man and he won't drink it. The best I could do for Minerve was to serve at the battlements, hurtling bolts at the French in the day and dropping the city's dead into the canyons at night."

"It'll be over in a matter of days. The path to the water is destroyed. They'll have no choice but to surrender."

"After Carcassonne surrendered, the devil's own hurt came on them."

Pedro put his hand on Tomás's shoulder. "Will you take comfort, *mon amic*?"

Tomás listened for a moment to the crickets fiddling in the night as the sound drifted through the linen-draped window.

"I don't think I deserve it."

"Then please just rest here in the dark for a while," Pedro said. "You can't think about this evil with every heartbeat. You'll find all your worries waiting for you in the morning."

"Why does it matter to God?"

"What?"

"Why does God care if you believe Jesus was truly a man or only the simulation of a man? It can't matter to God whether you believe this world is evil or whether you'll swear an oath. It should only matter that you try to live as Jesus taught."

He felt the king tense beside him. Pedro said, "It matters whether you accept the yoke of obedience to the Church. You can trust the Church to do the right thing, even if some priests go astray. You are arguing heresy."

This time when Pedro turned from him, Tomás felt a gulf of loneliness open between them.

"I'm sorry. I played the fool. Tell me what to believe when I err."

"I can't tell you what to believe," Pedro said.

"Don't turn away from me, *mon amic*. Your friendship is all that's keeping me reconciled to God right now."

"That's more burden than I can bear, Tomás."

"No, it's easy. Just don't turn away like everyone else has."

48

Mending Abrasions

"PLEASE TELL ME YOUR sister is well," Jean-Luc said.

Since he couldn't stand in his chains, he lay with his head in Isabella's lap while Father Anselm bandaged his wounds where the chains abraded his wrists and legs. Jean-Luc was filthy and stiff from immobility.

"She is fine." Isabella combed his hair to get out the worst of the dirt. "She came to Fontcours with your father. Then he brought her to Casa de Rossynols. They are good friends who bear each other up in their anguish for you."

"Don't tease, Isabella."

"It's the absolute truth."

"She's safe?"

"Yes, and you are both fools."

"She loves me?"

"When you die, God will have to pry her away so He can keep her in heaven and send you to hell where you'll feel more at home."

Jean-Luc whispered a prayer, unabashedly giving thanks to his creator. Then he sobered again.

"But what of Guillem?" Jean-Luc said. "He married Felicia when she loves me."

"*Bon Dieu!*" Father Anselm sat back on his heels. The usually tranquil priest looked aghast. He spoke rapidly, words pouring out in French. "I know better. Every sensibility warned me a secret marriage would come to no good. But she begged me. Pèire said he wanted it to happen, and Guillem kept reminding me that I heard Pèire say it. And he pleaded he couldn't bear to leave without marrying her.

What have I done? Guillem has been my dearest friend since Antioch. But now I have bound him into a faithless marriage."

"There's one thing," Isabella interrupted the torrent of words. "It's not Felicia who loves Jean-Luc. It's Beatriz."

"Beatriz?" Jean-Luc repeated her name. It seemed like a word from an unknown language.

"It was never Felicia, you fool. It's Beatriz who led you astray." As Isabella spoke, all the anger for her sister melted.

"I love Beatriz?"

"She lied about her name, just like you did. *Ai*, and she's carrying your child, which I believe you intended, didn't you? She and your father are waiting for you to join them so you can all enjoy heaven on earth together."

Jean-Luc settled back, sighing.

"Senhóra, I've been in hell and you just freed me."

"But you're still in chains. We have to get you out of here."

"And help me find that man I was chasing. I need to know who he is." Because it might be Yves. Gone mad, perhaps, but Yves.

49

Winded Horses and Nightingales

Gerard on the road to Casa de Rossynols, July 2

THE BRAVEST THING GERARD ever did in this mortal life was to get back on the horse for a second breakneck ride, returning to Rossynols. Hugues protested that Gerard needn't come along, but it was a waste of breath, for he couldn't sit idly while Beatriz was in jeopardy. The Celt from Senhóra Isabella's mercenaries appeared just as they were mounting to ride.

"We must get to Rossynols." Hugues shouted in his impatience to be on the road. "The women may be in danger from my brother."

Chrétien the Celt still detained them. "Where's Tomás? They said he came here."

"He's gone with Pedro," Gerard said.

"He wants nothing to do with me," Hugues blurted at the same moment. "Miquel thought—"

His face an icy mask, Chrétien stepped dangerously close to Hugues's prancing horse, one hand reaching out to calm the animal while he put his other hand over Hugues's mailed fist, which held the reins.

"No, senhór, Miquel insisted it wasn't you."

"How could you know?" Hugues's voice broke, so anyone in the yard could hear the plea in his voice.

"Because he raised me as if I were his son. Miquel insisted it couldn't be you we were hunting."

Chrétien let go of Hugues's hand to stroke the horse's face, blowing in its nose, having calmed both horse and man with a touch and a few words.

"I'll come with you," Chrétien said. "But we should bring Tomás and Sebastián, too. I'd have come sooner but Simon de Montfort's men detained me."

Then they wasted anxious moments before learning Pedro had already left the camp, with Tomás in his train of knights.

The bandy-legged knight Lázaro from Valerós said, "The boy went off with the knights Pedro sent. The king says he's protecting all of Pèire's heirs, taking them to Carcassonne."

"Where's Durán?" Chrétien said.

"He insisted on staying with Sebastián. We tried to argue, but he said you would follow and join them."

"We'll find them later," Hugues insisted. "We need to ride for Rossynols now."

While Hugues and Chrétien talked, Gerard tried to hear what the Celt said about his journeys, seeking Miquel's revenge with Tomás. But after they'd traveled a league, Gerard needed to devote his attention to overcoming the pain of riding, and so he heard almost nothing of the story.

It was long past dark when they arrived at Rossynols, their horses lathered and winded. Chrétien remained with the animals for several moments, helping the stablemen to calm and care for the beasts they'd abused on their ride. He caught up with Gerard before the viscount managed to hobble to the domus, following Hugues, who was roaring the house awake.

Guillem, the marshal of Valerós, came out to the inner court-yard first, having stayed behind when they delivered the women to Rossynols. Felicia, now strong enough to walk, stood at his side, her hand at his arm.

"Thank God, you're here! You're safe!"

Hugues sank to a bench, as exhausted as Gerard was. Hugues pulled his hands free of the mail mittens and then ripped free the laces on his coif, tossing it back and casting aside his sword. Gerard felt Chrétien at his side, begging to help remove the weight of his armor.

"By Our Lady, we were so afraid for you," Hugues said.

50

Release into Siege

ONCE THE MAYOR LEARNED from Isabella who lay in the city's dungeons, he claimed Jean-Luc as a hostage and denied any part in making him a prisoner. The chains were removed, but it took Jean-Luc a half day to stand and walk again. And Father Anselm worked to treat the chafed wounds from the iron bands, with scant water for washing.

"Senhóra, tell me again what happened after Tomás left Toulouse." Jean-Luc leaned on Isabella as they walked about the infirmary to stretch his abused and wasted muscles. "I missed most of the story that wasn't about Beatriz."

"Tomás talked the bishop into rejecting Renoud's accusations against me. They made him protector of Sebastián's land, including Fontcours. Then he and Sebastián went to get Father Anselm and the others out of Carcassonne. But Pedro talked him into coming here. Then he and Sebastián left Minerve the night I came in. From there, you know as much as I do."

Jean-Luc listened, and then held her injured hand in his, rubbing it in the way Father Anselm said to exercise it.

"When Tomás left the villa," he said, "he was deaf to reason, because of the lies Renoud told. What happened when he found you, Isabella?"

"It ended badly, as you tried to warn me."

Jean-Luc moved to embrace her, but she didn't relax into his effort to provide comfort.

"Something happened to him." Jean-Luc whispered in her ear as he held her. "Even before Renoud came into the room. He'd been so exuberant when we started the adventure. Then suddenly, Tomás wasn't himself."

"Chrétien say he's afraid of the dark. He went berserk, coming through the tunnel."

"That explains why he behaved so strangely," Jean-Luc said. "But, Isabella, he loves you."

Father Anselm laid his hand on Isabella's shoulders. "Tomás left here to find you, Isabella. It's only the canyons outside of Minerve keeping you apart."

She shrugged off their offers of comfort. "I saw what Tomás did to Renoud. It's more than a canyon between us."

"There wasn't that much to see after I laid Renoud out, prepared for the death-carts."

"He butchered him."

"No," Jean-Luc said. "Tomás stabbed Renoud in defense—before we learned anything. We heard only lies. It was done in a passion, but I wouldn't call it butchery, ma dòmna."

"Renoud's body was slashed and carved like a madman had attacked him."

"No, ma dòmna. Tomás delivered one swordsman's cut. Perhaps our enemy had enemies of his own. But whatever you saw, Tomás did not do that."

■

Standing on the battlements in the dark with Isabella and Anselm, they listened to the singing monks and watched the crusader camps. Jean-Luc said, "I prayed for God to make me forget. But Hugues de Beaurain caused me to be locked in a dungeon for how long?"

"Forty days. It wasn't Hugues," Isabella said.

"But my keepers told me as much. And I know now he's our quarry. He wept from Toulouse to Lastours and then all the way to Minerve after he learned Renoud died."

"I saw him when he learned Renoud was dead," Isabella said, "and he didn't care. And I saw Hugues when he learned you were in Minerve. He was crushed. He didn't know you rode with him. Hugues and Gerard are always together now. It can't be Hugues."

Jean-Luc frowned. "I wish that the heretic Montcava woman Hugues brought here would just tell us who our enemy is. Her secrets make her an enemy."

"You mustn't think so. Eloïse is the best help in my little hospice," Father Anselm said. Then he stopped to consider. "Perhaps Sebastián captured her interest, because she hasn't returned since the night he left."

"More likely she stays away because of me," Isabella said. "She fears me."

"That's not possible," Father Anselm said. "You're not a saint, but what have you ever done to her?"

Isabella spread her hands in the Catalan gesture of perplexity.

"I lost Eloïse, Tomás, and Sebastián as my helpers at the same time," Anselm said. "The same night I lost that man who attacked you, Jean-Luc. The men went over the wall, but Eloïse has simply stopped coming here. I thought barriers were breaking down inside the city, between Roman and goodmen Christians. But I seem to have deceived myself."

51
Going to St-Gilles

PRACTICING CLOSE BATTLE WORK while the horses rested, their swords bound in linen and leather to prevent dire accident, Pedro and Tomás switched positions. All twenty-four Aragón knights served as audience while their king learned the primary lessons taught by the Nizari swordmasters of the Outremer. Tomás and Pedro had switched positions in another way since they came together. Pedro, as thrilled as a boy to have a private friend, talked incessantly while Tomás remained silent, not speaking unless prodded to it by Pedro, except when they were alone.

"Is this the right stance?" Pedro said.

"Yes, if you want to convince a pig of a foot-soldier that you're slower and far more stupid than he is. But you'd better have a secret trick for coming out of it quickly."

Tomás attacked, his first feint showing the weak points in Pedro's stance.

"All right then," Pedro said when he got his balance again, "you may correct me."

Tomás nudged first the king's right foot and then his left into position, and ultimately set down his own sword and buckler to move the king's shoulders and elbows into the correct stance.

"You are capable of better work." Tomás spoke low, so all twenty-four knights didn't hear him upbraiding the king. "It's too late for you to learn speed, but you're conditioned and smart enough to learn proper form."

"But this way," Pedro murmured, "you have to touch me. I haven't figured out another way to get that yet."

"A weak excuse for mere sloth." Tomás stepped back. "Monsenyor, you need to master defending against two attackers."

He called over Cebrián, Marcos, and two other knights who'd be passable mates for the exercise. First, he paired two to fight against him, and then he asked Cebrián and Marcos to stage an attack for Pedro to defend against.

"This time, you'll also practice your battle cry, Monsenyor. When you strike, shout from deep in your belly."

"To frighten your foe?" Cebrián asked.

"To release more power," Tomás said.

Once the other men came on to the practice field, Pedro did much better, quickly mastering the points Tomás wanted to teach and disarming his two attackers in only a few deft motions. His practice partners bowed at the honor of working with the king, and then they all prepared to ride again.

"Are you proud of me for mastering my potential as a warrior?" Pedro grinned as they mounted their horses.

"You need to demonstrate a great deal more skill before I can share the real secrets of my swordmasters," Tomás said.

"You're too severe on me," Pedro said.

"I'd worry for my life if it depended on having you at my back," Tomás said. "You are too inexperienced."

"I'd like you at my back, but you insist on remaining inexperienced."

Tomás begrudged a laugh. Half a league down the road, Pedro would forget jesting and slip again into talking obsessively about the pope and Raymond's predicament, and how to gain the power he needed to stop Simon from taking more of the south. Pedro talked, and Tomás became the pupil.

"I hate this crusade," Pedro said. "Why can't we have the grand spiritual causes of our fathers and grandfathers?"

"What I hate about this crusade," Tomás said, "is how it looks like a war, and the cities smell like war, but there are no battles. No chance to fight on horse or on foot. Unless you count street fighting in Toulouse, which you can't count because there's no opportunity for either strategy or valor."

Pedro said, "You know I'm seeking a battle, in Andalusia. Will you come to Barcelona in the winter and help me prepare for it?"

"Perhaps."

"You're being coy."

"I'm never coy."

"Then you must be jealous that I asked your wife to come to Barcelona before I asked you."

"As I remember you telling the story, you couldn't tell the difference between a man and a woman. What should I be jealous of?"

"*Ai.*"

It would be several days' ride to St-Gilles. His headaches lessened as every part of his body healed: extracted tooth, sword cuts, Minerve deprivations. Most of the day, even in bright sun, he could see clearly; the veil had lifted. They rode a back route over rough ground, with a visit planned at Montpelhièr and a political need to pray at every chapel along the way, and to sup with every lord who needed to be noticed by the king of Aragón. Riding beside each other and then talking far into the night, Pedro frequently managed to find topics to discuss from which Tomás wanted to retreat. Near Maguelone, where a lord needed to be honored with a night's visit, Pedro resumed discussing a story Tomás told the night before.

"Your son's mother is a courtesan? Not a slave that a merchant was pimping?" This topic intrigued Pedro, who swore he had no bastard children to concern him.

"No, she entertained generals and sultans. It was years until I encountered another woman nearly so fine."

Pedro laughed in the way he did whenever Tomás humiliated himself. "You are a wonder, *mon amic.* Most times you're brilliant, but other times you are so blind you'd ride a horse breakneck into a wall. How old are you?"

"Twenty-five." Tomás answered, though Pedro knew exactly how old Tomás was, because a half day earlier they'd politely quarreled over whether being only eight years older allowed Pedro to assert the wisdom of age.

"I can understand you falling for such a story ten years ago, but you surely know better now. Perhaps in another ten years your vision might improve, if you can stay alive so long."

Tomás didn't want to give Pedro the pleasure of an answer, since he hated being baited.

Pedro said, "First of all, if she's a professional with high-ranking customers, she doesn't need the impoverished Tomás of Morella to pay the keeping of her child. She's probably rich as—"

"What?"

"I was going to say rich as a Cyprian harlot, but I didn't want to offend you."

"You are so despicably amusing."

"Seriously, a woman like that doesn't get a child unless she wants it," Pedro said. "She has your child because she wanted a pretty babe with a face like yours, not because the stars guide your fate."

Tomás tried to fit the facts into Pedro's reinterpretation, although he wanted to quarrel with Pedro over whether the king possessed sufficient wisdom about women to make such wild guesses.

"You might want to check your other women," Pedro said, "to see who else used you to make a prettier babe than she could get from her husband. And make sure your wife doesn't use the same trick."

"She can't have children."

"Then why in perdition are you married to her? The Church won't make you keep a childless wife. If you have to be married, you should at least get children out of it."

"I want to be married to her."

"You are a brave man. She scared the devil out of me."

"Must we talk about this, Monsenyor? My wife is a saint sent to live among demons. I don't know why God treats her as badly as He does."

"Sancta Maria, you are in love with her."

"Òc."

Pedro said, "It's not done in civilized society, you know, being in love with your wife."

"I'm not civilized. And I'm the worst husband in Christendom. Your wife should get on her knees and thank her Savior she's not married to me."

"I'd get on my knees in thanks if she were."

"This isn't humorous."

"Indeed. It takes all the fun out of my fumbled seductions. I had imagined that you follow the Church's new rules, which forbid men to love each other."

"It'd take a large stretch of imagination to think the Church could affect my choices."

"But far better than thinking that it's repulsion."

"Never on God's own earth. I just want to learn fidelity," Tomás said. "I'll choose Isabella as long as she's alive."

"I understand, I think. While I'd take you over my wife any day, I couldn't choose anyone over Aragón."

Tomás asked, "The Church made a rule against it?"

"At the Lateran Council after the last crusade, when Philippe and Richard went to Jerusalem. Though I am not implying the two events were related."

"Why does the Church care?"

Pedro held up his hand in the typical southern gesture of despair at understanding the whims of this world.

"I have to tell my brother he's going to hell," Tomás said. "Everyone always said Chrétien was the good boy and I'd go to the devil. I bet he doesn't know they changed the rules."

52
When a Brother Calls

Gerard at Casa de Rossynols, July 2

GERARD LEANED AGAINST ONE of the portico's pillars. Chrétien knelt before him to unbuckle the viscount's mail chausses, and then he begged the servants to bring water.

Marshal Guillem bit at his lower lip and stroked his mustaches, puzzled. The house began to stir as others came down to the inner court, where the sound of the fountain reminded Gerard how parched he'd been for the last several miles. Servants appeared to offer help.

François and Senhóra Paulette came in, with Senhóreta Katelina behind them.

"Welcome, brother! It's always good to see you, but it's a surprise you've come back so soon." François, always eloquent, exclaimed his welcome at length, while sending the servants scurrying for refreshments.

"I worried for the women," Hugues said.

Chrétien crossed to join Guillem and Katelina, so that all Gerard could hear was, "Tomás came out of Minerve, and Isabella went inside," before Hugues was roaring again.

"Where's Colomb? Where's Esak? I know they are all stopping here, and he'll speak to me now, before God and Man. I will know what he's doing."

François frowned. "Our brother left after midday. Business called him to Carcassonne and St-Gilles, don't you know. His church-lords call, and he's away. Colomb follows as usual. Family is several steps lower to Esak in importance, though Colomb always rides with him."

"When did they leave? Where is their next stop?" Hugues was on his feet, agitated and drawing up his sword and armor again.

Gerard felt his own cowardice wanting to cry out in protest. They couldn't chase any farther this night.

"Carcassonne for tonight," François said. "If you leave at dawn, you'll probably catch them tomorrow on their way to St-Gilles."

"How fast are they riding?" Hugues said. "We can catch them if we start now."

"As fast as one can travel with so many riders and a senhóreta along," François said.

"A senhóreta?"

"They were with the knights from Aragón, the ones who came for Senhóreta Beatriz. They had that nice young boy of Pèire Leteric's with them."

"*Dieu ait pitié!*" Gerard cried. "He has her!" *They've seized that beloved girl, who carries Jean-Luc's child.*

Hugues was already drawing his armor on again and calling for horses, before François finished his long exclamation of astonishment. Senhóra Katelina grabbed Chrétien by the shoulders, shaking him, a keening edge to her voice.

"What? Tell me what's happening. Why in the world are you worried about Beatriz?"

"It's our Crux Lunata enemies, ma dòmna." Chrétien called over his shoulder to Gerard. "No, monsieur. Hugues and I are enough. We can ride faster. Go to Minerve with Senhóra Katelina and guide your knights until we return."

"And mine." Hugues was half out the door. "My knights are yours to guide until I return."

53
Prelates and Priests

PEDRO LEFT MOST OF his knights at the edge of Montpelhièr and sprinted ahead to the palace, sending Cebrián and Marcos around front to announce his arrival while he chivvied Tomás through the back way to spy on his wife from behind the arras.

"But it's not spying," Pedro said. "We're just surveying the landscape before battle."

Tomás had been in the courts of the king of Cyprus and the Count of Antioch, and he appreciated the oriental splendor of those courts, even as impoverished as the king of Cyprus was and as desperately as the Count of Antioch lived every moment. But nothing in Tomás's experience matched this court. The marble hall was impressive, better furnished than any rich villa he'd ever visited, filled with a crowd of colorfully overdressed courtiers, all bustling about purposelessly and all focused on the small woman who held court from the center of the hall.

"Sycophants, every one of them," Pedro muttered. "It galls Maria most of all when I don't bow to her like her lackey friends."

The object of Pedro's contempt was a small woman of forty, her skin too sallow to match her henna-darkened hair and her expression pinched, like the dog in her lap, which growled at anyone who stepped too close. It snapped now at two courtiers who hurried across the floor to whisper to Maria, doubtless bringing the news of Pedro's arrival. Pedro got far too much enjoyment out of her shriek and the pandemonium that began when Maria's dog nipped the sleeve of a whispering attendant. The dog didn't let go when the attendant tried to hurry away to do whatever Maria instructed, causing the animal to be jerked from its mistress's lap. She shouted instructions in rapid order, so everyone nearby fled to do her bidding. A pretty young man in brightly colored silks and linen knelt at Maria's feet, taking instruction and a small purse from her.

"That's about enough of this entertainment." Pedro sighed. "I'd best go take my punishment. Please don't watch. I couldn't stand the humiliation."

For a change, it was Tomás who laughed at Pedro. Then he wandered away from the marble court, back to where Pedro brought him into the palace. The passageway opened on a portico overlooking the deserted courtyard where he expected Pedro's knights to arrive. The unmoving, hot air of July smothered him as soon as he stepped out of the palace, so Tomás longed to take off his armor, but he'd have to drag it around while waiting to learn where the knights would sleep. Instead, he found a bench in the deepest shade of the portico.

As soon as Tomás closed his eyes, he fell into a fugue. He saw Isabella in the siege, except it wasn't Minerve; it was Jaffa, where Greek fire poured into the town, and the battering of the siege engines thundered day and night. Another man died every second heartbeat from arrows and fire. If it wasn't Greek fire screaming through the air, it was a woman screaming over a dead soldier or a dead child. The black veils of the Outremer women fell around the loved one they mourned for the few moments before the death-duty crew picked up the body and bore it away. In his memory, he could smell the city the way he knew it as a boy: fire, offal, and the stink of unwashed, fear-stricken bodies mixed with the smell of death. They couldn't burn the bodies for lack of fuel. They couldn't bury them. As in Minerve, the men flung the bodies over the walls, but they didn't have engines to fling them far, so everyone smelled their decaying lost ones. Filth piled on the streets and flies lit everywhere, on the dead and living alike.

But Pedro insisted Minerve had surrendered by now. That meant Isabella was free and safe, sheltered by the Valerós knights who hated him. Perhaps she was on her way to Barcelona with the knights ready to serve as mercenaries for Pedro. He closed his eyes again, falling into despair over the loss of Valerós camaraderie, however short his friendship with those knights, however trivial its loss in the middle of this war that wasn't a war. All of Valerós despised him.

He pictured her face, masked with contempt when he spurned her. He opened his eyes again, to stave off remembering.

The pretty donzel from Maria's court appeared before him, dressed in brilliant woad-dyed blue and scarlet. He dropped to his knees by Tomás.

"Senhór, is no one seeing to your comfort? Can I do any service for you?"

"No, nothing," Tomás said. "I expected the knights to come here, but I must have the wrong courtyard."

"If there's any comfort I can offer, just ask." The doe-eyed donzel looked up; the moment for him to rise and move away had passed several heartbeats before.

"There's nothing, really."

"Can I help remove your armor? Ease the discomforts of the road? We understand you rode hard to come here."

The donzel touched Tomás's foot, where the leather riding-chausses covered his dusty boot-top. Then he touched the edge of Tomás's mail hauberk where it was exposed beneath his half-open surcoat. Tomás tried not to recoil, as he recognized what was happening. The donzel was perhaps Durán's age, but he had preserved a boyish appearance. Where Durán had all the experience of the Toulouse marketplace, this donzel apparently experienced only the shelter of court life. But where Durán possessed the guileless ease of a perpetual innocent, this donzel had the coy, hard expression of a long-time courtier.

"What's your name?" Tomás said.

"Jofré. I'm from Béziers. But luckily we were living in Montpel-hièr and missed the troubles there last summer."

"Your family?"

"Just my uncle and me."

"How interesting." Tomás waited for this false donzel to compromise himself.

"Hardly. Court life couldn't be more boring. But your life is so intriguing. I long to hear more, after we make you welcome."

Jofré again fingered the edge of Tomás's mail hauberk, and then traced the king's insignia on his surcoat. Tomás tried to imagine what degree of hell would be wrought on earth if it were really Pedro this donzel felt free to touch.

"You think I'm interesting?" Tomás said. "Is it the hauberk you find intriguing?"

"It's what's inside the hauberk that's interesting."

"Will it still be interesting," Tomás mused, "when you learn I'm only a bodyguard who wears the king's clothes while he's inside with his consort?"

Tomás's hands, free of gauntlets, rested in the folds of his surcoat, a far darker color than Pedro. Tomás enjoyed the spectacle as Jofré tried to mask dismay.

"A mestitz bodyguard." Tomás guessed *half breed* was the donzel's first thought. "Does your offer of comfort still hold?"

Tomás began to untie his chausses from the loops of his breeches, which wasn't much of a bluff. Just then several dozen horses thundered into the yard, and Jofré fled. Pedro's knights had joined an entourage of Churchmen, also traveling to St-Gilles. Tomás recognized several of them, including the prelate Arnau Amalric and his aide Thedisius, as part of the diplomatic deputation working to keep Ghuilhem of Minerve from resisting Simon. Seeing the stark, unforgiving faces of the Churchmen, Tomás moved back into the passageway he'd taken after eavesdropping on the marble hall.

Tomás stepped into an alcove as the Churchmen clattered past, all of them in too much of a hurry to stop and dust off the road grime coating their garments. The guards in the hallway didn't move when the priests, prelates, and their retainers passed, so Tomás guessed they were familiar visitors to Montpelhièr.

As he had with Pedro, Tomás stayed behind the arras to watch. He wanted to hear news from Minerve, since these men had ridden faster than Pedro's band. And whatever humiliation Pedro feared at his wife's hands would end with the entrance of the priests and prelates. Indeed, Maria and her coterie were sent packing after only the quickest of social exchanges.

▪

"The pope worries about foxes in the vineyards." Arnau thundered when they were alone with the king. "He should worry about—"

Pedro held up his hand. "Before we commence business, may we have prayer to bring God present among us?"

The oldest and most wizened priest among them accepted the king's request and began a long prayer in Latin, while Arnau Amalric fumed. The prelate was an imposing sight: large enough to have made a good warrior, with the visage of what must once have been a handsome man; but now a mass of wens and moles disfigured his face. Tomás did not believe a man's face was a picture of his soul, but he wondered what the change in the prelate's former good looks had done to the man's insides. As the prayer went on, Pedro assumed a placid, nearly beatified expression, as if he'd put on armor that the prelate couldn't penetrate.

"Amen," the wee priest said.

While the amens still echoed, Arnau began fulminating about Count Raymond of Toulouse. Pedro stopped him with a word spoken so quietly Tomás couldn't hear what he said.

"And what can you say to defend the treacherous count who holds court in a den of heretics?" Arnau said.

"You cannot condemn the man to me, and not just because he's my cousin," Pedro said. "Since you had him scourged last winter, and since he visited the pope, Raymond has been everywhere in the south, working to end all the problems with the abbeys. He made enormous reparation where your accounts claim he must. He's done everything to make good on the promises demanded when you scourged him."

"Yet Raymond doesn't act against the heretics in his county." Arnau's oily voice delivered threats even when he smiled. "While he allows them to thrive, he continues to lay heavy tolls on Church lands. Raymond simply hasn't met the terms of his penance."

"I know what the pope told you, Arnau. You must listen to Raymond. He didn't murder Pierre de Castelnau. And he didn't send someone else to do it."

"Raymond lied more than once." Arnau folded his arms over his broad chest. "He cannot be believed again. It's dangerous."

"What does that mean, my friend?" Pedro's voice sounded dangerous to Tomás.

Thedisius, the man closest to Arnau, said, "If the count demonstrates his innocence through lies or fraud, the whole work of the Church since the councils of Albi will be ruined."

"That's preposterous," Pedro said.

"After all the years of the Church's teaching, heretics flourish here as much as ever. Every southern lord has his back up, working against the Church to remain in the devil's mire," Arnau said.

"The lords have their backs up against the French invasion, plus a dose of resentment about the corruption of your own priests and bishops," Pedro said.

Arnau bristled. "You, Monsenyor, are hardly exempt. You ride across the countryside sleeping in the houses of known heretics, keeping the devil's own companions."

"You are quick to know whose hospitality I accept, Arnau. If any one of my seigneurs swears he's loyal to the Church, am I to outguess God in judging him?"

"We have reports."

"Meaning that you have spies everywhere? Even to spy on those like myself who are absolutely loyal to the Church?"

"Perhaps we understand 'absolute' to mean different things."

"Are you judging me? For what, Arnau?"

"What God Himself knows."

"And God Himself knows I do everything I can to walk in grace in His eyes."

"Then you yourself are deceived," Arnau said.

A messenger ran into the room. At his entry, Pedro rose. "Shall we go to dinner, my lords and friends? My wife longs to serve your pleasure."

The prelates and priests all left, Arnau still in a heat, leaving only the one small old priest with Pedro. Tomás started to depart, fearing he'd eavesdrop on something too private, when Pedro said, "How are things at St-Féliz-de-Fontcours, Pare Abát?"

Tomás was startled. The priest must be Isabella's old friend.

"Considering the tumult in our world, we are doing well," the priest said. After the oily Arnau, the old man's voice sounded sweet.

"There's hardly a moment's breath to enjoy life since Simon came to this country."

Pedro said, "You've always been a friend to the lords of the south, Pare Abát. Please help your brothers in the Church understand the damage they are doing to faith and trust in this part of Christendom."

"They cannot understand paratge, our patrimony and the honor that goes with it," the abbot said. "Our good Pope Innocent understands, because he comes from a strong family. These others, their sole knowledge of power is through the Church and their position. They don't see how the seigneurs believe the Church is seeking to destroy the very foundation of their lives and families."

"I hope they'll listen to your wisdom," Pedro said.

"And you, Monsenyor, what are you putting in peril?"

"I, Pare Abát? You've known me since I was a child when you came to visit my father. I was raised to choose the middle path and to praise God for the privilege of the yoke given me to bear."

"But what Arnau alluded to, those rumors are dangerous to you," the priest said, "especially since you made yourself such a favorite with the pope. After your confessor died last year, it's been hard for them to understand you or to know what you think. You haven't found another confessor to speak to the prelates for you. It's as if you are closing yourself off to the Church."

"That loss isn't what changed me, Pare Abát. Béziers left ice in my heart for this crusade."

"My son, your own treatise recommended the burning of heretics. It's cited in the laws now."

Pedro said, "I was nineteen and foolish beyond my years when I wrote that. If you only knew how I've anguished over it."

The abbot patted Pedro's hand, like the consolation an elderly uncle might give a child. He said, "Return to the close ties you had when the pope crowned you."

"Pare Abát, your brothers in the Church aren't telling the pope the truth about what's happening here."

"If you want to change that, you must be above reproach, Monsenyor. That's the only way you can help Raymond or the souls in the south."

"No one with sense would reproach me for the work I do." Pedro's voice was edged with steel.

"It's not your work but the rumors of your leisure that argue for reproach," the priest said. "You have a hard road, and you cannot allow yourself to slide into personal indulgence. Can you guess what my brothers in the Church plan to do at St-Gilles?"

"I hesitate to speak my thoughts," Pedro said. "I fear for Raymond, even though the pope insisted the legates listen to my cousin's pleas."

"Count Raymond of Toulouse won't be allowed to speak in his own defense."

"But they must listen!" Pedro cried, despair ringing in his voice. "The pope commanded it. Raymond worked hard to meet the penance laid on him last year. And he'll promise more."

"Any promises Raymond makes will be invalid without a sworn oath, and he cannot swear until the excommunication is lifted."

"But that's the purpose of this meeting. It's why the pope called everyone to St-Gilles."

"Thedisius, our brother among the prelates, will proclaim Raymond a perjurer, and a perjurer cannot be allowed to speak."

Pedro's howl echoed throughout the empty hall. It must have been heard as far as the stables. The abbot tugged at his sleeve, pulling the king down beside him.

"You must not confront my brothers here, for they'll know you got the news from me. Then I shan't be useful to you any more, Monsenyor."

Pedro paced around the abbot, agitated. "I'll leave and ride ahead of the legates. At least I'll have a chance to prepare Raymond. I appreciate your advice, Pare Abát."

"And my other advice, dear boy?"

"There's nothing else in my life upon which you should offer advice." Pedro joined the other Churchmen at his wife's dining table.

54

The Mass of the Holy Ghost

Jean-Luc inside Minerve, July 4

WHEN JEAN-LUC COULD MOVE with relative ease, he opened part of the seams on the Aragón surcoat Tomás had left behind, put it on, and went with Isabella and Father Anselm to visit the mayor, to demand to be put to use.

He stopped short when a ragged, black-haired woman bearing a jug crossed the cobbled street ahead of them.

"That's unlucky," Jean-Luc said. "I haven't walked in the open air for more than a month, and my first step out is an ill omen."

"What's unlucky?" Isabella glanced around. "You are the most superstitious person I know."

"Meeting a woman carrying a jug of water."

"It can't be water," Isabella said. "She's carrying something else. No one has that much water of their own, and they wouldn't parade it in the streets if they did."

Father Anselm said, "The mayor's house is on your left."

"I remember seeing Hugues lead his party there to spend the night," Jean-Luc said. "Just before they imprisoned me."

"It wasn't Hugues who did that," Isabella insisted.

At the mayor's house, it was Senhóra Isabella, as Pèire Leteric's child, who gained admittance for them to join the goodmen and goodwomen who'd gathered to pray. At first, no one in the room looked Jean-Luc in the eye, except he found kindly silver eyes following him. When he nodded, the white-haired woman lifted her folded hands to her lips in a kind of heretics' blessing.

"That's Eloïse of Montcava," Anselm whispered.

Isabella addressed the prayer circle. "This is our friend, the one we've been seeking. His name is Jean-Luc de Chartrain. His father is Gerard—"

"The viscount of Chartrain!" one old man exclaimed. He was skeletal-thin, with skin like parchment and a disarming, blissful smile. He took up Jean-Luc's hand in greeting, the way goodmen did with each other. When Jean-Luc did not respond, the man instead greeted him in the manner of southern knights. "I rode with Gerard in Edessa many years ago. You must be one of Pèire Leteric's bonfraires. I'm Calvert de Villeroi, an old, old friend."

The claim startled Jean-Luc. No one discussed the bonfraires openly, especially with strangers, yet he sensed a core of kindness in the man.

Calvert said, "I couldn't pass the challenge those rascals put before us, but I have every respect for the men who did. I especially respect your brother Anselm here, though we're on opposite sides of the pope's challenge."

"Thank you for your welcome," Jean-Luc said. "I've come to learn what I can do for you. I'm more used to being on the other side of the wall, but I've been inside a siege before. I was at Jaffa, and I have helped defend against sieges by the Angevines in the north."

"The last knight from King Pedro was at Jaffa, too." The mayor had received Jean-Luc in the coldest possible manner, and he spoke now with scorn coloring his voice. "His best advice was about how to sweep the streets and toss our dead over the walls."

Jean-Luc felt Isabella tense at the mayor's criticism of Tomás.

The mayor continued. "We were just discussing how your friend Anselm could help us. We all know how, in times of grave danger, a Roman priest can perform the Mass of the Holy Ghost. When that Mass is said, God must grant the petitioner's prayer."

"Even if it is counter to the laws of nature," Calvert said.

"There are clouds to the south," the mayor said. "We want Father Anselm to say that secret Mass up on the battlements, to make it rain."

Calvert said, "We can stay alive if a storm gives us sufficient water. Or if lightning strikes their war machines."

"I'm sorry, I can't do it," Father Anselm said.

"We know you need absolution for saying that Mass," Calvert said. "But in extreme times, can't one of your own Catholics grant you absolution? This is an extreme time. People are dying now and more will be dying soon."

"No, I mean there is no such magical Mass," Anselm said.

The mayor fumed. "I knew a wicked priest who said the backward Mass of St-Sécaire in a ruined church at Peyrian-de-Mer. For ten silver coins, he'd destroy your enemies. He told me about the Mass of the Holy Ghost. We know it's possible."

"He lied to you," Father Anselm said. "He lied about the Mass of St-Sécaire as well. There are no magical masses."

"You want us all to be destroyed." The mayor's wife sounded petulant as well as unreasonable, and Jean-Luc believed she spoke what the others in the room felt.

It was time to change the subject. Jean-Luc said, "My offer holds, to provide you any service or knowledge I can to help. We'll leave you to your prayers, with our apologies for interrupting."

Isabella and Father Anselm followed him to the foyer, as eager as he was to escape the mayor's house.

Senhóra Eloïse stopped them at the door.

"Please do as they ask," Eloïse grasped Jean-Luc's hand. Hers felt feverishly hot. "I'll tell you the name of the man you seek if you'll make it rain."

Isabella said, "At Laurac, you said your faith stopped you from telling me. You know that Tomás will kill the man."

"More women and children will die in this siege," Eloïse said. "If I give the name, perhaps I am giving up the salvation of the Consolamentum, perhaps even the hope of my own good end. But I will give that up if I can save some of the people here."

"Come out where your goodmen friends can't hear." Jean-Luc led her onto the portico. "We very much want to know your story."

Eloïse fixed her eyes on Jean-Luc and began talking rapidly and softly, so her voice didn't carry beyond the eves of the portico.

But Father Anselm stopped Eloïse before she could tell her story. "Don't be deceived, ma dòmna. We want to hear your story. But please don't think it will persuade me to sin against God. I cannot do what you ask of me."

"You can talk a man into anything, *ma bel criatura*." Eloïse folded Isabella's hand in hers and sounding warmer, more loving, more seductive than any woman who had ever talked Jean-Luc into anything he didn't want to do.

"Mother, I want to help," Isabella said.

"I'm a man of God," Anselm said. "I can offer simple prayer. I can join my prayers with yours, because I think we all believe in the same God. But I have no magic. And I cannot lie to you."

Eloïse kissed Isabella's injured hand, chafing it between her own palms. She reached out to tuck a lock of Isabella's hair, escaped once more from its kerchief, behind her ear.

"I wish you had been my own dear girl. I wish Melisinda had lived to see what a grand woman you grew to be. I wish only that you could leave vengeance and hatred aside. Come join the good-women. Our own end is so near now."

"Mother," Isabella rested her injured hand lightly on the woman's shoulder. "Though you and I are alike, my way lies with these men. They are my true brothers."

"I'm sad for you," Eloïse said. "This is not the path to the good end I wish for you."

After Eloïse returned to the mayor's house, Isabella said, "Father, I rather hoped you could be as deceitful as I am, at least until she finished the story."

"I'm sorry. I just couldn't lie to these people."

Jean-Luc said, "It doesn't matter. You heard how her story began. It's Hugues."

"It cannot be Hugues," Isabella said. "I'm weary with saying it to both you and Tomás."

"My prison guard said Hugues left me here on purpose and paid them to keep me in chains."

"I cannot believe that. What exactly did the guard say?" Father Anselm asked.

"That the old man paid them good silver to keep me here until the siege lifted."

"Perhaps they didn't mean Hugues," Anselm said.

Isabella said, "It couldn't be Hugues. He didn't know Simon was going to attack Minerve."

"Who else?" Jean-Luc considered his last journey with Hugues. "There was only that old priest. And Hugues's half-brother Colomb."

"*Ai Dèu!*" She clutched Jean-Luc's arm in a death grip. "Not Colomb. It's far worse."

Father Anselm looked puzzled. "You can't mean Esak? Hugues' little brother? But he's deeply devoted to the Church, has been ever since he returned from the Outremer. That's forty years ago."

Isabella sat, her face in her hands. "I've confessed every sin to Pare Abát. While he means to destroy all of us."

Jean-Luc sat beside her. "And we can't do one thing to stop him unless this siege ends today."

Father Anselm sat by Isabella too. "Which it won't. It doesn't seem that we can claim God is on our side, at least for now."

Jean-Luc had an arm around Isabella's shoulder, awkwardly offering comfort. "I don't think we should despair. Tomás is outside the city, still hunting."

She agreed. "And there's nothing Tomás wants more in life than to find that man and stop all evil."

55

Via com Dèu

TOMÁS WAITED FOR THE abbot to return to the courtyard, but the man continued to sit quietly, apparently waiting to be fetched by his retainers, so Tomás advanced on him.

"Pare Abát, please excuse my intrusion."

The little man glanced around, following Tomás's voice in the way a short-sighted person stares without seeing.

"How can I help you?" the abbot said.

"My name is Tomás of St-Joachim. We have a mutual friend, Isabella of Valerós, and I hope you might have news of her."

"You are a friend of poor Isabella?"

"I am—" Tomás sought the right name. "I am a knight of Valerós. We are sworn to protect her."

"How can you protect her from this great distance?"

"No one can help her now, except God. She's inside Minerve."

The old priest seemed startled. "How can that be?"

"God knows. The men of Valerós failed to protect her from her own impulses."

"If only she'd stayed in my house in Toulouse," the abbot said. "She was safe there."

"She never liked Toulouse." Tomás avoided exclaiming how unsafe she'd been in the abbot's house. "Do you have more news of Minerve than we have?"

"No, I'm sorry. But I'll keep her in my prayers."

"Thank you." Tomás considered prayer useless anywhere in the south, given the pope's incursion.

"Your voice sounds familiar. Do I know you?"

321

"We've never met before, Pare Abát."

"Come close by. My eyes are weak, and I'd like to see dear Isabella's friend. She has owned a place in my heart since she first came to Toulouse."

Tomás pulled the coif away from his face and knelt by the abbot's chair so the old man could see him.

And then a familiar expression crossed the abbot's face, as Tomás expected among lords and Churchmen: first, an involuntary repugnance, seeing how dark he was, and a flash of horror at the damage to his face. Then the mask of indifference descended, like the pulling of a curtain.

Tomás stepped back, disappointed. The old abbot might be Pedro's ally and Isabella's good friend, but he wasn't a friend to the dark *poulain* standing before him.

"You are that Moor she married." The abbot had no trace in his soft voice of the warmth he showed Pedro.

"*Òc.*" Tomás pretended the previous civility still existed between them, "though circumstances have parted us for the moment. Are you headed for St-Gilles with Pedro, *Pare Abát*?"

"No, I must return to Béziers on business. As soon as my retainers can find fresh horses, we're away."

"Then I'll say farewell. I need to take care of the king's armor."

Tomás rose to leave, but the abbot's voice stopped him.

"Are you the king's *bon amic* we've heard so much about?"

"I serve as his bodyguard. I wear his armor to confuse those who would attack him."

"And in his bed?" The abbot managed to sound like every censorious priest who had called Tomás to account as a child.

"Anyone who serves Pedro wouldn't repeat foolish or damning rumors about the king." Tomás tried to sound as contemptuous as his father always did.

"Some are paid to do just that." The abbot drummed his fingers on the arm of his chair, obviously impatient.

"The devil already has hell-fires burning for liars, traitors, and knaves," Tomás said. "Perdition is too good for such men."

"And yet, Pedro is too important for anyone in the south to tolerate a mestitz bastard leading him to perdition."

"Are you threatening me?" Tomás kept his voice free of emotion, since he'd been called that before. "Or only calling me names?"

"I'm stating the same facts that Arnau Amalric presented to the king. Except Arnau cares only about the appearance of things. I care more about what God thinks."

"And when did God call you to sit in judgment of kings, using rumors from paid liars and traitors?"

"Our pope was chosen to guide kings, as God's representative on earth. We are his minions."

"And where will God find another king who cares more about his people? Leave Pedro alone."

"It's you who should leave the king alone. Take your mestitz pollution as far from Pedro as you can. Go back to the Outremer. They don't care about the perversions of catamites there."

The abbot's coterie pounded in.

The lead knight—at first glance, Tomás mistook the man for Hugues, as he was the same height and color—hailed the abbot.

"We've traded for fresh horses and fed the men. Time to be away, Father Abbot."

The abbot rose in the creaky, slow way old men do. Tomás walked away without further leave-taking, searching for where Pedro's knights and retainers were being served dinner. Following the passage Pedro and the others had taken, Tomás found an upper gallery overlooking the lords at Maria's table. Too agitated to proceed, Tomás paced the hall for long moments. Then he saw the flash of blue and red beside Pedro, where fair Jofré leaned over to speak confidentially to the king.

Tomás asked directions of the guards in the hall for where the king's traveling knights could be found, and then he went in search of help to end the more ridiculous of the current plots against Pedro.

■

By the time Tomás returned with Cebrián and Marcos, Pedro had left the priests and prelates, and gone to exercise in the courtyard.

"Pedro gets like that," his wife was saying as Tomás and the others went in search of the king. "So much energy, all he can do is bash at swords with his knights."

Cebrián and Marcos were familiar with the palace, but the usual courtyard was deserted. Instead they found the king in another walled courtyard more suited to fine ladies wandering among the small arbor than to practice at arms. Dressed in chainmail, Pedro was wrapping his sword in linen to blunt it while talking with Jofré, the well-dressed donzel. A handful of other knights loitered at the edges of the courtyard, seeking the available shade at midday.

Without a word, the three knights of Aragón advanced on Jofré. Cebrián and Marcos seized him and carried him out of the courtyard. Behind the closed gate, they bound the man's hands and silenced him.

"Apologies for my inattention, Monsenyor," Tomás said. "I'm ready for practice when you are."

One of the loitering knights barred the gate as Tomás came to Pedro's side.

"You're jealous." Pedro grinned.

"Jealous? Of a fey *fadrin* who's paid by your wife? Didn't you see him in her court earlier?"

It took two heartbeats for Pedro to understand what Tomás meant and to stop smiling.

"What does she think she's doing?" he said.

"You'd have to ask her," Tomás said.

Pedro paced, angrily punching one fist into his palm in vexation. "I made her the queen of Aragón. She has two whelps from me. What more does she want?"

"You aren't truly asking me, are you?"

Pedro ignored him, still agitated. "She can't think I'd look twice at that pompous house-pet."

Tomás began to wrap his sword. "Practice the footwork I showed you while I'm getting ready."

Pedro stopped pacing. "But you didn't kill him. I thought you believed in no quarter."

"I've lost my stomach for it," Tomás said.

"What will you do with him?"

"Your messengers to Minerve are taking him along. They'll let him free in the crusaders' baggage train."

"That house-dog won't last a day in a siege camp."

"Perhaps the lad has skills he's never discovered."

Tomás had half his sword wrapped, thinking this little comedy was the last scene between them. Once Pedro exhausted his current rage, he'd leave for St-Gilles. And Tomás would return to Minerve. As he prepared to say goodbye to Pedro, he examined the knights loitering in the shade for the first time.

"Monsenyor, look at this." Tomás held up his sword to draw attention as he stepped to the king's side, and then dropped his voice. "These aren't your knights, Pedro."

Pedro glanced over at the men.

Tomás said, "Your surcoats, yes. But buckled coifs or not, these men are mercenaries in Aragón cloaks. See how they wear their swords? Your men never would."

"And we shall—what?"

"Stand back to back as I taught you. Remember how I said once that this is greatest thrill there is with another man?"

"There are six of them." Pedro began unwrapping his sword.

"It's the same as how you deal with two on one. There's just an extra man for each of us."

"I rather wish I'd gained the secrets of your swordmasters."

"There are two secrets." Tomás discarded the linen wrapping so his blade was bare again. He eyed the man he intended to take first: the one who carried a shield, since Tomás needed one of his own.

"The first secret?" Pedro demanded.

"Strike your foe. Second—"

"Let me guess," Pedro said. "Don't let your foe strike you?"

"You are a brilliant student, Monsenyor. Ready?"

"Now?"

"Move when I do. If we're going down today, we're going to-gether." Tomás dropped his voice. "As two brothers."

"I like the sound of that."

"You are not to give quarter, Pedro. This is a battle against your assassins, so we are killing them first. Except save the weakest to answer questions. Draw your sword, put up your shield, and move left now."

As soon as they stepped into battle stance, their foes understood they were being attacked. The man whom Tomás chose for the initial assault hacked at Tomás's legs but missed just as Tomás swung down from high guard to strike his prey's shoulder, toppling the man's head half from his body. Tomás snatched the man's shield and turned his attention to the others.

Pedro whooped as he struck down his first attacker, and the two of them began an exercise from the Nizari swordmasters, both striking more than they allowed strikes against them. As they scrambled through the hedges and flower beds of the ladies' garden, Tomás felt all his tension flow as power. It emptied the strain, apprehension, and dread carried from Toulouse. He'd regained the timing he'd sought since Famagusta. Two of his strikes needed better form, but he didn't linger on minor errors.

Pedro was winded when it was time to stop, holding his sword point at the last man's throat as the man lay on the gravel path, bleeding amidst lavender and rosemary.

"Who sent you?" Pedro panted. "For your life, tell me."

The man locked eyes with Pedro as he reached up with his gauntlet and pulled the blade into his own throat. Blood spurted onto Pedro's hand and splashed across his boot. Pedro yelped, stepping back surprised, then shocked. He stumbled away, being sick in the rockroses.

Tomás retrieved Pedro's sword and wiped it clean with one of the stolen and now ruined surcoats.

"You are so cold blooded." Pedro sank onto a bench near a small cypress, staring at his own bloody hands.

"Kings and popes should remember what their soldiers do when they send men to battle. They kill people. It's better than being killed. Or so I assume. Here, wipe your hands."

Pedro used the strip of linen that was supposed to wrap their sword for practice. Pedro had a bad cut on his brow, but most of the blood on his hands came more from a slice above his wrist, not from the suicide in the garden path.

"Let's get you stitched up." Tomás dragged Pedro to his feet. "Then we'll see if anyone in Montpelhièr recognizes your would-be assassins."

"They weren't trying to kill me," Pedro said.

"What do you mean, *mon amic*?"

"The ones I fought were pushing past me to get to you."

∎

Pedro refused the help of women who wanted to attend them when they returned, bleeding in Maria's inner court. Instead, they followed a physician to his cell in the outer reaches of the palace, where the man set leeches to drain away more blood. Then he stitched and dressed their wounds in the way of a man who had learned his craft on the battlefield. Tomás escaped with a hack on his right forearm, a modest slice on his left calf, and other minor cuts.

"Leave us." When the last bandage was tied, Pedro commanded away the physician and his apothecary companion. Pedro and Tomás waited in silence for their two healing attendants to depart.

"I'm going now, too." Tomás peeled away the linen stripping the apothecary had wrapped around a cut on his thumb. The linen would only prove a hindrance. "I hoped to travel with your messengers to Minerve. Perhaps I can still catch them if I ride hard enough."

"Must you go?"

"We both know that I must."

"You were warned off?" Pedro said. "Arnau hates to think there's any pleasure in my life because his is so barren. That's all it is. Jealousy and rumor."

"Yes, but my cautionary Churchman hates my black Moor's heart more than Arnau hates the idea you might be enjoying yourself."

"Enjoy?" Pedro said bitterly. "It all feels too desperate for joy to exist in this world. What will I do without you?"

"Wear your own armor. Cebrián, Marcos, and the others will protect you. Though you need to check again which of them you can truly trust."

"You know that's not what I meant."

Tomás rose to leave, throwing his gambeson and mail over his shoulder to put on later, carrying his sheathed sword in his other hand. Pedro followed him out of the physician's cell to a portico deep in the shadows across from the mews.

"Tell them you sent me on a mission, Pedro, so no traitor can make more of my leaving than it deserves. I'll take only my own armor and a horse."

"I'll send a clerk with a letter of passage for you. And you must keep the surcoat. You look good in it." Pedro's face kept its usual sardonic expression, but his voice was hoarse.

"But I'll feel like a target." Tomás tried to jest, too.

"Will you come to Barcelona in the winter?"

"If I'm still alive after the summer, I'm going to Cyprus. And then Cairo. There's business I need to attend to."

Pedro traced the scar on Tomás's lip. "Don't die," he said. "At least not before I see you again. I won't command you, but I'm asking you, as two brothers with the same heart."

Pedro kissed him, lightly touching Tomás's lips with his tongue. "If only the rumors were true." He let his kiss slip deeper, tasting faintly of wine and spices, until Tomás was lost at the edge of oblivion.

"Don't be afraid of the dark. *Via com Dèu.*" Pedro pressed at Tomás's chest, gently pushing him away while bidding him to go with God.

The king sprinted up the curving stairs into the palace, two steps at a time, and Tomás listened to him go, vaguely wondering if they'd be alive come winter or if God would end this wretched world before then, since it was so much trouble to keep it going. He breathed in the last of the comfort Pedro had left him. After half a moment of reverie, he began to think about how to get back to Minerve and turned to seek the stables.

But instead, he found Hugues de Beaurain, sword in his hand, standing in the shadows, dressed in Valerós colors.

Tomás drew his own sword from its scabbard as another figure stepped out of the shadows.

"It's not what you think," Chrétien said. "Nothing is what you think. We're hunting Hugues's brother, and we need you."

Lubos, Homesick

"PLEASE, FATHER, HELP ME! I want to go home, but I don't know where it is. Please help me find Aykuna and my girls."

He tucked the letter into Père-Izsák's saddle bags. His father had been short with him, scolding him for getting lost and being hurt. It took him more than a full turn of the moon to be free and find his father again.

Instead of greeting him like a father who'd lost a son, the knight-priest castigated him for carelessness. For being dirty. For forgetting what he was supposed to do next.

He scratched at the newest tattoo on his arm. Perhaps his father was right, since he couldn't remember the list of his tasks without being reminded.

But the spirits in his sword only sang, "Enough! Enough!" in that witch-language that his woman Aykuna spoke. He needed to go home to her. He'd leave now, but he didn't know the way. He didn't know the name of her country or her village, so he couldn't ask anyone for help. Except Père-Izsák.

He watched his good father from the distance, in the army where he was supposed to march, following Père-Izsák on his saintly mission. To serve God was the highest, most sacred duty. That's what his father taught.

But Lubos had done his duty, and his only mission now should be to go home to Aykuna. He tried to say one of her witchy prayers, but the bees buzzing everywhere made it impossible to get the words right.

PART SIX
Accidental Heretics

In Part Six

TO ARNAU, MY BELOVED BROTHER IN CHRIST,
As we teach under the guidance of His Holiness, original sin is transmitted to children through concupiscence. These heretics see birth and life on earth as the work of the devil and freely commit fornication, adultery, and incest in the manner of dogs in the street.

With no true notion of sin or understanding of redemption through the Resurrection, these heathens further the work of darkness while daring to call themselves goodmen or bonhommes. Their princelings and seigneurs decry the work of our enterprise, claiming that Philippe's word, in the hands of Simon de Montfort, is drenched with Christian blood. Philippe's forces, while serving as the Church's hammer, are castigated as dogs and pigs.

These seigneurs are spiritually destitute, having none of the kind of strength that is guided by faith. Pedro *El Católico* is at times like the dog that cannot bark, while these seigneurs howl in this wilderness of heresy.

I caution you: Do not believe oaths offered by any lords in this hereticated wilderness.

— Esak, your brother in the Lord
Seven days before the Feast of St-Veronica
7 July 1210

56
Béziers in Darkness

Tomás outside Montpelhièr, July 4

"HE HAS ALREADY LEFT Montpelhièr," Chrétien said. "We found out as soon as we arrived. We've been seeking you so we can pursue him together."

"You are traveling alone?" Tomás was still wary of Hugues, even though the old man sheathed his sword.

"We were attacked in Béziers and lost the Beaurain knights we had with us," Hugues said. "Your brother's skill allowed us to escape."

"Esak is headed for St-Gilles, as you were," Chrétien said. "We three can't hope to deal with him on the road. His entourage is too large. We'll find him in St-Gilles and ask other allies to stand by us."

"Or pay mercenaries," Hugues said.

"How did you discover him?" Tomás asked.

"I found your story disturbing," Hugues said. "Gerard and I spent a day remembering our old adventures. We recollected that my brothers and cousin had been particularly upset in the Outremer."

"François," Tomás said.

"No, my brother Esak. He was too young. They shouldn't have sent boys there. He believed Miquel was a bad influence on me. I never understood his animosity."

Chrétien said, "We went to Rossynols to be sure Beatriz was safe, and found he'd come with King Pedro's knights and taken her away."

"Except they weren't Pedro's knights," Hugues said. "He took Sebastián and Beatriz."

Tomás felt his gut tighten.

"And also Durán," Chrétien said. "When the false Aragón knights came to fetch Sebastián, Durán went with them, because they wanted to stay together as brothers."

"We must ride," Hugues said. "We can talk more on the road."

Hugues strode for the stables, but Tomás hung back, tapping Chrétien's shoulder.

"Durán told Sebastián," Tomás said in dismay. "Can't your brat boyfriend mind his own cat-licking business?"

"He believes Sebastián is his brother. It is his business."

"*Ai Dèu*, Sebastián knows! Can God not show mercy?"

Chrétien said, "How old does a boy have to be before he understands that his father made bastards? Sebastián never believed Nicolau to be a saint."

Tomás, hearing that Chrétien mistook his meaning, had one small consolation: Durán hadn't betrayed what Renoud said about Isabella, even to Chrétien.

Chrétien still glared at him. "Why do you think you're so much better than him? Because your father married your mother? Or because you're such a stud with a sword?"

"Nicolau was a—"

"No, I mean Durán. What makes you better than him? Is it loyalty? Fidelity? Virtue? Or your famous bravery?"

Tomás finally heard the insult he'd impulsively spewed. At the same time, he understood he'd crossed his brother long before this moment.

"Nothing. Not one thing on God's earth."

Chrétien gestured in the direction where Pedro had run up the stairs. "Some of us live in a world where you're just a pilgrim, like the tramps littering the streets of Santiago de Compostela."

"You don't understand. This was—"

"An exhilarating, thrilling experience, just between you and your new *bon amic*? And now you're going back to your wife, Parzival? Or, if she won't have you, another woman?" Chrétien whispered, but shouted at the same time. Not the teasing brother Tomás was used to. "It's been heard a thousand times before. Please notice, when you can spare the time, who you're hurting."

"I didn't do anything."

Chrétien clenched Tomás's wrist and rubbed at the bonfraires mark burned there, and then dropped his hand.

Tomás said, "I've been humiliated in every way possible in the past month, before God and man. How I spoke about Durán: it's one more humiliation I've brought on myself. I'm sorry, brother."

"Ask God to forgive you." Chrétien turned away.

Tomás grabbed him by the arm, spinning him around. "Chrétien, you have to—"

"What? What are you demanding now?"

"Give me your respect. I don't know what happened. I went into that room and lost everything."

"My poor brother."

"I cannot endure you turning away from me. What have I done that you can't forgive?"

"Honestly? You show no fidelity to the people who care for you. Like now. You jump from your wife to your king and back again like a flea."

"It's not what you think."

"You see that poor fellow over there?" Chrétien gestured to where Hugues checked the saddle and harness of his mount. "He says you look just like our father, who hurt him terribly for half a century. I see myself as just like him, and it frightens me to the bottom of my soul."

"Are we riding?" Hugues called to them.

·

"He was hiding from us in the Church, the whole time we were hunting a knight," Chrétien said.

"Why didn't Pèire or my father mention him?" Tomás asked.

Hugues said, "I doubt Miquel or Pèire ever thought of my brother again after he left the Outremer. Or if they knew Esak went into the Church. Neither would recognize him again."

They left Montpelhièr as quickly as they could. Tomás ate bread and cheese in the saddle, since Hugues couldn't be convinced to rest in Montpelhièr. At least age slowed Hugues down a bit, for which Tomás was grateful because the sword-slice on his calf hurt worse than expected. It throbbed as they jolted along the roadway.

"Which of the Churchmen is he? I saw the whole lot of them this morning." Tomás pictured the priests and prelates haranguing Pedro, though it was only Arnau Amalric's craggy face he recalled, with a vituperative voice behind the wen-wracked face.

"Esak is not remarkable," Hugues said. "If you noticed him at all, it's because he was the smallest among the older men. Few people ever realize we're brothers."

Tomás reined in his horse abruptly, which caused the others to circle back.

"Your brother is the abbot of St-Féliz?"

"Yes."

"He left at midday for Béziers, not St-Gilles." Tomás recalled the hatred and repugnance when the abbot saw Tomás's face up close. The man who'd sent false Aragón knights to attack him.

■

Arriving in Béziers at dusk, they gained entrance through the city gates because of the Aragón surcoat Tomás wore. Inside, they found the city had been torched but not razed.

In the heat of summer, the cinder ash on the streets stirred to hang in the air like a pall over the city. The old residents went to the hills—or to God—and the new residents claimed only small corners of their conquest. Villas and manses had new residents, but many buildings still had no doors other than animal hides hung as curtains. Nothing covered the windows. No new gardens had been sown. And there were no children anywhere. The only sounds were dogs barking in mews or chained in courtyards, and the clink, clink, clink of workers who sorted trash from good stones to rebuild the destroyed city.

They stabled their horses and began searching churches to find the abbot. The roofless Cathedral of St-Nazaire, where hundreds had been burned while seeking shelter, rested like a giant cinder, its insides blackened from fire. Rubble had been removed from the nave so the priests could hold Mass. Workers had swept the debris into the transept where they sorted stones to be reused. Hugues enquired after the abbot and, learning nothing, insisted they leave quickly. Outside, a street away, he leaned against a villa gate.

"I stood in the cinders last summer." Hugues rubbed at his face as he spoke. "I heard the screaming. I can still hear them."

In the marketplace, they bought food from street-vendors and ate on foot while seeking the abbot of St-Félix in three different neighborhood churches. As it turned out, it was not a problem to learn the whereabouts of the abbot. A sacristan in the third church pointed them to the neighborhood where the abbot was staying. The problem came when they were surrounded by mercenaries just after they entered the abbot's neighborhood. They did not successfully solve the problem.

Two knights against six attackers: possible in the garden in Montpelhièr. Three knights against twelve foes was not reasonable in unfamiliar alleys, especially when one of the knights was an old man who'd been pushed beyond endurance for days on end. They were shoved into an ancient villa in a deserted quarter.

"What's that smell?" Tomás asked as they were herded among tables and barrels cluttering the lower floor.

"Tallow," Chrétien said. "I think this was a candle factory."

"Shut up," one of their captors commanded, among the most eloquent of any words said to them.

Up two flights of stairs, they were cast into a stone-walled room and the door was barred behind them.

Locked in a darkened room.

"Are you all right, brother?" Chrétien's voice came from nearby.

"There's a window, and you're here. I'm fine."

"You don't sound fine."

"They stole our father's sword. It's bothering me."

"You were carrying the one Al-Samh made? From Castile?" Hugues sounded outraged, more than he had while they were being shepherded into their prison. "That sword is priceless. It's a travesty such mercenary filth touched it at all."

"We're mercenaries, too," Chrétien said.

"Taking pay to fight isn't what makes for filth among soldiers," Hugues said. "Esak will be made to suffer for all of this. I'm sorry to have brought this on us."

"We aren't down yet," Tomás said. "We're merely awaiting our chance, which will appear at the right moment."

They waited for their chance: studying how the guards opened the door to give them food and take away their waste. They calculated how they could overcome the four who invariably appeared at the door when it opened. They waited for a change in routine or a weak point to exploit, but such a chance didn't come.

A tiny slit near the top of the wall allowed in air and a modicum of daylight, but no sound from the outer world. They yelled for help when the door was locked; the first day, they shouted that they were vassals of Pedro d'Aragón; then they called out that they were French lords of the crusade; sometimes they cried out that they were helpless victims of thieves. The only response they heard was their jailers laughing on the other side of the barred door, joking about their hopeless efforts.

They spent a fortnight in a room that allowed just enough space to stretch and pace, with straw to sleep on. Soon, Tomás was nursing very ill men.

Hugues fell sick first, weak after the long days on the road and long nights of despair over his brother's actions. When Hugues first fell ill, Tomás spent every moment by his side, talking to divert his attention, and then holding Hugues in his arms, since they had no chairs or bedding. In the middle of the second night, Tomás felt Hugues fading, as if he might be falling into a feverish sleep.

Yet Hugues grabbed his wrist, though he was too weak to hold on. "How was it for Miquel in the end?" he whispered. "Can you tell me? Did he suffer?"

"No." Tomás lied, saying only what Hugues needed to know. "My father passed peacefully. Except he was pissed God made him die in bed instead of in battle."

Hugues sighed.

Tomás leaned over, speaking gently. "My lord, I know Chrétien reassured you, but I want to be sure you have no doubts. My father swore it couldn't be you who harmed us. He said it was impossible. Pèire Leteric said the same."

He felt Hugues relax in his arms. "Thank you for that, lad. Sweet Jesus in heaven, thank you."

"I didn't heed their advice," Tomás said, "and I'm sorry for the grief I caused you."

When Hugues didn't answer, Tomás assumed he'd fallen asleep, but after a long while Hugues whispered again.

"You are so like him."

"People say that. But I didn't know it because he was so changed after Damascus," Tomás said. "And I don't have the powers he did. No one follows my lead."

"Just let them know you care," Hugues said. "That's how both Pèire and Miquel won followers. Miquel took care of his men, but his special madness caused men to lose their hearts to him."

"I have only ordinary madness."

"You'll find your way. Pèire and Miquel didn't spring newborn as great captains of men. You must know that from Miquel's stories."

"No, Miquel didn't tell many stories when we lived on Cyprus," Tomás said.

"Will you humor me, if I tell the especially good tales?"

Until Hugues became very ill, Tomás listened to the stories he first heard from Pèire, and far more.

.

Hugues slept most of the time. Then Chrétien became feverish with camp sickness, too. At night in the darkness, with two fevered bodies propped against him, Tomás listened to his friends' labored breathing.

His father cradled Tomás, too. Sometimes he sang, in a way Tomás had forgotten, from the years before the siege at Jaffa.

"You aren't afraid?" Miquel whispered.

"This isn't the same as the infernal cellar on Cyprus," Tomás said. "I'm not going to die. I'm not alone like a mongrel cur."

"You screamed on Cyprus, even when I tried to comfort you."

"My friends are here. I've made peace with the vermin crawling in my shirt and hair."

"*Òc.*" Miquel still cradled him in the same way Tomás held Hugues. "These stone walls are too tight to admit rats."

"And we killed all the insects and kept the good spiders when our jailers first locked the doors."

"But you can't stop asking, eh, *fadrin*?" Miquel nudged him.

"What?"

"Why does your God allow it?"

Chrétien tossed in a fever and Hugues groaned with thin breaths. In the dark, Tomás traveled over the same ideas as in the cellar-prison on Cyprus, thinking how to answer his father.

"A bad situation, *peccador*," he whispered, calling himself a sinner. "There's no use hoping for Divine rescue. We aren't children."

"But I've always told you," Miquel said, "that there is no sin except betrayal."

"And that's why I'll live. I need to make it right with those I've betrayed." In the dark, he made a list: his brother and his wife. Now Tomás added Hugues's name to the list. And then he made the same resolve as in the dungeon on Cyprus: to kill his captors.

"This time it will be because of what they did to my friends," Tomás whispered.

"*Ai*, now you're getting it, *fadrin*."

·

In the dark, while Hugues slept, Tomás talked to Chrétien as he always had, over a thousand bivouacked nights, as if Chrétien could be sparked to join the conversation.

"Hugues knew our father a thousand times better than we did, perhaps even better than my mother. When we were younger, Miquel was gone all the time, while our mother taught us that he was a hero we should worship."

"Hugues's stories made me jealous." Chrétien's voice was racked from the illness.

"*Òc*. Hugues knew him and we never did."

"But can you imagine, fifty years loving a man?"

"Who just wanted to be friends?" Tomás said. After he and Chrétien quarreled in Montpelhièr, they hadn't spoken of it again. "*Jhezu del tron*, it breaks my heart."

Chrétien sighed in the dark when Tomás touched his hand.

"Maybe that's the third one," Tomás said.

"What?"

"Hélène hexed me. At Twelfth Night she condemned me to three heartbreaks. I didn't think anything could be worse than what happened in Famagusta. But I'd never cried when someone died.

I was never in love. I never felt my insides being ripped out when a friend turned away."

He listened to whether Hugues might be stirring and whether Chrétien might be better or worse. Then he spoke again, to stave off the silence.

"Now Pèire is dead. I've lost Sebastián and Isabella. My friendship with Pedro can't continue. And worst, I made a travesty of my oath to Pèire. I even lost the sword our father gave me."

Chrétien was breathing hard. He didn't speak.

Tomás said, "I can't bear to lose you, too, brother. I'll do anything to redeem myself in your eyes."

He groped for Chrétien's hand in the dark and felt the burning heat and paper-dry skin. He left Hugues for a moment to hold Chrétien upright and dab water on his lips.

"Don't die, Chrétien. *Ai Dèu*, don't leave me."

"I'm here, brother."

.

"For the love of God, water!"

Tomás begged their jailers to leave more water. He begged for salt in addition to water, hoping it would help keep the ill men alive. He begged for wastes to be taken away more than every third day. And he begged daily for help for Hugues. "This man is your lord's brother. You can't leave him to die like this."

He shouted up at the window at dawn and sunset, and at what he reckoned to be midday, like a *mu'addin* chanting from a minaret, calling the blessed to prayer. Except he couldn't call anyone around him blessed. He moved between his friends, holding one for a while and coaxing water into his mouth. Then Tomás went to the other man to wipe away the stains of sickness and fever as best he could, thinking that their evil jailers didn't need to bother with torture.

Then, amazingly, Hugues and Chrétien got better, and the three of them hunted for ways to stay sane.

They remembered every crusader hymn ever heard. Chrétien's voice wasn't what it should be, and the reed-thin sound of Hugues's voice singing "*Chanterai por Mon Corage*" plunged them into a morose reverie, until Chrétien said they should sing only at night.

Mostly they gambled. When they tired of dice, they matched hand gestures with a child's rhyme. They bet on the number of flies to land on Tomás's wounded arm when he removed the bandages. They bet on the number of stones making up each wall of their cell. (Tomás won, for he'd counted them while the others were ill.) They gambled for stories about best sword-play, best fight in the face of poor odds, best sexual conquest, worst defeat at arms, worst defeat in bed, greatest lie ever told, worst truth ever endured. They gambled for land. At first, Tomás spotted Chrétien with Fontcours and the Cairo fief. After a day, Chrétien owned all of Tomás's land and half of Hugues's estates. And then Hugues owned everything for a moment, but it sorted itself out again. Chrétien won both the guardianship of Fontcours and St-Joachim, which Tomás conceded only because in the final round, Chrétien abandoned cheating.

"You can keep Cairo," Chrétien said. "I let you win that one."

"Thanks," Tomás said. "I am giving it to Yusuf when I go there in the winter."

"Cairo?" Hugues was interested. "I haven't been there since— *bon Dieu*, it must be thirty years. Cairo is a city you can't forget."

Chrétien said, "You're going to Cairo, Tomás? When did you decide this?"

"I'm leaving the south as soon as all this is over," Tomás said. They'd been there a fortnight and no longer talked about Minerve, and they didn't talk about finding a way out of their cell. "I want to see Yusuf. Perhaps he might choose to come with me to Famagusta. Chrétien, please join me. Bring Durán."

"No, brother. I have to put Fontcours in order. Since I own it, I have to make it pay."

"The courts and Church will always think Sebastián owns it," Tomás said. "Though Sebastián says he doesn't want it."

"But you and I know that I won Fontcours in a fair game, so I have to be responsible."

"Perhaps I'll go with you," Hugues said. "I'd like to see Cairo again. Who is Yusuf?"

Like everyone else, Hugues joined in the effort to keep high spirits, but he'd aged a decade since they entered their prison. His skin was nearly transparent, his white hair lank from the illness and filth, and the flesh had melted away from his face and frame, so he appeared a living skeleton, rather than the hale warrior Tomás had confronted outside of Minerve.

Tomás told Yusuf's story, with the new interpretation he'd learned from Pedro.

"Does he look like you?" Hugues asked, an edge in his voice.

Before Tomás could answer, the scratching at the door announced their mercenary guards.

However, it was Sebastián and Durán who opened the heavy, barred door.

57
Writing Letters

ISABELLA CLOSED HER MIND to the threat of Pare Abát and her grief over Tomás's betrayal, since nothing could be done while the siege continued. When they were free, then she'd see Tomás again and ask him what happened that awful day. She'd tell him that her heart had softened, and ask if he was ready to hear the truth.

How could she nurse anger over misunderstandings with Tomás when people here were dying every day, when children cried from hunger? To keep her mind from grief, Isabella stayed busy helping with sick children and others who came to Father Anselm. Her truly useful work began when a young mother named Marieta begged Father Anselm to write a prayer for her, to use in a spell.

"You write the prayer on parchment, and I tie it around my waist," Marieta said. "My grandmother said it stops a woman's bleeding. It's two months since my baby was born, and a fortnight since the poor thing died. I must stop bleeding so I can care for the wee ones in our domus."

Father Anselm, ill over the past week, offered Marieta herbs: ergot and bayberry, but he refused to participate in spell-making for Marieta. But he seemed too tired to say more than no. Isabella, who did not share his scruples, offered to help Marieta and began to prepare a piece of virgin parchment for the prayer. Jean-Luc went with her to find feathers to shape into quills. This proved to be an easy task, since every goose and duck in the town had been killed, and the deserted fowl-pens hadn't been scoured by the children. No one made the remaining children do chores now. Marieta's grandmother brought two lamps with enough lamp-black to make into ink.

At the table, Isabella found it awkward but no longer painful to hold a pen. She wrote slowly, but the results were tidy, if not beautiful. It delighted Marieta, who kissed her for it.

Bertolomeu, a foot-soldier from Azille, came to the infirmary to have Father Anselm cauterize a wound from a crossbow bolt. He saw Isabella writing the prayer. After the priest treated his wound, Bertolomeu asked if Isabella would write a message for him.

"Just a short one. I want to leave a prayer for my mother. She doesn't know I'm here, and if I don't leave a message, she'll never know what happened to me."

Father Anselm said, "You mustn't believe that God will let us die here."

Bertolomeu shrugged but didn't reply. "Ma dòmna, can you hide it or protect it, so if they burn the city, someone will still find my prayer?"

Isabella promised to think of a means of preservation, and then wrote the prayer he asked for at the top of a new piece of parchment, signing the message for him since he could neither read what she wrote nor make his own mark.

And after that, her former duties were shifted to others, because first the foot-soldier Gautier and then Ponç and then almost every Catholic in the city came to ask for a note to be added, until she had to scrape a new parchment to hold more messages. Most asked her to write one more version of the basic message. Some contained confessions painful to hear and to write.

> I, Enric of St-Chinian, send my blessings to my mother Joana in St-Chinian and plead to be remembered by her in prayer.

> I, Bentivenya of Carcassonne, confess to God and beg of my brother forgiveness, for I lusted after his wife and sought to bring her to my own bed.

> I am Pascau of Minerve. I hurt my wife with my hand and words so that she fears my voice and my touch. May God forgive me in the afterlife.

A hundred sins and blessings. After the first five, she began writing smaller to accommodate them, and then smaller again on the second parchment. And smaller yet again, so room could be found for everyone to leave behind a word, a prayer, spilled sins.

"They all expect to die," Isabella said. "They expect to disappear from the world."

"Everyone is tired." Father Anselm bandaged the wounds at Jean-Luc's wrists and ankles, which were healing too slowly. "It's hard to hope when you're exhausted."

Hard to hope, indeed, after the animals began to fall down, bleating and dying in the streets and corrals and stables. Hard to bear, once the always-crying infants and children ceased crying. And the death-duty men had to take the little bodies from their mothers, who were too parched to cry.

Isabella lay down to rest, which she seemed to need to do often, though writing letters shouldn't be hard work. Across the way from where she slept, Father Anselm consoled a woman who'd lost a child. Moments later, he was consoling a child who'd lost her mother.

Lost. As if they could be found.

Isabella had been nine when her mother died, old enough to have memories of her, memories that had dimmed to flashes of laughter while playing in sunshine, chanting songs while they worked in the women's solar, riding through the rain to tend to chores in the village.

But nine was too young to have known her mother as a woman. Everyone said that Melisinda of Valerós, Pèire's daughter, looked just like her mother Anglesa, now long in the ground with no one to remember her since Pèire too had passed. Isabella closed her eyes to see her mother's face as she best remembered it, Melisinda praying in the chapel at Valerós when summer morning sun lit the altar. The day Pèire had come home from the Outremer and taken Isabella into his lap for the first time. Melisinda had copper hair, the same color as Isabella's, but it fell from her coif as silken floss instead of untamable like her daughter's wild mane. How else were they alike, Melisinda and Isabella? How could she ever know, since it seemed that they were both lost.

∎

Bertolomeu came back late in the afternoon, when Isabella's new parchment was almost full of prayers.

"Enego, that one-eyed bowman, was killed today. Did you know? A crossbow bolt went right through his good eye."

A common enough death. Isabella remembered the man from when she first came over the wall. His body had nearly been defeated by the last war, taking one of his eyes and half of one leg.

"Do you want me to pray for his soul?" Father Anselm was wrapping Jean-Luc's wounds once more. "The man often said he wanted to come for confession, but I never saw him down here."

"He was going to have the senhóra write a prayer for him," Bertolomeu said. "After supper, he said. But now he's dead. Perhaps you can write his prayer anyway, ma dòmna? I know what he wanted to say."

"Òc." She began whittling the point on a fresh quill.

"Then please write this, though it is very sad: 'I, Enego of Toulouse, confess that I perjured myself and caused a knight to be destroyed at Constantinople. I confessed this sin every day, but it is hard to believe God will take me to His heaven.'"

Jean-Luc, under Father Anselm's caring hand, cried out, then spoke again in the common tongue.

"*Qui s'ho creu?*" Who'd believe it?

"Believe what?" Isabella was startled by Jean-Luc's distress.

"This Enego. He's the man I've searched most of Christendom to find. Can I see him?"

Bertolomeu shook his head. "The death-duty men already put his body over the wall. They don't wait for the dark of night now."

Isabella kept writing for people.

But after another day, Marieta died anyway.

That day Ghuilhem the mayor sent for Jean-Luc, asking his help in the siege.

58
Avi! Avi!

"COME ON!" SEBASTIÁN URGED. "We have to find Beatriz and then leave quickly."

The boy offered three swords, but Tomás had his arms around the boy, trying to keep from weeping with relief. Chrétien embraced Durán and didn't try to keep from weeping. Then they got Hugues to his feet and out of the room, with the old man's arms around Durán's and Chrétien's shoulders.

"This morning I finally got close enough to steal back the dagger you gave me." Sebastián was in the highest of spirits. "I don't know why there are no guards today. Please hurry."

"By my father's hand, I am so glad to see you, *fadrin*," Tomás said. "We didn't know you were in this house."

"We heard you call every day," Sebastián said, "but we couldn't do anything."

"We're honored guests because he calls us his grandsons," Durán said. "But we had stern keepers."

"The man who stole me out of Valerós is here," Sebastián said. "But he's odd as a cuckoo. When he guards us, he makes us tell stories about what it was like when we were children. We call him Raoul, after the knight in the poem. You know, Raoul de Cambrai."

"Because he's mad as a pig-footed weasel," Durán said. "They shouldn't have left him as the only guard today."

"Raoul is tied up now," Sebastián said.

Still helping Hugues, Durán reached out to grasp Chrétien's shoulder. "*Ai Dèu*, you are so thin, *mon amic*."

"I had trouble keeping the food down," Chrétien said.

Sebastián ran ahead to check doors, calling for Beatriz. "I know she's here. She traveled with us, though they kept us apart. Because she's not his grandchild."

"Grandchild?" Tomás worried about what Sebastián knew. "Is that why he snatched you?"

Durán said, "He didn't say so at first. The abbot of St-Féliz came to our camp at Minerve, seeking Isabella. He was with knights the king of Aragón sent to protect us."

"Except they weren't Aragónese knights," Sebastián said. "I was so mad for not seeing it before we were on the road."

"And I should've known about the abbot," Durán said. "He used to visit my mother and give her money. He got me a job carving stone at the cathedral and was unhappy when I left to work in the markets. Why didn't I wonder why he bothered?"

"And Beatriz is going to have a baby," Sebastián said. "I'm going to be an uncle."

"Or a cousin. Or something," Durán said.

They finished searching the top two floors and descended to the ground floor.

"When we came to Carcassonne, he kept us in his room and explained how we were his son's children," Durán said.

Sebastián said, "And he wanted to give us everything since we didn't have a father to guide us."

"He cried while he told his story, but I wanted to pop him in his weepy face," Durán said. "Sebastián kicked me until I saw the right way to play it."

Sebastián jumped down to the landing, a self-satisfied expression on his face. "We love the abbot more than we loved our own father. Of course, Durán never met his—"

A wild-looking man stepped into the workroom, his arms around Beatriz and a knife at her throat.

Sebastián cried, "No, Raoul!"

Tomás grabbed the boy, as though he were threatening Sebastián with his sword.

Durán and Chrétien came down the stairs, awkwardly shifting Hugues while Chrétien brandished his sword.

"Leave me," Hugues said. "Help the others."

"It's only one leprous rabbit hiding behind a woman." Tomás recognized the man from Father Anselm's infirmary, the one who had chased Sebastián and other boys through the streets of Minerve.

Chrétien eased Hugues down on a bench against the wall with tenderness just as six more men came in with the abbot of St-Féliz-de-Fontcours. Durán stepped up behind Tomás, holding his sword in such a way he could hurt only himself.

Tomás whispered, "Follow Sebastián," and then tripped him. Durán sprawled at the feet of his grandfather and lost his grasp on the sword, which one of the mercenaries snatched up.

"*Avi! Avi!*" Sebastián cried, calling the man his grandfather. He struggled to get free from Tomás and embraced the abbot in the way Catalan knights greet each other. The abbot rubbed his hand across Sebastián's sun-bronzed hair and then gently pushed him aside. Sebastián dodged the motion and bent to help up Durán, who glared back at Tomás.

Chrétien said, "*Òc*, brat, betray us again. We knew you would."

Durán opened his mouth to speak, and then closed it, apparently understanding what he needed to do. He embraced the abbot. "We're so happy to see you, Grandfather. You came just in time to rescue us."

Caught up staring at the boys, wild Raoul lost track of his grip on his own prisoner, so Beatriz wiggled free and slipped in beside Tomás. As the man tried to grab her again, Chrétien's sword went up, stopping him.

"Forget her," the abbot said. "We'll leave this pack of vermin here to enjoy each other."

"Give me room to move," Tomás said softly. Beatriz stepped back by Hugues.

"Give you room?" the abbot said. "To roam Christendom, stealing innocents from the path of righteousness?"

The idea struck Tomás as so ridiculous he laughed aloud.

"You mock the idea?" the abbot said. "But the son of a jackal would, I expect. After I heard from my brother that a Moor married poor Isabella and murdered Renoud, I came as soon as possible to rescue her. But alas, you sent the girl to her doom inside Minerve."

Hugues said, "I never said that Tomás killed Renoud."

The abbot jerked at the sound of Hugues's voice, straining to see beyond Tomás.

"Hugues, is that you?"

"Yes, brother, you murdering swine. You left us here for a fortnight to die in our own juices. Yes, it is I."

"I didn't know you were here," the abbot said.

"You need better henchmen. We shouted it to them every day," Tomás said.

"Esak, your mercenaries tried to kill poor Isabella of Valerós. How could you sink so low?" Hugues's voice dripped scorn, and the abbot jerked as Hugues spoke.

"A lie!" the abbot cried. "I have always protected her. She's a darling of our domus. I worked with Renoud for years to free her from the snake's nest where Pèire Leteric imprisoned her."

"Isabella's only prison was the Montcava domus, where you planted your sons," Tomás said. "You failed to protect Isabella when she first came to Toulouse. Or did you teach your sons to take what they want from women, the way you did with their mother?"

Tomás talked while assessing the position of each armed man, determining how ready Sebastián and Durán were, judging the danger posed by the fidgeting, confused Raoul. Would Beatriz stay out of the way? He believed that he and his brother could still move as if they shared one heart and one mind, so Tomás prepared to seize control.

"You know nothing about what happened," the abbot said.

"But that's how we all got here, isn't it?" Tomás spoke sweetly, the way he'd learned years before, to distract men in a fight. "You once forced a little girl to do what she didn't want. You're a spit-licking weasel and a coward."

"You filthy *poulain*. You polluted our beloved Isabella. These children don't need to hear your slanders, too. God can't ask me to tolerate the devil incarnate." He motioned to the men behind him. "Lock them here and then we leave."

"Too cowardly to kill us outright," Tomás said. "Too cowardly to acknowledge your bastard sons in the light of day."

The abbot bared his teeth like a ferret in what was perhaps a smile. "You'll join your friend from Chartrain in hell. He is in Minerve, you know. Locked up and dying, if not already dead."

"We know he's there. I didn't know you betrayed him," Hugues said. Tomás felt Beatriz shaking beside him and grabbed her hand to stop her from moving.

The abbot said, "I recognized him when you sent me to free him from the town's constable, Hugues. I guessed then that he helped murder Renoud."

"Jean-Luc had nothing to do with it," Tomás said.

"You, *poulain*, did it all? You're the same soulless murderer as the fiend who sired you."

"Why hurt Jean-Luc? He was sinned against in Constantinople and then—" Hugues stopped. "*Bon Dieu*, you denounced him. What could you hold against that good knight? Or his father?"

"That 'good knight'?" the abbot said. "How can you be so blind? He made your wife into an adulterous whore, Hugues. He as much as killed Nicolau in Constantinople, just like he killed his own brother. He deserves to die, and his father deserves to suffer as I have."

Beatriz sobbed behind Tomás, the sound rising above Hugues's labored breathing and the shuffling of the impatient mercenaries. As she ran toward the abbot, shrieking, Tomás put out his hand to stop her, but wild Raoul kicked at his sword hand and sent the blade spinning away. Raoul snatched it and turned against Chrétien, who barely had time to parry the blade. A brace of mercenaries crossed their swords against Chrétien's. In the same moment three armed men immobilized Tomás.

The abbot had a small jeweled dagger, the kind women of the south keep for decoration, and he pressed it against Beatriz's throat, just where one's life pours out if cut there.

Sebastián rested his hand lightly on the abbot's, and spoke affectionately, in the quiet way one calms a spooked horse. "Grandfather, there's no reason to harm an innocent. She's not our enemy. Don't you agree?"

The abbot shivered as Sebastián touched his cheek. He let loose of Beatriz, pushing her to the floor at Tomás's feet. "Lock them all in the room over there," he ordered his men. "We must return to Minerve. I don't have time to waste on this filth. Come with me, brother. The legates have me carrying messages to Simon and the bishop of Toulouse." He reached out to Hugues.

"With you?" Hugues said. "I'd rather be in hell than anywhere on God's earth with you."

The abbot seemed surprised and dismayed. "I did everything for you, Hugues. Yet here you are, still following pretty boys into the mire of sin. Is there any hope for you?"

Towering over most of the men in the room, Hugues placed his hand on Tomás's shoulder, though the effort must have cost him dearly. Chrétien stood with him as if in solidarity, but in fact was ready to catch the old man if his strength failed.

"These men, like Miquel, are my true brothers," Hugues said. "I'll stay here with my bonfraires."

"It's you, *poulain*." The abbot spit the word in Tomás's face. "You did this, leading my brother back to an evil life. You subverted Pedro like Miquel did my brother. And you want to train Sebastián for the same life of sin."

Tomás said, "A man is what he is, Pare Abát. These men— Hugues, Pedro, my brother—they are what God made them. Only a weak man accuses another of leading him into sin."

The abbot struck him hard across the face with the handle of the dagger. Tomás's teeth cut into his cheek and he tasted blood.

"Jesus and the weeping angels! This is the best a coward can do?" Tomás sounded like his father. Then he lied. "I have a son, too. But he loves me, as your sons never did."

The abbot froze. Tomás had driven a wound home, but the man directed his men to seize Hugues.

"My brother will come with me and be saved," the abbot said.

Tomás kept speaking sweetly, hoping to create as much fury as he felt. "My son will find you next, Pare Abát. Wherever you go, there'll always be another Moor who looks like Miquel."

"Lock them up," the abbot said to his men.

Tomás said, "We'll keep coming, in your dreams and in the flesh, until one of us cuts out your liver and makes you eat it."

59

Prelude to Surrender

Jean-Luc inside Minerve, July 20

THE MAYOR'S WIFE'S DOG Mico lay under the portico, whining in misery. The brigades had ceased cleaning the streets, because no one possessed the strength or will to do it. Now the carrion of sheep, chickens, pet rabbits, cats, and other animals lay where they died. Maggots and flies became the only creatures enlivened by the work of the siege engines and the ever-chanting monks.

Hesitating before knocking on the mayor's door, Jean-Luc glanced down at Isabella.

"Do you want to stay out here?" he asked.

"It will be futile again, but I'll stay by your side because we need each other."

Since Jean-Luc had been freed, the affairs of Minerve consumed all his waking time. Only one captain of the city's forces still survived, and the men mostly climbed the battlements every day just to escape the misery of the streets below, even though the monks' voices rang louder at the top of the wall. Jean-Luc's first modest attempts to get the men back under discipline were embraced as if he offered food to the starving, because they longed for a leader. Although it could've been any man who made the effort, it was Jean-Luc who became de facto captain. The mayor thanked him, but Jean-Luc believed the men only wanted to stay busy while waiting to die.

Because Jean-Luc was a Frenchman, the mayor decided Jean-Luc could also advise on diplomacy.

"You know how those invaders think," the mayor said. But Jean-Luc didn't know, and anyway, the mayor invariably refused his

advice. A simple, inelegant balance guided each of their conversa-
tions: almost everyone in the city would follow Jean-Luc's sugges-
tions for how to survive this siege, and yet the mayor wouldn't
agree to what Jean-Luc recommended each day: surrender. Jean-Luc
knocked, and then they once more began the ritual of hospitality,
problem-solving, and refusal to capitulate.

"See who has water hidden away," Jean-Luc told the mayor. He
had little advice left to give. For many days he'd been working with
the men to rig ways to capture dew, but every new idea was as futile
as the last one. "You can easily tell who is hoarding, for they still
look healthy. Then make sure everyone knows the rules: one cup a
day for each person."

"What else?" Ghuilhem said.

"Tell everyone how the camp fever will come soon and kill us all,
whether or not we have water left."

"You don't know that for truth."

"Yes, I do," Jean-Luc said. "And you do, too."

"What can we really do?" the mayor said.

"Ask Simon again to let the women and children go."

"You know that's futile."

Jean-Luc knew what happened the day before, because he'd been
present during the negotiations, pressed in among the handful of other
hostages. Arnau Amalric came to parley, saying Pèire-Roger of Lastours had bowed to Simon de Montfort and surrendered his hostages.

■

"Let the women and children go," Ghuilhem the mayor had said in
the last parlay with the Churchmen.

"To let them spread heresy wherever they are?" When Arnau
Amalric scoffed, his ugly face made the sneer in his tone seem deadly.

"At least, let the children go."

"To let them breed contempt, spreading a foolish belief that their
heretic mothers are martyrs? Come, senhór, you have already drawn
the line. Total surrender is required of you and your city of heretics."

■

"I don't think it's futile," Jean-Luc said. "Ask Simon de Montfort, not Arnau Amalric."

"No," the mayor said.

"Then make sure the goodwomen keep preparing the winding clothes for the dead. Send your men around to tell all the mothers to say goodbye to their children, for they won't be seeing them again in this life."

"Senhór knight, you are cruel."

"The rest of the babies will die in the next two or three days," Jean-Luc said. "Then the last of the old people and those already ill. Within a week, all the smaller children will be gone."

"If we hold out only a little longer, the French will go home." Ghuilhem offered the imaginary shield everyone in the south had hidden behind for the past year.

"The men on the battlements talk of drinking their own piss," Jean-Luc said. "Most don't listen when I tell them they'll die sooner if they do."

"We won't give in to those devils. Better God take all of our souls," the mayor said.

"Those of your goodmen and goodwomen here who believe deeply, they welcome the chance to slip off their mortal shells. A few are consoling themselves by starving even faster than the rest of us, hoping to leave this world." Jean-Luc stared hard at the man. Rumor said the mayor's aged mother was one of those goodwomen.

"It's as they believe," the mayor said.

"But what of the others?" Jean-Luc pleaded. "What of those mothers who want to believe your black-robed teachers, but go up on the battlements to hear Father Anselm say prayers for their dead babies? Don't you hope to see another spring, however evil you think this world is?"

"We won't let the French make us into another Béziers," the mayor said.

"Simon wants you to bend to his will, not die. You're performing the massacre for him, by refusing to surrender."

"When I think of bending to Simon's will, the ghost of my father comes to shame me." Ghuilhem raised his hands in the common southern way of pleading with heaven.

"And what does the ghost of your mother say about all the children dying now?"

The mayor was weeping, or he might have been if there were enough water left in Minerve to make tears.

Jean-Luc said, "My friend, we believe in the same God. We still cry the same name when we ask for mercy. You must surrender."

The mayor folded his arms again in silent answer. With nothing more to say, Jean-Luc and Isabella returned to the rubbish-filled streets of Minerve.

60
Turning over Rocks

THE ABBOT'S MERCENARIES SHOVED Beatriz, Chrétien, and Tomás into a windowless room smaller and dirtier than the one they'd lived in the last fortnight. They beat Tomás, who fell to the floor and curled up to protect his head and middle. The mad Raoul delivered several good kicks before they barred the door and left.

When the ringing in his ears let up so Tomás could hear again, the only sound in the room was Beatriz crying as she wiped at Chrétien's face with the hem of her robe. The guards hadn't spared his brother.

Their new room had a much smaller slit for air, too small for even a child to pass through.

In the dim light of their new prison, Tomás lay still, trying to breathe. Every movement felt like a new attack, with stabbing pains in his belly and back that came from the brutal beating.

"It'll be dark soon," Tomás said.

"I'm here, brother. It will be all right," Chrétien murmured.

Beatriz brushed her hair back. "We need to find our way out before dark."

"Before dark? I'll settle for 'before we die of thirst,'" Tomás said.

She had a knife in her hands and tapped at the edges of the stones in the floor. Tomás blinked to see clearly. It was his knife.

"Where did you get that?"

"Sebastián pushed it into the pocket of my robe."

"It's my dagger. You're ruining it. What are you doing?"

"This house was built by crusaders. No crusaders with experience in the Holy Land would leave a room on the lower floor with only one way out. It makes no sense."

She scratched at the edges of stones, attempting to pry them up with the blade of the knife.

"How do you know crusaders built this house?" Chrétien asked.

"It's the domus for Felicia's family. Her uncle held it."

Tomás and Chrétien knocked and kicked at stones, listening for any that sounded different. Chrétien said, "You've been here before?"

"We visited when we were children. We didn't hear otherwise last summer, so we assumed the family was lost when—*Ai!*" she cried. One flagstone yielded to the blade.

Tomás and Chrétien worked the nearby stones free to reveal a wooden trap door. The last of the afternoon light from the slit high on the wall barely reached into the hole.

Chrétien had a hand on Tomás's shoulder. "We'll all go down together. Beatriz, you come behind Tomás so he knows we're both close by."

"Why? He's our famous protector knight. Or is he afraid of the dark?"

"*Òc,*" Tomás said. "I am."

"We're going down now," Chrétien said.

It took an eternity. Tomás focused on counting: fifty-two paces made with one hand against the wall and one on Chrétien's shoulder, softly singing "*Chanterai por Mon Corage,*" feeling the pull of pain in his belly, and then at last hearing Chrétien knock against wood.

"Who knows where this will take us?" Chrétien said.

"The street." Beatriz sounded more confident than Tomás felt. "We didn't go far enough to be outside of the city."

They were in an alley across from a church, the last one they'd visited while asking whether anyone knew where the abbot of St-Féliz-de-Fontcours slept in Béziers.

Tomás leaned against the stone wall of the church, panting, sweat from fear running down the back of his neck as he tried to gauge whether he'd done any better in the darkness this time.

"The daylight is gone," Chrétien said. "The gates are barred so we can't get out of the city tonight."

"We have to go back into the house anyway," Tomás said. "We may find arms or food."

They next worked to break into the villa from which they'd just escaped, finding a way over the wall and through the doors of the deserted and undefended household. They searched the rooms for what would help their journey, finding the surcoats they wore when captured and a single sword. No food. No armor.

And then they set the house afire.

Beatriz said, "If Felicia can't have it, neither can our enemies."

As the Frankish conquerors of Béziers flooded out into the streets to keep the fire from spreading to their own stolen homes, the three refugees slipped into the shadows. They found an alcove in one of the unrepaired churches where they could sleep. And Tomás and Chrétien took turns creeping through the city, one seeking food and whatever else might aid their journey while the other man stayed behind with Beatriz.

In the morning when the city gates opened, two scribes and a tall Celtic mercenary set out afoot on the road to Carcassonne.

.

"We're alive," Tomás said.

Chrétien said, "I managed to piss without passing out. That weasel Raoul kicked me right in the kidneys."

"When did he have time? He tried to kill me with his boots."

"I haven't been so bruised since we first trained with our swordmasters in Cairo."

"But the abbot has Sebastián."

"And Durán," Chrétien said. "He has Durán, too."

"But they're together," Tomás said. "God at least granted that bit of luck."

They whispered so their voices wouldn't carry to Beatriz, who was attending to nature in a nearby cypress stand.

"Thank you for saying so," Chrétien said. "And not saying the other thing."

"What?"

"Sebastián will be protecting Durán, not the other way around."

"I never even thought it."

"Are they safe, since they're his grandchildren?" Chrétien said.
"They are both happy to find a brother."

"Except they're only cousins," Tomás said.

"No, I'm sure Renoud believed Nicolau is Durán's father. He treated Sebastián more like his own—*ai Dèu.*"

"Never say it."

"That's what rattled you into killing Renoud? That's why—*ai Dèu.* Poor Isabella."

"Please don't speak of it. Only Father Anselm and Katelina know. The abbot seems ignorant of it."

"But Durán must know," Chrétien said. "He stayed behind and heard all. Why didn't he tell me?"

"Because he's a better man than I am. He's faithful to Isabella."

Beatriz came down the path to join them. Since she was so small, one could already see the outline of the baby growing in her belly, even through the scribe's robe she wore.

Speaking again, to cover the jealousy he felt, Tomás said. "Jean-Luc had better be alive. Beatriz blames me for leaving him in Minerve."

"Because, *punxor*, you're a cock-up. And after Raoul's work last night, you're even uglier than you were before." Chrétien laughed at him, which felt consoling.

"I'm fortunate Beatriz didn't leave me in the house before torching it. I swear she wants to kill me."

Chrétien said, "The only people who don't want to kill you just haven't met you yet."

"*Òc*, I'm the biggest fool who ever cocked up his own life. Do you think I'm a sodding arsewit, like everyone else does?"

"You know I'm not one to indulge in obsequious praise."

Beatriz joined them. "Let's go. We won't get to Minerve sitting on a rock in the sun."

·

At night, they couldn't travel safely on foot, and when they stopped to find a protected place to sleep, Beatriz insisted they turn over every rock in the area to check for scorpions.

Chrétien had the first watch, since he said it hurt worse to lie down than to sit as guard from the top of the boulder pile that hid them from the road. Tomás showed Beatriz how to spread her robe to serve as a cover against the dew. Then he began to spread his own cloak, with the pain of his cracked ribs magnified by fatigue from their long walk.

"Sleep over there," Beatriz said.

"Senhóreta, I'll sleep here, close by, solely to protect you."

"Chrétien is keeping watch. I won't have you beside me."

"You used up your ration of complaints for the day, senhóreta. This is not negotiable."

"You cannot command me."

"By all laws of Church and king, I can, ma dòmna. I am the consort of the only married child in your domus. Until you marry or come of age, you are ruled by me as much as your sister is."

"She's not my sister, and you are the world's poorest excuse for a consort. I won't have you this close to me."

"Jesus and the weeping angels. You can't walk too fast, because it's jarring. You don't like your bed because of scorpions. You won't eat the food we find because it makes you throw up. I spent a month on the road with your sister, and she never complained once, except to regret how her clothes smelled of horse when she had to sleep in them. She was happy to bathe in a stream."

"If you would find a stream to bathe in, I'd give thanks to God. It would be much more pleasant."

Tomás exploded. "How could any man endure being around you long enough to give you a baby?"

"Maybe he had less barbarous sensibilities than you. And far better manners."

"Are you calling me a barbarian? Your sister is as civilized as any woman in Christendom. She never complained about my sensibilities." Tomás seethed. "There's nothing wrong with my manners."

"I wouldn't know. I've never seen them."

"I'm sleeping beside you for your protection. My manners aren't in consideration."

Tomás, glad to be free of his scribe's robe, lay in just breeches and shirt, letting the night air cool his body, hoping it would cool his temper. He turned on his side, his back to the rankling senhóreta of Castell-de-Valerós. Pain wracked him, so he had to lie on his back again, facing the stars.

"Am I to believe you could protect me?" Beatriz wouldn't let him rest. "It was I, with Sebastián's help, who got us out of that house."

"I swore to Pèire I would protect his children." Tomás bit his tongue for having answered her.

"Heaven forbid you are ever my enemy," she said. "Everyone knows what you did to my sister. It's pathetic that she's still in love with you."

"How do you know? Did she say anything?" Even as he spoke, he felt he'd fallen into a trap.

"No. But I could tell."

"And you're an expert about love because you got the loneliest man in the world to go to bed with you?"

"I didn't send the person who loves me into the greatest peril in Christendom."

"And I won't be so barbaric as to compare that with what you did to Senhóra Katelina," Tomás said. "Nor was I ever so uncivilized as to let a poor leper think he slept with his best friend's betrothed."

"No, you merely humiliated the only woman on earth aberrant enough to care for you."

"Here's my knife, senhóreta. Just cut my throat so I don't have to listen to you anymore."

Beatriz kept silent for several long moments. Then she said, "Since we must go on together, we'll forget what just happened."

"How can we forget?"

"I'll apologize and then you'll apologize."

"When every goat in town dies. Ai Dèu."

"I'm sorry I brought it to your attention how you hurt Isabella," Beatriz said. "I'm sorry I didn't tell Jean-Luc my name, even if he didn't tell me his. Now it's your turn."

"I'm sorry I was ever born. I'm sorry my mother didn't leave my father to rot in that Syrian citadel. I'm sorry my grandfather ever came into the same county as my grandmother."

"Without a doubt, you'd be as extravagant in humility as you are in conceit."

Tomás pondered joining Chrétien at his guard post. He considered leaving Beatriz at the first religious house they could find. Then he remembered the nights they traveled with Isabella, which was false nostalgia.

"I'm sorry I sent Katelina away, so that you went to find her. It made Isabella run after you." Beatriz spoke quietly, just above a whisper, but there was no trace of a whine or complaint in her voice. "This whole nightmare is my fault."

"I believed that for a long time. But no. Your anger just started things a few moments sooner than when those Montcava bastards stole Sebastián and burned the wool bar at Valerós. No one blames you for being angry, senhóreta."

"Katelina came to Fontcours," Beatriz said. "When you left the Vale of Roses, you thought Katelina had been murdered, but she hid in the infirmary among the sick Valerós knights left behind. She rode with them to Senhóra Paulette's, and then to Fontcours with Guillem after he left Carcassonne. Blessedly, she forgave me. And Isabella did, too, I hope."

"Will she forgive me? Believe me, I know what my sins are."

"Perhaps, if she's alive. Is Jean-Luc still tortured, believing it's Felicia he loved?"

"Isabella must have found him by now and told him. And I think they're alive. Wouldn't we feel it if they died?"

She pressed her hand against his mouth. "Please don't speak of it."

He gazed up into the stars, wanting to be lost in sleep. After a long while he heard her sigh and turn over beside him. "Perhaps my sister is stupid enough to forgive you."

"She's not stupid," Tomás said.

"But she forgets things. That's your best hope."

61
Fever

"WE'RE GOING TO DIE, aren't we?" Isabella said.

"It seems so." Jean-Luc didn't feel as defeated as Isabella sounded. A thin strain of a psalm to the glory of God drifted to where they talked, carried down by Anselm's sail. "But faith is all I've had for so long, I can't quit now."

"Did you convince the mayor to surrender?"

"I don't know. What would convince you if it were Valerós?"

"Nothing. I never would. Come back to the infirmary with me," Isabella said. "I want to sit with Father Anselm. He's not well."

"Yes. And I want to see you drink your water instead of giving half of it to others."

"I only give it to the nursing mothers."

"Their children will be dead soon. It won't help. You'll just join them sooner. Have you eaten?"

"There's only cheese and old bread. It makes one thirsty."

Joining Father Anselm, they found he'd closed the infirmary, his last patient having died. The priest was pale and hot.

"It's a touch of camp fever, I fear," he said. "I sent everyone away so it wouldn't spread from me."

"It'll be through the whole town soon," Jean-Luc said, "and it won't have come from you."

He helped Isabella make the priest comfortable.

"I'm always the healer, not the one in the sick bed," Father Anselm said. "I make a poor patient."

"We'll get along well then. I'm a poor physician," Isabella said.

Father Anselm rested his hand on hers. "I saw you with the mothers today, trying to help them with their children."

"I'd rather be on the battlements," she said. "But the men don't want me there, after so many asked me to write their confessions."

"It happens," the priest said.

"Let me do as you did for me," Isabella said, "when you prayed for me and saved my life."

Father Anselm said, "I need prayers. Someone should intercede for me, since I've given so many absolutions while excommunicated for remaining here."

Jean-Luc wrapped his hand around Anselm's wrist, where the mark of the bonfraires had been burned. "Now we are brothers in more ways than just this one."

"It hurts," Father Anselm whispered. "Being cast out when I'm only doing what I believe God wants me to do. I couldn't leave these people."

"You have the hardest way of all," Jean-Luc said. "I can't blame the Church for applying the law, since men lied in accusing me."

"I admire you for keeping your faith when you were cast out of the fellowship of men."

Jean-Luc grasped the priest's hand more tightly. "Since you're already outside the Church, will you—" He stopped, since it was too much to ask for absolution when he'd been excluded from the communion of saints.

"Hear your confession?" Father Anselm whispered. "Of course. Isabella, perhaps you could leave us?"

"She may as well stay. She knows most all of it. Or has guessed."

Jean-Luc knelt beside Father Anselm and felt the priest's hand settle over his head.

"Bless me, for I have fallen short of the glory of God."

And he told it all, until his voice ripped raw, just like when he'd confessed to the young woman in his loft over the smithy at Valerós:

What he'd done to his brother. And then his cowardly escape from home, after he saw the same expression of surprise and horror on his father's face as on Yves's face when he died.

The nights of doubt that gnawed at his soul, when he was barely able to keep from cursing God.

The years of betrayal, thinking he was in love with his lord's wife and acting on his carnal desires for her.

The faithless act of adultery against Beatriz, when he lay once more with his lord's wife.

"And for your liaison with Beatriz?" Father Anselm said.

"Since Constantinople, I've spent every moment longing for mercy," Jean-Luc said. "I can believe God forgives me, but I didn't find comfort until Beatriz came to me. That wasn't a sin. Except I doubted her afterwards. Father, I need forgiveness for that."

After, Jean-Luc finally slept.

.

Before dawn, Father Anselm's fever cooled. He dozed off.

"Come sleep beside me," Jean-Luc said to Isabella. "*Bon Dieu*, don't act like a spooked cat. I only want a friend by me. I don't want to be alone any more. And neither do you."

She did as he asked, lying down awkwardly beside him, both in their sweat-stained clothes.

"Isabella, I'm worried. Your mind is wandering. You mustn't share your water ration with others."

"I'm fine. I'm distracted from worrying about Father Anselm."

Jean-Luc rolled onto his side and, despite the heat, pulled her closer to him, rocking her in his arms. He felt the sharp bones of her thin shoulders and hips as he whispered to her. "It feels odd to lie by a woman again."

"I think about him only when I'm trying to sleep."

"That's when we most need comfort, isn't it?"

"When we lay down at night to be free of this mortal world?" She whispered, too. "I lie here at night, thinking I'm imitating death by escaping into sleep. It can't be so bad to die."

"Do you find comfort in prayer, Isabella?"

"Not for a while now."

"Beatriz and I pray to the Virgin Mother. She can help you know God's beneficence. She can intercede for you.

"But you shouldn't need an intermediary," she whispered. "That's one teaching of the goodmen that I understand. We don't need a priest to lead us to God. But many just put their teachers in place of the priests to ask for intercession. I want to do it myself, to speak directly to God. I want Him to explain His faithless nature."

"This is heresy," Jean-Luc said. It was the same sort of thing Yves used to say. He held her closely, wanting her to stop thinking.

"No, I like how God has so many contradictory aspects. I like trying to understand how God could be good when the world holds so much evil. I like thinking God doesn't always care, yet sometimes He punishes me."

"There aren't contradictions. Our faith is just too weak to understand. I believe the pride of a fallen angel created confusion and evil, like in my own life. I believe God permits it because He has faith we'll find our way back to Him."

She squirmed in his arms. "If I didn't already know that God is capricious, I'd go mad explaining the contradictions day after day."

"You like the confusion, Isabella, because you believe you're smart enough to think your way back to God."

"Òc," she said, "if I have enough time. Though I haven't figured how to think my way back to my husband, so I don't know why I have the hubris to think about God."

"You need water and food, Isabella. Your mind isn't clear."

"Things are much clearer to me every day." Isabella moved closer to Jean-Luc, settling into his arms. "It's as if the air is lighter. The sunlight has substance, like fog or smoke. With each breath, I can feel the light coming inside me."

When he felt her fall asleep in his arms, it startled him into wakefulness, wondering if this was the last time he'd feel a woman's heartbeat under his hands and her breath whispering like the wind across his arm. He fingered the braid in his hair that entwined Beatriz's strands with his, as he often did to find comfort. He worried about Isabella's bright-eyed but confused musings, fearing she was falling ill. He wondered whether Beatriz was safe and whether their child would look like its mother, then wondered what his father would do with a child in the house, especially if Jean-Luc wasn't there to join them.

Then, strangely free of worry, he wondered whether his two friends sleeping here in the infirmary were waiting to be free to begin life again, or merely waiting to die.

62

Nunc Dimittis

WHEN ISABELLA RETURNED TO the infirmary at sunrise, when the monks' changed to a new song, she found Jean-Luc stoking a charcoal fire in the brazier.

"What are you doing?"

Jean-Luc fanned the fire with a small hand-bellows.

"Father Anselm drifts in and out. When he was last lucid, he had an idea, so I want to fill his wish. Where have you been?"

"With the mothers on the battlements."

Feeling light-headed, she sat beside him. She'd been with the goodwomen and Catholic mothers on the wall, praying over the children consigned at night to God's care. After so many days, she still couldn't fathom what it must be to lose a child.

"I feel so sorry for them," she said. "Afterwards, I went to see Eloïse and her friends. They are all praying, too, but it confused me, to go from the weeping mothers to these goodwomen who seem content that we're all about to die. They pray just as fervently as the mothers, but they seem transported with joy."

"The goodmen and their closest followers stopped eating several days ago. They're probably hallucinating about God from sheer starvation," Jean-Luc said.

She could feel the heat from Anselm's fever before she even touched him.

"Pray for us, O Holy Mother of God," she murmured.

"That we may be made worthy," Father Anselm said. "I'm not drifting. We want you to join our bonfraires while I can still say the prayers, ma dòmna."

Jean-Luc came beside them. "I'll say the prayer. Save yourself to just give us the blessing, Father."

The priest agreed, his hands folded over Isabella's as Jean-Luc repeated the long prayer Isabella first heard in the cellars of Castell-de-Valerós. Then Father Anselm gave the benediction every priest says at the close of a Mass.

"This is our oath," Father Anselm said. "You must put your hands on the cross and repeat after me."

Jean-Luc offered his sword to serve as the cross. Isabella put one hand on the cross-piece while Father Anselm grasped her other hand in prayer.

"*Sodalitas, fidelitas, virtus.* Upon my honor I swear absolute loyalty to my brothers when called to arms."

Isabella repeated his words, her heart aching for how weak Father Anselm sounded.

"I swear on the name of Our Savior and on St-Jordi to stand by my lord and king. I swear to stand ever ready to serve as a defender of the poor and of the Holy Catholic Church."

Isabella felt the priest's hand tremble as she spoke. Jean-Luc held her hand as he stamped the hot crossbow bolt onto her wrist. She cried out, and then felt ashamed to show her pain when the priest was suffering. Jean-Luc embraced her, to comfort them both, just as the door at the top of the stairs was thrust open.

"Senhór Ghuilhem commands your presence!" a voice shouted. "There isn't a moment to lose."

Jean-Luc bounded up the stairs. Isabella wondered faintly where he found the strength. She settled beside Father Anselm and repeated the same prayers he'd taught her as a girl. There was only enough water for her to wet the priest's lips. Her throat felt parched from all the praying, and her head ached, throbbing in time with the burn on her wrist. But there was nothing to do except sit and wait, as they had for weeks.

She fell into a dream, knowing it was a dream. Sebastián called to her. Pèire began another of his lie-and-boast tales of crusading. But she was seated too far away to hear.

She roused from the false dream. After again wetting Father Anselm's lips, she said a prayer automatically, without attending to the words, eager to drift again and hear Pèire tell the story. And then Tomás was there, smiling as he had at Anfos's cottage, as if he cared for her. She could see his lips move when he said something, but she couldn't hear the words. She reached out to touch his lips.

"They're probably all dead now."

She heard the words, and it made her think she too was dead. This was what it was like: almost like being alive, but you couldn't see well.

Then Jean-Luc appeared among the faces of all her other friends who must be dead now. But she heard him speak.

"Minerve is surrendering. Help me carry Anselm up the steps."

63

Chartrain Avant

A QUARTER TURN OF the sun after dawn on the feast of St-Mary Magdalene, the monks ceased singing. Murmurs passed around the camp. Soon, Gerard heard the news: the mayor signaled Minerve's surrender. By midday, men were obeying Simon de Montfort's command to break up the crusaders' camp. All makeshift shelters, the woven pine-and-broom sun-covers, and cooks' stocks of firewood were demanded for the pyres.

Beatriz returned to Gerard's camp just as Simon's men departed to harass the next encampment to yield up its wood and trash.

"Hello, Father," Beatriz said. "We're safe."

Relief rushed through his blood as Gerard embraced her. He'd forgotten how small she was, for how large his worry had been.

Miquel's son, who brought her to Gerard's camp, barely said *bon día* before he dropped into a black rage over Simon's command.

"Simon can't—not again! He's preparing a burning, isn't he? Does Pedro know? Is he back from St-Gilles? Can't the king stop that monster?"

Beatriz appeared to be well, but Tomás and Chrétien had taken severe beatings from either the crusader army or rebels. Both had the grey, haggard look of men campaigning too long on short rations.

"Is there word of Jean-Luc and Isabella?" Beatriz asked.

Gerard said, "Not yet. But they are bringing out the hostages and the Catholic defenders soon. We shall see them then." He tried to see past Chrétien. "Has Hugues joined his men? Where is Sebastián?"

"Hugues is with the abbot," Beatriz said. "And the abbot still has Sebastián and Durán."

Chrétien said, "Hugues has been ill. The abbot's men carried him away."

"I should have been able to stop him." Tomás ceased raging over Simon's men gathering wood for a pyre, his face a picture of grief.

"Impossible," Chrétien said. "The abbot left us to die in a house in Béziers, but we escaped and walked here."

"Did he hurt you?" Gerard asked Beatriz, wondering how a woman walked from Béziers to Minerve in her condition.

"He only kept me locked in a room and frightened. Tomás and Chrétien fared less well."

Gerard described the message he'd sent to the bishop of Toulouse about Esak's evil doings. "We must also tell the bishop what happened to you. But no one will attend to our story until this business in Minerve is over."

"We have to find Isabella," Tomás said.

"Don't worry, lad." Gerard put a hand on the man's shoulder. "Under the terms of surrender, everyone goes free who will say the creed. All will be well before the day ends. We have to struggle only with our impatience."

"Do you believe that, monsieur?" Beatriz said. "If you believe it, I will, too."

"Jean-Luc is French," Tomás said. "Ghuilhem will claim he was a hostage. If he's alive."

"I know he is," Beatriz said.

"Let me get food and wine for you," Gerard said. "There isn't water to wash, but we can find clean surcoats. Senhóreta Beatriz, what are you wearing? We need clothes for you, too."

"It's a robe Tomás stole from the farm laundry yesterday. It's a bit large."

"A surcoat is best for you too, senhóreta, so every man can see you belong with—"

"The conquerors?" Tomás's voice burned with bitterness. "We don't want anyone mistaking us for the wretches they plan to burn. We must find Isabella."

Gerard convinced them to take cheese and bread, and then they gathered a dozen Valerós and Chartrain knights as they picked their way among the camps to the road trailing down the canyon and back up to the gates of Minerve. People rushed to see the punishment of the rebels and heretics.

When trumpets sounded, it was the harsh, deep trumpets used to rally men in battle.

"They're bringing out the hostages," Gerard said, excited.

His words were lost as Simon de Montfort and another French lord came out of Minerve. A tremendous cheer went up among the French crusaders, who greeted Simon as a great conqueror.

"Who the devil is the other man?" Tomás muttered.

"It's my son," a small woman beside them said. Gerard glanced down at the old woman, recognizing Mathilde de Garlande from the Pays de France. "Bouchard de Marly. He's been hostage at Lastours this entire season. Pèire-Roger, the lord there, surrendered his hostages last fortnight. Simon wanted to honor Bouchard along with the hostages from Minerve."

A cheer rose again when a trio of men walked through the gates: Jean-Luc with two others, all of them with fleur-de-lis surcoats thrown over their shoulders. Jean-Luc looked as if he'd suffered through the throes of hell. Gerard felt his heart thump, the same as the morning his wife first presented Jean-Luc as a newborn infant. He pulled Beatriz close to him, wanting to shout out his son's name.

"Do you know the others?" Chrétien said to Tomás.

"They lived at the mayor's house, but I didn't know they were hostages. Perhaps 'hostage' in the common tongue means a seigneur who repents of dallying with rebels."

"Likely the mayor presented them to Simon as hostages to protect their families." Gerard swallowed hard, amazed he could speak.

"Why isn't Isabella with them?" Tomás said.

As cheers went up again for the hostages, Jean-Luc scanned the crowd. When he saw Beatriz and Gerard, he dropped the surcoat and ran to them, wrapping first Beatriz and then his father in his arms.

"O Father, I love you," his son murmured in his ear.

With his son's arm around him, Gerard breathed a prayer while feeling the boy's bones, sharp from starvation. Then Jean-Luc greeted Beatriz as if seeing her were his only hunger.

"*Chérie*, don't let me go again."

After a moment, Simon turned in impatience and spoke to his men, who surrounded Jean-Luc and urged him on. Beatriz and Gerard walked at his side. Tomás and Chrétien followed with a gaggle of Gerard's own knights.

"Where's Isabella?" Tomás demanded Jean-Luc's attention several times. "Where's Father Anselm?"

"She's with the women." Jean-Luc glanced away from Beatriz for only a moment. "The mayor begged me to come out as a hostage, and I couldn't find Isabella or Anselm to bring them along. They will bring the Catholics out at midday."

"Why so long?" Tomás said.

"They are saying the creed for the priests who travel with the prelate. It will take time."

"This is unendurable."

Following the road up the plateau, they came to where the Church leaders were encamped behind the pavisses and barricades, where no arrows or missiles could reach from atop the walls of Minerve. As Jean-Luc and Beatriz whispered to each other, Gerard moved away to give them a private space.

Then once more the unpredictable Moor had his sword in his hand, roaring at a passel of mercenaries in the road who wore Montcava colors. Gerard wished the son had inherited more of Miquel's grace, sure Tomás would drag them into a problem with the bishops' and prelates' men. Then he saw Sebastián, who looked exactly as Pèire Leteric had when they first met as boys.

Tomás shifted his stance, prepared to take on the six mercenaries surrounding the boy. In a heartbeat, Chrétien was at Tomás's back, and in another beat, three of the mercenaries were bleeding in the dirt. Sebastián and his brother sprinted free to join the ring formed around Beatriz by Gerard's own men.

Just as quickly, they were all surrounded by the prelates' guard, who cried the Peace of God while forcibly restraining all of them. It took three men to immobilize Tomás.

"You, sir, aren't you the Moor who is King Pedro's bodyguard?" one man shouted.

Tomás said, "I am the regent of Montcava. These men holding my son are not my knights. Take these false knights away and leave us the two donzels of our domus."

One of the prelates' guards said, "You're wearing Chartrain colors. The viscount's men don't brawl in the dust like rabble."

Gerard stepped forward to settle the peace. "These men have just come from chivalrous service to my son's wife. It is as they say. These others are false knights who stole the true heirs of Montcava."

At Gerard's word, the false knights were taken away. Sebastián and Durán were both breathless with excitement. Durán said, "The abbot came to get Senhóra Eloïse and Isabella from Minerve. He means to take them away with us."

Sebastián said, "He had his men inside Minerve this morning with the French, trying to free them."

"But they didn't succeed."

"Then crazy Raoul quarreled with the abbot and carried us away," Sebastián said, "but you found us."

Tomás and Chrétien hugged the two boys, both so happy it wasn't clear they listened to what Sebastián and Durán said.

"Where is the abbot?" Gerard said.

"Right there." Sebastián pointed to a pavilion at the south end of the prelates' camp.

Tomás drew his sword, but Chrétien yanked at his arm, holding him back. Tomás jerked to get free, but Chrétien just grasped his arms more tightly.

"Brother, think. Half the south wants to hang the mad Moor who murders priests."

Torment crossed the young man's face. Gerard felt confused, seeing Miquel's face replicated beside the young incarnation of Pèire Leteric. Miquel would never reveal either irresolution or anguish.

Sebastián tugged at Tomás. "I don't think the abbot cares if he dies. What worse can we do to him?"

"Killing him isn't worth the trouble," Chrétien said.

Durán said. "If you try to kill him, he'll just steal your soul like Renoud did."

"Leave him to me," Jean-Luc said.

"No, you have too much to lose," Tomás said.

"We have to seize him," Gerard said.

At Gerard's command, Chartrain knights defeated the mercenaries guarding the abbot's pavilion and then encircled Beatriz outside the tent to protect her.

Tomás said, "Senhór Gerard, please leave us a brace of your knights while you fetch the prelates' men to take the abbot away."

"You are sure?" Gerard hesitated, his sword still unsheathed.

"Handing him to the Church is the right thing to do. Though I don't know how long I can hold my resolve. Everything in me wants to cut him open the way my father was done."

"Take Beatriz, Father," Jean-Luc said. "Leave me your sword."

"No, I want to stay with you." Beatriz spoke with the same fierce heat as the men.

"*Chérie*, I don't want you to see this. Please take her as far from here as you can, Father."

"I can't bear to be away from you so soon."

"Yes, you can," Jean-Luc said. "Aren't you a crusader's wife? Aren't they braver than the men they're married to?"

64
Endura

Isabella inside Minerve, July 22

IT WASN'T A DREAM. The light had grown too bright. It shimmered around people's faces, making it hard to tell who she was with. She helped Jean-Luc carry Father Anselm up from the infirmary, and they laid him on a pallet under a portico. The whole time they worked their way up the steps with the priest, Jean-Luc talked.

"Simon will let anyone go who says the creed of the Apostles. His soldiers are coming soon. You must stay with the women, and I'll be going with the men."

Isabella saw his lips move, but only understood half of it.

"Sancta Maria, Isabella. Go find the women you prayed with last night. Tell them they'll be safe if they say their creed. All of you must stay together. Help them not to be afraid."

As they came out onto the city streets, voices shrieked and cried everywhere. People moved in all directions, but everyone was so enfeebled it could scarcely be called running.

"The women are in the church, Isabella. Go there now. Father Anselm will be safe here until the other men come for him."

A soldier motioned for Jean-Luc to follow.

"Isabella," he called as he ran off, "go now!"

She crouched beside Father Anselm and held his hand, the way he had held hers in Laurac. She no longer had water to wet his lips. She tried to share the wetness of her own mouth, but when she licked her hand, there was nothing there.

A man knelt beside her. The old crusader who first made her welcome in Minerve. He said, "I heard Anselm was ill. We didn't know it had come this."

"There's no water. We can only pray."

Other men joined him.

"We should say the final prayers," one said.

Another man spoke. "We've done nothing but say those prayers, day and night for eternity."

The old crusader whose name was Calvert said, "This man is special. We want him delivered into God's hands. He was a good man, however his allegiance fell."

"The woman must go," another said.

They began to say the final goodmen's prayers over him.

"No." Isabella's lips cracked as she spoke. She lay down beside the priest, entwining her arms around his neck.

"You mustn't let your woman's flesh come between man and God," one said.

She could hear Father Anselm's light, raspy breath and felt his chest rise as he inhaled. "You can't say those prayers over him. You must not."

"Is it ever such?" a man said. "Woman forever corrupting man, trapping souls here in the world of evil."

She had no strength left, but they couldn't lift her away from the priest, and instead they carried Anselm and Isabella as a single load and deposited them amidst a crowd of women who all prayed together, holding hands.

Afraid to let go of her friend, she stayed wrapped around Father Anselm, listening to the prayers.

"We don't need to be afraid if we believe." What did Jean-Luc say that she must tell the women? "We just have to pray and tell them what we believe. We'll be fine."

"Come, pray with us," a warm, kindly voice said. "Leave your friend. God will tend him."

A white-haired woman helped Isabella to her feet and pulled her into the circle of praying women. Isabella embraced them, held up more by the women's locked arms than standing on her own. She sang and prayed with them, though she felt so exhausted, she just wanted to lie down beside Father Anselm and sleep until either God took them or the French let them live again. But Jean-Luc told her to help the women, to pray with them so they wouldn't be afraid.

The circle of women held her up, and she sang until she felt dizzy. Her cracked lips felt moist again. Licking her lips, she tasted salt and iron from her own blood.

The French came then. She broke away from the women to stay with Father Anselm, though the women urged her to remain with them. That's what Jean-Luc told her to do, but she worried about Father Anselm.

"Sancta Maria!" one of the soldiers shouted. "They have a priest here. God knows what vile things they must have done to him."

65
Another Cain

SEBASTIÁN AND DURÁN WENT inside the pavilion. Tomás and Jean-Luc stepped behind them, so they saw the joy on the abbot's face when the two boys appeared. The abbot's delight shifted to anger and dismay when first Jean-Luc and then Tomás and Chrétien appeared.

"Now you noble knights will quarrel over who will slay me." The abbot sneered.

"I long to take that honor," Tomás said.

"No," Jean-Luc said. "Let the Church deal justice. We'll pass the days till then, thinking about you in hell."

The abbot stared at Jean-Luc. "*Ai*, Cain, I find pleasure each day in meditating on the pain I've dealt my enemies."

Tomás said, "Didn't you hear what happened in Minerve? Jean-Luc found valor where you meant to deal pain, Pare Abát."

The abbot gazed at Tomás with intense hatred. "Any worthless mestitz children his Saracen concubine gave him will inherit nothing. Miquel's name is now as meaningless as sand across Christendom."

"My son lives, and so will Jean-Luc's," Tomás said. "Yours are carrion for bone-sucking vultures."

"Indeed, I didn't get all the satisfaction other men get from their sons. They didn't rise to become great men. But I have hope in my grandsons." The abbot's eyes flicked over to Sebastián and Durán. "They will avenge me on you."

Durán laughed at him. "Old man, you are as bad as your bastard Renoud, believing Senhóra Isabella was in love with him. All she wanted was to stick a dagger in his belly."

The abbot's smile faltered, then vanished as Durán embraced Chrétien, more as lovers do than as gentlemen greet each other.

Sebastián said, "When you're dead, I'll stand on your grave in the churchyard and shout, 'Don Miquel of Fontcours is my grandsire!'"

"This abbot," Jean-Luc said, "will not find himself buried on hallowed ground."

■

"Sebastián." Tomás called him over, returning the dagger Beatriz had used to free them. "You saved our lives, *cavaller* Valerós."

He wanted to give Sebastián his borrowed sword, too, to remove temptation. He remained a sword's length away from the abbot, studying the man to see how such a small wretch of humanity could cause so much pain.

"Before the Churchmen come to rescue you, O damnable Pare Abát, pray tell who you sent to harm Isabella. Especially the man who hunted her at Valerós. Was it the same man who killed the priest in the Valerós latrines?"

"I would never harm the senhóra."

"No? You left it to your sons to do it for you?"

"Never. She's the wife of my son. She's the cousin of my beloved and stands equal to her among the angels." The abbot closed his eyes, as if keeping private thoughts.

It struck Tomás like a sword's blow: the abbot didn't know about Renoud and Isabella, and he didn't know who hunted her. Tomás let his hatred seep away so he could do the right thing, free of the beguiling passion to kill the man. It wouldn't be an act of anger, as with Renoud, just the passionate fulfillment of a promise made in the name of his father's honor. He could feel the blade go in; he'd watch the abbot's face as his soul was cut free of its moorings to sail away with the devil. When Tomás pulled the blade free, he'd wipe it clean with the hem of his tormentor's robe and then wash it in a stream. The last of the man's blood would seep into the ground and rivers of the south. Isabella and Jean-Luc—and the ghosts of Miquel and Pèire if they watched—would be free of the man's malice forever. His hand and arm could feel it, the most divine sensation of the best thrust and slice he might ever make, the jolt up his hand and the release as he followed through and then pulled his blade free.

A groan came from behind the tent's dividing curtain. Jean-Luc thrust the curtain aside with the point of his sword. He returned with Hugues resting against his shoulder.

·

"I'm so sorry for your troubles," Hugues said. "If only I'd taken better care."

"None of it was your fault, my lord." Jean-Luc murmured his dismay at finding Hugues so ill.

"I should have recognized the lies." Hugues brushed aside any consolation. "I could have cut short your suffering, and your father's, if I'd succeeded in pleading your cause with the king."

"I don't deserve your kind attentions," Jean-Luc said.

"There isn't a better knight in the Pays de France. I wish I had a son like you. None of you deserved my brother plaguing you with revenge over petty slights."

The abbot's face was twisted up in a red rage, the first emotion he'd shown besides scorn. "Murder my son? Cuckold my brother? Who thinks such slights petty?"

"The man who murdered Pèire Leteric's son? Who cuckolded my father?" Tomás said. "The man whose own life is a tissue of perjuries and deceits?"

"You filthy mestitz *baquelar*." The abbot sniffed, ferret-like. "Your bonfraire sodomite father robbed my brother of his innocence. You now try the same with my grandchild."

"Is everyone else's joy a sin," Tomás said, "because you can only get children by raping another man's wife?"

Tomás missed seeing the petite jeweled dagger in the abbot's hand until the abbot lunged for him. Tomás stepped aside so that the abbot fell against him, almost as if they were embracing.

Hugues let out a sigh behind him, like the sound of a lover finding release, and then his head lay on Tomás's shoulder.

"*Aiieee!*" the abbot screamed, stepping back from Tomás, the ferret's smile replaced by a mask of horror. Tomás caught Hugues in his arms, bumping the jeweled knife where it stuck in the old man's lower ribs.

"You killed the best knight in Christendom," Tomás murmured.

"*What hast thou done?*" Jean-Luc cried out in Church Latin. "You are another Cain."

Tomás sank to the ground under Hugues's frail weight. The man was still breathing, foamy flecks at his lips. Tomás held Hugues again, as he had in Béziers. He brushed the lank locks of hair away, trying to wipe Hugues's lips and mouth so he could breathe freely.

"You were always so beautiful," Hugues whispered. His fingers traced Tomás's lips. "And I loved you so."

Tomás touched Hugues's cheek, knowing the man mistook him for Miquel. "You'll be well, *bon amic.*"

"Not this time," Hugues murmured. "*Via com Dèu.*"

·

While Jean-Luc howled in rage and grief, Tomás found his arms were too full to draw his sword. Instead, Tomás wept. Holding Hugues, he cried the tears he held back when his father died, when he'd been too full of his own pain. He wept for their final goodbye when he and Pedro pretended it was only a farewell. And he wept for Hugues, for fifty years of lost love.

"Help me, brother," he called to Chrétien, who came and lifted the marquis's sparse weight off him. Then they worked together to lay out Hugues's body. They folded Hugues's surcoat neatly over him and laid a sword at his side so he appeared as a valiant knight. Then Tomás glanced up and saw the execrable abbot, guarded by Jean-Luc, weeping, his wizened face drenched in tears. Tomás again had the beguiling desire to murder him.

"You and I are so much alike, *poulain*," the abbot said.

"Nothing is more untrue," Tomás said.

"I sold my soul to pursue revenge, like you. I loved a woman more than she loved me. You endure the same hell, rejected by both man and God. My love will walk out of Minerve into Simon's pyre. Your wife will walk out, but not into your arms. And your royal *bon amic*—"

"If loneliness defines hell, then you never defeated my father." Tomás cut him off. "Miquel had a wife who loved him with each breath every day. Pèire Leteric found the same solace in Katelina of Naxos."

"But that's what you'll never have, *poulain*. God has a special hell for you."

"My father Miquel says God is indifferent to my paltry failures."

"The Church will burn the woman who holds my soul," the abbot whispered. "There'll be nothing left for God to judge."

"There is a hell, and your soul will burn there," Jean-Luc said.

"The Church will judge our own!" Arnau Amalric's gravelly voice thundered.

As the prelate burst into the pavilion, Tomás and the others bowed their heads in the Catalan style, not bending their knees. Pedro hovered behind Arnau, his eyes on Tomás.

"What's this I hear from our lord Gerard of Chartrain? Abduction? Perjury? Murder? Villainy on top of heresy? Or do the two go in hand together down the lane?"

The abbot didn't speak, only stared at Tomás, his eyes burning. Tomás's hand still itched with the desire to send the man to the devil.

"Are you the men he has persecuted?" Arnau demanded. Close up, closer than Tomás had been in Montpelhièr, the prelate's face proved to be even more fantastically distorted by wens and moles and other blemishes. Heated from the exertion of hurrying to the pavilion, the man's face dripped perspiration among the shapeless folds of flesh.

"You?" Arnau's hot breath blasted on Tomás's face at the same moment that the king of Aragón stepped behind the prelate, with Cebrián and Marcos on either side of him. "Who are you?"

"Tomás of St-Joachim, a knight sworn to Pèire Leteric of Valerós on the Aragón frontier, a seigneur who himself swore fealty to Pedro d'Aragón." He didn't look at Pedro while claiming fidelity.

"Do I know you, Tomás of St-Joachim?"

"No, Monsenyor. I was on the last crusade as far as Zara. But there was no opportunity for us to meet."

"And of what do you accuse this man?"

"He murdered his own brother just now, as we all witnessed. The marquis Hugues de Beaurain lies here, dead at this man's hand."

"A Cain hiding among the Church's flock, eh? What else do you hold against this man?"

"The abduction of Pèire Leteric's heirs and of the heirs to Font-cours and Montcava in Toulouse."

"Toulouse, eh? Are these heretic lands?"

"No, Monsenyor. The heirs, who are standing right here, are happy to say their creed for you." Tomás claimed it, while not knowing if Durán could or would say a creed.

"What of Pèire Leteric? I remember his name from Simon's roster of seigneurs sheltering heretics. They say he murder one of Simon's gold-dousers."

"The abbot is the perjurer who placed Pèire's name on Simon's roster. Pèire's people are as loyal and Catholic as any in Aragón. And we have already rendered the accused murderer of your priest to Pedro *El Católico* for resolution." Tomás again avoided Pedro's eyes.

"Are there more crimes?"

"I can't prove them to you." Tomás kept his eyes away from Pedro, focusing on the prelate. "But he raped my father's wife, though she won't swear to it because she's become a heretic. He destroyed the Viscount de Chartrain's son through perjury in Constantinople. He sent men to attack and murder my father and Pèire Leteric's son."

Jean-Luc said, "But he hid his path so well we can't show you a single over-turned stone to prove it."

"It's of no consequence." Arnau waved his hands to indicate the insignificance of the travesties that had injured every person Tomás cared for. "The Church will hold him for the sins of Cain. But we need to go watch the healing fires. Can you hear them making ready?"

Tomás had blocked the sounds clattering outside the pavilion: the shouts and cries of men; the thunder and cracking of the wood and trash being piled to receive the heretics.

"The disappointed lords of France are still out there arguing with Simon," Arnau said. "I've given every heretic a last chance to say the proper creed. The crusader lords think my offer will keep them from their booty. But it's as I told them. Most every fool has refused the chance of salvation." Arnau was smiling in the abbot's face now. "And how about your salvation, Pare Abát? I could ask you to speak for yourself, but you are a perjurer, so how can we believe anything from you?"

"Persuade the abbot to tell us whether he's in league with anyone else," Jean-Luc said.

"Ah!" Arnau said. "They've kindled the fire. Can you smell it?"

Tomás shuddered at the expression of joy on the man's face. *Never trust a man who smiles at the idea of another's death.* That's what Miquel said.

Arnau prodded the abbot with one of his sausage-sized fingers. "How about answering, as our hero from inside Minerve asks? Who else is working evil with you?"

The abbot pointed at Tomás.

Pedro pushed aside the abbot's hand. "My seigneur has endured evil at your behest. Leave my knights alone."

Tomás stared at the red lunar cross above the back of the prelate's hand, not hearing clearly what Arnau said next.

"Carry the abbot to my tents. We'll take him to a Church court," Arnau growled. "Or do you want to plead mercy for this man, too, good king Pedro?"

Pedro said, "No, Arnau. The Church needs to show people how it punishes its own."

A voice rang out from the roadway. "The heretics are prepared for judgment!"

The prelate's lumpy, ruined face cracked with the joy as he rushed out of the pavilion, charging ahead of the men who seized the abbot. Those men pushed the abbot past Tomás.

"My son had your wife," the abbot said, "and I bought your soul, *poulain,* when you sold it to the devil to buy revenge."

"And you presumed to scold me while you live in evil?" Pedro said. Tomás kept his hand on the pommel of his sword while the prelate's men led his enemy away.

.

After the abbot left the pavilion, Pedro lingered behind. Sebastián was nearest to the king, and Pedro greeted him in the Catalan style.

"I'm sorry for your troubles, my young friend. Is all well with you now?"

"Thank you, Monsenyor. We are still waiting to fetch my mother from Minerve. May I introduce my brother to you? This is Durán of Montcava. He'll be the seigneur there, if the courts are ever free to attend to such things."

Durán's eyes darted to Sebastián, obviously astonished. He tried to imitate Sebastián's homage to the king, but Pedro was taking his hand as one Catalan knight greets his equal, creating an awkward moment where Durán was uncertain how to finish his bow. But Tomás could guess what Pedro saw: a handsome young man with a quick smile and an indefatigable desire to please.

"I'm honored." Pedro once again changed a man into his loyal vassal in a heartbeat, by offering a handshake, kind words, and respect. "Sebastián saved my life. I owe him an enormous debt. I heard you shared Sebastián's travails. Please consider me your ally, Durán of Montcava, if you need one."

"Thank you, Monsenyor." Durán behaved decently in a strange situation. "This is Chrétien of Cyprus, who is Tomás's brother."

Chrétien tried to step back, folding his arms rather than greet the king, but Tomás had told too many stories late in the night. Pedro grasped Chrétien's hand as one knight greets an equal, not giving Chrétien the opportunity to even lower his head.

"And this is Jean-Luc de Chartrain," Sebastián said.

"Ah, the man who talked Minerve into surrender." As Pedro saluted him, Jean-Luc demurred.

Then no one stood between Tomás and Pedro. Tomás stepped back as Chrétien did.

"You won't greet me, *mon amic*?" Pedro spoke in the same tone he used when Tomás came out of Minerve and Pedro tried to calm him. *Will you take comfort, mon amic?*

"For your own safety, no. Avoid me like the leper I am."

"Is that what you prefer?"

"I prefer not to harm you in any way, Monsenyor. Your enemies will use me to hurt you."

"What happened after Montpelhièr? You look awful, Tomás. Did you murder someone again? Not a priest, I hope."

"The opposite. I failed to, when I should have."

"Are you still in thrall to your revenge?"

"No, I chose to forego revenge in favor of justice. But when I see that pyre, I have doubts about the Church and justice. What should I believe, Monsenyor?"

Pedro didn't respond to the provocation. Instead he said, "Will I see you when the Valerós knights come to Barcelona?"

"No, Monsenyor. I intend to leave the south as soon as I can."

"I'm sorry you've come to hate this country, *mon amic*." Trumpets sounded nearby, drowning out Pedro's words. "They are bringing the people out of Minerve. Do you want me to greet your wife and your other friends?"

"Pedro, are they going to burn these people?"

"Only those who won't say their creed."

"I know all of them." Tomás fought the desire to cry out. Grief over Hugues still choked him. "They were my neighbors and some are my friends. The people among them that you call heretics, they are old women, young wives, cousins, brothers. They're ordinary, innocent people. Please make this stop."

"No, Tomás, I can't."

"God damn your Church for it, Pedro. God damn you for not stopping them." Tomás rocked in anger, his arms wrapped tight in frustration.

"I believe He has damned me." Pedro's voice dropped. "Have I lost your friendship? Did Arnau and Simon also destroy that in their zeal?"

The trumpets sounded again, followed by a roar from the crusaders outside the gates.

"We have to find our people from inside the city," Tomás said.

Pedro murmured his assent. "I'll send men to be sure the marquis receives the honor he's due." Then he signaled to the other men in the room and departed with Cebrián and Marcos.

"I met a king," Durán said.

"They're just men who put on their breeches like everyone else," Chrétien said. "Only it hurts worse when—"

Tomás interrupted, impatient. "Sebastián, will you come with me? Can you trust me again?"

"Òc. But before we see her, tell me what happened between my mother and you."

Before Tomás could answer, Durán said, "Renoud told Tomás terrible lies, worse than how he lied to us."

"But I should never have listened." Tomás was grateful for the partial truths Durán now told. "Father Anselm proved what a fool I was. I trespassed on her trust."

The trumpet calls bounced from the castle walls to echo in the canyon below Minerve.

"Let's go! Chrétien, Durán, fetch the Valerós knights to join us at the gates. Sebastián and I are going there now." Tomás had hold of Sebastián's arm and was already running.

"I'm coming, too," Jean-Luc said.

66

The Promise of the Pyre

Tomás outside Minerve, July 22

EVERYONE IN THE INVADERS' camp came out in excited hopes for a good view, so Tomás, Sebastián, and Jean-Luc could only make progress by squirming through the bustle and commotion of Brabançon mercenaries, *routiers* from Maine, and even Greek *coterels* in the pay of a Norman or Frankish lord from the Pays de France. The footsoldiers shuffled into place shoulder-to-shoulder with knights and lords, since only the prelates and Churchmen could command a better view of the pyres prepared at the bottom of the canyon.

It was a festival. Since they could now all pack and leave the overheated plateau, there was no need to hoard the wine, which flowed freely from botas and leather flasks passed hand to hand among the men. Everyone on the outside was happy to end the boredom of the siege, and even happier at the prospect of a burning.

Because of the sense of celebration, most men were good-natured about the jostling as Sebastián and Tomás wiggled through the blade-thin spaces left between bodies. People recognized Jean-Luc from earlier and parted at the sight of him. The three of them came to the edge of the road leading from the gate into the canyon, arriving just as the last of the Catholic defenders departed the gates. A coterie of women followed a priest carrying a large wooden crucifix.

"Have you seen her?" Sebastián shouted across the way to the Valerós knights.

Benito called back, "They've taken all the Catholics out. We saw Father Anselm, but we didn't see her."

"No!" Sebastián cried.

Tomás looked to the gates as a surge went through the crowd.

A shout. "Swine of Satan!"

"Devil's offal!"

The air thundered with catcalls as the gates were thrust further open and a pack of Simon's men surrounded the heretics they led out of the city.

The men came first, stripped naked as the day they came into the world, walking in front of the jeering crowd. Despite the catcalls and their obvious state of dehydration and partial starvation, the men all walked upright—when not shoved or manhandled by the guards—chanting a prayer together and smiling as if beatified. The men were forced to the farther pyre, where Arnau Amalric shouted at them, offering them a last chance to say their creed and renounce the devil.

In a brief, accidental moment of silence, the reed-thin voice of Calvert said, "We're not afraid to die for what we believe."

Arnau laughed, true to the person they'd met in the abbot's pavilion, and called, "The devil will know his own."

Another thunder of catcalls drowned the prelate's words as the women came out the gates, stripped and forced to walk naked in front of the mob. From the hollows around the eyes of many of the women, especially the older ones, these women were starved and had refused water to hasten their end. If Simon didn't burn them today, most would die within a day. Among them was the mayor's aunt, who carried water to the men on the battlements most afternoons. Another had once gone with Tomás on death-duty, the night her child died.

He was already weeping when the last of them came through the city gates. Isabella, her hands bound, walked alongside Adalyde of Toulouse, with Miquel and Eloïse at her other side. Eloïse leaned against Miquel, his arm wrapped around her for comfort.

"That's my mother!" Sebastián cried, his voice breaking into a childish, high register. "She's not one of them."

"That woman isn't a heretic," Jean-Luc called. "She's a Catholic subject of King Pedro."

Tomás pushed past the guards to go to her, but one of the men thrust up the pommel of a sheathed sword into his sternum, throwing him to the ground.

"Every one of these heretics chose to be here." Simon de Montfort stood over Tomás, stepping on his hand.

"She's not a heretic," Tomás said.

"Then she's free to recant and step out."

"She's mad with thirst," Jean-Luc said.

The small woman who'd been beside them earlier pushed past Simon, with the kind of personal gesture only a close acquaintance could make. "Simon, you're a fool. That woman is a Catholic."

"Mathilde, stay out of this," Simon said. "This is not the business of any woman."

"I've lived most of the year among these people, trying to rescue my son while you did nothing. I know how they think. And you're making a fool of yourself by creating martyrs."

Tomás ran with Mathilde to where soldiers were shoving women onto the pyre. Sebastián pressed to his side.

"By the grace of God, come down from there," Mathilde called, her attention fixed on Isabella.

"Leave them alone!" a soldier shouted. "They want to die!"

"And we want to watch!" another called.

"Isabella, please come down," Tomás called. "*Ai Dèu*, she can't hear my voice. Sebastián, call her. She'll hear you."

"Mother, come down. For the love of Our Savior and Lord, please come down."

Jean-Luc called out, too, but he called Adalyde's name and the names of other friends from inside Minerve, calling as a captain does to marshal his men's attention in battle. Mathilde cried just as passionately, her attention focused on any woman who turned when she shouted.

"If you love our Lord and Savior, there's no reason to die!" she called. "Please come down and pray with me."

Tomás and Sebastián shouted together, calling Isabella's name. Only once did she turn as if she heard them, then stared off to heaven. She smiled in the same way as the beatified heretics, though Tomás saw the same shadow on her face as on Hugues's when it seemed sure he'd die in Béziers.

Flames licked the bottom of the pyre.

"Watch the devil take these women." Arnau Amalric pushed the abbot of St-Féliz-de-Fontcours to stand in front of him, the prelate's heavy paw at the abbot's neck. "This is the fate of women who steal men's souls."

"Eloïse!" The abbot cried, struggling to move toward her but held back by Arnau's men. When they wouldn't let loose of him, he fell to his knees. He cried out her name again.

Eloïse nestled in Miquel's arms, while the abbot screamed her name over and over, begging her to come to him.

Tomás and Jean-Luc called Isabella's name. "Isabella! Valerós!"

Adalyde supported Isabella in an embrace, but then nudged Isabella forward. "Go to your friends, *xiqueta*. You aren't ready to leave this world yet."

A soldier thrust Adalyde further up the pyre, cursing her as a heretic, condemning her to the devil. She held up a hand in blessing. "How can we be afraid to leave the devil's world to join God?"

Jean-Luc called Adalyde's name and pleaded with her, but Adalyde joined the prayer her friends chanted, all of them gazing up to heaven.

Isabella glanced around wildly, as if lost. "Mother?" she called. "Where are you? Sancta Maria, please find me. Mother!"

Mathilde de Garlande pushed past Simon and the soldiers to scramble up the slippery slope of trash and branches to Isabella, grabbing her bound hands and flinging her down from the pyre with more strength than possible for an old woman. As Isabella tumbled down the slope, Mathilde grabbed two other women who responded when she called to them.

"Let her alone!" Mathilde shouted when one of the soldiers reached for Isabella. "In the name of our Savior, leave her alone."

Tomás knelt to help Isabella up, wrapping his Chartrain surcoat around her nakedness.

"She has to say her creed." Simon challenged Mathilde and blocked Tomás from bringing Isabella away from the pyre.

Tomás felt the heat of the crackling twigs and straw behind him, knowing every bit of wood the soldiers gathered was dry tinder, ready to flare hot. He spoke in her ear. "Isabella, say your creed, just like you say it for Father Anselm. Say, 'I believe.'"

He started the words in Latin, hoping to say it with the same rhythm as Father Anselm so she'd speak the lines automatically, like a child does. And for the greatest relief of his life, she did as he asked.

Before she came to the last line, Simon walked away, apparently disappointed to lose a victim.

"I believe in the resurrection of the body and life everlasting."

"Get her away from here!" Mathilde shouted at Tomás. The fire roared up, too hot to stand near.

Carrying Isabella, he scrambled up the slope of the canyon to the road, Mathilde behind him with the other two women. Jean-Luc still shouted names, commanding people to come down. Then his voice broke as the roar of the fire and the collapsing mount of twigs thundered through the canyon.

As Tomás stopped at the rim of the canyon to get her dressed in the surcoat, Isabella chanted as if she were still saying her creed.

"O my dove in the clefts of the rock," her voice rasped deeply, jagged with thirst, her lips cracked and bleeding, "in the secret places of the stairs, let me see your face, let me hear your voice."

"Isabella!" Jean-Luc called to her, coming to help hold her up.

She glanced at Jean-Luc, her eyes red from smoke. "For sweet is your voice, and your face is comely."

"Get water for her," Tomás called over his shoulder.

"Mother!" Sebastián hugged her, tears running down his face, filthy with dust and smoke.

"We have to get away," she said to Sebastián. "You must be very quiet and very good. We have to run away."

"Isabella," Tomás said, "you're safe now. Don't be afraid."

She looked straight through him, as if seeing through a ghost, her eyes too large in her thin face.

"*Ai*, my husband! It's you who wanted me to die."

"No, Isabella. It's me. Tomás."

"Don't let him have Sebastián." She screamed, tearing at him and everyone around, trying to get past him, shrieking that she wanted him to die. "Let go! He can't take Sebastián. Stop him before he gets Sebastián."

Jean-Luc wrapped his arms around her, holding her tight. "Be still, Isabella. You're safe. No one will hurt Sebastián."

The Valerós knights came.

"Just give her this wet cloth to suck," someone said. "She'll be sick if she drinks too much."

Jean-Luc said, "I should never have let her out of my sight. She was ill from thirst."

"I'll carry her." Tomás reached for Isabella.

Half of Valerós came between him and his wife. The bandy-legged knight Lázaro pushed him aside, and tall Bonanat gave Tomás a rude, painful shove.

"You heard her, *punxor*. She wants you gone."

The shove spun Tomás around. He stumbled to get his footing, trying not to retch at the smell of burning flesh wafting on the air. Jacques and Thierry, his Norman friends, caught him between them, steadying him.

"*Bon Dieu, mon ami*," Thierry said. "Let's go from this place. Burgundy pays better, without the disgrace."

Tomás saw past the two Normans where the wild Raoul in a Montcava surcoat stepped away in retreat, holding Tomás's father's sword. Reaching for the borrowed sword he carried, Tomás pushed past his few friends and the many carousing crusaders, intending to take no quarter, seize back his sword, and then go home.

67
Vespers

EVEN BEFORE THE CALL for vespers, Gerard slipped away. He'd seen Jean-Luc at the pyre shouting until he was hoarse, exhorting people to say their creed and go on living. And he'd seen his son hold his lover in his arms and look up to heaven with horror and grief carved on his face, not the expression of a man happy to be safe again.

The guilt grasping Gerard's heart felt as wrenching as when Jean-Luc had left his house years before. He'd spent the summer worrying about Pèire's women. And his son. And Hugues. He'd considered this miserable crusade only what a soldier did to support his Church. But his son, a sworn Catholic knight and the French hero of Minerve, tried to marshal the heretics of Minerve to leave the pyre, the way one marshals men to an orderly retreat in the face of a massacre.

Gerard didn't understand what his son was doing. He didn't understand when Jean-Luc refused Simon's invitation to his pavilion. He didn't understand why there was no joy on Jean-Luc's face as he embraced his lover.

"Come to the prelates' pavilion with me." Gerard spoke to the two lovers. "The bishop of Toulouse will say a special mass tonight."

Jean-Luc refused. "I don't want to pray with priests." Gerard must have shown his perplexity, for his son spoke in his ear, where Beatriz couldn't hear. "They were just people who loved God, Father. They were neighbors and mothers and aunts, and this is the worst Christendom has ever done."

At vespers, Gerard didn't go to the special Mass. He drifted alone in the dark, finding his way among the paths through the broom to the canyon's edge, staring down at the pyre and up at the formidable walls of the city that had held life and misery the day before.

He found a stone outcrop for a seat and silently said the usual prayers one does to bring God present. Other figures came to the canyon's edge, as silent and still as he, heads bent in prayer. Trying to pray for something larger and less selfish than his son's life, which was all he'd prayed for years, he couldn't find a prayer large enough.

"All the golden angels have been dancing in darkness." Pèire growled in Gerard's ear, as if he were there. "Pray for sunlight."

Miquel's words from long ago echoed in the canyon. "He's so concerned with every sparrow that falls, He has no time for men."

"What's the use?" Gerard murmured aloud, startling a figure seated near him.

"Pardon?" It was Pedro d'Aragón, shrouded in unmarked armor, unrecognizable if one didn't know the man's voice.

"He's so concerned with every sparrow that falls, He has no time for men."

Gerard didn't mean to repeat such things aloud. Certainly not to the pope's own vassal. But Gerard didn't care about his sudden foray into heresy. He kept seeing the pain on Jean-Luc's face and hearing his son's voice commanding the heretics to come down and save themselves.

"One must have faith that God cares," Pedro said, "to keep from going mad. Pretend if you must, when it's too hard."

"Monsenyor, I can't pretend that it wasn't me with the dozen lords who went along as Arnau and Simon commanded. Many lords seem too greedy to notice that we're murdering our neighbors."

"Simon isn't greedy," Pedro said. "He truly believes he's doing God's work."

"That's the worst jest the devil has played in this whole mess."

"I hope to foil the devil by praying for mercy," Pedro said.

Gerard tried that, first for the souls of Minerve, and then for the French crusaders. But then he descended into his usual petty prayers, asking only that his son might find respite.

Lubos, Alone

FATHER, FATHER, why have you forsaken me? Where have you gone? Why am I all alone?

PART SEVEN
Sodalitas, Fidelitas, Virtus

TO OUR MOST HOLY FATHER,
The siege of Minerve has ended. Although your hammer in the Languedoc, Simon de Montfort, sought to treat these rebels with leniency, but he listened to my caution about future problems if rebels were not punished. We permitted the Catholics to go free, with great generosity, allowing anyone who would say the creed. Most so-called Perfects among the heretics refused. Some entered the flames of their own volition. We shall not in the future allow such exhibitions of erroneous self-righteousness.

— Arnau Amalric
Your servant as the abbot of Cîteaux
One day after the Feast Day of St. Mary Magdalene, July 22
the Eleventh Year of Your Pontificate

68

Miserere

IN HIS FATHER'S PAVILION, Jean-Luc tried to listen to everyone's stories, but he couldn't distinguish the words. He tried to stay awake, because it felt like desertion, leaving Beatriz and his father, but he couldn't fight off sleep.

When he woke in the dark, he felt her fingers on his neck and smelled the sunshine caught in her hair. He pulled her close, to feel her heat against his chest and loins, in the same way he used to take comfort by remembering her.

"*Chérie*, talk to me so I know it's real."

She kissed him, touching him everywhere until his senses became confused, feeling her soul in the night, hearing her smile when he traced the lines of her face. As tiny and delicate as he remembered, except for the small mound of belly under his hand. He parted her legs and she sighed when he joined her, her hands caressing his back, and he fell deeply in love with her again, the same as a dream where you fly like a goshawk over valleys and oceans. But it was more like sleep than making love.

He lay beside her, his arm on her shoulder. "I remain outside the Church. We can never convince the bishop to let us marry, *chérie*."

Beatriz whispered, "The bishop needs only to ask the pope to return you to the communion of saints. We are already married."

"Our child will be grateful. But I must have slept through it. Was this last night?"

He caressed her back, the narrow shoulder blades, and the soft skin at the base of her spine, thinking this was a foretaste of heaven.

"No, it was years ago. Your father hosted an old-fashioned sort of wedding at Fontcours. The kind where the bride is only eight and the husband leaves soon after for another country."

"I can't believe my father would agree to such subterfuge."

"Katelina, my mother, had to write the marriage articles. She's not as good as Isabella, but she could sign Pèire's name and Father Anselm's."

"Did I enjoy myself?"

"You got drunk as a lord. They had to carry you into your marriage bed. Fortunately, the bride was too young for consummation, so she wasn't disappointed by your performance."

He smiled, an odd feeling on his newly shaven face. Beatriz, his ever-efficient nurse, had him shorn of his lice-infested hair and beard the night before, almost as fast as she had him watered, fed, washed and his wounds tended, her consoling finger tips lifting most, but not all, of the burden weighing him down.

"For all the searching I did, I may as well have never left, *chérie*. The only man I found who could free me died inside Minerve."

"Then it's good how divine inspiration caused our fathers to marry us before you were excommunicated. Nothing can part us since we were already united."

"My father never told a lie in his life."

"He couldn't rest easy with the idea of your child being a bastard. And he has found it easier to be economical with the truth since Felicia and I came into his life."

"Felicia. Is the real Felicia well, my little liar?"

"Guillem left with her to return to Valerós before the siege lifted. He wanted her as far from the invaders as could be."

"Did you know Guillem is a goodman?" Jean-Luc said.

"But a weak sort, who'd let a priest marry him to his lover. I'm sorry my lies hurt your friendship."

He kissed the length of her arm, pausing to rest in the crook of her elbow. "I lied about who I was only to protect you, *chérie*."

"As I did."

"It was only the second worst thing I did. The other was not to trust you, after you swore you'd cast your lot with mine."

"I didn't make a very good crusader wife. I wept a great deal when no one could see."

A voice cried out, a too-familiar sound in the night.

"It's Isabella," Jean-Luc said. "She has bad dreams."

"Sebastián spent most of the night at her side. I'd better go to her."

"Let me come with you. I can't stand you so far away."

"How long until she sleeps peacefully? Or walks around without fingering the dagger in her pocket?"

Jean-Luc considered. "I think a long while."

•

After dawn, while men packed to go north, their forty days' crusade service paid in full, and while Jean-Luc breakfasted with his father and Sebastián, the king of Aragón came to visit.

After ritual greetings were done, Jean-Luc said, "Tomás isn't here."

"I've come to see you," the king said. "When my men tended to the Marquis de Beaurain, they found this."

He unrolled a piece of parchment with ill-written scratches sprawled at an angle. Hugues de Beaurain had consigned all his possessions, the rights and rents of all his villages, and his title to the living son of the Viscount de Chartrain, as if Jean-Luc de Chartrain were the marquis's own son, to recompense a great knight who'd been destroyed through perjury. Everything should go to Jean-Luc, except for Hugues's house in Antioch, which he gave to Tomás of Morella.

"It's already been announced in the Beaurain camp," Pedro said. "His men expect you to lead them home."

"But I can't. This paper isn't witnessed, and I'm still excommunicated. I can't prove the truth about the abbot's perjury."

Jean-Luc stopped just short of proclaiming gratitude for the barrier excommunication placed between Hélène and him. Then he saw his father reading over Pedro's shoulder.

Of course Gerard knew about Hélène.

Because Hugues had known.

"This is exactly what Hugues wanted," Gerard said. "We talked about it often after we misplaced Jean-Luc inside Minerve."

Pedro said, "Anselm, the priest from Valerós, is in my camp. He told me your story. I've already sent intercessions to the pope for both of you."

Pedro gestured to Gerard, who brought ink and pen from his own writing box. In an astoundingly brazen manner, the king witnessed the document with his own signature, dating it for the feast of St-Mary Magdalene. Then Gerard signed it, too.

"This is too much." Jean-Luc considered how his father perjured himself twice in a single summer.

Pedro, mistaking his meaning, said. "You were born and raised to take such burdens, like your father and Pèire Leteric."

Gerard said, "Hugues always had strong stewards. I'll help his widow go to the Beaurain estate in Arles while you take our two armies north. How many times have I heard Hélène say how the Pays de France is too cold for her?"

"That's kind of you, Father." Jean-Luc felt ashamed that Gerard wanted to rescue him, not Hélène. Yet his mind immediately galloped off at the idea of leading two armies, his father's and his own, rather than pitying the pouting widow.

69

Consolateum Redux

"BONJORN," THE HERALD SAID. "Pedro *el Rei* salutes the Master of
the Valerós knights."

"I'm not the master. I can call him for you." Isabella's raspy voice
was still weak. She felt sick and shaky and disreputable, though
Beatriz had dressed her respectably in a linen robe. Beatriz stayed
by her site, which Isabella appreciated, so some one might catch her
if she fell.

Pedro offered Isabella his hand in greeting, the same way he'd
greeted her the first time they met, as one knight to another.

"I've sent some of my men to help protect Valerós." Pedro
smiled, as if they were friends. "I did it because the Master of the
Valerós knights signed a contract to send the best knights to Barcelona. To teach my young knights how real crusaders do their work."

"The greater part of Valerós belongs to Beatriz." This was the
first time Isabella had said it aloud, which might be why it hurt her
already raw throat. She'd had plenty of time to prepare for this, to
let go of Valerós as her home, as Sebastián's inheritance. "I cannot
muster the knights without her leave."

"I don't care to hold Valerós," Beatriz said. "I'm going north
with my husband. You care more about Valerós than any queen cared
about Jerusalem. And as Pèire decreed, Sebastián is Master of
Valerós. You love Valerós, Isabella. I love my husband."

"That simplifies things," Pedro said, "since Don Tomás showed
me Pèire's final charter. Senhóra Isabella, will you bring your knights
to Barcelona come winter, as we agreed?"

"My knights will come, as I swore they would." Her blood heated for the first time since she'd taken ill in Minerve. Valerós for Sebastián! This was true salvation, true freedom. "I have to tend to business at Arracheuse. It's all I have, and as steward, I need to see to its business."

"What about Montcava and Fontcours?" Pedro said.

"Sebastián feels as Pèire always did." She glanced at Sebastián, who nodded in answer to her unasked question. She'd lost all the timidity she'd felt weeks before, when she bargained with Pedro to sell the Valerós knights as mercenaries. Pedro was just a man. With immense power, but just a man. "Sebastián is giving his portion of Montcava to his brother Durán and—what's the other boy's name? Henri. They can fight with Hélène and her brother Louis and the three dozen cousins who each have a piece of Montcava."

"Neither my mother or I will ever enter Toulouse or Montcava again," Sebastián said. As exhausted as she was, her son's resolution buoyed Isabella's spirits. Their minds and hearts were joined on this.

"You are letting your emotions overcome good sense," Pedro said. "Sebastián, keep your seigneur's portion of Montcava. We need sensible lords in the Languedoc, to help end this soon."

"I intend to be a warrior, not a landlord," Sebastián said.

"Then find a steward and join my seigneurs in Barcelona this winter." Pedro folded his arms, which seemed to mean he was commanding Sebastián, not suggesting.

A voice outside the pavilion said, "Do as your king says, *Cavaller* Valerós. Keep the land that belongs to you."

Tomás, looking even worse than the day before, pulled a half-naked man along with him into the pavilion. The man, stripped to only his under-linen, was battered, bruised, and defiant. Isabella knew her sympathy should be roused by so much injury, but that must have been burned out of her inside Minerve.

A long row of tattooed crosses covered the man's left arm, the tips at the end of each cross dripped blood-red crimson crescents.

"It's the wild man I tackled in Minerve." Jean-Luc held Beatriz close to him. "The same ghost we fought with the bandit-crusaders."

"It's Raoul!" Sebastián cried. "He's the man who snatched me."

"*Ai*, no!" Isabella jumped, feeling like a gazelle frightened out of its hiding place.

Tomás grimaced, his damaged face as twisted as the rictus of a dead man. "He murdered the priest Clémence at Valerós. And the lay-brother at Fontfroide, and the nun at the Vale of Roses. It's the man Anselm nursed in Minerve, not knowing this *baquelar* trapped Jean-Luc there. And what else?" He prodded the man. "Tell Senhóra Isabella you killed her horse and tried to kill her."

"She caused all this," the man croaked.

Isabella drew back, wishing for shelter. But Beatriz was in Jean-Luc's embrace. Only Pedro stood near, and however much horror she felt, she couldn't touch a king just to feel safe.

"You scrofulous cur." Tomás shoved his captive. "We discussed this all last night. Tell Sebastián the truth."

"Tell me what?" Sebastián had his hand on his dagger. Isabella sought who surrounded Sebastián. Was he safe?

The man, seething with hatred, searched between Tomás and Isabella, as if he wanted to murder them both. "My father wanted Sebastián to be with him. Renoud stole the lad from me. That witch-woman lies—"

"No!" Isabella's voice ground like rocks tumbling in a flood. She heard in his voice who this monster was. She wanted him gone before anyone said his name. Before he might harm or frighten Sebastián in any way. "Take him away. Or kill him. You said you wanted to."

"I can't," Tomás said. "He's already dead."

The wild man said, "It's all her fault, flaunting her urchin ways, acting like she's as good as a man."

"She's better than most. But you are born of a race of lepers." Tomás had his hand on his sword pommel, his fury palpable.

"I want my son," the man said. "I want my witch-wife to die."

"Please explain," Pedro said.

Jean-Luc tightened his grasp on Beatriz. "The wrong brother came back from the dead in Constantinople."

·

Isabella dug her hands in her pockets, grasping what she could to still her anger. Clenching her fist still hurt her ruined hand, but she let pain anchor her. She refused to feel fear. He'd already wrung too much of that from her.

"You aren't my father," Sebastián said.

"I am Lubos. I fight for the Crux Lunata. And for my father, Père-Izsák."

Tomás kicked him. "No, *baquelar*. We talked about this. Your father is Esak de Beaurain. Tell us your real name."

The man boiled with hatred, mute.

"You are Nicolau of Montcava," Tomás said.

The man shrugged away from where Tomás prodded him. "That whelp is my son. Renoud and that witch tell lies."

She glanced around the people crowding the pavilion, wanting to rest her eyes somewhere safe.

Sebastián glared in anger.

Tomás's scarred lips twitched with scorn.

Gerard seemed horrified, offended to the core.

Pedro's eyes flitted from person to person, watching with sophisticated distain.

Beatriz nestled in Jean-Luc's arms like a startled child.

Only Jean-Luc appeared to understand. "You have at least four brothers here, ma dòmna. Whatever you want, we will do. *Sodalitas, fidelitas, virtus.*"

Gerard, who stood nearest to that man, drew his dagger. "You have only to name what you want us to do, ma dòmna."

Tomás said, "No, that's not fair. Don't make her decide."

Pedro glanced around, uneasy now. "You can't kill this man just because a woman asks you to."

"Why not?" Jean-Luc said. "You heard the evil he's done. God should have left him dead in Constantinople."

"He should be called to justice by his lord," Pedro said.

"Raymond of Toulouse is still excommunicated. He can't serve up justice."

Tomás said, "The spite-faced viscount Simon de Montfort is lord of Minerve now. Jesus in heaven knows he is incapable of justice."

Jean-Luc said, "Tell us what you want, ma dòmna."

"You can't..." Pedro started to protest again, but in the same moment Nicolau pushed against Gerard, taking his knife.

"You jackals cannot judge me. You'll murder me like you did my brother."

"Your brother lost a fair fight," Jean-Luc said, "when he tried to murder us."

"Monsenyor, you can't let them kill me," Nicolau pleaded with Pedro. "I want my son."

"You don't have a son," Tomás said. "Your life is a dung heap. You don't exist. We can't kill you because you are already dead."

"Everyone has forgotten you," Jean-Luc said. "Montcava will be wiped from memory."

"You aren't my father," Sebastián said again. "You're only the bastard son of a renegade priest."

"Your witch-mother poisoned you against me." Nicolau glared, Gerard's knife in his hand.

"Leave Sebastián alone," Isabella commanded.

"He's my son. I'll see him dead before you steal him from me, witch-woman."

"No." Her voice shattered. "He isn't your son. Never was."

"There's not a drop of your blood in my veins," Sebastián said. "Don Tomás is my father. I'd rather eat dust than be your son."

In a heartbeat, Nicolau had the knife poised to throw.

Her dagger in hand, Isabella stepped through the motion as she'd learned it. Push upward under the rib cage, shove, twist. But at the last moment, it was too late to stop Nicolau. His knife flew toward Sebastián.

Pedro reached out his hand, as if commanding the knife to stop.

•

Jean-Luc found once again, at the moment it mattered most, he could do nothing, not even pray, to stop the blade from plunging into flesh. With both arms around his wife, he couldn't protect anyone else.

•

Life-long habit led Gerard to step between the king and danger, wrapping around Pedro to save him from harm. The king shuddered at the sound of the knife striking flesh.

•

411

Tomás thrust Sebastián to the ground, his arms outstretched to cover the boy.

As they always said, it didn't hurt. Tomás had felt both sword and knife sufficient times to know you don't feel it going in. Just a stunning, bruising thump in his side, more surprise than pain.

Isabella begged him, her hands at his face.

"Don't die. Please, for the love of God, you can't die."

And Sebastián was crying.

Jesus and the dancing angels. Tomás needed to tell the boy he was too old now to cry. He held up his hand for quiet, so he could be heard and found a Greek blade just below where his heart used to be.

70
Kestrels and Crows

Jean-Luc outside Minerve, July 27

TWO DAYS AFTER MINERVE surrendered, a heatwave settled on the plateau, stealing energy from people and animals, so that the only possible work was to find shade, and then sit and swelter.

Late the next day, a hot, dry sirocco wind from Africa blew over the plateau, carrying desert sand that rubbed skin raw while the armies packed and began their journeys—northward for any army that claimed to have completed its forty days of service; toward Termes and Toulouse for any men called by Simon to pursue submission of another city.

After the sirocco scoured the plateau for two days, lightning flashed through the night. The rain released a perfume of wet dust and thyme, without any unholy masses being said to herald the torrent.

When the rain stopped, Jean-Luc listened in the pre-dawn for first the nightingale and then the lark. With most soldiers departing the plateau in the past few days, except for stragglers like the Chartrain and Valerós camps, the birds and other animals came back. Frogs croaked in the canyon, refreshed by the night's rain. The wind and rain, though, hadn't washed the remains of the crusaders' filth and trash from the plateau.

Through the heat, wind, and lightning, Beatriz had done the work—or supervised others—to stitch up Tomás and keep him alive. After the rain, when dawn light made it possible to tell one shadow from another, Jean-Luc called Beatriz and insisted that she sleep. At the tent where Tomás lay, Jean-Luc chased Sebastián to bed, uncertain whether the boy had slept at all the past four days. Then Jean-Luc and Chrétien coaxed Isabella to sit by the cook's early-morning fire and eat breakfast. If only from pacing, Isabella must have walked a dozen leagues in the past few days.

Alone beside Tomás's makeshift sickroom, Jean-Luc threw back the tent flap to let in the rain-freshened air. A murder of crows wheeled across the sky, coming back with the dawn from wherever they rested at night. The pyres had burned so hot only ashes remained, and the crusaders had torched the brush in the canyon where the people of Minerve dropped their dead. That left nothing in the canyon bottoms for the carrion crows, ravens, and jackdaws, but they held a carnival every day, gleaning among the deserted campsites.

Kee. Kee. Kee.

Jean-Luc searched the sky for the crying kestrel, then found it gliding above the city tower. It soared down into the canyon. Perhaps the mice and grasshoppers had returned.

Inside the tent, it smelled of the pennyroyal and rue Beatriz burned to block the smell of the crusader camps. Tomás coughed and then gasped in pain, his eyes open for the first time.

"Hey, arsewit. Back among the living?"

Tomás's eyes followed the sound of Jean-Luc's voice.

"Hurts to breathe, doesn't it? I took a blade at Antioch in almost the same way. It was half a year before I could laugh. But you're so tough, you'll be chewing your own food by Michaelmas."

Tomás coughed again, and Jean-Luc knelt to wipe the man's mouth free of sputum.

"The worst might be over, swordsman. If it's not, then I call on you as a knight of honor, please don't puke any more blood in front of the women. Though for myself, I'd rather spit red than piss red."

Tomás, startled, searched his face. Jean-Luc guessed the man hadn't yet assessed his own pain. So, he kept talking, since he didn't have a clue how to offer comfort.

"Beatriz didn't care about the blood once she knew you'd live. But listening to someone drown from the inside is never pleasant."

"Is he dead? Nicolau?"

"He never returned from Constantinople alive."

Jean-Luc saw no reason to revisit how his father convinced Pedro to confirm that it had only been one of the abbot's mercenaries attempting a final attack.

"Isabella was upset with you for bleeding all over the pavilion. Though she didn't get sick until Beatriz and Katelina started sewing you up from the inside out. Gerard walked her around the trails in the gorse to keep her away. Beatriz says Isabella watched them stitch her up after Sebastián was born. That's why she has a great fear of blood. Even if it's leaking out of a mooncalf knight like you."

He held the cup for Tomás to drink, and then wiped olive oil on the man's cracked lips as Beatriz had done for days.

"Too bad she couldn't just faint like you, eh, *mon ami*? You took the weasel's way, but at least we didn't have to hold you down while Beatriz plied her needle. What did you say, swordsman?"

"Shut up, Jean-Foutre."

"Glad you're better."

"What day is it?"

"Two days after the Feast of St-Christopher," Jean-Luc said. "We've been arguing for three days whether the saint would bear you to safety or the ferryman would row you to hell, *pécheur*."

"Is Sebastián all right?"

"Yes, except he's worn out from waiting on you day and night. Blessed Mother of Jesus, do not weep. I can't take anymore tears. I've had to comfort all those women and my father. And even Chrétien and Sebastián. And you—you're not a damned Catalan sheepherder who cries at good news or bad."

"Tell me who died."

"We're all fine."

"I mean inside the city. I saw who they burned. But who died before the surrender?"

"*Bon Dieu*, Tomás, please don't ask."

"Tell me."

Jean-Luc said their names, a different list from the one he recited for Isabella the first night they waited by Tomás's bed. She had wanted to know who they burned. Answering Tomás, Jean-Luc couldn't name five of those lost before Tomás wept again, and he continued weeping while Jean-Luc named those who'd perished at the battlements or from illness.

"I met that man Enego," Tomás said. "The one you were searching for. He volunteered for death-duty, though he was too mangled to be of use. I had no idea—"

"About his part of my troubles in Constantinople? It doesn't matter now."

The two men listened to the larks and frogs and crickets taking back the plateau and canyons for their own. A dragonfly hovered outside the tent opening, its evanescent body catching the first rays of sun and glowing green.

·

"Why are you here?"

Isabella's hoarse voice outside the tent jolted the two men from reverie. Tomás reached out for Jean-Luc's hand, his fingers too weak to grasp anything.

"He's my seigneur. I have business with him." The mellow sound of Pedro's voice startled Tomás again, his eyes darting, and Jean-Luc regretted he hadn't been outside to waylay the king, who came twice each day, seeking news. "I want to help his friends."

"Help?" Isabella's voice cracked. "God forbid you ever mean us harm. My priest is excommunicated and my son lived under siege for weeks because you tried to help. You promised to protect my family, and they ended up imprisoned in Béziers. Your help is dangerous."

"Make a beggar of me if you must, senhóra. I want to know he's all right."

"He's alive." Her voice shattered, like pottery cast to the pavement and shattered in a thousand pieces.

"There's no reason for us to quarrel, ma dòmna. He's already made his choices."

"Under your inveiglements."

"Inveiglements? Senhóra, every single one of his choices came from being married to a woman like you. If it were me, it would cause a host of unfortunate choices."

"A woman like me would never marry someone like you. I'd never agree to be locked in my own castle while you—"

"Stop! This is unseemly." Chrétien's voice broke in between Isabella and Pedro. "And I can't believe it's me complaining about bad behavior. He needs to see Tomás, Isabella. Step aside."

"Then at least stay with him, Chrétien. Sebastián will go wherever Tomás goes. Keep their king from sending them out on another venture on the road to hell. Please."

When Pedro stepped into the tent with Chrétien, he greeted Jean-Luc in the French style. Jean-Luc then made a weak excuse about his wife needing him. He'd already given his best advice to Tomás. His own fate lay on the road north, with his new wife and his father and his new army.

71

Sodalitas, Fidelitas, Virtus

Tomás outside Minerve, July 27

"YOU DON'T NEED TO get up on my account." Pedro mocked Tomás in the way he used to, whenever cajoling him for being too morose.

"*Bon día*, Monsenyor."

Tomás still found it painful to speak, every breath and motion sending pain shooting up his middle.

"The secrets of your Nizari swordmasters did not serve you well, *mon amic*."

Chrétien thumped Tomás's forehead with a knuckle, as their father used to. "You told him the Nizari secrets?"

"Only the basic rules, Chrétien. Please tell Pedro anything else he needs to know to stay alive."

"Monsenyor—that's what I call you?" Chrétien had never behaved in so familiar a way with Hugues.

Pedro said, "What do you know that Tomás didn't pound into me in the practice ring?"

"Your enemies are closer than they should be. But that's not a Nizari secret. While Arnau Amalric lives, your life is in danger." Chrétien turned to Tomás. "Do you remember when Arnau fetched the abbot away? Arnau also bears the *crux lunata* sign."

"The mysterious brotherhood of knights?" Pedro asked. "The demons Tomás claims have pursued you to hell and back? Didn't the arrest of the abbot end that? I'm not part of his old vendetta."

"No," Chrétien said. "His new one. Look at this letter that the abbot's devil left in Valerós." He had the Wolf-letter that Tomás had given him. Pedro read it aloud.

We'll take your cubs from your den.
Your Rock won't help you.
My Wolf topples that one next.
God won't come to Aragón,
when Aragón is Gomorrah.

"We think—Isabella and I—that the Wolf was the brute Tomás captured, who's been terrorizing us. The Rock is you, Monsenyor." Chrétien folded his arms like he did when stepping back to watch Sebastián practice the battle moves he taught.

Pedro looked bemused. "Arnau has been jealous of my easy friendship with His Holiness, Innocent. But I don't see the need for vengeance on Arnau's part. Although we disagree strongly over his methods, Arnau is pursuing the Church's work."

"Arnau has the abbot now, and Esak's brother Colomb rides in his train," Chrétien said. "And each of the three bore a tattoo with the lunate cross. They are false knights of the Crux Lunata."

Tomás murmured, "'If God had a care, He'd never have let those wolves, the Knights of the Lunate Cross, come to be.'"

"God has a care." Pedro rose up in a heat.

"I'm quoting my father," Tomás said.

"Miquel's blasphemy aside," Chrétien said, "Arnau and the abbot mean you harm."

"Except the abbot is dead," Tomás said.

"No, brother, he's not. Arnau had him in his coterie when he left Minerve. The abbot's hands weren't even bound."

"*Aiieee*, the legate can burn half of Minerve and yet keep that wolf-devil alive?" Tomás jerked up in anger. The searing pain laid him back; he bit his lip to avoid humiliating himself in front of both Chrétien and Pedro.

"Peace, *mon amic*." Pedro rested a hand on Tomás's shoulder. "I'll heed your caution. What of you? Are you still going away?"

"As soon as possible."

"I shall make things right, Tomás. Let me do more for you."

"There's nothing, Monsenyor."

"For your friends then."

"Only Chrétien and Durán are staying in the south. I'm going to seek my fortune where it's safer."

"Stay, please. Come to Barcelona, Tomás. Bring your wife with the Valerós knights."

"You know I can't, Monsenyor."

"It's cruel for you to blame me for Minerve."

"If you intend to stop Simon from creating hell on earth, you must keep away from lepers like me."

"You want to sacrifice our friendship for the good of Aragón?" Pedro's brows twitched into a frown. "What really happened after Montpelhièr?"

Tomás took a deep breath, which hurt beyond belief. Seeing that, Chrétien rescued him and told Pedro the story, first about Hugues and Chrétien finding Tomás and chasing the abbot. Then how they lived for a fortnight, ill in a tiny cell. And then the fumbled escape, losing Sebastián and Hugues to the abbot, and walking half-starved from Béziers to Minerve.

Tomás said, "Hugues died mistaking me for my father, still in love with him. And you heard how Hugues's friendship with my father twisted the abbot over decades of hate."

Pedro glanced at Chrétien, then stared at Tomás. "You won't come to Barcelona because you think I'm in love with you?"

"No." Tomás shook his head, which shot pain along his left side. "Because of Miquel's and Hugues's bond, Esak launched a siege of vengeance. Arnau is likely to attack you however he can, and I refuse to be that excuse. So, if you feel you must take care of someone, take care of my brother."

"I have a brother," Pedro said to Chrétien as they studied each other. "But we weren't raised in the same house as children, and hardly see each other more than every other year."

"I have a brother I'd die for," Chrétien said. "If he doesn't get me killed first."

"Viscount Gerard described how you and Hugues tried to save Pèire Leteric's children. I want to make you a knight of Aragón."

"But we failed," Chrétien said. "I fared no better at chivalry than my brother."

"They are safe now. I want you for an ally. Unless your fealty to the king of Cyprus forbids other oaths."

"You have my brother's oath, and that's the same as if I gave you an oath myself," Chrétien reacted as if challenged, because he hated the king of Cyprus for an ill-turn done to old friends in Famagusta. "I am as incapable of betrayal as Tomás is."

"However, you are remaining in this country," Pedro said. "I want to reward your service to the marquis and Don Tomás. And I want to hear your oath for it, as is the custom in the south."

Chrétien stood as he would when preparing to sing for a night's supper. He bowed first to Tomás and then bent his knee to Pedro. He rendered his oath as if it were a chant or the words from one of his songs. But he broke the formula every southern knight would use to make a vow.

"I, Chrétien de Cyprus, son of Numa of Syria, a mercenary and jongleur of no renown, but now the guardian of Fontcours and St-Joachim—"

Pedro interrupted. "St-Joachim belongs to Tomás."

"My brother lost it to me in a dice game in our Béziers prison. I'll take better care than he would."

Pedro waved him on, rubbing the line between his brows.

"I will be true to you, Pedro *El Católico*, king by Grace of God of Aragón, son of Sanchia Castile, Count of Barcelona and Roussillon, vassal to Innocent the Third of the Holy Roman Church—"

He continued citing the full string of titles to which Pedro could claim, showing a poet's strength of memory by calling out every iota of the king's heritage, throughout which Pedro refrained from his usual impatience.

"From this moment until God parts my soul from this body, whether He chooses to do so out of caprice or wisdom or a lost gamble with the devil."

Pedro had nodded assent at each incanted line, then accidentally nodded at the minor blasphemy.

Chrétien continued, each phrase and line rendered as poetry. "I'll hasten to protect and defend you from your enemies, in good faith and without the deceit for which the seigneurs of the south are famous throughout Christendom and all the lands of the Turk and the Saracen, as God is my witness and helper. Else let me burn in hell through eternity with Judas Iscariot."

The phrase was supposed to be *in good faith and without deceit.* But Pedro accepted the vow, laying his hand on Chrétien's head, thinking the oath finished.

Chrétien hesitated. "Now I'm supposed to promise to render my castle whenever you ask for it, but I don't have one."

"I don't have a spare castle to lend you," Pedro said. In the middle of the oath, the two men decided they liked each other. "Promise to render whatever you have that's most valuable."

"Then I swear this in solidarity, fidelity, and faithfulness," Chrétien said, "as truly as a crusader swears to lay down his life for his own brother."

The last he said in Latin. Hearing the words of the bonfraires, Tomás said, "Chrétien, you can't share beyond our brotherhood."

"Peace, brother. It's the right words if he still has your oath, too."

"Do I?" Pedro almost touched Tomás, but then stopped.

"For whatever it's worth, Monsenyor."

"And I still have the silver I won off you the night you saved my life. You'll want to try to get it back one day, *mon amic.*" Pedro glanced from Tomás to Chrétien. "You might need it if you give everything away to your brother. If what you claim is true."

"It's true,' Chrétien said. "But before you go, there are two more secrets we must share, Monsenyor. About our Nizari swordmasters."

"Yes?" Pedro was as eager to hear it as Sebastián would be.

"First, there is no such thing as Nizari assassins," Tomás said.

"But the stories everyone tells—"

"Are false," Chrétien said.

"Our swordmasters in Cairo were charlatans. They succeeded by pretending to be more than they were," Tomás said.

"Our last secret is that we've found their approach to fighting works for us, my brother Tomás and me. Pretending to be more than we are." Chrétien folded his arms, satisfied to share their secrets.

"I might one day need to make use of that secret. Who knows what the future holds?" Pedro laughed at them both. Then he was gone, his words echoing behind him. *"Via com Dèu."*

72

Another Surrender

Isabella outside Minerve, July 27

ISABELLA GAZED AT THE horizon. The hot summer air was already thickening again, once more hiding the Pyrenees on the horizon in a haze of hot dust. A pair of golden eagles soared up on the draft from the plateau's heat.

Heat and dust could be an excuse for how slowly she sorted through jumbled thoughts. Even with Pedro's guards nearby, she stood just outside the tent where Tomás lay, unabashedly listening, to hear whether Tomás planned to join Pedro again. She remained as still as the wall lizard and grasshopper that clung to the tent's side.

However, she didn't quarrel when Jean-Luc asked her to come talk with him outside his own tent. Beatriz and Katelina hailed them from inside, too busy packing to join them.

"Are you prepared to leave?" Jean-Luc asked. "Everyone plans to depart early tomorrow."

"I don't have anything to prepare." She still needed to *know* something before she could *do* something. But she didn't want to explain her thoughts. "Everything I've worn or slept in or touched, every horse I've ridden since May-day, it's all borrowed. I travel at the mercy of the Valerós knights."

"Beatriz will make sure you have what you need. My father Gerard will give you a horse." Jean-Luc hesitated in a way she recognized—he was about to admonish her. "Isabella, I heard your quarrel with Pedro this morning. Please give up on your jealousy. You and Sebastián must render Castell-de-Valerós and Arracheuse to Pedro, so he can protect your people."

"I can't ask Sebastián to give away his birthright. Pedro already sent knights to protect Valerós. That should be enough."

"We both know the Church and the French won't stop. No one can raise an army large enough to resist what Simon and the pope intend. You'll need help, and Pedro is your best friend."

"My best friend? *Ai*, God help me." She protested, but weakly. Every memory of Minerve reminded her that Valerós needed all the help it could find. Still, she clung to her wish for independence. "Valerós is too far up in the backcountry hills. The crusade won't come there."

"You know nothing will stop Simon. The prelates will urge other greedy French lords to crusade, summer after summer." Once Jean-Luc began, it was like he wanted to pound these cruel truths into her. "Next summer, or the one after that, you'll have to stand on the battlements at Castell-de-Valerós and decide whether to surrender your heretics or let the whole valley and its villages die. Who will you surrender when they demand your heretics? Ermessen and her family? Guillem and Felicia? Or will everyone resist together, and you'll go out at night to pray with mothers who've lost their children?"

"Stop!" She fumbled with the folds of her borrowed robe. "Can't you and Beatriz protect Valerós? You're French. Simon's crusaders will leave us alone if you take it. That was Pèire's plan when he wanted Gerard to marry me."

"Beatriz and Katelina are coming north with me. And Valerós belongs to Sebastián. It remains his if you render Valerós castles. Pedro will give it all back to Sebastián when this fiasco is over."

"Pedro took Tomás away." Just three days ago she'd been bold enough to address Pedro as an equal. Seigneurs in the south were supposed to be equal with their king. Yet to her own ears, her voice sounded like a jealous Toulousain fishwife.

"No, he didn't. And Tomás came back for you. He almost died for you. It's time to do what you must. To save Pèire's people."

At the pavilion where Tomás lay, the flap slapped open. Pedro emerged, greeting his guards.

"There's Pedro. Do it now, Isabella. Hand in hand with Sebastián, while you're strong. Do it now so you don't have to beg later."

She rose and put her robe in order, adjusted her headcloth, and wiped her face on her sleeve. She called Sebastián to join her, and then, pretending to be as brave as any seigneur on the battlements, she hailed the lord to whom Valerós owed service.

"Monsenyor, we beg the pleasure of rendering the Valerós and Arracheuse castles. We hope that you can protect our shepherds and weavers and children, if it's ever needed."

Pedro kneeled to accept the rendered Valerós castles, acting in a humbler way than she'd managed in rendering the castles.

"Thank you for your kindness, Monsenyor."

"Thank you for trusting me." He smiled, but that frown line in his forehead deepened. "Shall we say adios until you join the Valerós knights in Barcelona?"

"Òc, Monsenyor." Sebastián answered with all his enthusiasm. "The Valerós knights shall see you there by All Saints."

When the king left them, Isabella sent Sebastián off to rest, despite his argument that his place was beside Tomás.

One more surrender was required that day.

73

Barceloneses to Bezants

IN THE DIM LIGHT of the tent, Miquel sat cross-legged by Tomás's pallet, not speaking. He hadn't said a word since Béziers, but he hummed *"Chanterai por Mon Corage"* while he rested his hand on Tomás's shoulder.

Isabella's voice carried from across the way.

"Go to bed, Sebastián. There's nothing more God or man can do here. Get some sleep."

She sounded even more hoarse than usual. Her voice aroused all the trepidation he'd avoided as long as he had Miquel nearby.

Miquel ceased humming. "I'll leave you now, *fadrin*. You don't need me."

"Have mercy, Father! Please stay!"

Tomás begged aloud, just as Isabella threw open the tent flap.

"Praying, Don Tomás?" She was as translucent as Miquel, and so thin that the whisper of the wind at Miquel's departure might waft her away.

"No, though Father Anselm and Pedro both tried to change my ways." He swallowed to keep from begging her mercy. That's what he should do: admit to being a scabrous weasel, whining like a spit-licking dog.

She towered over him with her arms crossed, her grey hawk's eyes boring into him. "They say you were there when Mathilde pulled me from the pyre. That you made me say my creed. And that's what saved me."

"You were in a passion."

"Indeed. I've never known such ecstasy. I saw the light burning around the throne of God."

"You still believe more than I can." He should confess what a leper he was.

"Yes. Except that day it turned out to be the flames of the pyre." She seemed annoyed, hostile in the same way she used to be. Which was comforting. Familiar. "Chrétien says you are leaving this country as soon as you can travel."

"It's true," he said. "I'm going to Cairo to find my son Yusuf, and then to Cyprus, where my mother is. I can't stay here."

"None of us can stay here." Isabella made a deprecating motion, the same hand-wave Pèire Leteric used, but her grey eyes smoldered, so angry he flinched when she came close. Pain shot up his side.

"I swear by my father's hand I never betrayed you, ma dòmna, except for that one horrible day at St-Sernin. For which I beg you to forgive me. Even though I don't deserve forgiveness."

Again, she waved as Pèire would, disparaging his oath; her sleeve slipped, showing the mark of the bonfraires burned on her wrist. "Stop. You made a mistake, for which you've paid more than just recompense. But this—this desertion?" Her voice tore. "*Sodalitas, fidelitas, virtus.* That's what you swore. And you claim to be a man of paratge? A man who swears on his mother's honor?"

"*Òc.* But I can leave now. Miquel's need for revenge and Pèire's call to protect his children, both are complete."

"You're running back to Cyprus?" While she talked, she paced like a feral creature, her hawk's eyes flashing. "You saved Sebastián. Chrétien told me how you cared for Hugues in Béziers."

"I did my duty." Confusion rushed through his mind, like a small animal scrabbling in a cage. What was she scolding him for?

"Then why do you want to leave like a deserting, faithless coward?" She spread her hands in the Catalan gesture of perplexity. "Who are you running from? Sebastián? Pedro? Me?"

"Running? I'm leaving because I don't have a place here. And it's not safe in this country."

"It's not safe for any of us. You aren't special." She rubbed at her wrist, as if it hurt her. "Chrétien bet gold bezants against silver barceloneses to that you still love me. So, why run away, *amador*?"

"*Ai.*" Warm blood ran in his veins again. He'd misunderstood her again, but in a less treacherous way.

·

"*Amador*? You still want me, ma dòmna?"

"'Want' is too tiny a word." Isabella did what she hadn't while Beatriz nursed him. She touched his hair, traced the tender line that sliced across his face, the edges of his lips. He flinched, like he always did. Except now, he was shrunken from almost dying, his skin like ashy slate instead of burnt umber.

"I'm confused, ma dòmna. What are you saying?"

"Do not go away from me again. We have a contract. We made promises. I've lost so much else…" She had to stop, not wanting to betray herself with tears. She cleared her throat, spoke with more humor than she felt. "Anyway, since I met you, I've almost died six times…"

"I think it's seven." He coughed, which clearly pained him.

"And I hired you to protect me, Don Tomás. Since I haven't torn up that contract yet, I want…I need…I hope…I expect you to remain with me. To keep me…" She stroked only his hand, the way she did when they were alone, the precious few days they spent together. "Alive. Even when I don't need rescuing."

"As you wish, ma dòmna."

His dark eyes cleared. His face had more of its usual color. He understood. When he struggled to sit up, she pressed him back. He lay still a minute, biting his lip while waiting for pain to pass. When he couldn't speak for several moments, Isabella fumbled with her braided belt, attempting patience, wanting to hear the smoky tones of his voice. Hoping to hear yes. But then, surprised.

"But, ma dòmna, before we go to Barcelona with the Valerós knights, can we first go to Cairo? While I've been lying here, I've been making a plan to fetch my son."

"Before that, *amador*, we also have to retrieve the horse we left with Anfos up in the hills." She gripped his hand, the only part of him she felt sure she could hold without adding to his pain. "Then we need to help with the harvest at Valerós and Arracheuse, to make sure our people don't go hungry this winter."

428

"I'm not much of a farmer. And didn't I hear that Guillem and Felicia are taking care of Valerós?"

"Òc, but I need to see Valerós again to be sure life on God's green earth goes on. I need that as much as I need to be with you. *Eu vos amor.*"

∎

"Slow down, donzel!"

Sebastián didn't look back. Jean-Luc had developed a bad habit, always telling him what to do. Sebastián had rejected such father-mongering since he left Toulouse.

"I'm not a donzel!" he called back. "I'm a knight of Aragón, sworn to Pedro *El Rei* and Don Tomás of Morella and—"

"Don't charge in without announcing yourself."

"I belong at my master's side."

When he threw back the tent flap, prepared to take up vigilance, Sebastián found Isabella sitting on the camp stool that he'd begun to think of as his own after long nights watching over Tomás. She seemed to be mending her belt, braiding the thin strips of leather. It was peaceful work, but her chest heaved, as if she'd just run a great distance.

Tomás sat up, pulling the coverlet up hastily, like a girl might do, as if Sebastián hadn't seen him naked, having bathed his master throughout the days and nights of fever. However, Tomás was flushed now, instead of pale as death.

"Are you well, senhór? You don't have a fever?"

"I'm quite well." That claim seemed exaggerated, given the awkward way Tomás jerked when he reached to offer a bonfraire's handshake. "I must thank you for your care."

"Every bonfraire knows his duty." Sebastián imitated the gesture Pèire used, turning his palm down to disclaim any glory.

"Don't we though?" Isabella murmured. She was still looking at her lap, braiding and then unbraiding and braiding again that belt Beatriz had given her.

No one spoke, so the only sounds came from the camp—people banging baggage or shouting for help amidst the clang and pole-smacking noise of tents coming down. And the buzz of flies and bees in counterpoint with the clacking of crickets in want of mates.

"Don't you have chores, *fadrin*? Or at least practice at arms?" Tomás asked.

"No. Chrétien and Durán are packing to go to Fontcours, so there's no arms practice. They'll ride out tomorrow with Gerard and the men from Chartrain. Jean-Luc is preparing the Beaurain army to move, now that it's his to command. And if he's not busy doing that, he's mooning over Beatriz."

"You could help Beatriz and Katelina pack," Isabella said.

"They've already done everything. The only task Beatriz seems to have is sewing up a gambeson and hose for Jean-Luc. Or maybe today it's a new shirt. Anyway, she follows him everywhere." Sebastián didn't add how uncomfortable it was to sit beside Beatriz, knowing that Valerós was his only because she preferred to follow Jean-Luc north.

Tomás stared off in space, perhaps beyond where Isabella sat. "Didn't I just hear Jean-Luc call to you before you came in?"

"Yes, but that's because he insists on ordering me about every time he sees me."

"He's Perseus. You're Corax." Tomás touched the bonfraires' brand on Sebastián's wrist.

Sebastián understood Tomás's point and could see that the movement hurt him. He stood up straighter. "I don't think any French lord has any business telling a seigneur of the south what to do. Even if he's one of our bonfraires."

Neither Tomás nor his mother answered. They seemed to be too busy looking at each other. Sebastián hesitated for a moment and then said, perhaps too loudly, "The French army and their henchmen burned the goodwomen from Minerve. Including Senhóra Eloïse and Senhóra Adalyde, who never hurt a soul. *Avi* Pèire always said this crusade is just about Normans and *francimands* stealing our land."

"Hush," Isabella said. "Not all the Churchmen and their informers have left Minerve yet."

However, Sebastián found that once he started to speak his mind, he couldn't stop. He dropped his voice to a whisper. "How can you burn people and take everything they own just because you don't like how they pray?"

"*Jhezu del tron*, with all the weeping angels in the golden heavens." Tomás sounded like *Avi* Pèire, cursing when annoyed. "The devil might know, but I don't."

"I hate Simon for this," Sebastián said. "And the Church."

"You saw the people going to the pyre." Isabella spoke just above a whisper in that hoarse voice. She seemed almost healthy again, no longer the specter that haunted the campsite while they waited to see if Tomás might live. "They weren't filled with hate. We must honor their faith. It wasn't the Church who did this. It was just men."

"Men who tell lies everywhere," Sebastián said. "We never saw anyone inside Minerve desecrate the Host or kill babies. Who cares how they choose to eat? How they choose to—"

"Die." Tomás finished his sentence. "Simon has sown enough terror to make it so that daily life is worse than each man's vilest nightmare. Worse even than mine."

Isabella dropped the belt she'd been braiding and laid her hand on Tomás's. After a moment, she folded her fingers within his. Sebastián glanced between his mother and his master, trying to see what had happened.

"Are you leaving tomorrow?" Sebastián asked, speaking to Isabella. "I can't stay here any longer. There's nothing to do, and it smells so foul."

"You don't have to travel with me," Isabella said. "Are you going to lead your knights to Barcelona? Doesn't Benito have Valerós men ready to travel? Especially now that Father Anselm has rejoined our knights?"

"From what Pedro said, I believe that's what I should do." Sebastián guessed at what she wanted him to choose—to go to Valerós or Barcelona? A dull thought.

"Benito can lead them across the mountains without you," Isabella said. "I'm curious to see Cyprus first, though. Aren't you?"

"And Cairo. Come with us, Sebastián," Tomás said. "You might not have another chance to see Cairo."

"You're both going? Together?" Sebastián asked.

"Of course, we're going together," Isabella said. "Tomás and I are married. We go everywhere together."

. . .

Lubos's Successors

THIS IS THE FIRST of the tales that the jongleurs sang and the grand-mothers told about the union that spanned the Pyrenees between Morella and Valerós, and then crossed the Great Sea to Cyprus and the Outremer.

Jean-Luc, Beatriz, and Katelina rode north to the Pays de France. Tomás and Isabella rode with Sebastián to Castell-de-Valerós, with the jangling of chainmail and harness and the horses' hooves beating time like a heartbeat. Then later in autumn, just before All-Saints, the three rode down the ragged granite trails from Valerós and headed for Narbonne, to sail to Cyprus and then to Cairo.

They say the new house of Morella y Valerós had much to offer the Kingdom of Aragón, while Pedro worked to mount the Recon-quista with allies from Castile, Navarre, and León.

But that's another story.

END BOOK 2 • ACCIDENTAL HERETICS SERIES

Next in the series:
BOOK 3: CRUX LUNATA

Heretics' Glossary

A

Affinity (canon law): Kinship by marriage; at the time of this story, affinity and consanguinity restricted marriage to fourth degree relationships. A man, for example, could not marry his brother's widow.

Ai Dèu: O God.

Angevines: The Plantagenet dynasty that ruled from Ireland to the Pyrenees. The Angevine empire grew through the marriage of Henry II and Eleanor of Aquitaine.

aqua vitae: Medieval ethanol, typically made by distilling wine.

aventail: A chainmail curtain to cover the neck and shoulders.

B

baquelar: Villainous rogue.

barcelonese: Coinage under the Count of Barcelona.

bezants: A Byzantine coin.

Bogomils: A medieval Gnostic sect, believing a dualist view of Christianity, seemingly arising in Macedonia.

bon amic: Good friend, or boyfriend.

bon Dèu; Bon Dieu: Good God.

bon día: Good day.

bon nuoit; bona nuèch, bon vèspre: Good night.

bonfraires: A brotherhood.

bonhomme: What the so-called heretics called themselves. This story uses the English version, goodmen.

bonjorn: Good morning.

booty: Treasure; the primary way crusaders financed their armies or paid their mercenaries. Rather than "looting," these cultures considered booty as legitimate plunder.

Brabançon: A mercenary from the Low Countries, with a reputation for lawlessness.

brioix: Bread.

C

cançós d'amor: Troubadours' love songs.

cançós d'Arturo: Songs of the Arthur legend.

cançós de guèrra: Troubadours' songs of war.

Candlemas: Feast of the Purification, February 2; one of the pre-Christian fire festivals.

Catalan: In the Middle Ages, a language and culture, not a political entity.

cavaller: Knight.

Cistercian Order: The White Monks, a reformist Benedictine order, who stressed manual labor and a return to the Rule of St Benedict.

common tongue: The Romance language of the Languedoc in the Middle Ages, often now called Old Occitan.

compadre: "Shared parent," like a godparent-godchild relationship.

consanguinity: Laws governing the degree of relationship that would prohibit marriage among people with a shared ancestor. A convenient reason for marriage annulment among European ruling classes, since they were all related, and a "fourth degree" relationship could conveniently be discovered.

cor dolç: Sweetheart, an endearment.

cortezia: The southern value of grace and courtly honor.

crozada: Crusader; Crusade Song.

Crux Lunata: A (fictional) secret brotherhood, whose symbol is a lunate cross, featuring lunar crescents at each terminus; both a pagan symbol and war tokenism imported to Europe by returning crusaders, adding the Islamic crescent in heraldic and other symbols.

cuirass: A rigid armor covering the torso. At this period, it was still made of leather.

D

deniers: A French coin.

Deus vult: God wills it! (A motto of early crusaders.)

Dieu ait pitié! God have mercy.

domus: Household; specifically, the larger economic household of a titled landholder.

don: A courtesy title for a gentleman from the landed classes.

donzel: A young gentleman, in training for knighthood.

Doutz Jhezu: Sweet Jesus.

duenna: A governess or chaperone.

E

E vos: And you?

el meu amor: My love.

el meu capità: My captain.

esbirros: Hired bodyguards.

eu vos amor: I love you.

F

fada: Fairy.

fadrin: A lad, a term of endearment.

Fontrevists: Members of the Order of Fontevrault, whose abbeys included separate communities of men and women, led by a monastery abbess.

francimand, francimandalha: Frenchman.

Franks: Colloquially, at the time of this story, a reference used by Muslims and others for Western European people.

fustian: A heavy cotton fabric.

G

gambeson: A padded jacket worn under armor or alone as a defensive covering.

garderobe: The inner privy of a castle.

gavatx: Bird's crop; throat-speakers. An insult indicating a northerner who speaks the local tongue badly.

goodmen, goodwomen: A reference to the people whom the Church called heretics; now commonly called Cathars.

Greek fire: An incendiary of naphtha, pitch, and sulfur.

H

hauberk: A chainmail shirt.

hereticated: Having decided to adopt a heresy.

hola: Hello.

Hospitallers of Jerusalem: A Christian military order, founded in Jerusalem to care for sick pilgrims; later given a charter for defense of the Holy Land.

I-J

Jhezu adouçar: Sweet Jesus.

Jhezu del tron: Jesus in heaven.

Jhezu y Maria: Jesus and Mary.

jongleurs: Medieval minstrels who sang the troubadours' songs.

K

kalila: Sweetheart, an endearment.

Knights Templar: A monastic crusader military order, the most elite of the crusader armies.

L

Latins: Colloquially, how the Muslims referred to the invading Western Christian armies.

loophole: A slit in a stonewall that allows light and ability to shoot arrows while protecting the defender.

M

ma dòmna: My lady.

mangon: A catapult design in use since Roman times.

mangonel: A large siege engine.

marquis, marquesa: A lord (and his wife) whose land is on a frontier border, and so must be a capable defender.

mestitz: A person of mixed heritage.

mignotta: A prostitute.

mon frère, mon fraire: My brother.

Monsenyor: An honorific, such as for a king.

Moors: People from northern Africa who settled on the Iberian Peninsula under Muslim leadership. Colloquially at the time of the story, a person of dark complexion.

morabatin: Gold coins in Aragón. A horse at that time would cost about one hundred morabatins.

N– O

Nizari: A legendary assassin cult at the time of the Crusader states.

Normans: Descendants of the Viking Northmen who settled Normandy, and later invaded Britain in 1066.

òc: Yes.

P

Pare Abát: Father abbot.

paratge: A concept in Troubadour culture of kinship and justice, more than honor: natural balance, harmony, "what is right."

Parzival: From the Arthurian legend, the knight who heals the Fisher King and goes to the Grail castle with Galahad.

peccador: Sinner.

petraria: A rock hurler powered by a bow.

pinxo: Bully.

poulain: A colt; colloquially, a word used among Latins in the Outremer to describe children with crusader fathers and local mothers.

punxor: Prick.

Q – R

quiquid: Whatever.

qui s'ho creu: Who'd believe it?

Ransomers: A monastic order of knights in the Crusader states.

rebec: A medieval stringed instrument, imported into Christian Europe via Andalusia. At the time of the crusades, it was likely referred to as a lyra.

rendability: A practice, at the time of this story, of a king (or other leader) demanding that an independent lord make castles available to the king, in exchange for the king's promise of protection.

renrén: Fool.

S

Sancta Maria: A woman's oath, calling on Saint Mary.

Saracen: Colloquial term for Muslims used in Europe.

schismatic: For members of the Holy Roman Church, a common way to refer to members of the Eastern Orthodox Church.

scrofula: Tuberculosis of the neck; colloquially, part of an insult.

seigneur: A man of rank who rules lands and a household.

Seljuks: Fighters from a Turkish-Persian empire.

seneschal: A steward.

senhór, senhóra, senhóreta: Titles of respect.

simony: Paying for an office or position in the Church.

Sodalitas, fidelitas, virtus: Motto of the bonfraires: fraternity, fidelity, virtue.

squire: In the southern lands, a fighter of rank between knights and foot soldiers, for his lifetime. In the southern world, squires did not rise to become knights.

surcoat: A long coat worn over others clothes or armor.

T– Z

Turcopoles: Mercenary mounted archers in the Crusader states.

Venetians: The instigators and financiers of the so-called Fourth Crusade to conquer Constantinople.

viech d'ase: Donkey's cock.

viscount: A European noble rank, above a baron, below a marquis.

woad: A plant used to create a blue dye; grown as a cash crop around Toulouse.

xiqueta: Child, an endearment.

Place Names

Valerós, Fontcours, Montcava, and the Vale of Roses exist within the world of Accidental Heretics, but nowhere else.

A

Aleppo: One of the oldest continuously inhabited cities. In Syria, at the end of the Silk Road, Aleppo was besieged twice by crusaders but never conquered.

Antioch: Conquered early in the First Crusade, it was battled over among multiple successive crusader rulers until it was abandoned in the face of the Mongols. Antioch lay on an important trade route until the Mongol conquests interfered.

Aquitaine: A duchy in what became southwest France after the time of this story. It was a key part of the Angevine empire under Henry II and Eleanor of Aquitaine.

Aragón: In the mid-thirteenth century, a union of the Kingdom of Aragón and the County of Barcelona established the dynastic Crown of Aragón, with tributaries across the Languedoc at the time of this story.

Aude: A river in the southwest of what is now France that flows from the Pyrenees to the Mediterranean.

B

Barcelona: A territory on the Mediterranean, now approximately the political entity of Catalonia, for which Pedro II held the title Count of Barcelona.

Béziers: A Languedoc town that controlled most of the east-west trade route, and that was infamously burned by the invading crusader-terrorists in a massacre.

Bram: A fortified town in the Languedoc attacked by the French crusaders in 1210.

Byzantium: The Greek-speaking Eastern Roman Empire, with Constantinople as its capital, including Macedonia, Greece, and part of Turkey at the time of this story.

C

Lastours: Castles and villages north of Carcassonne that formed a center of resistance to the French early in the Languedoc crusade.

Carcassonne: A fortified city in the Languedoc, which surrendered to Simon de Montfort in 1209.

Corbières hills: Foothills in the southwest of the Languedoc that lead up to the Pyrenees.

Constantinople: Capital of the Eastern Roman Empire, sacked in the Fourth Crusade, becoming the seat of Norman rulers for the next fifty years.

Cyprus: A Mediterranean fiefdom conquered by Richard the Lionheart, who then saw it as not worth the bother and sold it to the Knights Templar, who then sold it to Guy de Lusignan.

D–F

Dalmatia: A region on the eastern Adriatic coast, portions of which were under the control of Venice in 1204.

Edessa: An Armenian city, ruled by various Crusader lords and under frequent attacks by Turks. First of the Crusader States to be lost.

Famagusta: Tomás's home on Cyprus.

Fontfroide abbey: At the time of this story, a Cistercian monastery near Narbonne.

H–J

Holy Roman Empire: The successor in central Europe to Charlemagne's empire, including during the late Middle Ages parts of Germany, Burgundy, Italy, and Bohemia.

Iconium: An ancient city in Asia Minor, now Konya, Turkey.

Jaffa: The southern part of what is now Tel Aviv, captured after the First Crusade, conquered by Saladin, and then reclaimed by Richard Lionheart. After fighting off Saladin, crusaders held the city until 1268.

Jerusalem: Captured by the crusaders in 1099, recaptured by Saladin in 1187, traded back and forth for several decades until finally captured by the Mamluks and lost forever by the crusaders.

L

Lagrasse: A town in the lower foothills of the Pyrenees, centered around the abbey of Sainte-Marie de Lagrasse.

Laurac: A village in the Aude valley.

Limoux: A town in the Languedoc, on the river Aude.

M

Maine: A province in France, under Norman and Angevine control until lost to King Philippe in 1203.

Montpelhièr: A walled city in the Languedoc, near the Mediterranean, with the second oldest university in Europe.

Morella: A town near Valencia, taken from the Moors by El Cid, lost again before finally becoming part of Aragón in the Reconquista.

N

Narbonne: A rich Mediterranean port in the Languedoc that was the seat of the bishop and home to a significant Jewish community.

Naxos: A Greek island in the Aegean Sea, alternately under Byzantine and Venetian rule.

O–R

Outremer: The Crusader States, the land overseas.

Pays de France: The historic personal domain of the king of France; most of this area became the province Ile de France.

Peyriac-de-Mer: Site in the Aude region of a Cistercian monastery.

Pieusse: A Languedoc village overlooking the Aude, on a main road to Carcassonne.

Poitiers: A county in west central France, whose county governed the Aquitaine and Poitou.

Provence: A county on the Mediterranean under the rule of the counts of Barcelona.

Quéribus: A stronghold on the Aragón frontier in the Corbières hills.

Rhône: The major river running from the Alps to the Mediterranean.

Roussillon: A county in the Languedoc, under the Count of Barcelona at the time of this story.

S

Sicily: A Norman kingdom during much of the Crusades era, after Normans conquered the Arab rulers of Sicily and southern Italy.

St-Gilles: Site of a Benedictine abbey to the east of Montpelhièr.

St-Sernin: A Romanesque basilica in Toulouse.

Syria: An Arab land in Western Asia, with districts captured, recaptured, and carved among Turks, Seljuks, Byzantines, and Crusaders.

T–Z

Termes: A stronghold castle in the Aude valley, attacked by Simon de Montfort in 1210.

Toulouse: A county in the Languedoc, whose count owed allegiance to the king of France at the time of this story. The city, a major trade route between the Mediterranean and central France, was a bishop's seat.

Zara: An island in the Adriatic where Venetian and French mercenaries rioted in rebellion, while camped and awaiting ships to advance of the crusade to conquer Constantinople.

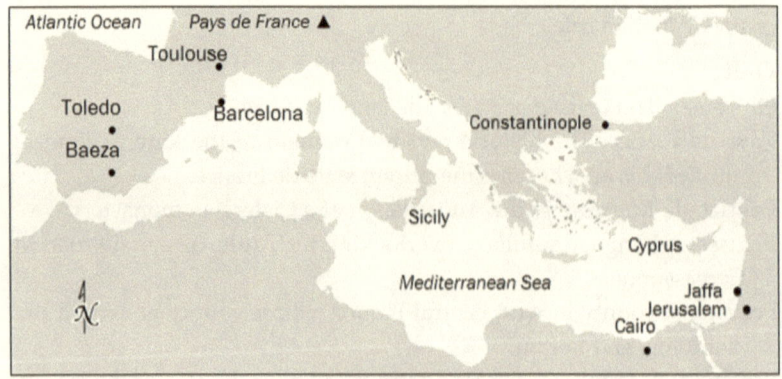

Crusaders' World ▪ 1210

About the Author

E.A. STEWART is an American writer whose *Accidental Heretics* series explores intrigues in France and Spain in the thirteenth century. Annie Stewart worked for many years as a technical writer and project manager in Pacific Northwest software companies.

Ms. Stewart lives and writes in Seattle.

www.eastewartauthor.com

Acknowledgments and Notes

Thanks to Ajax Bell, Elizabeth Bjorkman, and Laurie Cropp.

Author's Note:
King Pedro II of Aragón was in Iberia in 1210, gathering an army and then laying siege to Ademuz near Valencia, in response to an Almohad incursion. However, this is fiction, and I chose to have Pedro witness the outcome of his youthful plea to burn people for heresy. Since I brought him to the Languedoc, I found other ways that he could make himself useful.

The Cathars: Dualist Heretics in Languedoc in the High Middle Ages by Malcolm Barber, Pearson Education Ltd., 2000.
The Perfect Heresy: The Revolutionary Life and Death of the Medieval Cathars by Stephen O'Shea. Walker & Company, 2000.
Medieval Warfare Sourcebook by David Nicolle. Arms & Armour, 1997.

About the Accidental Heretics Series

Lost in the Languedoc Crusade

Find this series in your favorite online store
or ask your independent local bookseller.

ACCIDENTAL HERETICS SERIES
Book 1: *Bone-mend and Salt*
Book 2: *Trebuchets in the Garden*
Book 3: *Crux Lunata*
Book 4: *Song of Valerós*
The Mad Woman of La Catalane: A Novella
The Blue Door… and More Accidental Heretics Tales

LEGENDS OF VALERÓS SERIES
Wheel and Serpent: 1
Traitor: 2
Hero: 3

To learn more about
the Accidental Heretics series, visit:
www.eastewartauthor.com

From Jugum Press

HISTORICAL AND CONTEMPORARY FICTION

Nzinga, African Warrior Queen by Moses L. Howard

Nzinga is a brilliant leader during a time of violent upheaval. This fictional biography brings to life the 17th century flourishing African kingdom, now lost, where early explorers' maps of West Africa call out: "Here reigned the celebrated Queen Nzinga!"

Nine Volt Heart by Annie Pearson

He said, "I love you." She said, "You don't even know the real me." He said, "Great song lyrics. Key of G? Can we try close harmony?" Jason and Susi meet by accident in Seattle. Secrets, songs, and stalkers quickly entwine their lives in unpredictable ways.

This Charming Man by Ajax Bell

A chance encounter with an intriguing older man inspires Steven Frazier with visions of a more rewarding life. A vibrant snapshot of Seattle in the early 1990s, this story captures the drama of coming into one's own as an adult.

A Summer in Peach Creek by Michele Malo

Teenaged Faith travels to Peach Creek, West Virginia for a visit with relatives in 1932. When a scandalous murder occurs, Faith discovers the corrupt underbelly of Logan County. As summer progresses and peaches grow, Faith finds her own moral center.

PERSONAL VOICES IN HISTORY SERIES

Journey into Gold Country: Memories of a Forty-Niner

by Ralph Buckingham; foreword by Charles Barker

The California Gold Rush, remembered sixty years later by a New England younger son who went to seek his fortune.

We Were Walimu Once and Young, edited by Brooks E. Goddard

True stories from the Teachers for East Africa and Teacher Education for East Africa experience in the 1960s.

Find print and ebook editions:

www.jugumpress.net